A NEXT GENERATION NOVEL

RESCUE Us

J.M. WALKER

IBSN: 978-1-989782-32-3

Rescue Us (Next Generation, #7)

FAMILY TREE

Angel and Genevieve "Jay" Rodriguez
(Grit, King's Harlots #1/Grim, King's Harlots #3)
Angelica "Gigi"
Ryder
Meadow

Asher and Meeka Donovan
(Stain, King's Harlots #2)
Aiden
Ashton

Coby and Brogan Porter
(Rude, King's Harlots #4/For You, King's Harlots #7)
Zachary "Zach"

Dale and Maxine "Max" Michaels
(Numb, King's Harlots #5)
Piper

Vincent "Stone" and Creena Stone
(Rust, King's Harlots #6)
Luna
Vincent Junior

Greyson and Eve Mercer
(Greyson, Hell's Harlem #1)
Jaron

Tray and Zillah Lister
(Tray, Hell's Harlem #2)
Beatrix "Bee"

John and Beatrix "Trixie" Butcher
(Hell's Harlem Series)
Cyrus
Samson "Sammy"

WARNING: The heroine is a human trafficking survivor, so if you have triggers, please read with caution. Do NOT take this warning lightly.

DEDICATION

Angie:
I told you I could make you love someone more
than Garrith.

PROLOGUE

Ainsley

EYES DOWN.
Palms up.
Breathe.
Don't make eye contact.
Don't utter a single word.
Do as you're told.
Breathe.
Don't talk back.
Survive.
Repeat.

No matter how much time had passed, I played the rules over and over in my mind. They were engrained in me like scars on my soul. No one could see these scars of course, but I could sure as hell feel them. Every time I went to bed at night and closed my eyes, the rules were there.

The faces.

The cold, vacant eyes.

The men.
The other victims.

Before I fell asleep, I was always left with *his* eyes staring back at me. They were dark, cold, and soulless. I could never understand how someone could be as evil as him. I heard about monsters. In the news. In movies. From friends. Teachers. My parents. But I always brushed it off. It would never happen to me. There was no possible way that I could ever run across someone like these men who took girls and boys against their will, all to make a buck. I hung out with friends, had a buddy system whenever we went anywhere at night. But we should have had one during the day. No one would grab me if the sun was up, right?

I was wrong.

I tried to forget and move on, but I couldn't.

I could still feel their hands, their bodies, parts of them I never wanted, but got just the same. They were forever etched on my very being, much like the scars on my skin.

Although they all terrified me, there was one man who stuck out the most amongst them all. I never knew his name; I never even saw his face. He always wore a mask that was made out of leather. But I remembered his eyes. I would recognize those eyes anywhere. They were soulless, black like most of the clothes I wore. I could still remember the smell as he breathed heavily against my ear. I could feel the smooth texture of the mask as he rubbed his cheek against mine. We may not have known his name, but he was there, constantly. He made us refer to him as Master. That was only when we were allowed to speak of course.

"How are you doing?" I was asked on multiple occasions ever since I escaped, but I never answered. How did they think I was doing? I didn't speak. I no longer had a voice. I was a shell of the woman I used to be. She was still here. I knew she was. I could feel her. But she was cowering somewhere in the deepest parts of me. She had been broken, her will shattered. I missed her, the part of me that had once been fierce and strong-willed. Not knowing how to find her, I went through each day trying not to think about how much I had changed. How much *they* had changed *me*.

"Ainsley."

I jumped, finding Jay Rodriguez staring back at me. She gave me a small smile, her voice gentle but firm. Lines sat at the corners of her eyes and mouth, like she had spent years laughing and smiling. I wished for that. No, I longed for it. The happiness I once had.

"You have nothing to fear here," she told me. "Do you understand?"

Of course I understood but it didn't mean I wasn't scared nonetheless.

Her face softened. "You're probably scared shitless right now."

My eyes flicked to hers. I swallowed hard, nodding.

"I get it." She crossed one knee over the other. "I won't even begin to say that I know how you feel because I don't. But just know that any of us here are always willing to listen or just sit with you, even if you don't want to talk."

Talk. I hadn't talked in years because I had never been allowed to. He preferred it that way. Although he liked when we called him Master, he much preferred to hear our screams instead. It was one reason I stopped making a single sound. It almost cost me my life a few times, but I refused to give him that satisfaction. I needed some sort of control over my life, even if it was something small like the use of my voice.

"There's a reason I called you here," Jay said, flipping through my file.

I nodded again because I didn't want to be rude. It wasn't her fault I turned out this way. Silent. Mute. It was theirs. The men who had taken me and others captive. The monsters who would forever haunt my nightmares. The bastard who organized it all. If I could get my hands on him and knew I would survive, I would kill him.

"How about you just let me talk, explain myself, and we'll go from there," she added.

I nodded and looked down at my hands. American Sign Language was my way of communicating. The silent language had always fascinated me, so I learned it as a child and thankfully became fluent before I was taken. I never knew how much I needed this language until now.

I sighed, knowing that some of the fuckers who took us were able to get away. I gave the cops whatever information I had, but I didn't let it occupy my thoughts all the time. I couldn't dwell on it because I knew that no matter what, sex trafficking would never end.

Jay stood from her chair behind the large oak desk in her office. She went up to the window that looked out onto the back of the compound. "I was kidnapped by my husband's boss."

My eyes widened at her words.

"I was found rather quickly but it still fucked with my head." She looked at me then, the lines on her face hardening as the memories rushed through her. "Now, I know it's still not the same as what you went through of course, but I just want you to know you aren't alone. Everyone here has their own story. Don't ever forget it."

I looked down at my hands on my lap, nodding slightly. I wanted to thank her with my words, but I couldn't. The doctors and therapists said it was due to the trauma I endured. Maybe so. But I had never been a talker. Even before everything happened. I liked being quiet and preferred to stay in the background, listening to everyone else. I hated being the center of attention. It was one of the reasons why learning ASL meant so much to me.

"I want you to know that you always have a home here. You have made so much progress since you arrived. I'm proud of you. Now, last month, per your request, we set you up with an apartment at the building run by our staff. You were also given a monthly allowance as well," Jay stated, heading back to her desk. She opened my file once again, glancing down at it before meeting my gaze once again.

I nodded.

"Do you feel safe at your apartment? If not, we can keep your room here. I can't imagine that things feel even remotely normal when it's only been eighteen months since…"

I winced, forcing myself not to let those dark thoughts invade my mind.

"Do you feel safe there, Ainsley?" she asked gently.

I shrugged. Truth was, I didn't feel safe anywhere.

"You probably don't feel safe anywhere, do you?" she asked, taking the thought right out of my head.

I looked down at my hands, shrugging again.

"Okay. It's settled. We will keep your room here for when you need to feel more secure. Now the reason I wanted to speak to you is because we'd like to offer you a job. If you wish."

My head snapped up, my eyes welling at the thought of making something more of myself.

She laughed lightly. "I can tell by the look on your face that you weren't expecting that."

I shook my head quickly.

"Although, we often communicate in writing, you are fluent in American Sign Language. According to your file, you learned it as a kid but only started using it consistently after you were rescued."

Rescued.

I almost scoffed at that single word. Sure, I, along with others, were saved from those men, but there were so many of us who weren't. Some committed suicide because they couldn't handle being out in the real world. Years of conditioning were so engrained in us, we didn't know how to cope without being told what to do. It was fucked up to say the least.

Picking up my phone, I started typing. It was the way I communicated with people when they didn't know ASL. Not that I expected everyone to know it of course, but it was a nice surprise when I came across someone who did. Jay even provided me with a therapist who could communicate with me using ASL.

I was sick one summer when I was a kid and couldn't play outside. I read every book in my grandmother's house a handful of times. She always told me I was too smart for my own good. Maybe she was right.

One night over dinner, she and my grandpa were talking about ways to challenge me. I was acting out because I was bored. Whatever virus I had, just wouldn't go away no matter what we tried.

My grandpa suggested jokingly that I learn another language.

My grandma laughed.

They didn't think I could do it, but I did. I learned ASL because it fascinated me but also because there was something about it that I needed. I just didn't know it at the time.

"And you succeeded in learning it," Jay added in awe.

I nodded, placing my phone back on my lap.

"Well, the job we are proposing is that you teach others here how to sign. Once you are comfortable with that, I'm sure we could find more work around the center for you too, to fill your time, help us out."

I gave her a small smile, appreciating all she was doing for me.

"Would you like that?"

Picking my phone up again, I typed out a single word that I had been trying to get answered for years. No one knew the damn answer but hopefully Jay could at least answer it for this situation.

Why?

She went to the couch by the far wall and patted the spot beside her.

I moved from the hard chair and joined her.

Jay turned toward me, giving me her full attention. "I know you've had it hard and are trying to make a life for yourself. I'm not even going to pretend to know what you're going through but I'm offering to help in any way I can. That's what we do for everyone who comes here. We don't close our doors on anyone. Even when it's someone who just needs to get away because the demons in their head are too loud. You don't have to have experienced recent trauma for us to take you in. It could be a childhood experience or a current experience. It doesn't matter. Our doors are always open. As you know, we have quite a bit of trained staff who deal with all sorts of mental health conditions, trauma, PTSD, and more. Now that The Dove Project has gotten quite successful, we're able to get doctors, therapists, psychiatrists and everything else that we require to help those who need us, but some of our residents still need to find their voice, or may want to learn a new skill while they are here. For this reason, the other owners and I have sat down and would like you to be part of the staff here. Offering ASL would be a wonderful addition to the team, and you are the only person we feel is right for the job."

I tilted my head, searching her face for any indication that she was lying. I had learned over the last few years how to read people. That was what happened when you had nothing else to do and had to remain silent instead. You kept quiet, listened, and watched. Everything.

"You're probably wondering why we want to hire you." Jay laughed lightly. "In addition to your knowledge of ASL, you're young and I think you can relate more to the other survivors here. They'll see that there is a chance for a normal life. All of you are strong." Her voice cracked, her eyes welling.

A part of me wanted to reach out and console her but I didn't know how. My emotions were locked up tight. I wasn't even sure when the last time was that I cried. And laughing? That was almost non-existent anymore.

Thank you, I signed.

Jay smiled. *You're welcome.*

My lips twitched, a tiny smile forming on my face at the fact that she had been trying to learn ASL.

For me.

While we filled out the paperwork, I couldn't help but wonder what would have happened to me if I hadn't been introduced to The Dove Project. It was owned by Jay and her friends. They started the company years ago after they had worked with their husbands and brought down a human trafficking ring. I didn't know their individual stories, but I did know that they all experienced their own personal trauma. Some more than others. I could see it in their eyes and the eyes of their husbands. They tried masking their pain with whatever vice they could and even though it had been a long time, it was still there. It would always be there.

I was thankful the center had grown as much as it had and that I was handed information for the center from the social worker at the hospital. I couldn't stay in that city. I couldn't even stay in that state. When I first wrote down my need to leave, my social worker did her research and returned with the information on The Dove Project. I agreed that it was the place for me and she set it up.

I wasn't sure what would have happened to me if that raid had never occurred at the brothel. The only thing I currently knew, as safe as I thought I was, someone was likely looking for me. Maybe someone would always be looking for me.

I also knew that one day, the monsters would come. Whether it be the ones in my head or the ones lurking in the dark corners of my room. It was only a matter of time before they came to collect. I just didn't know who would be first.

The ones in my head.

Or *him*.

ONE

CYRUS

I DIDN'T USUALLY VISIT my parents' gravesite by myself, but my brother was off doing who knew what, and I didn't feel like waiting for him. He typically joined me, was the first one to arrive most times, but not today. For whatever reason, pussy was more important to him. That was the excuse he always made anyway but I knew that it went deeper than that. He missed them. Both of us did but their deaths affected us in different ways.

Our parents had been gone for over twenty years, but that didn't mean it hurt any less.

Both shot and killed within a year of each other, the agony over losing our mom and dad when we had been so young, would forever be etched on our damn souls.

We had different ways of coping with that loss. Sammy fucked through anything he could stick his dick into, and I fought. I also drank a bit at times but fighting was better and helped me deal.

Glancing at the headstone one last time, I took a deep breath, swallowed my sorrow, and headed back to my bike. It had belonged to our father. Even though it was old, the machine purred like it was brand-new. Keeping up on the maintenance helped and I would ride it into the ground if I had to.

My phone took that moment to buzz. It was later in the afternoon and while most were getting dinner ready, I was itching for more. Something else. Something different. Something I never had before.

Checking my cell, I saw a text from my brother.

Sammy: The kitties are in full swing tonight.

My brother's choice of words when it came to women, was interesting to say the least. I couldn't wait for the day when a woman brought him to his knees.

Me: On my way.

Sammy: I'll keep them warm for you.

I rolled my eyes, stuffing my phone back in the pocket on the inside of my leather cut.

Sammy's views on women changed depending on how they acted. Most threw themselves at him, so he would fuck them and leave. Pussy was pussy. His words. I knew there was someone out there for him and I had a feeling that he had already found her. Especially since he had become moodier over the past few months. A lot of shit went down in the last year. Things we never even saw coming. They never affected us directly but seeing family members almost lose each other and a child at the hands of vile human beings, we upped the protection and remained as quiet as could be as a result of it.

My brother was now on edge and searching for something much like I was, but I didn't know what. I didn't think he knew either.

I wanted a good girl. Someone who was okay with sitting at home on a Friday night and watching re-runs of *The Office*.

Someone who enjoyed the simple things in life. Like a home-cooked meal or that first cup of coffee in the morning. But I also wanted someone who had a passionate part of them just the same. A part that they would only let me see. I wanted her at my feet when the moment called for it, but also at my side.

I wasn't happy being single anymore and had been looking for that special someone for a while, but something was always stopping me. Endless dates were a recurring thing for me until our cousin asked both Sammy and me to watch over his girl and daughter. I didn't mind as it was distracting, and Piper Michaels was like a little sister to us anyway.

Slipping on my helmet, I straddled my bike and let out a sigh as the engine roared to life. Driving the distance to Rouge, the strip club Sammy was at. The length of time it took to get there eased some of the tension resting on my shoulders.

When I arrived at the club, it was pushing seven at night. It was still too early to be attending a strip club, but I never said anything and just went with it. I also had to look out for my brother. He was a hothead and was going to get himself mixed up with the wrong woman one day who had an ex that was larger than him. Sammy was a nasty fighter and one of these days, he was going to get himself hurt or worse.

"It's about time you showed up." Sammy butted out his smoke on the bottom of his Shit-Kicker and pushed away from the wall.

Killing the engine, I pulled off my helmet. "Why are you here so early?"

"I was bored." He grunted, pulling a pack of cigarettes out from the inside of his cut. He lit up another smoke, took a deep inhale, and let it out through his nostrils. The spicy scent of the tobacco wafted into my nose. He was stressed about something. It was the only reason he was currently chain-smoking.

"You're always bored." I slid off my bike and placed the helmet in the side storage compartment before locking it back up.

"Nah, brother. It's getting worse."

I straightened, slowly looking at him over my shoulder. "What's wrong?"

He shrugged, puffing away on that damn smoke.

"Sam." I went up to him and took the smoke from between his fingers before bringing it up to my mouth. Inhaling the sweet, spicy bliss, I let the smoke settle deep in my lungs before blowing it out slowly between my lips.

"Nothing's wrong exactly. I just…" He looked at the building behind him. *Rouge* sat in large red letters above the door. It had been our home away from home for years. We knew the owners and the women who danced. We even knew the regular customers. If new people came into the club, we made it a point to get to know them as well.

"You're wanting something more than just easy pussy," I told him.

"Is that what you want?" he asked, still looking at the building.

"I've been wanting it for years, Sammy." I clapped his shoulder, handing him back his smoke.

"Why? Women are difficult, brother." He stuck the smoke back between his lips. "They usually come with baggage or a large fucker for an ex."

"That's because you go after women who aren't readily available." I went to walk past him when a thought came to me. "How's Red?"

His dark eyes locked with mine. "I have no idea what you're talking about."

I chuckled, shaking my head and heading into the club. Sammy followed because I knew he would. Even though I could hear him grumbling shit about the woman he was currently hung up on, he followed because he wanted to see her. She was a dancer and only ever went topless if the owners demanded it. It didn't happen often because even when she was clothed, she could move and had the men drooling at her feet.

Once Sammy and I were seated at our usual booth, his mood changed. He scowled, glaring at everyone who walked past our table.

"Seriously, Sam. Chill the fuck out." I stared at my twin. "What the hell is your problem?"

He crossed his arms under his chest, staring out at the dance floor.

I followed his gaze, finding the reason for the sudden change in his mood front and center on the stage.

Red was moving her body to the music. She swung from the pole, did tricks and moves most would kill for. Though she was beautiful, she never did it for me. Not that I was opposed to strippers or anyone for that matter, the attraction just wasn't there. She never even looked at me anyway. Her eyes had only ever been on my brother. Like they were now. I saw a smirk spread on her face as her eyes locked with Sammy's while she danced. When she was done, she blew him a kiss and quickly left the stage.

Glancing back at him, I saw his shoulders slump like he was relieved no one was watching her anymore.

"You two have a history?" I asked, even though I knew he wouldn't tell me. We were close. Hell, we were twins. We were identical but now that we were older, you could easily tell us apart. I became bigger and he became moodier.

"Not yet we don't," he mumbled.

"But you want something. From her." I wasn't one to pry but if it distracted me from my own shit or lack thereof, I was down for it.

"I want to beat her ass for dancing like that on stage and choke her until she knows who she belongs to." Sammy's eyes snapped to mine. "Does that answer your question?"

I sometimes questioned my bother's sexual exploits but if it was consensual between him and his partner, who was I to judge?

"Just make sure you have a damn safeword," I warned.

"I know that," he said, signalling the waitress.

"Hey guys," the waitress, Kelly, greeted, coming up to our table. "The girls were just asking about you. You going to play nice tonight, Sammy?"

"I always play nice if they give me what I want," he said, letting his eyes roam down the length of her.

"Well…" She hesitated, probably knowing that there was no point in arguing with him because truth was, my brother was sick in the head. "I'll get you your beer." She spun on her heel before either of us could respond, and headed to the bar.

"Why do you have to scare the girls?" I asked, wondering about him sometimes.

He only shrugged.

I loved him but sometimes I worried he would be alone forever, and that no woman would be able to handle his level of kink. Whatever kink that may be. We were close. More than brothers. We were best friends. But when it came to sex, that shit was private. I had heard about twins sharing women but that had never been our thing. I was a selfish guy. When I had a woman, I wanted her to focus solely on me and no one else. Sammy was the same. He had women, several women in fact, offering him up threesomes and more, but he never went for it.

Ever since Red started working at *Rouge* months ago, I actually hadn't seen my brother with anyone. He used to take them home, but that hadn't happened in quite a while. Maybe she was the reason for his change in mood.

"I haven't been to the club in a while," he muttered, voicing his thoughts out loud.

"Neither have I." There was no reason to either when I didn't have someone to go with me.

Sammy and I were members of a BDSM club called The Rope. No one knew of our lifestyle. Hell, even the women we had been with outside of the club, didn't know. Both of us had one goal in mind when we explored our kink; that was to get a submissive. But it hadn't happened yet, so our visits to The Rope were few and far between.

"You heading to The Dove Project tomorrow?" Sammy asked, changing the subject.

"Yeah. Greyson thought it would be a good idea for us to help. Jaron liked the idea, so he'll be there too." We had been on edge lately. After almost losing Jaron Mercer, the newest president of the Hell's Harlem MC, we needed something to take away the stress. Most of us either drank or fucked it out. A few of the guys had an old lady to go home to, so I was sure that helped them deal. But Jaron's father knew that a lot of us were still single, so he was trying anything to help us work through the stress.

I would give my left arm to be able to go home to a woman. Someone who greeted me at the door with a smile on her face. I imagined that she would kiss me, and I would take it further than that. It had been so long since I had a woman beneath me.

"Cyrus?"

I jumped, finding Sammy staring back at me. "What were you saying?" I asked as Kelly brought us a pitcher of beer.

He tilted his head, eyes that mirrored my own, bore into me. "Daydreaming?" Sam added once we were alone.

I sighed and looked out at the large room. The dancers mingled with customers. Waitresses served drinks and food.

The owner, Candace, was there tonight and she barked orders at her staff while her husband, Ronny, worked on the books in the back.

"I need something," I heard myself say.

"Like what?"

"A woman." I locked eyes with my brother.

"There are a lot of women here who would be more than willing to go home with you, C."

I grunted. "That's the problem."

Sammy scratched his jaw. "I hear you, brother. I'm sick of easy pussy."

Before I could comment anymore on it, the rest of our crew rolled in.

Hell's Harlem had members across the country. While we didn't have a lot of members in this area, we could still pack the bar. Especially when members visited from out of town.

"I think I'm going to call it a night." I rubbed the back of my neck, trying to ease some of the anxiety resting on my shoulders.

"You just got here," Sammy pointed out as Jaron joined us.

"What's going on?" he asked, sliding into the booth beside Sammy.

"Cyrus is ditching us early." Sam took a swig of his beer, his eyes moving back to the stage.

"I'm just not feeling it tonight," I explained. "Not that I have to give you a reason, fucker."

Jaron chuckled.

"How's the family?" I asked Jaron, needing to take the subject off of me.

"Good." Jaron grabbed Sammy's beer and drank the rest of it before placing the empty glass back on the table in front of my brother.

I expected him to make a snide remark about it, but instead Sammy stared out at the vast room surrounding us.

"What's with him?" Jaron asked, nodding toward Sam.

"He's pining." I was almost jealous of the fact that there was someone he wanted when there was no woman I was even remotely interested in. I had been looking for months and my brother wanted nothing to do with relationships. But yet, Red caught his attention, and he couldn't stop scowling.

"Just go talk to her," Jaron suggested.

"Do either of you know anything about her?" Sammy asked, ignoring him.

Jaron and I glanced at each other.

"No," I answered. "Should we?"

"I thought you already talked to her." Jaron poured himself another beer from the pitcher, let out a sigh, and took a long swig.

"No but I'm about to." Sammy gently nudged Jaron. "Move."

Jaron rolled his eyes. "Grumpy fucker." He slid out of the booth, letting Sammy out before sitting back across from me.

"Be nice," I called out.

"She doesn't want nice," Sammy muttered, walking toward his latest conquest.

"Have you met her? This Red?" Jaron asked.

"Not officially. She started working here a few months ago and whenever she dances, it pisses Sammy off." Not that I understood exactly why. "How's Piper doing?"

Jaron smirked. "Perfect."

I chuckled, shaking my head. "How's she feeling?"

"She said she feels okay, and that this pregnancy is different than with Brynlee. I don't know how different, but she thinks it might be a boy." Jaron sat up straighter at that thought. "I'm happy either way. I'm just glad I'm here for this one."

"Me too. Sammy and I kind of forced ourselves into her life, so we could watch her for you. I'm surprised she never told us to go fuck ourselves." I remembered back to when we first met Piper, the only woman who had ever captured Jaron's heart. That wasn't a good night, but Jaron had saved Piper from getting attacked by a so-called friend at the time. It could have gone down much worse than it had but they still lost each other for a bit as a result of Jaron's rage.

"She loves you both like brothers. Besides Bee, she's the only one who can tell Sammy off and get away with it." Jaron laughed.

"Oh yeah." I had a feeling that Red would be able to tell Sammy off as well. He needed it. Our cousin Bee had told Sammy that she hoped he would find someone who could knock him down a peg or two after he had given her a hard time about the man she had fallen in love with. Now, you would never know that Sammy and Bee's husband, Tanner, hadn't gotten along at first.

While we sat in silence, I mindlessly sipped at my beer. The guys were mingling with the dancers, drinking, and having a good time. It was a way for us to relax. Taking a night off was needed.

I finally called it a night, said goodbye to Jaron and a few of the guys, and made my way out of the club. The stench of smoke and sweat, lingered beneath my leather cut. A hot shower would be the only way to get the smell off of me.

As I was making my way to my bike, a slight movement caught my eye.

Sammy was standing with Red by her car. She was glaring up at him with her hands on her hips. He leaned down toward her ear, muttering something that made her eyes widen.

I wasn't sure what it was about her that pulled him in, but I knew my brother. He was hooked and the fact that she turned him down, probably made him want her even more. I knew because it would be how I would react.

I couldn't wait for the day that I met my match. I wasn't submissive in the least but if the right woman came along and told me to kneel, I would. And I would beg at her feet until she gave me what I wanted. And more.

TWO

Ainsley

THE DOVE PROJECT WAS my safe place. Literally. No one judged. No one asked questions. Technically they weren't allowed to, but they could have pulled me aside and asked. They never did, thankfully. I almost wondered why. I didn't talk and hadn't said more than a few words in a very long time. Not by my choice really. I was conditioned to be silent and only speak when spoken to. But now that it was so deep in my head that I wasn't allowed to talk, I just stopped altogether and chose to speak through American Sign Language instead. I learned it as a girl but never took it seriously until it was my only way of communicating as I got older. I wondered if I would ever speak again. Maybe one day. With the right person. The right man. Someone who was patient and kind. Someone who pushed me but didn't expect anything in return. Who gave and took only when I allowed it.

I found that while I could still communicate, a lot of people or most people actually, were put off by my lack of words. Several times I had come across those who assumed I was deaf just because I used ASL. Then I would catch them talking about me. It was useful sometimes, especially before. Then. Back when I wasn't free.

Shaking my head, I forced those thoughts to the back of my mind. I couldn't go there.

Inhale.

Exhale.

Repeat.

My heart started racing.

Inhale.

Exhale.

Repeat.

Blowing out a slow breath, I closed my eyes and mentally counted to ten. The hairs on the back of my neck tingled and I realized then I was being watched.

Opening my eyes, I found the darkest pair of eyes staring back at me. My throat dried. My heart jumped. My stomach did a little flip, sparking feelings I had never felt before. Not ever in my twenty-seven years of existence.

The eyes heated, almost like they were looking into the deepest parts of my soul. It was as if they were trying to reach a part of me that had never been revealed to anyone because I had no idea it even existed until *them*. But they never let me embrace that part of me. They assumed it was unnatural and took parts of me away only because I was inexperienced in my sexuality at the time. I reacted to a rough, firm touch and it backfired on me. It resulted in me being called horrible names and worse.

The man's mouth twitched like he was holding back a smirk. He was standing outside with another guy who looked like him. They must have been brothers, or they were definitely related in some way at least.

While the first guy with the smoldering eyes continued staring at me, the other one followed his gaze. But when he looked at me, it made me feel small. Worthless even. I wasn't sure why but for whatever reason, he didn't like me. I didn't even know him. Never met him before in my life but by the way his brother, I could only assume, was looking at me, he didn't like it. He muttered something, pulling the other guy's eyes from mine. I almost whimpered at the loss. I couldn't explain it. I wasn't even going to try but I found that I liked his eyes on me. But clearly, his brother didn't.

"Ainsley."

I jumped, finding Piper Michaels standing a few feet away.

"Sorry." She laughed. "Didn't mean to scare you." She came toward me, cupping her swollen stomach. When she reached the counter I was standing behind, she placed a hand on the edge and blew out a slow breath.

I raised an eyebrow.

"I'm fine. Promise." She gave herself a shake. "I ate something I shouldn't have and it's making me nauseous."

Going up to her, I placed my hands on her stomach. I wasn't a touchy person. Hell, I didn't even like it when others touched me but to feel life growing inside her was something else entirely.

"Jaron thinks it's a boy," she murmured. "We'll both be happy with whatever it is though."

I smiled at her when I felt her unborn baby kick my hand. I had met Jaron Mercer a handful of times when he picked Piper up from the center. He had always been nothing but nice to me even though he never spoke much. My eyes flicked back to the two guys standing just outside the doors. I noticed then that they were wearing leather cuts. Maybe they were part of the same club Jaron was, but then I wondered why I hadn't met them before. Our town wasn't overly big even though it continued to grow with each passing year.

"Do you want kids, Ainsley?"

I swallowed hard at the question. It was harmless, I knew that, but it didn't make it hurt any less.

Piper's face fell. "Oh God, that's super inappropriate of me. I'm so sorry."

I shook my head, giving her a smile of reassurance. Truth was, I *did* want kids, but it would never happen for me.

Letting out a sigh, I pulled away from her and went back behind the receptionist's counter. Our usual receptionist only worked a few hours a week since finishing school and advancing in her career. I filled in for her when I wasn't teaching ASL classes. Even though I didn't speak and liked sticking to myself, I enjoyed working behind the counter and seeing people when they came through the front doors. Especially when they were usually quiet themselves. My demeanor was calming, I was told.

Whenever I helped at the front desk, Jay had the calls forwarded to her office. I tried insisting on just staying behind the scenes but both her and one of the therapists told me that it would be good for me.

"The bigger one is Cyrus and then his twin brother is Sammy," Piper explained, pulling me from my thoughts. "Don't let his gentle name fool you though. He's kind of an ass." She laughed. "But I love them like brothers."

I wanted to ask for her to tell me more but when they turned toward us, I changed my mind.

Piper waved.

They came inside.

And all the air was sucked right out of my lungs as the one named Cyrus stared at me.

"How's my third favorite girl?" Sammy asked Piper, pulling me from his brother's intense gaze. Sammy went up to Piper and drew her in for a hug.

"Third?" She pushed away from him and smacked his arm. "Why am I number three?"

"Because Bee is number two. I knew her first. And then your daughter is number one." He clutched his chest. "She stole my heart."

Piper giggled, shaking her head. "One day a woman will steal your heart too, Sammy."

The smile fell from his face. "Unlikely."

While Piper and he continued talking, I saw out of the corner of my eye that Cyrus was shifting closer to me. My stomach felt like there were butterflies flying around in it the closer he got.

"What's your name, pet?" he asked me, his voice low.

My eyes snapped to his, almost expecting him to be talking to someone else. But when I realized that it was only me and him and that Piper and Sammy were no longer around, my heart pounded.

That single word. *Pet.* It did something funny to my belly. Something I had never felt before. Something I never thought I would feel. Ever. And especially not for a man.

Desire.

For a man.

A stranger.

Cyrus tilted his head, watching me.

Out of habit, I lifted my hands to sign my name but then realized that he wouldn't know what I was saying. My name was on the tip of my tongue, but I couldn't say it. I tried, God I wanted to tell him, but it was like my mouth wasn't connecting with my brain and the words wouldn't come out.

"You understand me?" he asked gently.

I frowned. Did he think I spoke another language?

I nodded, pulled my phone from my purse, and began typing. When I was done, I showed him the screen.

My name is Ainsley.

His eyes moved across the screen before meeting mine once again. "It's nice to meet you, Ainsley." He stuck his hand out. "I'm Cyrus."

Chewing my bottom lip, I tentatively reached out my hand and returned his handshake. His touch was firm, his calloused thumb brushing over the back of my hand.

"You don't speak?" he asked, keeping his hand wrapped around mine. The question held no hint of judgement.

Shaking my head, I pulled my grip from his and went back to my phone. I had every intention of typing up a reply, but his throat clearing stopped me.

Do you use American Sign Language to communicate? he signed slowly. He fumbled over a few of the words and hand signals, but I got the gist of what he meant and the fact that he tried, did something funny to my heart.

My eyes widened.

His lips pulled up into a smirk. "Surprised, pet?"

I nodded quickly.

He chuckled, the sound deep and growly.

For the first time in a very long time, I smiled back.

I wanted to ask him how he knew ASL, but our conversation was cut short when Piper and Sammy stepped into the lobby. Sammy had a scowl on his face while Piper was on her phone.

"What's going on?" Cyrus asked them, taking a step toward me.

He was standing so close, if I made a sudden move, my shoulder would brush just beneath his chest. I could smell the cologne coming from him. It was spicy mixed with a hint of leather.

My eyes flicked to his leather cut, noticing a Hell's Harlem logo sitting on the left breast with vice-president just beneath it. He obviously knew Jaron, Piper's fiancé.

"Jaron wants you two to come over for dinner tonight," Piper said, confirming my thoughts and looking up from her phone.

"He probably wants me to watch Brynlee so you two can have some alone time," Sammy said, rolling his eyes.

Piper grinned, her cheeks turning pink. "We did that once."

"Yup and I'm never letting it go." Sammy wrapped his arms around her shoulders and kissed the top of her head.

Watching the exchange before me sent a flutter of unease rushing through me. I wanted that. Family and friends. People you could trust with your heart and emotions. Someone I could trust with my body and soul. But I was so damn broken, there was no way that could ever happen.

"You may be free of us now, but you will never forget. I will come back for you."

The words had only been a whisper at the time, but *he* was right. I hadn't forgotten.

My palms became sweaty, my heart was racing to the point it felt like it was trying to escape my chest.

"Breathe, pet," Cyrus murmured beside me.

I turned, needing to get out of here. Needing to get away from people's eyes and just escape. I needed to be by myself for fear that someone would see my vulnerability and take advantage of it.

"No." Cyrus's voice was firm. "Breathe."

Squeezing my eyes shut, I shook my head. My body vibrated, the anxiety slicing through me like tiny little shards of broken glass.

"Look at me, pet."

That rough demand forced my eyes open.

"I said, look at me. *Now.*"

A soft whimper left me, but I did as I was told and was met by a dark, stormy gaze.

"Breathe," Cyrus said gently, taking a deep inhale before blowing it out slowly.

I did the same, repeating after him.

Inhale.

Exhale.

Repeat.

"Again."

Inhale.

Exhale.

Repeat.

My heart finally started slowing down, the need to leave no longer there.

"I got you, pet," he whispered, reaching out and running his thumb along the pulse point on my wrist.

That single touch sparked something inside of me that had been dormant for so long.

"We should go, Cyrus," Piper suggested. "Jaron is here anyway." She came up to me and picked up my phone. She quickly typed something on it and showed me the screen.

You good?

I nodded, my heart warming that she cared.

She smiled. "Take care of yourself, Ainsley." She handed me my phone, spun on her heel, and went up to Sammy. "Let's go."

He hesitated, his eyes locking with mine. They flicked between his brother and me, a deep frown settling between his brows.

Cyrus didn't budge.

That fact alone made me stand up straighter. I jutted my chin, refusing to back down from his incessant stare.

His mouth spread into a smirk, something flashing in his eyes.

Piper muttered something to him, gently pushing him out the door. I watched as she was greeted by Jaron. Before she even made it to their car, he had her in his arms. She threw her head back. Even though I couldn't hear her, I could feel her laughter and for the second time that day, I smiled.

THREE

CYRUS

SHE WAS ABSOLUTELY BREATHTAKING. Especially when she smiled. As cliché as it sounded, it lit up her whole face and reached her eyes. I woke up that morning in a shitty mood only to meet this beautiful woman and have her smile pull me out from under the dark cloud that constantly hung over my head.

Her blonde hair was pulled back into a messy ponytail with loose strands framing her face. Her lips were a light pink and freckles sat on her nose and cheeks where the sun had kissed her skin. She appeared to be small under the ripped jeans and baggy sweater she was wearing but I knew that if I let her, she could force me to my knees, and I would comply.

Willingly.

Once I realized that Ainsley didn't speak, I racked my brain with the sign language I had learned as a kid. Thankfully, I had practiced often and kept up on it as best I could, but it wasn't something I let most know. Even my own brother didn't know I knew ASL. But when Ainsley realized that we could communicate without her having to constantly use her phone, the hope dancing in her eyes made me realize that I had kept up on the language for a reason.

But her panic attack bothered me.

And the way Sammy looked at her, bothered me even more. Not because he wanted her. I knew he didn't. He had someone already in mind, but he looked at Ainsley like she was beneath him. I didn't know why. He had peculiar tastes when it came to sex. I only knew because I had walked in on him one too many times. I had seen women in all sorts of positions but one thing I had noticed over the years, he always kept his clothes on. It wasn't something I questioned him about. Obviously, we were close but it was a line that neither of us crossed and we liked it that way.

A tap on the window pulled me from my thoughts. Sammy scowled, nodded once, and in not so many words, told me to hurry my ass up.

I looked down at Ainsley.

While she was pale, her cheeks held a glow that I found I wanted to explore and make the rest of her glow just the same.

Blood pulsed through my cock, making it jump the longer she stared up at me. Clearing my throat, I backed up. "It was nice meeting you, pet."

Something flashed in her eyes at the term of endearment.

Proud of myself, I left the building and was met by my grumpy as fuck brother.

"Who is she?" he asked, following along beside me as we walked toward Jaron and Piper's car.

"I just met her the same time you did," I told him.

"You gonna hit that?"

I stopped, turning on him. "I don't *hit* women. That's you."

He rolled his eyes. "I don't hit women either. Hitting involves punching and shit. Spanking is a different story."

"Still considered hitting." It didn't if it was a kink and that was your thing, but he was pissing me off.

"It does not." His scowl deepened. "Tell him, Jaron."

Jaron chuckled, pulling Piper closer to his side. "I'm not saying shit."

Piper looked between us. "As long as it's consensual between all adult parties, who cares?"

"Exactly." Sammy punched my shoulder. "That's why Piper's my favorite."

It was my turn to roll my eyes then.

They laughed but I wasn't feeling it. I loved Sammy. He was more than just my brother. He was my best friend. But he had become moodier over the past few months, and it affected everyone around him. I wasn't sure what his deal was, but it was annoying as fuck.

While they continued talking, I looked back at the building. The Dove Project was a center to help human trafficking victims. While they sometimes helped domestic abuse victims as well, it was mostly for those who had survived being taken.

I couldn't see Ainsley from where I was standing but I could sense her. Was this how it was with my parents? Were they attracted to each other right away? While it hurt to think about them, I'd heard over the years that my mom had started a rumor about herself to get my dad's attention. Making a mental note to find out more, I turned back around.

"We should go." Jaron cupped Piper's stomach.

"I'm feeling like pasta." Piper paled. "Wait, never mind."

We laughed.

"We'll find something to help settle your stomach, babe." Jaron kissed the side of her head.

"I didn't have morning sickness like this with Brynlee." Piper shook herself, blowing out slow breaths. "It only lasted the first couple of months with her but this one has been nonstop and it's kicking my ass."

"It's almost time," Sammy reminded her. "And then you can go back to making more babies."

"Oh God. I need a break." Piper laughed. "But not from the trying to make babies part." She waggled her eyebrows.

Jaron lightly smacked her ass. "Good. Now let's go. Gotta feed my girl."

Piper shook her head, a wide smile spreading on her face.

Heading to my bike, I glanced back at the large window. When I saw Ainsley standing there, I stood up straighter and popped the collar of my hoodie beneath my leather cut.

She waved.

I nodded once.

"Do you want that?"

I frowned, glancing at Sammy. "Want what?" I asked, looking back at the large window. When Ainsley was no longer standing there, my frown deepened.

"A relationship and a family."

Straddling my bike, I ran a hand down my face. "One day." I just wanted a good girl. A wife. Kids weren't a priority on my list but if it happened, I would be happy. At the moment, I just wanted a relationship.

Sammy nodded, throwing a leg over the seat of his own bike.

"Do you want the same, Sammy?"

"I have you."

I scoffed. "That's not the same."

"No, I guess it's not," he murmured.

"What about Red?" I asked, knowing that I was taking a chance by asking him about her.

He stiffened. "What about her?"

"Have you asked her out yet? Wined and dined her? You know, the usual shit that you hate doing."

"No but if anyone deserves it, it's her."

"What are you waiting for then?" I asked, surprised that he was opening up a bit about her. It was one thing I had learned about my brother. He talked about the women, all of the women, but when it came to Red, he kept that shit closed off. He must have really liked her because I didn't know anything about her. Just her nickname and that she worked at Rouge.

"I'm waiting for her to make a move," Sammy admitted, pulling on his helmet.

"Why?"

"You ask a lot of questions, brother." He hesitated. "If she makes a move, then I'll know." He turned on his bike, revved the engine, and drove off leaving me wondering what the hell was going on with him.

Something deep within me told me to go to Ainsley. To talk to her. To get her to sign, so I could learn more about her. I wanted her words, but I wasn't lucky enough to get them from her. Maybe one day. Maybe never. Either way, there was something about her that I craved. I could sense that she kept a part of herself hidden. I would earn her trust, so she would reveal all to me. No matter how long it took.

Once I arrived at Jaron and Piper's place, I saw Sammy sitting on the front patio bench.

Killing the engine, I pulled off my helmet and hung it over the handlebar. "What's going on?"

"They're busy." Sammy picked up a bottle of beer off the patio floor. "Jaron said to give them thirty."

I chuckled, shaking my head. "Must be nice." I went up to Sammy and joined him on the bench before taking the bottle from him.

Jealousy coursed through me. Not that they were having sex. I could get that anytime I wanted. But to have that partner, a companion to come home to. That was what I wanted. I had wanted it for years. A part of me blamed my brother's active lifestyle for my lack of settling down. Another part, the real part, blamed myself, fearing that it wasn't something I deserved.

"What's Red's real name?" I heard myself ask, taking a swig of the beer.

"Amber."

My head whipped around, not expecting in the least for Sammy to tell me that.

His eyes met mine. "What?"

"I wasn't expecting you to actually answer me."

He shrugged. "It's not a secret."

"It kind of is, Sammy. No one calls her by her real name." It was like our father. No one called him John except for our mother. She had been the only one to get away with it. Everyone else got a fist to the head.

Before I could ask any more about this mysterious woman I had only seen in passing at Rouge, the front door opened.

"Is it safe now?" Sammy asked, rising to his feet.

"It was always safe." Jaron chuckled.

"We weren't doing anything," Piper called out from the kitchen.

"If you weren't doing anything, then why the hell did you make me wait outside?" Sammy picked up the six-pack of beer off the porch and headed into the house.

"Because even though you're a grumpy ass, you're talkative and we needed a moment alone." Jaron smacked his arm. "Not that I have to explain anything to you."

"Right." Sammy grunted. "You should really learn to respect your elders."

I only shook my head, following them into the house. Closing the door behind me, I clicked the lock into place. I went to join Jaron and Sammy in the living room when I was stopped short by Piper.

"Hey," I said, because I didn't know what else to say. She was staring at me like I had stolen a cookie before dinner.

"Hey yourself." She rubbed her stomach, blowing out a slow breath. "I just wanted to talk to you about something."

The hackles on the back of my neck rose. "You do?"

"I do," she murmured, her eyes meeting mine. "I saw you talking to Ainsley and calming her down after her panic attack."

"You saw that?"

She nodded. "She gets them often and can usually talk herself down." She paused. "She's had a hard life, Cyrus." She scowled, shaking her head. "It's not my place to say but just don't be shocked if she wants nothing to do with you or..." She waved her hand between us. "...this."

"I just met her today, Piper." I wasn't sure what she was getting at, but I didn't like it.

"I know. I'm not warning you against dating her, but I do suggest taking it slow. I also don't want you getting hurt. That's all."

I went up to her and kissed the top of her head. "I appreciate that but I'm a big boy. I can handle it." And one day, I would love to be able to handle Ainsley. Even just her name could bring me to my knees.

"What's going on?" Jaron asked, heading to the kitchen.

"Nothing." I shot Piper a look. I didn't need them in my business over a woman I had only just met and found hot as fuck. That was all it was. She was beautiful. It wasn't like I was in love with her or anything. I knew her name and that she didn't speak. That was it.

Piper sighed, patted my arm, and followed her fiancé into the kitchen.

"Careful, C," Sammy said from the dining room table. "You might walk in on them doing something."

"For the last time, we weren't doing anything." Piper rolled her eyes. "My back was hurting, so Jaron gave me a massage. It's cooler out here, so I was sitting on the couch. We didn't want you to see me topless, if you must know."

"Does it still hurt?" Sammy asked, concern evident in his voice.

She sighed.

Jaron chuckled.

For someone who didn't want a relationship or a family of his own, my brother had a big heart. He had spent years building up walls around himself and it would take a strong woman to break them down.

"Not at the moment." Piper went up to Sammy and grabbed his hand. "But he's kicking."

"He?" Sammy and I asked at the same time.

"We don't know. We want to be surprised, but something's telling us it's a boy. Either way, I don't care." Jaron clapped my shoulder.

"Here." Piper placed Sammy's hand on her swollen stomach. "Feel that?"

Sammy nodded, staring at her abdomen. "Jaron, I'm not going to have to sleep with one eye open for touching your girl's stomach, am I?"

"No." Jaron laughed. "I know whose cock Piper's riding at night."

"Just at night?" Piper threw at him.

"Touché." Jaron went back to the kitchen and joined me a moment later. "Here," he said, handing me another beer.

I clinked it against his before taking a long swig. "You happy?"

"Fucking finally," he muttered, pulling back his beer.

I only grunted because what the hell could I say? Jaron and Piper had struggled in the beginning. Hard. He asked us to protect her after he was thrown in jail for saving her from a monster. That monster was dead and gone, but the fucker got off too easy if you asked me.

Add to the fact that Jaron and Piper almost lost their daughter in the process. None of it was fair.

"Listen, I never thanked you."

My back stiffened. "Thank me," I repeated. "For what?"

"For protecting her." He nodded toward Piper and Sammy. "For taking care of her and our daughter."

My chest tightened. "You don't have to thank us for that shit, Jaron. You're family, which automatically makes her family as well."

"That's the truth," Sammy chimed in.

"Either way." Jaron went up to Piper and pulled her into his arms. He kissed her head before looking at both of us. "We almost lost our daughter. I can't…we can't thank you enough for helping us through that."

"Fuck," Sammy muttered.

The air in the room suddenly became thick. It was suffocating as the mood went from light and humorous, to heavy as hell.

"You don't have to thank us," I insisted. "For anything."

While Piper got supper ready, we had laughs, talked, and laughed some more. It was needed after all of the months of heartache Piper and Jaron endured. Even though he wasn't there in the beginning to witness it all, he knew about it. Because both Sammy and I made sure to tell him. There wasn't a day that went by where we didn't tell him. He needed to know that Piper, his girl and the mother of his daughter, needed him. She lived. For him. He had to be strong to get back to them. The love they shared was something I strived for. Something I needed. Ever since I was a little boy, I never believed that girls had cooties. I wanted what my parents had. I wanted that unconditional love I knew I could get with the right person. I just had to find her.

While the rest of the night ended up in a blur, I couldn't help but think back to Ainsley and Piper's warning of her. It made me wonder what that was about or if Ainsley had trouble with the law back in the day and was trying to make a better name for herself. Either way, I didn't care. I just knew from the moment we met, there was something in each other that both of us needed. What it was, I couldn't be sure, but I hoped, no, I damn near prayed, we would find out.

Some way or another.

FOUR

Ainsley

I WAS BEING FOLLOWED.

I wasn't sure by who, but I had spent months looking over my shoulder, so I knew the tells. It also wasn't the first time I had been followed either. While it happened more times than I cared to admit, there was always something familiar about the person too, but I could never figure out what exactly. I was always able to outrun them and find a public hiding place, but a part of me wondered if it was what they wanted. I had a feeling this person made it so I felt like I could always escape them. They were taunting me, letting me think I was in control when really, I never had been. I knew that one day eventually, they would catch up with me.

Hairs tingled on the back of my neck. They stood up straight, almost as if they were giving their silent little warning.

That feeling of being followed was always the same. Your stomach clenched, your chest tightened like the lone voyeur was using your discomfort for their personal gain.

It was an uneasy feeling, knowing you're being watched but you couldn't figure out by who or why. In my case, I did know. It was someone from my past. From my years in that hell. I had been reassured by the authorities that I was finally safe, but was I really? They couldn't give me a definitive answer on everyone who had escaped or who had a hand in the trafficking or their whereabouts, so I knew it was only a matter of time before at least one of them caught up with me. Add to the fact I never even stepped foot off of American soil, being trafficked within my own country made it almost seem worse somehow.

All I knew was that ever since I left the center fifteen minutes ago, I was being followed. Every time I looked over my shoulder, I didn't see anyone out of the ordinary. But the farther I walked and the faster I picked up my pace, the more intense that same feeling became.

I should never have left the center, but I needed out of there. Sitting inside the same four walls day in and day out, could be detrimental to a person's sanity. I needed to see something different. I loved the center and what it stood for. Everyone had been nothing but kind to me. I stayed there long past my shift until I had nothing else to keep me busy and decided to walk home. It was still early in the evening; the sun was high in the sky and my apartment was only a few blocks away. Walking and getting some fresh air was good for me, but today I regretted not taking a cab.

Once I turned the corner of another block, I recognized a familiar deli that I had never been to before but heard about often. Picking up my pace, I ran to the front doors. My eyes flicked to a beautiful motorcycle in the parking lot, my thoughts suddenly conjuring up a dark stranger. I wasn't sure who the bike belonged to but a part of me hoped that maybe one day I could go for a ride on the back of Cyrus's bike.

Before I could dwell further on a certain man, I was inside the deli. The bell above the door indicated my arrival, making my cheeks burn as patrons looked up from whatever they were doing.

With my head down, I held my bag to my chest and took a step down the aisle.

Looking over my shoulder, I saw a man in a hood coming toward the front of the deli. My heart picked up speed. I knew him. I didn't know how I did but familiarity scratched over my skin like little knives, reminding me that I would never be rid of that place and my captors. No matter how much I tried, they would always be a part of me. It was what they wanted. They made it so and because of them, I would always be looking over my shoulder.

"Ainsley?"

I jumped, spun around, and found Cyrus standing in front of me.

Oh, thank God.

I remembered that he knew some sign language, but I couldn't remember how fluent he was. But I still took a chance anyway. Pulling the strap of my bag over my shoulder, I lifted both hands.

Help me.

Cyrus frowned, his eyes flicking above my head before returning to me. "Tell me."

A shiver raced down my spine at the deep command. *I think that man has been following me.*

Before I could say anymore, Cyrus closed the distance between us and wrapped his arm around my waist.

It had been a long time since I felt the contact of a man, let alone someone as intense as the one standing in front of me. When I looked for the sense of fear that he would hurt me and got nothing, I let out a slow breath of relief.

His eyes dropped to my mouth. "I got you, pet."

My breath caught at the term of endearment. He had called me that when I first met him. I never understood why. Maybe I never would. But right now, I was thankful he was there.

He was much larger than I last remembered. I never noticed when I first met him weeks ago, just how big he actually was.

Cyrus bent at the waist, leaning toward me. His mouth pressed against my ear, his breath hot and inviting.

I could hear my own heart pounding in my ears, I was surprised he couldn't hear it himself.

His mouth slowly moved down the length of my jaw. "Trust me," he murmured against my skin.

As soon as the chime above the door jingled, indicating someone's arrival, Cyrus crushed his mouth to mine.

My eyes widened, a small gasp leaving me. It was the only invitation he needed before slipping his tongue between my lips. The kiss deepened, pulling a moan from the back of my throat.

He grunted his approval, nipping my bottom lip. The sharp pain, although minimal, sent a jolt of pleasure through my nerves.

"He's gone," Cyrus murmured, breaking the kiss and pulling away from me.

The sense of loss I felt at him no longer being close, set off alarm bells inside of me. I couldn't give myself to him, or to anyone for that matter. I was broken, a shattered mess and I didn't know how to fix it. I didn't know how to fix *me*.

Cyrus stared at me, his eyes dark and molten with lust.

My cheeks burned at the intense scrutiny coming from him.

"Have breakfast with me," he finally said, breaking the unnerving silence between us.

I swallowed hard at the rough demand but found myself nodding. *It's not breakfast time.*

His face was impassive as he glanced at the booth. "It is when you haven't eaten yet and this deli serves breakfast all day. Haven't you ever had pancakes for supper?"

I shook my head.

He gave me a small smile. "You should."

Something switched between us then. Something fast. Something heavy. And I wasn't sure how I felt about it.

Clearing my throat, I slid onto the red leather bench and placed my bag beside me.

"Tell me who that man was," Cyrus said, sitting in the booth across from me.

When I went to lift my phone to type up a message for him, his hand covered mine. My eyes snapped to his, my heart jumping to my throat at the gentle touch coming from him.

"If you sign for me slowly, I can understand. Please."

The demand was soft but firm. It opened up something inside of me. Something I wanted to explore.

I took a breath, pulled my hand from under his and began moving my fingers.

I don't know. I think he started following me about three blocks ago. I didn't actually see him though and I came in here because I didn't know what else to do. Then I saw you and…

Cyrus smiled. "You're safe here and with me."

Somehow, I believed him.

You understand me?

He nodded. "I'm rusty but I can understand most of what you're saying."

I can sign slower or text you. Oh God, now I was hinting for his phone number.

"I like that idea too, but I still want you to sign. It'll help me remember." He pulled his cell out of his leather cut, typed a few words on it and slid it across the table.

My eyes dropped to the phone. Giving him my phone number would hint for more wouldn't it? Would he think I was leading him on if I didn't want anything to come of this? Would he be like the other guys I had come across who would think I was a tease just because I smiled at him or gave him my number? It was how I ended up in that hell anyway. All because a guy hit on me, and another swooped in like a hero. He ended up asking for directions and used the excuse he was new in town. The next thing I knew, I was in the back of a van with him deep inside—

"Ainsley." Cyrus's gruff voice pulled me back to the present. "Take your time, pet."

I glanced up at him, wringing my hands together in my lap. I could do this. I could be normal.

"I won't pressure you into giving me your phone number," Cyrus added. "Whatever you're thinking, get it out of your head. I just want to be able to communicate the easiest way with you. Whatever you want and that's best for you."

His voice, although deep and firm, was also soothing in a way. He was giving me control and I found that it set me on edge. I wasn't used to that. Even now that I was safe and out of that hell I had spent years living in, I wasn't truly in control. Not of my life. But this moment right here with Cyrus, even though it was something small, like giving him my phone number, I was in control. I could say no, or I could say yes. It was *my* choice.

Reaching for the phone, I typed my number in it and handed it back to him.

"Thank you, pet." He typed something on his phone before stuffing it back inside his leather cut.

My phone dinged a second later.

Unknown number: Now you have my number.

I smiled, adding him to my contacts list under *Handsome Stranger.*

Once that was settled, I looked around me. The deli was small and quaint. It reminded me of the older days with the checkered black and white floors and tablecloths.

"Did you want something to eat?" Cyrus asked, taking a sip of his water.

I was going to say that I wasn't hungry when my stomach rumbled.

He chuckled. "What would you like?" he asked, handing me the menu.

I decided to take him up on his advice and chose chocolate chip pancakes with a coffee. I'd never had breakfast for dinner before. Even back when I was a kid, my parents had strict rules about having the proper meals at the right times.

My stomach twisted, wishing I could see them. My mom and dad. We had left things on a bad note, and I never got a chance to tell them I was sorry. For being a typical teen. For not listening to them. For not going home like my mom had begged before it was too late, and I was taken from them.

'My parents,' *I wrote on the piece of paper.* 'Where are my parents?'

The social worker gave me a sad smile. "They were in a car accident, *Ainsley. They're gone. They've been gone for more than a year.*"

I was alone. I had no one. Not then. Not now. Not—

"Ainsley?" Cyrus frowned, his jaw clenching.

My cheeks heated at being caught daydreaming. Although it was more like a nightmare. A nightmare that I was constantly living no matter how much I tried waking up from it.

"This place makes the best pie," he said, trying to distract me. "Did you want to try a piece instead of breakfast?"

I shook my head, appreciating the thought but preferred an actual meal instead.

Cyrus helped me place my order and thankfully, the waitress never gave any sort of judgement. Not even when she asked if I wanted anything else with the pancakes. I pointed to the options on the menu instead of actually voicing my answer out loud. She just smiled and nodded and went to put our orders in.

Cyrus took another sip of his water, watching me over the rim of his glass.

My heart jumped as he stared at me. *Where did you learn ASL?*

"I learned it as a kid," he told me. "A boy in my school was deaf and while the other kids ignored him, I made it a mission to learn so I could communicate with him. I think he appreciated the gesture. He left for a special school a year later, but I was determined to continue learning it. It hasn't come in handy until now though." He winked.

My cheeks burned.

"When was the last time you spoke?"

Shifting in my seat, I looked down at my lap. Picking at a string on my ripped jeans, I shrugged.

"You don't know?"

I met his gaze then. *Why?*

Cyrus sat back in the booth, resting his hand on top of the table between us. "I don't know, pet. But I find that I want to get to know you. I want to know your truths. Your hobbies. Your likes and dislikes. I want to know what movies you like. What music you listen to and if you like to read."

I almost laughed at him wanting to know what kind of music I liked. My music tastes were heavy. To say the least.

I searched his face for any sign that he was lying or hinting for more, but truth was, I couldn't tell. I ended up trusting the wrong people before and I paid for it.

My chest tightened, remembering some of the other girls I had been locked up with. I hadn't thought of them in so long. I never even knew their names.

"Run. Run as fast as you can."

The words slid into my mind, like tiny shards of glass threatening to cut away every bit of the sanity I had left.

We didn't know each other's names but even though that was the case, we still knew everything there was to know about one another when it came to us being in that world. But I didn't know them outside of it. I didn't even know if any of them were still alive. If they were, I prayed they had good lives. I prayed they survived.

"Ainsley?"

I jumped, finding Cyrus staring back at me. Clearing my throat, I grabbed my phone.

I haven't said more than a handful of words in years. I actually don't remember when the last time I said a full sentence was.

But I did. It was before. Before everything happened and I was taken. Before I was shoved into a life most would never see or even know about. It was safer that way if you asked me.

Cyrus's eyes moved along the tiny screen on his phone. "It's been that long?"

I don't trust anyone enough to give them my voice.

Something flashed behind his eyes. Before he could respond, the waitress brought over our food.

Cyrus thanked her.

I gave her a small smile.

While we ate in silence, I wondered why Cyrus was suddenly thrown into my life. I had been living at the center for well over a year and working for a few months now. How come I never saw him before?

Me: Do you work at the center too?

I tapped my phone.

His eyes slid to his cell sitting on the table beside him. "No, I don't work there. We started volunteering there only just recently. You would have met or at least seen Jaron more because Piper works there. Sammy and I never went with him until now. Jaron's dad wanted us to do something nice in the public eye. We've been through some shit with the previous mayor, so we're being good boys at the moment."

I mulled over his words. Price Davies, the old mayor of our city, had suddenly disappeared. There was much speculation as to what had happened to him, but no one knew all of the details. I wondered if Cyrus knew more than he let on.

"How long have you been working there?"

Me: Almost 3 months.

Cyrus picked up his phone and began typing.

Handsome Stranger: You don't want to sign?

Me: I always worry that someone can understand. It's odd, I know. I guess I'm paranoid.

I was surprised my truth came out so quickly, especially when I didn't know him.

Handsome Stranger: I get that.

Placing my phone on the table in front of me, I watched him. I found that since I hadn't spoken in quite a while, my other senses kicked into overdrive. The scent of his cologne made my nose tingle. His muscles bunched under his long-sleeved shirt as he shifted in his seat.

"You're staring, pet." His eyes lifted, catching mine.

My cheeks burned. *Sorry.*

His lips pulled up into a small smirk. "Don't apologize. I like your eyes on me."

My face heated even more. I was sure it was bright red but even though that was the case, I couldn't help the smile pulling at my own lips. It amazed me how much I smiled both of the times I had been around Cyrus. Even though I didn't know him overly well, there was something about him that called out to me. I found myself wanting to get to know him more. What made him tick? Was he close with his brother? Did he know why, for whatever reason, Sammy hated me? As much as that bothered me, I wanted to know everything there was to know about Cyrus more.

"Eat your food." Cyrus nodded to my plate. "It's going to get cold."

While we ate in silence, I noticed how comfortable it was to just sit there with him. He never demanded for me to talk like a lot of people did when they first met me. I assumed he would eventually, but for now he let me text him or sign. Whichever I felt like using at that point in time.

When we were done our breakfast, Cyrus asked for the bill.

I reached into my bag to grab some money for him when his hand covered mine. My eyes shot to his.

"This is my treat," he said gently, his calloused thumb running back and forth over the edge of my hand.

I shook my head, not wanting him to think I was a freeloader.

"Trust me. I am honored that you agreed to have breakfast with me, pet. I would never make you pay." He pulled his hand back and tossed a couple of bills onto the table.

Thank you, I signed, even though those two words would never be enough.

"You're welcome." He slid out of the booth, came to my side, and held out his hand.

I looked up at him, chewing my bottom lip.

"Trust me." He had said those words a couple of times already and while I had to be cautious, a part of me did in fact trust him. Maybe eventually, all of me would.

(Cyrus)

I wasn't expecting to see Ainsley today. I was going to grab something to eat and then head over to the center to see if she was still working. I wanted to ask her out on a date. It would have been forward of me, but I wasn't getting any younger. I had been ready to settle down for years and while I didn't know Ainsley, I wanted to see where it could possibly go with her. If anywhere at all.

It was later in the day, but I didn't sleep much anymore, so having breakfast at this time, was normal for me.

Piper had reminded me a couple of times already during the week, to leave Ainsley alone. I appreciated where she was coming from but at the same time, I refused to listen.

I didn't believe in love at first sight, but I knew what attraction was and I was definitely attracted to Ainsley.

When she showed up at the deli, frantic and worried, it took everything in me not to go after the bastard who had scared her.

A man wearing a hoodie had come into the deli, only to stop when he saw her standing in front of me. I didn't see his face but there was something off about him and I knew that it wasn't a good thing.

Before I kissed her, movement across the room caught my eye. A man was sitting in a booth, looking directly at me. I didn't know him, had never seen him before in my life. But something was odd about the way he stiffened when the other guy came into the deli after Ainsley and how he stared at us after that bastard left.

Ainsley's ragged breaths at the time, had pulled my gaze back to hers.

Kissing her was something I never planned for. Knowing she was timid, I half-expected her to push me away and slap me but when she had opened up to me instead, that single submission called out to the Dom in me.

Now we were done our breakfast and I was waiting for her to slip her fingers in mine so I could gently help her out of the booth like a gentleman.

Her teeth grazed over her bottom lip, her dark eyes locking with mine.

"Trust me," I told her again.

She grabbed her bag, holding onto it like it was the only thing she lived for, and slipped her fingers in mine. Letting me pull her out of the booth, I made sure to remain standing close, so she could get used to me being near her.

Her breath caught, her body brushing against mine.

My dick stirred to life, jumping behind the fly of my jeans. Well, that was new. It had been a long time since a woman caused any sort of reaction in me, I almost thought my dick no longer worked. Now it was the second time my body reacted to hers.

The scent of something sweet, wafted into my nose, making my dick twitch.

"Come," I said, my voice raspy. With my hand in hers, I walked us out of the deli and into the late afternoon sun. It had been a warmer day with a nice cool breeze billowing around us every so often. "Were you walking home?" I asked her.

Ainsley nodded.

"I'll take you." Thankfully, I had taken the SUV after Jaron asked me to drop off a load of supplies to the center. I hadn't made it to the center yet and would do that after driving Ainsley home and making sure she was safe.

She shook her head.

When she went to pull away, I tugged on her hand. "I'm just going to drive you home and make sure you get inside safely. I won't come in. But I also won't leave until I know that you're inside and your door is locked." My tone held no room for argument. I was a patient man and, for her, I would learn to become even more patient, but when a frantic woman ended up in my arms because someone was following her, I made sure to do everything I could to see that she was safe. Whether I was attracted to her or not.

Her eyes darkened. Something was hiding deep inside her. I knew because I felt the same thing.

I learned rather quickly that she was naturally submissive. Whenever I made a demand, no matter how big or small it was, her pupils would dilate, and her breath would catch. I wasn't sure if she noticed but I did. It had been something I trained in. While I didn't practice the lifestyle day in and day out at the moment, I had been looking for a submissive for a while. A good girl. A pet. When I first used the term of endearment on Ainsley, it just felt natural. The pet name had fallen from my lips like I had been calling her that for years, even though I only knew her for a short time.

With her hand in mine, we walked to the large black SUV I owned with my brother. Even though I was the only one who drove it, Sammy's name was still on the registration. I often wondered why he never got his own car, besides the bike he owned, but never questioned him on it.

When we reached the passenger door, I opened it for Ainsley.

She was looking anywhere but at me.

Wanting to test something, I gave her hand a tug. "Eyes, pet."

Her gaze shot to mine, her cheeks turning pink.

Blood rushed through me. I found her. Fuck me, I found her. Was this how it was in the beginning with all of the couples I knew? Did they feel this intense attraction for their partner right away or did it happen over time?

"Interesting," was all I said because hell, what else was there to say? If I actually voiced the thoughts running rampant in my head, they would scare her off before I even had a chance to ask her out.

She tilted her head, a frown settling between her brows.

I chuckled, reaching out to brush my thumb along the edge of her jaw. "Don't worry about it, Ainsley. You'll understand. In time."

Stepping away from her, I went around the SUV to the driver's side. I needed to put some distance between us before I continued touching her. I wanted to unleash the passionate vixen inside of her but that would have to wait. Making a mental note, I vowed to earn her trust first.

No matter how long it took.

FIVE

Ainsley

"YOU CAN'T TRUST PEOPLE."

Yeah, no shit. I often wondered how a lot of these therapists got their degree whenever they pointed out the most obvious thing. It was like they thought I didn't know that I couldn't trust people and was just figuring it out for the very first time.

I shook my head anyway.

"Use your words, Ainsley."

My eyes shot to his. A man. Not that I had sworn off men completely but coming from what I had, you would think I would have been set up with a female therapist at the hospital, but life was cruel and that wasn't the case in this situation.

Crossing my arms under my chest, I stared at him. He was older, maybe mid-forties, with gray sprouting from the dark hair on his head. The longer I stared, the more I realized that this wasn't working for me.

"When was the last time you said something?" he asked, writing in his notebook.

I didn't answer because what was the point? He would demand that I actually speak.

Trauma was not an excuse to become silent. His words.

I remembered back to that session. It didn't last long, and I left shortly after, never to see him again. I couldn't even remember his name. He didn't deserve that much.

It was late one evening during the week. I sat on the couch with a glass of white wine, reading a classic novel, and listening to music. The heavy bass and the growl of the singer slid into my ears, easing the constant anxiety resting on my shoulders. Every time he screamed, I felt almost at peace.

"How the hell does a quiet girl like you listen to this kind of music?" Ashton Donovan shook his head. "I'll never understand it."

"Don't listen to him," his twin brother, Aiden, said. "You listen to whatever you want."

I only nodded, shoving the ear bud back into my ear as the guys went back to work on the construction they were doing on the center.

My heart warmed at the memory. The twins had become what I would once consider friends. Now I just assumed they, along with everyone else, put up with me because I was just there. It was a cynical way of looking at things but having been through hell, my emotions and my heart were closed off. To everyone. Or they used to be until I met a handsome stranger.

Cyrus had been on my mind constantly. I hadn't seen him lately, but we spoke a bit through texting. Just simple things like how our days were going or what we were watching on TV. Nothing super important but those little conversations, meant a lot to me. I found that I wanted to see him, but I had been too nervous to ask him if he wanted to go get a drink or a coffee. I also missed his commanding tone and gentle, but firm, touch.

A sudden ding came from my phone, startling me.

My eyes widened when I saw who was texting me. Cyrus. The very man that had invaded my thoughts ever since I met him. It had been a couple of days since we last texted, so I was surprised to get a message from him.

Handsome Stranger: Hey, pet. How are you?

I swallowed hard, loving that term of endearment.

Me: Hello. I'm fine, thank you. How are you?

Handsome Stranger: Good too. You've been well?

My stomach tumbled that he cared so much about my well-being. When he drove me to my apartment after we had breakfast for supper together, he walked me into the building even though I insisted that he didn't have to. He even walked me up to my floor and waited at the end of the hallway, making sure I entered my apartment safely.

It was the sweetest thing anyone had ever done for me. Even though it happened a few weeks ago, I constantly thought about it.

Me: Yes, keeping busy at the center. You?

Handsome Stranger: Busy here too but nothing overly fun. Some shit went down. That's why I've been quiet the past couple of days. I'm sorry for that.

I frowned, not understanding why he felt the need to apologize for something that wasn't his fault and also, it wasn't like we were together. He didn't need to keep me in the loop over things he did.

Me: You don't have to apologize, Cyrus.

Handsome Stranger: I do, so I am.

Me: Apology accepted but it's not necessary.

Handsome Stranger: Thank you.

Me: Is everything good now?

Handsome Stranger: It will be. In time.

Me: I'm glad.

Handsome Stranger: Any plans for tonight?

Me: Listening to music, reading, and having a glass of wine.

Handsome Stranger: What kind of music do you like?

Chewing my bottom lip, I hesitated in responding. I wasn't sure why. It didn't matter what I listened to, but a lot of people judged. They assumed that heavy metal was all angry and filled with hate. While that may be the case in a lot of the genre, it wasn't in the bands I chose to listen to.

Me: Heavy metal but black metal is my favorite. Or deathcore. Depending on my mood.

Handsome Stranger: You would get along with my cousin. She likes that kind of music too.

Me: But not you?

Handsome Stranger: Not so much. But I don't judge.

A breath I didn't realize I had been holding, left me.

Handsome Stranger: I would like to see you again, pet. I'm sick of texting. When are you free next?

I thought a moment.

Me: If it's not too late for you, you're more than welcome to come over. I'm not doing anything overly exciting tonight though.

It took everything in me not to erase the message and make plans to see him somewhere public, but Jay had told me to put myself out there. Slowly anyway. Something told me it was different with Cyrus. He didn't judge. He never demanded for me to speak when I wasn't ready to.

"Cyrus seems to be interested in you," Piper told me one afternoon.

I only stared at her, neither confirming nor denying it because really, it wasn't like I could.

"Whatever happens," she patted my hand, *"I can vouch for him. He's a good guy, Ainsley. And if he dates anyone, I'd be happy to see him date you."*

That conversation took place a couple of days ago. I appreciated hearing her words. Maybe I could trust him like he said.

Handsome Stranger: I'm on my way.

My eyes widened, my stomach dropping. I almost expected him to turn me down.

Quickly tidying up, I took a glance around my small living room. It was clean but definitely looked like it had been lived in. Magazines were on the coffee table; three bottles of water were on the end table. A plate of cookies sat on the other.

I was going to put the water and cookies away but thought maybe he would end up wanting some.

Letting out a small sigh, I turned off the music and threw on a sweater when my phone dinged.

Handsome Stranger: I'm here.

I buzzed him in once I heard that familiar beep. While I was the one who invited him over, I was still nervous. I never had a man over before. Was this too soon? Was there a rule on when I should have a man over, if ever at all? Should we have met up somewhere else instead? Piper vouched for him, so that was enough, wasn't it?

Taking a deep breath and then another, I unlocked the door and stepped out into the hall.

The elevator doors dinged. A moment later, Cyrus stepped into the hallway. A deep frown had settled on his face making my stomach twist. Something was wrong.

He looked my way and paused.

What's wrong?

His face softened as he came toward me. "Don't worry about it. Just a weird feeling, that's all."

Just the sight of him took my very breath away. He was dressed in a black hoodie with light blue jeans that were ripped at the knees. He wasn't wearing his leather cut and that fact alone, almost made him seem more lethal.

Swallowing hard, I backed up a step when he started walking toward me.

Heading back into my apartment, my heart jumped to my throat when the door shut behind me.

"Ainsley."

I turned at the abrupt use of my name. *You sure it's nothing for me to worry about?*

"I felt like I was being followed. I don't like that shit. Makes me itchy." Cyrus remained by the door, almost as if he were waiting for something. An invitation maybe? I already let him into my home, so I wasn't sure what more he was wanting.

I started wringing my hands in front of me, unsure what to do. If he was being followed, that could mean whoever it was knows where I live. So many thoughts started bouncing around in my mind. Who was this person? Should I be worried? Should I call the police?

"Hey." Cyrus's smooth deep voice brought my attention back to him. "Don't worry, Ainsley."

I took a deep breath, let it out slowly and nodded. *Did you want a drink? I have beer, wine, water, juice.*

"I'll have what you're having," he answered, coming toward me.

I nodded, heading to the kitchen to grab him a glass of wine. Even though he didn't look like a guy who drank it, I liked that we shared something in common.

Grabbing a glass from the cupboard, I pulled the bottle from the fridge and made my way back out into the living room.

Cyrus was sitting on the couch, looking at the book I was reading. "Jane Austen. Good choice."

Sitting beside him, I poured a glass of the white wine from New Zealand I had fallen in love with, and handed it to him.

"Thank you." He clinked his glass against mine and took a sip, his eyes never straying from mine.

My cheeks heated.

He winked over the rim.

Taking a sip from my own glass, I leaned back against the couch. Happy and content just to sit there in silence with him, I liked having him in my home.

"How long have you lived here for?" he asked, breaking the comfortable silence between us.

Placing the glass on the table in front of us, I turned toward him. *A few months.*

"There's some heavy-duty security here," he pointed out. "You even have a security system in here. You don't see that a lot in apartments."

I lived at the center for over a year but wanted to have something I could call my own, I signed slowly for him. *I don't make enough to buy a house. Jay and the other ladies who run the place, had their husbands look into an apartment building for those of us at the center that are ready to move out. They made sure it was safe for us. Angel, Jay's husband, said that if he wouldn't want his wife or kid living there, then it wasn't good enough.* It had been sweet of him to look out for me, like he did his own. Jay's eyes had welled at that, and I was sure that if swooning was actually a thing, she would have done it.

"That's good." Cyrus placed his glass on the table beside mine. "I'm glad you have people looking out for you."

Me too. I remembered back to our conversation, wondering if everything was actually okay with him. *How is everything? I'm surprised you didn't have plans tonight. Especially when it's Friday.*

What are you implying, pet? he asked, raising an eyebrow.

My body buzzed over the fact that he signed for me. I only shrugged, unsure as to how to answer him.

"There's a strip club I usually go to with my brother, but I wasn't feeling it tonight. He's been in a mood, so I told him to go get laid." Cyrus shook his head, running a hand through his dark hair. "He's a stubborn ass though and won't go after the one woman he wants."

Sounds confusing.

"Yeah." His eyes dropped to my mouth. "But enough about him. What would you spend your night doing if I wasn't here?"

A smile pulled at my lips. Jumping from the couch, I headed to the TV stand and opened the bottom cupboard before pulling out the item I was looking for.

"You play video games?"

I laughed, nodding quickly.

His eyes widened a touch. "You laughed."

My neck heated, the smile falling from my face.

"No." He rose from the couch and came toward me. Pulling me to my feet, he cupped my cheek. "Never feel ashamed over laughing. I'm just surprised. I haven't heard a sound leave you yet. Thank you for giving that to me."

Covering his hand against my cheek, I pushed my face into his big palm. His thumb brushed along the edge of my jaw, dipping lower to run under it.

"Has anyone ever told you how beautiful you are?" he asked, his voice low.

I shook my head.

"Well, you are, Ainsley." He took a step closer. "So fucking beautiful."

Tilting my head back, I stared up into his dark eyes. They were filled with lust, desire, and so much more. Feelings I had never seen before. Not directed toward me anyway. I had seen Jaron look at Piper like this, like she was the only who mattered in his world. Besides their daughter and unborn baby, she was. She was his life and he the same for her. I wanted that. But I had never gone out and looked for it because the guys at the center were just as broken as I was. And any of the guys who worked there had their own shit to deal with.

"Ainsley." Cyrus's voice was low and deep. With his hand against my cheek, he didn't take it further.

Licking along my bottom lip, I watched as his nostrils flared. He caught the movement, a low rumble leaving from somewhere deep inside of him.

Placing my hand on his chest, I felt the beating of his heart beneath my palm. My mouth tingled, itching to feel his running along mine. To feel his tongue deep in my mouth like our moment at the deli. But that had been different. It was all for show anyway, since I had been followed. Wasn't it? It wasn't like he actually wanted to kiss me. Did he?

"Your move, baby." Cyrus's hand dipped lower, wrapping around my throat. No air was cut off as he stared deep into my eyes, but the move alone made me feel safe and protected.

I fisted his hoodie, pulling him toward me.

He lowered his mouth to mine, the kiss soft and gentle. Not like the man standing in front of me. He was rough around the edges but was kinder than I expected. It just proved you shouldn't judge someone based on their exterior.

Although the kiss was just a peck, I breathed him in as best I could. I took his strength and power, embracing it to the point everything fell away around us.

Cyrus pulled away, placing a soft peck on my nose and then my forehead. "Let's play one of your games."

Blowing out a slow breath, I nodded. Lowering to my knees, I rummaged through my games before finding the one I liked playing the most.

"What's your favorite type of game to play?"

I looked up, finding him standing only a few feet away. He was looking at the rows of movies I had on a small bookcase.

But when I looked down, I suddenly realized the position I was in. On my knees. In front of him. It looked bad. Very bad.

Jumping to my feet, I hugged the game against my chest, taking a step back.

His head whipped around. "What's wrong?" He came toward me, but I only continued backing up. "Ainsley, stop."

My back hit the wall, my eyes closing tight. Memories rushed through me. Painful, agonizing, downright brutal memories. They controlled and took, not giving me any sort of solace in return. One man specifically ruined my life, while the others watched or assisted. Because of him, I had nightmares. Because of him, I wasn't the woman I once was. Because of him, I would never see my parents again. Because of him I wouldn't be able to tell them how much I loved and missed them and how sorry I was.

"Breathe, baby." Cyrus's gentle voice slid through me. The game was pulled from my clutches and replaced with rough calloused hands. "Open your eyes."

Doing as I was told; I was met by Cyrus's handsome face. I noticed then how his nose was a little crooked. A faint light pink scar sat on his upper cheek. Maybe from being hit too hard.

"What just happened?" he asked, releasing my hands so I could answer him.

I wasn't thinking, I signed slowly for him when really, I just wanted to rush the words out, so we could forget this ever happened in the first place. *I didn't want you wondering if I was hinting for more. I'm not ready. Not for that. Not for any of that. I like when you kiss me, but I can't handle anything else, Cyrus. I'm sorry. Please don't think—*

Cyrus grabbed my hands, pulling me against him. He wrapped his arms around my body, hugging me tight. "I would never think that of you. I don't know who hurt you, but you have nothing to worry about. Not when it comes to me." He leaned back, cupping my face. "I like you, Ainsley, and I would like to take you on a date. If you'll let me."

I nodded.

"Also, what just happened, was not your fault. I would never hint for more. Not like that. Not when we just met. I'm sorry for making you uncomfortable and for scaring you."

Before he could say any more, I grabbed his hoodie and threw my arms around his thick neck. I wanted to thank him for having patience with me. Sure, we only saw each other less than a handful of times so far but that was beside the point. I knew how some guys worked. I shouldn't have assumed that Cyrus would be the same way, but I didn't know him enough to know how he was with his partners.

"You're welcome, pet," he murmured, placing a soft peck on my cheek.

Clearing my throat, I pulled away from him and picked up the game. I popped it into the console before turning on the TV, while he went to the couch.

I grabbed both the controllers and joined him.

"Racing game?" he asked, once the title of the game and the credits appeared on the screen.

Putting the controller on my lap, I tapped his arm.

His eyes flicked to mine, a spark of interest flashing behind them.

Racing games are my favorite. They ease my anxiety and help distract me.

"Makes sense. I like to fight to ease my anxiety." He laughed, shaking his head. "Don't look at me like that."

I scowled, unsure as to how I was looking at him.

He chuckled, leaning over and kissing my nose. "The other guys always look worse than I do, baby. And I have scars which I've come to learn are sexy as fuck."

Does your brother know? I wasn't sure exactly why I asked that, but I needed to know that Cyrus had someone rooting in his corner for him. And that he had someone who could take him to the hospital if needed.

"He does." Cyrus turned back around, looking ahead at the TV. "I was the bad influence and got him into fighting originally but he's dirty. He wouldn't think twice about wiping the ground with my pretty face. We're close. Too close sometimes. We've shared a room and lived together ever since we were born. Even at the clubhouse, we have a room together. Our apartment is the only thing separating us. He has his own room and thank fuck for that. The women he brings home…" Cyrus shook his head. "Anyway, we need some sort of privacy." He looked at me then. "Does that make sense?"

It does but to be honest, I wish I had a sibling that I wanted to keep things from. I wanted to tell him my history and why I wasn't overly close to anyone, but I couldn't. I didn't want to scare him away or for him to think that I was only looking for sympathy.

"Are you close with your parents?"

My chest tightened. *We became estranged and before I could make things better, they were killed in a car accident by a drunk driver.*

"I'm sorry, Ainsley." A dark shadow passed over Cyrus's face. "We lost our parents when we were young. Our mom was killed and then a year later, so was our dad. It's been hard but we've had people looking out for us thankfully, so we weren't thrown into the system and separated."

I'm sorry for your loss too. I cupped his shoulder, placing a soft peck on his cheek.

"Thank you," he murmured, his voice thick. "This conversation suddenly got heavy." He smirked.

It has but thank you for letting me learn something new about you.

Cyrus grabbed my hand and brought it up to his mouth. He kissed the tips of my fingers, his eyes locking with mine. "Thank you for the same, pet."

When he released my hand, I kept my fingers against his lips. I noticed another faint scar in his upper lip. Maybe he had been punched, which caused his lip to split and never healed properly. The skin was slightly raised but he was right, his scars were sexy.

"You need to stop looking at me like that," he muttered.

Instead of asking him what he meant, I leaned forward, pushing my mouth against his.

He cupped the back of my neck, slipping his tongue between my lips and deepening the kiss. It turned fast and frantic, like both of us were experiencing a kiss for the very first time.

While his mouth was locked with mine, I was vaguely aware of his other hand on my hip. His fingers inched beneath my shirt. As soon as they came into contact with my skin, I jumped away from him and bounded to my feet.

Alarm bells rang in my head.

Too soon. Too damn soon.

"Ainsley."

I shook myself, blowing out a slow breath.

"Come here."

I turned toward him.

Cyrus held his hand out. "Please."

I'm sorry, I can't do more. I can't. I just need time. I can't give you more. Not yet.

"I want whatever you are willing to give me." His face softened. "I didn't come over here to have sex, pet. I came over to get to know you better. Sure, sex would be nice, but we only just met. I don't even know your last name."

A soft laugh left me. *Cloet. I'm Ainsley Cloet.*

"Nice to meet you, Ainsley Cloet." His smile grew. "I'm Cyrus Butcher. Now, can you come here please? We can play this game, cuddle, kiss, cuddle some more, but I promise, I will not pressure you into doing anything you're not ready for."

Why not?

His smile fell. "What do you mean?"

I mean, most guys would push for more. In my experience, that's how it is anyway.

"I don't know who or what the fuck you're going on about, but I am not him. I am not the bastards who hurt you. I feel like you're telling me that things were taken from you without your permission." He stood, coming toward me.

Before I could lift my hands to respond, he crushed me to him.

"I'm a patient man, pet." He placed a hard peck on my mouth. "This is your show. You make the first move. I'm just along for the ride. Got it?"

I nodded quickly, my body buzzing at feeling every inch of him pressed up against me. I swallowed hard when I felt a large bulge twitch against my lower stomach.

Cyrus leaned forward, his mouth brushing along the length of my ear. "I won't pressure you, baby, but I also won't apologize for how my body reacts to you. My dick has a mind of his own. He's suddenly become a fan of yours."

A laugh bubbled through me. I pushed away from him, smacking his stomach playfully.

A wicked grin spread on his face, and I knew right then that I could fall for Cyrus.

And I could fall hard.

(Cyrus)

Before Ainsley could get away from me, I was on her. My fingers dug into her ribs, laughter shaking through her. It was a beautiful sound and one that I planned on making leave her, often.

I had no idea that even being in a kneeling position would conjure up images from whatever it was that she went through. It wasn't something I would do and definitely not until she let me.

Giving Ainsley some reprieve, I stopped tickling her.

She wiped under her eyes, a huge smile on her face.

Her shirt was wrinkled and out of place, her hair was a mess around her head but fuck me, she was stunning.

Thank you, she signed, mouthing the words at the same time.

I kissed the spot by her ear. "You're welcome, baby."

Stepping away from her, I mentally patted myself on the back when I saw the shiver rippling through her.

Heading to the couch, I picked up a controller and moved through the game until I came to the two-player option.

Ainsley joined me, gently nudging me in the shoulder.

I smiled down at her, wrapped an arm around her middle, and pulled her against me.

She sighed, her body relaxing at my touch.

We played like that for hours. She kicked my ass most times but to be fair, I hadn't played a video game in years.

Eventually, Ainsley started yawning. I realized then that it was pushing almost four in the morning. I turned off the game and went to pick her up from the couch when she jumped away from me.

"I'm just going to put you to bed. Did you want to walk instead?" I asked her gently.

She nodded, chewing her bottom lip.

Holding out my hand, I waited. This was all her. I made my first move by kissing her. It was her turn to make the second by giving me even a small sliver of her trust.

She tentatively placed her hand in mine, letting me help her to her feet. I kissed the back of her knuckles.

"I just wanted to thank you for tonight, pet," I murmured.

Ainsley pulled her hand from mine and cupped my cheek. *Thank you.*

When she disappeared down the hall, the sound of her door shutting a moment later made me release a breath I didn't realize I had been holding this whole time.

I had a lot of work cut out for me when it came to earning her trust but it was something I strived for.

I was going to head home but after having a couple glasses of wine, I decided to stay and sleep on her couch. I didn't want to overstay my welcome, but I also wanted to be safe.

Quietly closing the door behind me, I made my way back out to the living room.

Turning off the light, I laid on the couch, sent Ainsley a text that I was still there so she wouldn't be startled in the morning. I also texted Sammy, letting him know that I wasn't coming home. Like usual, he was still up and made some remark about me finally getting laid. I only rolled my eyes and didn't respond.

I made a mental note to talk to him about the way he had been looking at her the first time we met. It didn't make sense, but I couldn't dwell on it. Tonight, had been the best night I'd ever had with a woman. Especially one I hadn't slept with. As much as I wanted her, I meant what I said when I told her I wouldn't pressure her.

This was Ainsley's show. She was in control.

Whenever she gave the go-ahead, I would be there.

Ready and willing and I would show her that not all men are monsters.

SIX

CYRUS

"SAMMY! SAMMY! WHERE ARE *you? Cyrus, where's your brother?"*

I shot upright, a cold sweat coating my skin at the recurring nightmare I had since I was a kid. "Fucking hell." I rubbed the back of my neck, blowing out slow even breaths.

Trying to ease the anxiety resting on my shoulders, I checked the time on my phone. It was only seven in the morning. Longer than I usually slept. But the fact that I actually slept, said something.

Glancing around me, I frowned when I realized I wasn't in my bedroom. Memories from the night before came rushing back.

I had gone to Ainsley's place and spent the night after having some wine. Giving myself a shake, I laid back down.

My phone suddenly rang, startling me.

Sammy's name flashed across the small screen, my stomach twisting, knowing exactly why my brother was calling me.

"You have a nightmare too?" I asked, my voice still rough from sleep. They say that twins have a different connection that went deeper than just being siblings. I would have to say that I agreed. Whenever we had a nightmare, one of us called the other. We just knew when the other was hurting. It went past just being empathetic. We were a part of each other. Literally.

"Yeah." He inhaled, paused, and let out a slow breath. "Same dream as usual?"

"Yup." I pinched the bridge of my nose. "I thought you were going to try and quit."

"I hardly drink. I don't drink coffee. This is my only vice. Lay off, brother."

I chuckled.

"You still smoke too, shithead."

"Not as much as you," I reminded him. To Sammy, smoking was a part of him. It was like the cigarette was an extension of his body. As much of an ass he could be, he didn't smoke around others who didn't and was courteous of pregnant women. He had a big heart but masked it with his crude words and vulgar humor.

"Truth." He paused to take another drag. "Where did you spend the night?" he asked, his voice strained.

"At a friend's place." I figured that was a safer answer than explaining to him who Ainsley was to me. It wasn't like he gave me a whole lot of information on Red either.

"A friend?" Sammy snorted. "Come on, Cyrus. I know you went to a woman's place."

"Nothing happened. I had some wine, so I didn't want to drive. I haven't slept with her if that's what you're implying."

"Huh…I wonder what that's like. I think Piper is the only woman I'm actually friends with that I haven't fucked. Bee doesn't count, since she's family."

"Tanner would have your head and Jaron would cut you up into little pieces, very slowly, and feed you to pigs while you're still alive." I chuckled at the thought. "He'd make you watch."

"Well, that's pretty graphic."

"What did you do last night?" I asked, changing the subject.

"Nothing. Went to the club and came home."

"Alone?" I sat up and left the couch in search of coffee.

"Yeah, man. Red wasn't working and I didn't want...well, it doesn't matter."

"You like her."

"Nothing's happened. I introduced myself, got her name, asked her to come home with me and she hasn't. She's got baggage..."

"And you want to help her carry it," I finished for him.

"Something like that, C."

"Have you slept with anyone since meeting her?" I recalled how he hadn't brought a woman home in quite a while.

"Gotta go, brother," he grumbled, disconnecting the call.

I laughed to myself, shaking my head. Shoving the phone back in my pocket, I searched through the cupboards until I found the coffee and got it ready.

While it was perking, I leaned against the counter when a movement caught my eye. Ainsley was coming down the hall toward me, rubbing her eyes.

My body stirred. She was wearing pajama shorts and a tank top. She must have changed some time during the night after she went to bed. I hadn't seen her in that little amount of clothing before. She usually wore baggy clothes. While she wasn't dressed up and her hair was a mess around her head, she was fucking flawless.

Clearing my throat, I waited for her eyes, needing them on me.

Her gaze landed on me, her eyes widening.

"Morning. You didn't check your phone, did you?"

She shook her head.

"I texted you that I was spending the night. Didn't want to drive after all that wine, so I slept on the couch."

She nodded, giving me a small smile. *Sleep okay?* she asked, closing the final bit of distance between us.

I grabbed her hands, wrapped mine around them, and brought them up to my mouth.

Her lips parted, her eyes staring into mine.

"Knowing you were near," I kissed her fingertips, "helped me sleep."

So many questions danced behind her eyes at my confession. I had no idea what was going on with me or why this woman affected me the way she did but I couldn't control it. There was something about her that I needed. Something dark, strong, so damn strong, that I would spend the rest of my days searching for it if I had to.

"I made coffee," I told her, releasing her hands and putting some distance between us before I did something she wasn't ready for.

Thank you, she signed. She grabbed a mug, made her coffee, and went to the balcony door. She looked at me over her shoulder, waiting, and like a good little boy I followed.

(Ainsley)

To say I was surprised to see Cyrus again that morning, would be an understatement. But the fact that he didn't want to drink and drive, even though he didn't have that much wine, made me respect him even more.

When I went to the balcony, I hoped he would get the hint and he did. I was thankful for that because I didn't want him to leave just yet. I enjoyed spending time with him. Even though our friendship was new, I still considered him just that. I never met someone who was as patient as him. We kissed a few times and I found that I wanted more. No, I needed it.

When he joined me on the balcony, he went to the railing and let out a heavy sigh. My chest tightened. Was something bothering him?

He gave himself a shake and joined me on the patio couch. I had set up the balcony as a little reading nook that I used during the warmer weather. It wasn't much but it allowed me to get outside more and gave me more space. It also got me out of the apartment.

Cyrus wrapped his arm around my shoulders and kissed the side of my head.

My stomach tumbled.

"Will you go on a date with me?"

My head whipped around, finding his dark eyes staring back at me. They were hopeful, wishing for my yes.

You asked me that already.

"I know. I'm asking again because it's a new day and I want you to be sure."

Yes, I want to go on a date with you, I signed which earned me a smile.

"You've made me a very happy man, pet." Cyrus waggled his eyebrows.

I laughed, shaking my head.

He chuckled, pulling me into his arms. "A very happy man," he murmured.

His hot breath fanned over the side of my head. Just the sound of his deep voice, eased the stress that had become a permanent fixture on my shoulders.

Cyrus placed his mug on the table beside him then pulled me closer. He cupped my shoulder, pushing his thumb into the spot at the base of my neck.

I pulled my hair to the side, giving him better access.

"Trust me, pet," he whispered.

I wanted to. God, did I ever want to. But I needed time. A lot of time. I was never told when it would be too soon to move on from my trauma and the shit that happened to me. Everyone was different. I could only take it one day at a time. Cyrus said he was patient but there was no way in hell he would wait. Not forever. It wouldn't be fair of me to ask that of him.

"What are you thinking about?" Cyrus asked, handing me his phone. "Type it out," he said, opening up the notepad app on his phone.

I took the phone from him as his hands massaged my shoulders and the back of my neck. I stared at the blank screen, not knowing what to type.

"Tell me how you feel," he said as if he could read my thoughts. His fingers continued pushing and kneading my muscles, sending a flush of heat washing over me.

Good. That feels good.

A soft moan left me.

"What are you doing today?" he asked, his voice husky.

I have to go to the center. I'm teaching an ASL class. I'm also teaching them that they don't have to talk until they're ready.

I wasn't a therapist by any means, but I had experience. I considered taking some courses online and maybe one day I would, but for now I was happy just doing what I could at the moment.

"Is it hard teaching them when you don't speak yourself?"

It can be but I have an assistant who understands ASL as well, so that helps.

"I'm glad she's there to help you."

My fingers hesitated over the small screen before I began typing again.

He. My assistant is a guy.

Cyrus stiffened behind me, the sudden wave of jealousy coming from him, slamming into me.

"He, pet?" Cyrus repeated, his voice gruff. "What's his name?"

Cheesy. I don't know his real name but he's nic—

"Cheesy?" Cyrus snatched the phone from me and shoved to his feet. "You got some explaining to do, boy," he told whoever was on the other end of the phone. "How do you know Ainsley Cloet?"

I never had a man become jealous over me being close with another guy. Cheesy and I had become friends. He was young and I looked at him like a little brother. Whatever Cyrus was worried about or was jealous over, didn't make sense.

Cyrus's dark eyes met mine. "You friends?" he asked who I could only assume was Cheesy on the other end of the phone.

"That it?" He waited. "Good. Keep it that way." He hung up and came toward me at the same time I rose to my feet.

Listen, whatever you think is going on, isn't. He was vetted by the owners of the center. I don't think they would hire just some random guy. So, I don't appreciate you accusing me of shit when I haven't done anything. It's not like you and I have put a label on this either. We've never said that we're exclusive or committed to each other, Cyrus. You've asked me on one date and kissed me a few times. But it's nothing more than that.

"Slower, babe." He frowned. "I can't catch everything when you go fast."

I huffed, throwing my hands up in the air and went to storm past him when he caught my arm.

Cyrus spun me around.

I don't like this jealousy rolling off of you, Cyrus.

"Fuck, Ainsley. Slow down."

I shoved him away, glaring at him.

"Keep your dirty looks to yourself, pet. Maybe if you actually spoke, we'd be able to communicate better."

My eyes widened, his words slapping me in the face.

Cyrus scowled, shaking his head. "Shit, that's not what I meant."

Lifting my hands, I curled them into fists and gave him the signature Ross Gellar sign for *fuck you* and stormed back into the apartment.

SEVEN

CYRUS

I WAS AN ASSHOLE.

I shouldn't have been jealous. Hell, I had no reason to be. Like Ainsley said, we had never put a label on what we were doing. We weren't official. We weren't boyfriend and girlfriend. Whatever the fuck you wanted to call it. I called Cheesy because I had assumed it was him. It wasn't like Cheesy was a common nickname. He had stuttered over his words and quickly said that they were just friends and how his dad wanted him to give back to the community.

I should have taken her word for it but the jealous possessive side of me came out faster than I would have liked. Truth was, I had never been jealous over a guy being friends with whoever I was interested in. Not that there had been many women I was interested in over the years anyway. Ainsley was a first for me.

The hurt written all over her face for my little outburst was not something I wanted to ever put there again, but the words slipped from my mouth before I could stop them. Now I wanted to shove my foot up my own ass and go dig myself an even bigger hole.

Putting my hands in my pockets, I headed back into the apartment in search of the woman I was quickly becoming obsessed with. She had me unraveled. I had asked Jaron before how he knew he was in love with Piper, and he said he just knew. That didn't overly answer my question. My chest tightened, wishing my parents were here to help me. To guide me. I imagined my father telling me to do whatever it was I could to make it up to Ainsley. Although we had lost them when we were kids, I still remembered the love they had for each other. It was something I wanted for as long as I could remember.

"What's wrong with mom?" Sammy asked, shoveling a spoonful of cereal into his mouth.

Dad sighed, taking a sip of his coffee. "I messed up," he told us. "So now I'm trying to figure out how to get back in your mother's good books."

"You're fighting?" I asked, my stomach twisting. Mom and Dad hardly ever fought.

"You mean, you fucked up and now you're begging for Mom's forgiveness?" Sammy asked, his question pulling a deep chuckle from Dad.

"Something like that." Dad sat forward, narrowing his eyebrows at my brother. "You need to watch your mouth, Son."

Mom took that moment to come into the dining room. "What's so funny?"

"Your son is calling me out on my shit," Dad told her.

Mom stood up straighter. "Good. That means we're raising our boys well."

The memory hit me hard. It came on so quickly that it took the breath right out of me. It left this ache where the hole had been ever since they were both taken from us. Fucking hell, I missed them.

I could almost hear my dad as if he were there, telling me to go to Ainsley and make it up to her for what I had said.

She was in the kitchen, opening and closing drawers looking for something, but when she couldn't find whatever it was, she would slam the drawer closed.

"Looking for something?" I asked, slowly making my way toward her.

Her head whipped around, her gaze searing into me. If looks could kill, I would have been dead on the spot. She may have had no voice but fuck, could she speak with her eyes. Her feelings swam behind her dark gaze. They toyed with me, tempting me to go closer and fall within them.

As if my body had a mind of its own, it took a step toward her.

Ainsley turned toward me, placing her hands on her hips.

"Listen, I'm an asshole, alright?" I ran a hand through my hair, shame resting on my shoulders over the shit I had said. "I'm not used to this."

She frowned, tilting her head. Confusion was etched in her beautiful features. If I was an artist, I could spend the rest of my life drawing or painting her. She was breathtaking.

The closer I got, the more I could see the freckles on her nose and cheeks. I could also see the hint of caramel in her blonde hair that was around her head in messy waves. The lighting in the kitchen was fluorescent and I could have thanked whoever set it up that way because I could see Ainsley. I could see more than she probably realized as well. Her nipples were hard beneath her tank top, making my mouth water for her.

"I've never liked a woman like this," I confessed, inching closer to her. "Like you."

She took a step away from me, backing up until she hit the edge of the counter.

I took that as my chance and closed the distance between us. She couldn't use her words, well she sure as hell was going to listen to what I had to say. Boxing her in, I placed a hand on either side of her, gripping the edge of the counter.

"I like you, Ainsley. I want to date you. I want to spend time with you. I wanted to sleep with you last night, but I also didn't want to scare you. I wouldn't have hinted for more. I just wanted to be with you." I reached out, cupping her jaw and forcing her head back. "Eyes, pet."

When they landed on me, her lips parted.

"I wanted to lay beside you. You've opened up feelings in me that I can't explain but I know that I've definitely never felt them before." Lowering my mouth to hers, I breathed her in. My dick jumped, pushing against the fly of my jeans.

My phone rang somewhere in the distance, ruining our little moment.

Breaking the kiss, I crouched until we were at eye level. "I *am* sorry. Can you forgive me?"

She chewed her lip, her eyes searching my face. She reached out, brushing her thumb along my mouth and closing the distance between us. When she pressed her lips to mine, that was the only indication of a *yes* that I needed.

"Friday," I murmured against her mouth. "I'm taking you out for dinner. I'll pick you up and drop you off. All the lame shit they do in the movies."

A breathless laugh left her.

I grinned, grabbed her hands, and brought them up to my mouth. "Okay?"

She nodded.

"Good." Pulling away from her, I went to get another coffee when I felt a tap on my shoulder. Looking down at her as she stepped up beside me, she lifted her hands.

I accept your apology, she signed slowly for me. *I'm not used to this either, so I'm sorry too.*

Don't be, I responded.

She smiled, nudging me in the shoulder with hers.

We made another coffee and spent the rest of the morning playing one of her video games before she had to get ready to go to the center. I found myself wondering what her actual voice sounded like. Was it high-pitched or husky? Was it soft? Either way, I prayed that one day I would be blessed enough to hear it but until then, I would never take my time with her for granted.

Later that night, I headed into Rouge to meet up with my brother and a few of the other guys. I would prefer if we went somewhere else, but I had to give it to the owners; the drinks were cheap, and the women were decent looking. If that was what you were looking for anyway. I just wanted to spend time with Ainsley.

I sent her a quick text, letting her know I was thinking of her.

Me: I hope your day went well.

The dancing dots appeared almost immediately.

Pet: It did, thank you. How was yours?

Me: It was good too but uneventful. Now I'm at the club with a few of the guys and I'd rather be with you.

Pet: You're at a strip club but you got jealous over the fact that my assistant is a guy?

I stared at her text, not unexpecting her to actually call me out on my shit. I think that right there, made whatever these feelings I had for her, grow. Immensely.

Me: I'm a dick and I'm sorry for how I reacted.

Pet: You just there for drinks?

Me: What are you asking me, pet?

The dots danced, stopped, danced again.

Pet: I'm having a moment of jealousy myself.

Me: You have nothing to worry about. Just here for drinks with my brothers. But thank you. I'm glad I'm not the only one.

Pet: I'm confused.

Me: Same, babe. Same.

Pet: Enjoy your time with your brothers. Be safe.

Me: Always. I'll see you soon.

"What or who put that grin on your face?"

I looked up from my phone as Jaron sat down across from me. "Nothing and no one."

He chuckled, taking a sip of his beer. "Right." He looked around the room, his body shifting in the seat.

"Something wrong?" I asked, my stomach twisting. Just once I would like an easy night.

"Not exactly."

I frowned. "What do you mean?"

"I think I pulled a muscle." He moved again, wincing. "And it hurts like a bitch."

A laugh boomed through me. "Too much sex?"

"No such thing my friend." He chuckled. "Piper is due anytime and I think she's just dying for the baby to come, so she's trying everything to make that happen. I usually love the attention, but my dick feels like I got fucked by sandpaper."

"She's in the safe zone, so if the baby comes now, both of them would be okay."

Jaron raised an eyebrow. "How do you know that?"

I shrugged. "I read and know things."

"I thought her fourth month of pregnancy was bad." He looked down at his lap. "We'll make her kiss you better later, buddy. Don't worry."

"I think you need to get out more," I laughed.

Jaron chuckled.

"What's so funny?" Sammy asked, joining us with Cheesy at his side.

All humor left me as I stared at the guy who was apparently friends with my girl. Leaving the booth, I went up to him.

His eyes widened. He lifted his hands, trying to ward me off. "Cyrus."

I only smirked and smacked his hand away. "You going to slap me around, Cheesy?"

He swallowed hard. "Listen, whatever you're thinking—"

Closing the distance between us, I hooked an arm around his shoulders and led him away from the crowd.

I was vaguely aware of my name being called but I didn't give a shit. I needed to let Cheesy know just who exactly Ainsley was to me and to find out how far their friendship went.

"Cyrus, I swear nothing happened."

"We're going to take a drive." He was a good kid and did well for the club. He would eventually patch in and become a full-fledged member but for now, he was going to help me.

"Where are you taking me?" he asked, his voice shaking.

I stopped us just outside my SUV and cupped his shoulders. "You think I'm going to hurt you."

"I…" He thought a moment. "Yes."

"I won't but I need to ask, are you just friends with Ainsley or are you interested in her?" My possessive side was coming out and I wasn't sure how I felt about that. This thing with Ainsley was new but something in her, called out to something in me. I needed to make sure that no one stood in the way of me getting closer to her.

"We're friends and no, I'm not interested in her," Cheesy said, his dark eyes moving back and forth over my face. "Is she yours?"

"She's a woman, Cheesy. A human being. Not an object. She doesn't belong to anyone. Not even me." But as I said the words, I did, in fact, consider her mine. Not as an object. But as a partner. I wanted her to be my submissive and my Old Lady. I wanted her in every single way I could have her.

"I know that." Cheesy shoved out of my grip but it was only because I let him. "We are friends. I help her with her classes and she's also helping me with ASL. Jaron wanted me to volunteer there to make a better name for us in the public eye."

I nodded. "So he's making you help with the non-physical labor, while the rest of us do the hard work?"

He rolled his eyes. "He's not making me do anything. I actually like it. But yes, I don't know my way around a screwdriver. I wasn't raised to know that shit."

"I can teach you." The words left my lips before I could stop myself. I liked him. He was raised well and had a good head on his shoulders. His father was a cop and I heard that he never judged his son for wanting to be a biker.

"Really? I've always wanted to learn but my dad's too busy. He's tried but he doesn't have any patience at all." Cheesy laughed to himself. "I remember one time he was trying to teach me how to change out a lightbulb and I electrocuted myself. I'm kind of accident prone."

"Well, I'll help you." I opened the passenger door. "Get in. You're going to help me first."

"Where are we going?" Cheesy stood back, looking between me and the door.

I rolled my eyes. "If I wanted to hurt you, I would have done that already. Now get in."

"You guys leaving?"

We turned as Sammy came toward us.

"Yeah, heading to The Ring and Cheesy is going to help me." I gave his back a couple taps. "Aren't you, buddy?"

"I don't know what The Ring is but okay." He narrowed his eyes at me. "Unless this is a catch."

"Nah, man." Sammy chuckled. "I usually do it but now it's your turn. I just came out for a smoke. Gonna hang here for a bit."

Meaning, he was going to stalk Red and hope tonight would be the night that she paid him some attention.

"Get in," I told Cheesy and went around to the driver's side of the SUV.

"Be gentle with him," Sammy called out, heading back toward the entrance to the club.

As I slipped into the driver's seat, Cheesy opened the passenger door. I bit back a chuckle at his hesitation. "I promise nothing bad is going to happen. I just need your help with something."

"I'm not going anywhere with you until you tell me what exactly The Ring is," he said, lifting his chin in defiance.

"Really?" I asked, raising an eyebrow.

"Yes. The ladies like me, so I know they'll have my back if I say that you were mean to me." He smirked. "Besides, you know what I have below my belt. I can convince any woman to do what I want."

I groaned, rolling my eyes. "Don't remind me, fucker."

He laughed. "Not my fault you walked in on me while I was changing."

"I'd say that I'm jealous, but I like what I have." I grinned. "The piercings help too."

The guy was born with two dicks. Two. And I was the lucky bastard who got to see both of them. Even though it was an accident, I'll never get the image out of my head. He talked a big game, but I had a feeling that sex was harder to get for him than he let on. A lot of women didn't want both holes filled at the same time. It sucked but it happened.

He grimaced. "I'll never understand anyone who does that."

"The women like it," I said, starting up the engine. "Listen, are we going to talk about our dicks all night or are you actually going to come with me like I asked?"

"You didn't answer my question," Cheesy reminded me.

I sighed. "The Ring is the name for a large room in an empty warehouse where a bunch of us get together to fight and blow off some steam."

"Isn't that what sex is for?" Cheesy asked, slipping into the vehicle finally.

Once he shut the door, I pulled the vehicle out of the parking lot before continuing. "It is but sex can also come with a price. Besides, not that I have to explain myself to you or anyone, I'm sick of casual sex. I'd rather be celibate."

"I can't say the same for your brother," he mumbled.

"What Sammy does on his own time is neither of our business. As long as he's safe, that's all I care about."

"So what do you need help with then?"

"I need you to collect any money I make, hold my towel and water," I explained.

"And bandage your booboos?"

"No." I chuckled. "I do that shit on my own." Eventually, I hoped that Ainsley would help me with them but for now, I would take care of it myself.

"Good because I love you, man, but that's too close to comfort for me."

I agreed with him.

"So, why did you ask me to come with you and not someone else? Is it because of Ainsley?"

A sour taste filled my mouth at the thought of him knowing her better than I did. "I need to keep an eye on you and your dicks, so yes, it's because of her."

He scoffed. "Trust me, she's not interested in me. Before I even knew that you two knew each other, she was telling me about a guy she met and how he saved her. That was you, wasn't it?"

I passed a glance at him, finding him staring back at me. "Uh…I guess?"

"You guess?" He chuckled. "It's none of my business but I know it was you she was talking about. She's not close with anyone. Even though she's been working at the center for quite some time. She hardly communicates with anyone."

"But she does with you," I pointed out, unsure as to why that still grated on my nerves.

"Yes, but it's only because she looks at me like a little brother."

Leaning my elbow on the windowsill, I rubbed my jaw, driving with one hand. "Really."

He shook his head, letting out a huff. "Trust me, Cyrus, she's not interested in me. At all. But can I ask how you saved her? She never talks about anyone. Not from her past or even people she knows now."

"There was a fucker following her. I don't know who he was and neither does she. She ended up at the deli I was having breakfast at." A question came to mind, and I knew I shouldn't be asking him and should be asking Ainsley instead, but I needed something. "How much do you know about her?"

"Nothing much really. Just that she hasn't said more than a handful of words in years and that she's been working at the center for a while. She used to live there but wanted to feel somewhat normal, so she moved into her own apartment."

"The security in that place is top notch. I was impressed."

"You've been there?"

"Yeah." I looked at Cheesy when he didn't answer but only stared at me instead. "Why?"

"No one knows where she lives, Cyrus. Only the ladies who own the center. That's it."

"Huh." I wasn't sure if that was a good thing or not. Should I be proud of the fact that Ainsley trusted me enough to know her address? No, it couldn't be that. I drove her home the second time I saw her. It didn't make sense for her to trust me so quickly.

"Either way, if you hurt her, I'll kill you."

I chuckled. "Right." I glanced at him when he didn't respond. "You're serious."

"Of course, I'm fucking serious. Now tell me, who are you fighting tonight?"

Jumping from foot to foot, I shook out my arms. Leaning my head from side to side, I shivered when the hard crack rippled down my spine. I lived for these moments. The time before the fight when I hadn't met my opponent yet. I didn't know if he was bigger or smaller than me. I didn't know if he was a dirty fighter or played it safe. I preferred the former. The 'anything goes' type. It helped me work out that familiar edge when sex was currently off the table.

My phone took that moment to ding.

Pet: Just wanted to say hi and I hope that you have a good night.

A shit-eating grin spread on my face. It was like she knew. It was like she knew to text me at the perfect moment so it would give me the strength I needed to beat this fucker.

A part of me hoped I could get this done and over with, so I could go back to Ainsley's place, but I didn't want to push myself on her either. I was sure I would see her at the center, or I would text her in the morning and make plans to meet up before our date.

"Cyrus."

A punch to my shoulder forced my head around.

Cheesy grimaced. "You're distracted. I don't know much about fighting but even I know that it's not a good thing when you're not paying attention to where those fists are flying."

"I'm fine. Just be there to collect the money when I win." Sure, it was cocky of me, but I had a driving force behind me that usually made me win.

Anger.

I channelled it and called it forward, letting it control my actions until my opponent was writhing on the ground beneath me. It usually called for death but that wasn't my thing. I could get paid more if I killed the guy, but I didn't care about that. Even when the crowd started chanting for me to kill him, I refused. I didn't kill innocent people. Even though most of the guys earning a buck or two here, were ex-cons. I still didn't kill them.

When a whistle suddenly sounded, the crowd parted like Moses parting the Red Sea back in the day. At the other end, I saw who I was fighting. I had never met him before, and he wasn't that much bigger than me. He was tatted up, had eyes filled with hate, and a cocky grin on his face.

The crowd formed a circle around us.

I could feel Cheesy at my back, his nervous energy sparking this need to get this done and over with quickly. I liked the kid, but I wouldn't bring him back here. I would go by myself first if I had to, but I couldn't deal with the nerves rolling off of him.

"Cheesy, stop twitching. I'll be fine," I told him.

He grunted. "Sure, come back alive and then we'll chat."

I reached a hand out, keeping my eyes locked on the fucker at the other end of the circle. When a bottle was placed in my hand, I took a long swig and handed it back to Cheesy without even looking.

Another whistle sounded, forcing my legs forward.

The other guy did the same.

I usually took it slow and wore them out a bit, but tonight I wasn't feeling it. When he finally got close enough, I cocked my arm back and pushed it forward with so much strength, he wasn't expecting when my fist hit his jaw.

He was knocked back a step, blood pouring out of his nose. But it was like he didn't notice, or he didn't care. He yelled, charging for me.

"Come on, fucker. Show me what you got," I taunted him.

He yelled again, swinging and kicking. His foot got my shin, sending agony shooting up my leg. He was uncoordinated and messy and that posed for a dangerous fight.

His fist got my cheek and then my mouth. I got a couple of punches in myself, but I couldn't figure out his moves when he just kept swinging like a fucking mad man. When his fist connected with my eye, stars danced in my vision. I shook my head, trying to gain control of the fight. Luckily, when I opened both eyes I was still able to see but the area around it, hurt like a bitch.

Grabbing hold of the guy, I forced him to the ground and knelt on his back. He kicked and thrashed beneath me.

Reaching for his arm, I pulled it behind him. I kept pulling until he screamed, begging for me to stop. "You need to gain control of your moves if you want to fight here like the man you think you are," I told him.

"Fuck you," he growled, spitting out blood.

"Fuck me?" I chuckled, pulling his arm back until a pop sounded.

His screams became louder.

"Suck it up, buttercup. It's only a dislocated shoulder. It's an easy fix." I pulled myself off of him, offering out a hand.

He pushed to his feet, slapping my hand away. "Next week, be here. I'll fucking end you."

"Right." I scoffed, turning away from him. "Your threats are cute." I continued walking back to where Cheesy stood, ignoring the guy behind me as he yelled profanities and whatever else he could think of.

"Did you really have to do that?" Cheesy asked, handing me a towel and a bottle of water.

"Do what? The guy's lucky I didn't kill him like everyone here wanted." I took the towel and water from him. "Collect the money, Cheesy."

I left the building, ignoring everyone and anything around me. My body hurt and I could use a good massage but for now, I would just suck it up until I could get Ainsley's hands on me. If that ever happened. There was something about her that kept the passionate part of herself hidden. But I made it a mission to seek it out and bring it forth.

No matter the cost.

EIGHT

Ainsley

"AINSLEY, HOW'S MY FAVORITE quiet girl?"

I rolled my eyes but couldn't help but smile as Cheesy came into the large room. *I'm the only quiet girl you know, I'm sure.*

He chuckled. "Maybe so but it still doesn't mean you can't be my favorite."

I shook my head, when a thought came to me. *I'm sorry about how Cyrus reacted.*

The smile fell from Cheesy's face. He looked over his shoulder, almost like he expected Cyrus to jump out of the shadows. "Uh…it's fine." He looked back at me. "I explained that you're helping me with my sign language and I'm helping you teach others. Jaron wants me to be a good boy, so here I am. My dad's a cop anyway, so I'm sure he doesn't mind that I'm helping you."

I tilted my head, staring at him as he rambled.

"I'm rambling, aren't I?" He laughed, running his hand through his light brown hair.

I gave him a small smile. *It's okay.*

He sighed. *Your boyfriend has me nervous.*

He's not my boyfriend. I really liked the sound of that though.

Leaving the large hall where the meetings were held, I went to the receptionist's desk with Cheesy following behind me.

"Well, whether he's your boyfriend or not, he sure made it known for me to back off."

Stopping at the desk, I turned toward Cheesy and placed my hands on my hips. I waited for him to continue. The words were on the tip of my tongue like they usually were, but the more time passed where I didn't say anything, the more I didn't actually want to. Not until I met Cyrus.

Cheesy opened his mouth to respond, when his eyes flicked over my head.

I followed his gaze, finding a large black SUV pulling into the parking lot. My stomach tumbled.

When it parked, Sammy left the passenger side, lighting up a smoke as soon as his Shit-Kickers hit the ground. His head lifted, his eyes looking my way. I wasn't sure if he could see me from where he was standing but it sure as hell felt like it.

I shifted from foot to foot, not liking the hatred rolling off the man I didn't know.

"Don't worry about him," Cheesy mumbled. "He's a good guy but he's just angry at…well…life right now."

I didn't believe him, but I never questioned it. There was something deeper, something else going on with Cyrus's brother. It wasn't my business, but it still made me leery of the guy.

"I'm going to go say hi," Cheesy said, backing up. "If I don't come back, send a search party."

I nodded. *Good luck.*

Pulling up a chair, I started typing away on the computer.

Setting up a few appointments for Jay, Brogan, Meeka, and Maxine, the ladies who owned the establishment, I was lost in my own little world when a dark shadow loomed over me.

My stomach started doing somersaults, my heart picking up speed.

Breathe, Ainsley. Breathe. I told myself that mantra over and over until the shadow disappeared.

"Hey."

I looked to my left, finding Cyrus crouching beside me.

"You good?"

My eyes widened when I saw that his lip was split, a dark bruise sat under his right eye while a small bandage sat on his left cheek.

What happened? I reached out to touch him, wanting to make sure he was okay.

He grabbed my hand, running his thumb along the edge of it. "Don't worry about it, baby."

I pulled from his grip, brushing my fingers over his mouth before signing, *How's the other guy?*

He chuckled. "Went to the hospital last night with a dislocated shoulder and a broken nose. I offered to pop them both back into place, but he refused. Apparently, I'm a big meanie."

Was this a random fight or are you an actual fighter?

"None of the above, pet. I fight to take the edge off at the moment."

Do you get paid for it?

"Yes, but I don't keep the money," he explained.

What do you do with the money?

"I give it back to the community. A random bookstore, a library, a funeral home. I gave a homeless person five-hundred bucks before." He shook his head, chuckling at a memory. "He offered to buy me a steak as a thank you but I ended up treating him to a few drinks instead after getting him cleaned up. One of my favorite moments."

My heart swelled. *That's pretty amazing.*

"I don't do it for the recognition, but I do love helping when I can. What are you doing here?" he asked, nodding to the computer screen.

Besides teaching ASL, I'm also the receptionist. I guess seeing my face first, helps ease people's anxiety. I shrugged.

"Trust me, pet. Seeing you first thing would definitely be the highlight of my day too."

I stared at him. Even though you could clearly tell he had been in a fight, he was still gorgeous. He looked like he walked right off a GQ magazine. I bet he looked delicious in a suit.

He tilted his head. "Why are you looking at me like that?"

I'm imagining you in a suit.

His lips pulled into a grin. "Really? Well, I guess you'll have to wait until our date, so you can see me in a suit then."

My cheeks burned, my eyes widening at the thought.

He chuckled, rising a touch and leaning toward my ear. "Tell me what else you're imagining me in or..." His lips brushed along the shell of my ear. "Not in."

I shivered at the soft touch.

His laugh deepened, rumbling through every inch of me. "So, Ainsley, you ready for our date?"

You'll really wear a suit? I asked him, wondering why he would agree to such a thing.

"Babe, I'll wear a fucking garbage bag if it puts a smile on your face."

I laughed, standing from the chair as Sammy and Cheesy entered the building. My laughter quickly died at the scowl on Sammy's face. It amazed me how they were twins and yet, were nothing alike.

"What's so funny?" he demanded, looking between Cyrus and me.

Cyrus rose to his full height, stepping up behind me. "What's your deal?"

"I don't have a deal." Sammy stared at us.

As much as I didn't want to, I was the one to look away first. I went to walk around Cyrus when he caught my arm.

The touch was gentle, but it forced me to look up into his dark eyes.

"I wasn't kidding about that date, pet," he said. "Tell me when you want me to pick you up and I'll be there. In a suit."

I could feel Sammy staring daggers into the back of my head, so I did the only thing I could think of. I pulled my phone from my pocket and typed up a response.

Yes, I'm ready for our date. I'm done work at 6pm tomorrow evening.

"I'll pick you up at seven."

I nodded, stood on tiptoes, and placed a soft peck on his cheek. The scruff from his light beard tickled my lips. Before his brother could say or do anything else, I left the room.

(Cyrus)

As I watched Ainsley leave and disappear down a long hall, a throat clearing forced my head back around.

I found Sammy and Cheesy both staring back at me. "What?"

Cheesy shook his head. "No issues from me, man. You're bigger than me. We're cool," he said quickly.

"You're bigger than me too but I don't give a shit about that. What's going on with you and her?" Sammy demanded, like it was any of his business.

"I like her if you must know, brother." I lifted my hand before he could speak. "I love you but right now, you're being a fucker. Whatever happens between Ainsley and me, stays between us."

Sammy's frown deepened, something flashing behind his eyes. "Cheesy, you got somewhere to be, don't you?" he asked him, not taking his eyes off of me.

"Yeah. I'll go see if Ainsley needs help," Cheesy muttered, heading down the same hall Ainsley had

"What the fuck is your deal, Sam?" I asked him once we were alone.

Instead of answering me, he left the building and headed toward the SUV. He lit up a smoke, the spicy scent hitting my nose as I followed him. Every cell in my body told me to turn around and go to Ainsley. Not to talk but to just be with her. To be around her. She had an air about her that calmed me. I understood why she was placed at the front. Victims could see her first and would find that sense of calm they needed. It made me wonder if she ever had that for herself. Not that I knew her whole history, but I wasn't stupid. She didn't stop speaking just for the hell of it. Something happened. I would make it my personal goal to earn her trust enough that she could share that piece of herself with me. To let me into her darkness. To be the light she needed.

"I have no idea what you're talking about." Sammy went up to the SUV and pulled open the passenger door when I slammed it closed.

"Talk to me," I demanded.

He took a puff of his cigarette and let out the smoke slowly, blowing it in my face.

My jaw clenched, a sharp pain shooting up the sides of my cheeks. "If you weren't my brother, I'd have you on the ground already."

"You wouldn't do that shit here." Sammy chuckled. "You wouldn't want your precious little girlfriend to see that side of you."

I took a step closer to him until we were nose to nose. "Try me."

His eyes widened a bit.

I had a good twenty-five pounds on him. Even though he worked out as much as I did, he could never gain the muscle I could. I often used it to my advantage, especially when he was being a shithead.

"Try me, Sammy." I waited for him to respond. When he didn't, I continued, "You better keep those dirty looks to yourself and worry about your own personal life. Maybe I should approach Amber myself and tell her that she deserves better." It was a low blow, but he was pissing me off and I'd had enough of his shit.

Sammy lifted his chin, sticking the smoke back between his lips. "Do what you want, Cyrus. Anything you say won't stop her from craving my dick."

"Why the hell are you so damn crude when it comes to the woman you clearly have feelings for?" I was all for dirty talk and telling my partners exactly what I wanted and how I wanted it but Sammy…he took it to a whole other level.

"She likes it," he mumbled, stepped away from me, and opened the door to the passenger side of the SUV.

I stared at him, wondering what the hell was wrong with him. I realized then that Amber would need a whole hell of a lot of patience to break down Sammy's walls.

My phone dinged, interrupting my thoughts.

Pet: You good? You and your brother looked like you were having a heated conversation.

I let out a heavy sigh before responding.

Me: He's a dick. Ignore him.

Shoving my phone inside my leather cut, I joined Sammy in the driver's seat and drove us to the Hell's Harlem clubhouse. He was silent the whole way, puffing on that damn smoke of his. When he finished one, he lit up another. He was stressed about something. I knew, because it was the only time he lit up smoke after smoke.

"What's going on with you?" I asked once we pulled into the driveway in front of the clubhouse.

"Do you think Mom and Dad would still be together if they were alive?"

My mouth fell open, taken aback by his question. Clearing my throat, I nodded. "I do."

Sammy looked at me then. "How?"

"They loved each other. I know we were young when they died—"

"Killed, Cyrus. They were fucking killed. Murdered. Shot. Taken from us before their time." Sammy left the SUV, slamming the door shut behind him.

I let out a hard sigh, knowing he was right. Maybe it was why he was so damn grumpy lately. It was as though the more years passed where our parents were no longer with us, the moodier he became.

A woman left the large house, running toward Sammy. I realized then that it was our cousin, Bee. When she reached him, he picked her up and spun her around.

I left the SUV, heading toward them, still pissed over how my brother was acting, but would leave it alone. For now.

"Cyrus." Bee rushed to me.

I chuckled, crouched, and held my arms out.

"God, it's been too long." She threw her small body around me.

I lifted her into my arms, hugging her a little longer than I intended.

"Hey." She wiggled out of my grip, staring up at me. "You good?"

"Yeah." I hooked an arm around her shoulders, leading her to the house. "How's the family?"

"Good! Manuel is with my dad and mom, and Tanner's inside," she said, nodding toward the house. "We're taking a little trip just the two of us, so my parents are babysitting for the weekend."

"That sounds fun." I hugged her into my side as we walked to the front doors of the clubhouse. "Let's get in there before my brother murders your husband for just existing."

She snorted. "Whatever. Sammy likes him. He just won't admit it."

"Sammy won't admit anything that has to do with him being nice," I corrected her.

"True." She laughed. "I take it you're still fighting?"

"Yeah." I forgot about the bruises on my face. "I made Cheesy go with me this time."

"Oh, I bet he loved that." Bee shook her head, a wide smile forming on her face. Her head of curls swung with the movement. "Poor thing. You guys are mean to him."

"We are not," I said as her husband, Tanner, took that moment to join us.

"How's it going?" I asked him, pushing his wife into his arms.

"Good. Quiet," he said, hugging her to him.

"Quiet's good." And that was the truth. They had it hard in the beginning when Tanner was accused of killing someone from our club. While his name was being cleared, he and Bee ended up together. It had amazed me how even in the most inappropriate of times, love could still bloom.

While Tanner and Bee mingled with everyone, I slipped away quietly and made my way down into the basement. My muscles were itching for some pain, even though I had put them through a lot the night before with the fight and all. Maybe I should have gone to The Ring again.

I pulled my phone out of my back pocket, checking to see if there were any fights tonight and if I missed any calls or texts.

"Cyrus, wasn't expecting you here tonight."

I lifted my head as Greyson Mercer came down the hall toward me. He was wiping the back of his neck with a towel.

It was true. I had been staying at the apartment lately, but something pulled me toward the clubhouse instead. Sammy never even mentioned anything when I had driven us there. Maybe he was feeling it too.

"We were at the center." Which wasn't really a reason seeing as the clubhouse was nowhere near it. "We dropped off a load of supplies for Piper and…I just didn't want to be at the apartment tonight."

Greyson nodded once. "I get that. How's your brother doing? Eve said he's being an ass lately. More so than usual."

"I don't know really." But I did know. A bit anyway. Just not enough to explain what was going on because the truth was, it was none of my business. "Tanner and Bee are here. I'm going to get a workout in." I went to walk by him when his next words stopped me.

"Sammy never goes to your parents' gravesite."

My head whipped around. "How do you know that?"

"Just because I'm no longer president, doesn't mean I don't know things," Greyson said, crossing his arms under his broad chest. "Jaron told me."

"How does he know?"

Greyson closed the distance between us and cupped my nape. Turning me around, he led me to the gym. "Jaron's become a little paranoid after everything went down."

"Understandably so."

"I agree. He's had people keeping an eye on things."

I stared at the man who had been my brother's and my guardian since our parents died years ago. "What are you telling me and how come I didn't know?" I was the vice-president of Hell's Harlem. Jaron never even approached me on the topic.

Greyson opened the door to the gym and stepped aside so I could enter. "He didn't tell anyone. I only found out because I was at the cemetery and saw an SUV I had never seen there before. Three guys were in it but never said a word. The driver told me to ask my son about it. So I did and I'm telling you what I know."

"He's had us watched to keep us safe?"

"Basically." Greyson smiled, the lines in his face, softening. "I guess he didn't want it obvious that he had people watching everyone but with Price disappearing, he's being extra cautious."

Price Davies who used to be the mayor of the town Piper grew up in, had it out for Jaron and his family. I understood his fear and his need to do everything he could to keep those he loved safe. I just wished he had told me so I could help.

"Don't be mad at him, Cyrus." Greyson gave my shoulder a squeeze before heading to the door. "He did it to protect both you and your brother." And with that, Greyson left the room.

Sitting on the nearest bench, I called Jaron up.

"Mercer," he said on the first ring.

"What's this I hear you've been having us followed?" Well, I guess there was no point in beating around the bush.

"Shit. My dad told you, didn't he?"

"Why didn't you tell me, Jaron? I'm your damn VP. Sammy's the enforcer. We're your best friends." I laid back on the bench, staring up at the white ceiling.

"I know." Jaron let out a hard sigh. "I'm sorry I never told you two. I should have. I know that. But with everything…I just figured it would be better if it was only me who knew."

"Who are the guys who's been watching everyone?"

"Not everyone, Cyrus. Just my girl, you and Sammy, my parents, Piper's parents...the usual."

"They must be good if I had no idea that we were being watched this whole time." I sat up as Sammy stepped into the room. "Who are they?"

"Just guys trying to make an extra dollar or two," was all Jaron said.

"Fine, don't tell me," I mumbled.

"Listen, they saved Piper and I, so I'm returning the favor by paying them to keep an eye out on things. But don't even bother approaching them and asking them for information. I won't even tell you how long it took for me to find them and get them to agree to work for me."

"You used Rowan, didn't you?"

"I have no idea what you're talking about." Jaron paused. "I have to go, and you can tell Sammy but please don't tell anyone else. Don't need any issues for being paranoid."

"Got it." We said our goodbyes and I placed my phone on silent so I could get a workout in uninterrupted. I still wondered who these guys were that Jaron paid to watch us, but I let it go. If it came down to it, I could contact Rowan Crane and get the information from him. His parents had been hackers when they were young, and he continued on with the family legacy after his parents retired from that hidden talent of theirs. Or so Rowan said, but I firmly believed that his parents still used their computer skills and just never told him about it.

"Was that Jaron?" Sammy asked, pulling me from my thoughts and heading to the treadmill.

"Yeah." I explained to him that Jaron had us being watched for our safety.

"Huh." Sammy stabbed a button on the machine and started running. "I had no idea."

"Neither of us did."

We spent the next hour working out in silence. Nothing was said between us, but I couldn't help but wonder what was on his mind. After our parents died, I had fallen into myself. I became well acquainted with Jack Daniels after my eleventh birthday and spent many drunken nights with only a bottle to keep me warm.

When I was getting ready to leave the gym and go take a shower, I checked my phone and smiled at a new text from Ainsley.

Pet: I hope you're having a good evening. Should I wear anything special tomorrow?

Me: I am, thank you. I hope you are too. I'm wearing a suit as requested, so whatever you want to wear is fine with me.

Pet: You don't have to wear a suit, Cyrus. I was mostly kidding.

I chuckled to myself. She wasn't kidding. I remembered the spark in her eyes when we had talked about it. Sure, I hadn't worn one since I was a kid, but I would wear one for her.

"What's so funny?" Sammy asked, wiping a towel down his face.

"Nothing." I shoved my phone into my pocket. "I'm calling it a night."

"Really?" He raised an eyebrow. "It's early."

"It is," I said, heading to the door.

"What's with you?"

I stopped, spinning on him. "Me? What's with you, Sammy? You're grumpy as fuck, snapping at everyone and anything. Is it that time of month or some shit?"

"I'm fine," he muttered, shoving past me and leaving the room, slamming the door shut behind him.

If my brother thought I was going to chase after him, he was mistaken. He knew where to find me if he wanted to talk. Until then, I was going to focus solely on trying to earn Ainsley's trust.

NINE

CYRUS

IT WAS FINALLY FRIDAY, and I was getting ready for my date with Ainsley. I had about an hour before I had to pick her up and I wasn't anywhere near being ready. I was showered and shaved but that was it.

I looked at the suit laid out on my bed at the clubhouse. I had never been on a date before. Most of the women I had gone out with ended up in my bed back at the apartment only because I had nothing better to do. I didn't even have to ask and they were there beneath my sheets, waking up and wanting more, but I could never give them what they wanted. No matter how much they tried. There had never been anything about them that I needed or even wanted. Not until I met Ainsley, did I ever once think I would settle down anytime soon. As much as I wanted it, it hadn't happened.

Grinding my teeth together the longer I stared at the suit, my jaw ached. I wished my parents were here. I imagined my mom telling me that everything would be fine, and that Ainsley was lucky to be going out with me. Truth was, *I* was the lucky one.

My dad would probably say something like, 'You got this, Son.'

My chest tightened, a lump forming in my throat that I would never hear those words from him.

Giving myself a shake, I headed to the door. When I opened it, I was met by a scowling Sammy. "What's wrong?"

He pushed past me, stopping at my bed. He looked from the suit to me. "Date?"

I didn't answer but I didn't need to. He knew.

"With that quiet chick or someone else?" he asked, like there could ever be anyone else.

"Her name is Ainsley," I bit out.

He nodded once, coming back toward me.

I stepped in front of him, blocking him from getting to the door. "What's wrong?"

"Nothing." But he wouldn't meet my gaze.

"Sam." I cupped his shoulders. "You always talk to me. Or you used to. What is going on?"

"We're not women, Cyrus." His dark eyes snapped to mine. "We don't need to talk about our shit."

"What is wrong with you?" I searched his face for a sign. Anything. Something that could give me a little insight into what the hell was pissing my brother off. "Did something happen? Are you in trouble?"

He patted my cheek, a slow smile creeping onto his face. "Don't worry about me, brother. Have fun on your date. Tell Ainsley I said hi." He pushed out of my grip, only because I let him, and left the room.

I stared after him. My brother. The other half of me. The single person I could never live without. I didn't think he would ever understand how much he meant to me.

Leaving the room, I went after him to try and talk some sense into that head of his. Once I reached the main floor, I looked around the large room. Sammy wasn't anywhere to be found.

"You looking for your brother?" Cheesy asked, carrying a case of beer behind the bar. "He just left. Not sure what his problem was but I thought he was going to kick my ass just because I asked him if he was joining us for supper tonight. Eve had me ask." He shook his head.

My phone took that moment to ding.

Sammy: Heading to The Ring. Sorry about before. Have fun on your date, brother. I mean that.

Me: What's wrong?

Those three little dots danced. They continued dancing for a few minutes before I got a response. I was about to put my phone away when a text finally came through.

Sammy: I miss you.

Me: I'm here. Always. It's you and me against the world, brother.

Sammy: You and me. I hope that never changes, C.

My throat closed. Fucking hell, Sam.

I didn't bother responding. Not yet anyway. I needed help with my outfit first. The lady at the store this morning, said it looked good, but I had a feeling it was only because she was hoping I would fuck her. I rolled my eyes at the thought. I had even told her I was going on a date tonight, but she still inched a little closer and kept her hand on my shoulder a little longer. And stared at me like I was going to fulfill every single fantasy she ever had. It pissed me off to the point I was tempted to call up my brother and sick him on her.

Heading to the basement, I found the very people I was looking for.

Greyson, Catch, and Tray were watching movies with their wives. It had been something they did quite often lately. Now that Greyson was no longer president of Hell's Harlem, he could live his life like a retired man, spending his time with his wife.

"Hey, Cyrus," Greyson said first. "Everything okay?"

"Yes, but I actually need to steal your wives if that's okay." I waited for the badgering of questions. I knew it would come once they saw me in the suit, but it didn't matter. If it made Ainsley happy, I would be willing to wear anything to put a smile on her face.

"Really?" Eve looked back at Greyson. "I've seen this movie already anyway."

"Same," Zillah and Sara said at the same time.

"Besides, it's not like it's a horror movie," Zillah added, rolling her eyes.

Her husband, Tray, chuckled.

"Rude," Catch muttered.

He had been the only one out of all of us who liked romantic comedies. He was teased about it quite often, but it never stopped him from watching them over and over. *The Princess Diaries* was his favorite and if he could, he would watch it on repeat. It was highly amusing.

"I won't keep them long." I stepped to the side. "Ladies." I thrust my arm out, waiting for them to walk past me.

"Cyrus."

I turned at Grey's deep voice. "What's up?"

"You talk to your brother?" he asked. "He's been in a mood, fighting with the prospects just for shits and giggles. I love him like a son but he's starting to really piss me off."

"I'll talk to him." I left the basement and went up the stairs before Greyson could ask me any more questions about my twin. Truth was, I had no idea what was going on with Sammy.

"So, Cyrus, what's going..." Sara's words trailed off as she handed me a bottle of water. "You shaved."

I lifted a hand to my jaw. "Not completely." I didn't like the clean-shaven look. Not for me anyway. But I definitely trimmed and cleaned up my beard.

"It looks good, Cyrus." A hint of amusement flashed in her eyes. "What did you need us for?"

"Follow me." I walked past them and up to the room I shared with Sammy. "I have a date tonight and I need your help in making sure I look okay." I stopped when I realized that no one was following me.

"You have a date?" Eve whispered, looking between Sara and Zillah.

"Yeah." I frowned. "Why do you three seem shocked?"

"We're not shocked exactly." Zillah laughed. "It's just…"

"You've never asked us for help on one of your dates before," Sara explained. "You've always done it yourself."

"I've never been on a date before," I told them.

"Then why did you get dressed up before?" Eve asked, confusion etched on her face.

"This is the first time I've worn a suit for a woman," I explained, and I couldn't wait to see Ainsley's face.

"Okay, maybe you never wore an actual suit, but you still looked nice," Eve pointed out.

Zillah laughed, shaking her head. "It's because he was trying to impress the ladies, Eve."

Eve smacked her forehead. "Oh God. Of course."

I chuckled, shaking my head. "Most of the ladies I know, and I use that term loosely, aren't worth the trouble. I haven't worn a suit since…" My dad's funeral, and my mom's a year earlier, but I didn't say that. "It doesn't matter." I went to my bedroom door. "I just need to make sure it looks okay."

"You must really like her if you're needing our help," Sara said, coming toward me first. "You do, don't you?"

"I do." I pushed open the door to my room and grabbed the suit off the bed before the ladies could see it. "I'll get changed and then I need your honest opinions."

They looked between each other.

"When have we ever lied to you?" Sara asked. "That's my husband. Catch thinks he's being funny but usually, he's not."

"I'm bigger than him, so now I can just kick his ass," I pointed out.

"I heard that," a deep voice yelled from the hallway.

We laughed.

"I'm going to get changed," I said, when I saw the time. I had to pick Ainsley up in a half hour. Not waiting for the ladies to respond, I rushed to the bathroom.

A soft knock sounded on the door as I was doing up the tie. Satisfied with how I looked, I opened the door. "What do you think?"

Eve stared up at me. "I…" Her eyes welled.

"Shit, don't cry." I pulled her in for a hug because I didn't know what else to do. "Is it that bad? I can find something else to wear."

A muffled laugh left her.

Sara and Zillah came up behind her.

"You look like your father," Zillah whispered.

My throat closed up. "Oh."

"It's true." Sara's hand fluttered to her throat. "I didn't know your parents, but I've seen pictures. You look like your dad so much right now, it's unreal."

"You look like Butcher did on their wedding day," Zillah added. "Tray showed me pictures and, Cyrus, you could be your dad's twin."

"Whoa, ladies. I like her but I'm not proposing anytime soon." I laughed but the idea of putting my ring on Ainsley's finger didn't actually sound so bad. Although, I would rather have my collar around her throat first. I imagined holding the end of a leash while she crawled on the ground for me. A hot shiver raced down my spine. Clearing my throat, I gave myself a shake. "Anyway, you sure this looks okay?"

"Yes." Zillah sighed dramatically. "But we do need more babies around here. So hurry up and make this girl fall in love with you."

"I'll see what I can do." I couldn't help but chuckle. Zillah and Tray had a grandson but with them living so far away, they didn't see them as much as they would have liked. Jaron, Piper, and Brynlee didn't come by much either even though they definitely tried to.

While Sara and Zillah talked about babies and plans for my future love life that I didn't know about, I looked at Eve. She stood off to the side, wringing her hands in front of her.

"Is this okay?" I asked her gently, looking down at myself. I loved them all. They took on the role of being mothers to me and Sammy without even needing to, but Eve was who I looked to for guidance most. She was there when my mother died. She was there for it all. My mom saved her and Jaron. She sacrificed her life for them, and I found because of that very reason, it brought us closer somehow.

I never usually cared what I looked like, knowing the woman wouldn't be seeing my face for long anyway. It was an asshole trait of mine and one I wasn't proud of but most of the females I had slept with only got my dick. That was it. Not my gentle touches, my kind words, or my need to wine and dine them. These traits, they were all for Ainsley. There was something special about her and while I didn't know what it was, I went in with open arms, hoping to one day find out.

Eve shook herself, a shuddered breath leaving her before she gave me a wide smile. "It's perfect, Cyrus." She came up to me and grabbed my hand, leading me to a floor-length mirror in the corner of the room. She stopped us in front of it and leaned her head against my shoulder, meeting my gaze in the reflection of the mirror. "They're right you know. I saw your dad in a suit once. He took your mom out on a date. She insisted that he didn't need to dress up for her. You want to know where they went?"

I nodded quickly.

"To the backyard." Eve laughed lightly. "The guys did up the yard for them and everything. Greyson and I even let them use the little house in the backyard so it could feel like they were at a hotel in a way. It was so romantic. The guys teased your dad and said they would have to up their game."

My heart swelled at the image she was painting for me. I hated asking about our parents, knowing it hurt to talk about them, but every time I got a piece of information, I soaked it up. Sammy on the other hand, would leave. He didn't want to hear it. He was pissed that they left us even though it wasn't their fault. At all.

"Where were Sammy and I?" I asked as Zillah and Sara came up on my right.

"You were with Greyson and me. I was still pregnant with Jaron at the time. We spent the night watching movies and both of you fell asleep on your blankets and pillows you had on the floor. You don't remember that? You would have been around eight I think."

"Mom died shortly after, didn't she?" The air suddenly became thick around us.

"Yeah, she did." Eve turned me toward her, straightening my tie. "I loved your mom. She took me under her wing and helped me through one of the darkest times of my life. She saved Jaron and me. I know…" Her chin wobbled. "I know I've said it before, but I am sorry for the shit I brought here. If it wasn't for me, your mom—"

"Stop." I pulled her into my arms. "It's not your fault. Everything happens for a reason." Neither Sammy nor I blamed Eve for her ex killing our mom. That thought never even crossed our minds.

"You be good to this girl." Eve pulled out of my arms and straightened my jacket. "I don't know what's going on with your brother but I'm sure we'll find out in time. Whatever it is, I know he'll come around. He's just…he's sad right now and is using his anger to mask that but I think there's a lady in his life and it's driving him crazy because he doesn't know how to deal with these feelings."

"How do you know that?" It wasn't like he ever talked about Red.

"Trust me." Eve patted my cheek. "Us ladies know things but don't worry about him. You need to take care of yourself. You helped Jaron and Piper when needed and I can never thank you enough for that, but you need to focus on yourself now."

"I don't know how to but I'm trying," I muttered.

"I know. I can see that. Especially since you're standing here in a suit for a lady, I'm assuming you hardly know."

I nodded.

A sad smile crossed her face. "Sammy took your parents' deaths the hardest, but he won't admit it of course. He likes to hide his feelings. It'll take a strong woman to shatter his shell.

And whether he's found her yet or not, it'll happen." She cupped my cheek. "You like this girl."

I nodded again because what else could I even say?

"You're taking her out for dinner and then what else?"

"Just dinner. I'll pick her up and drive her home and make sure she gets inside safely as well." Taking Ainsley out on the date was my move, but anything more than that and it was all up to her. I may have spent the night last time we were together after having too much wine, but it wouldn't happen again until she was ready.

"You are so sweet."

"She's a lucky girl."

"I can't wait to meet her."

When all three of them spoke at the same time, I could only laugh. "I'll tell you all about it tomorrow. But right now, I really need to go." I gave myself one final look in the mirror.

"You're handsome," Eve said, giving me a hug. "Your parents would be so proud of you."

I hugged her back, squeezing her a little longer. I thanked the ladies for their help and left the room with them at my sides.

Once we reached the main floor, it was a little more packed with people than I expected.

Whistles sounded once I was noticed.

"Fucking hell," I muttered.

"Ignore them." Eve laughed, following me to the main floor. "You look handsome. Go have fun on your date."

"Well don't you look pretty?" Catch came up to us, wrapping his arms around his wife.

"He does look pretty." Sara kissed his cheek. "Let's go finish our movie. Can't wait to hear about your date, Cyrus."

I sighed, suddenly feeling exposed standing out there in the open.

"Date?" Greyson took that moment to join us.

"Yeah. She's someone I met at the center," I told him, waiting for him to warn me much like Piper did. I wondered then if Ainsley let it be known she was going on a date with me tonight and if Piper had said anything to her.

"Interesting." Greyson threw his arm around Eve's shoulders.

"I expect her home by eleven."

I bristled at the sound of Cheesy's deep, but teasing, voice. I glared his way.

He shrunk into himself, sipping at his beer.

"That's what I thought." I stood taller, left the house, and went to pick up Ainsley.

TEN

Ainsley

MY STOMACH WAS FILLED with butterflies, my palms were sweaty, and my heart felt like it was about to burst right out of my chest.

I had never been on a date before. Ever. I had never even been asked out. And I sure as hell never had a man who looked or acted like Cyrus show any interest in me. He was different. Although he looked lethal as hell, there was a gentle side to him. He was the type who would walk an old lady across the street but wouldn't think twice about killing you if you crossed him or those he loved. Sure, I hadn't known him for long and I didn't know him overly well, but what I did know, I liked. He had a strong, powerful side to him that I craved. A part of me wanted him to tuck me into his arms, keep me safe, and never let me go while the other part of me wanted him to use his body on me the way I knew would be nothing I had ever experienced before.

My phone chimed, interrupting my little fantasy about the man I was lusting over.

Handsome Stranger: Hey, pet. I'm outside your building.

My stomach did a flip. Oh God.

Me: Heading down now.

I took a deep breath, gave myself one last look in the mirror, and made my way to the door. There was no point fussing over what I decided to wear seeing as Cyrus was here already. So my dress would have to do.

I settled on a knee-length, body hugging, blood red dress. The sleeves were long, and the neckline was high. It didn't show anything off but my curves. Curves I hadn't let anyone see in years. It wasn't too fancy but also, the only dress I owned. I usually went for ripped jeans and an oversized shirt or sweater, but if Cyrus said he was going to be wearing a suit, I figured I would dress up too.

My hair was pulled back into a low messy bun at the nape of my neck with some strands falling down around my face. I tucked one behind my ear, nervous as to how tonight was going to go.

Once I reached the main floor of my apartment building, I took another deep breath. I could do this. I could live a normal life and not be consumed by my demons and the darkness that threatened to swallow me whole day in and day out. I had to. For fear that I would finally lose myself like *they* wanted. Like *he* had promised.

Once I reached the main doors leading to outside, I was stopped short by Cyrus leaning against the driver's side of a beautiful car. I didn't know what kind it was, not being up on my types and styles of vehicles, but this one was stunning. It was black and older. I had seen cars like this in movies and shows before. I didn't know the make or year of course, but I did know that it was a muscle car and a popular one at that.

While the car was gorgeous, I couldn't help but let my eyes linger on Cyrus a little longer than I had intended.

He was wearing a suit like he promised. It was navy blue and hugged his big body in all the right places. It was like the suit was made solely for him. He wore black aviator sunglasses and was looking down at his phone.

My feet carried me toward him before I could stop myself.

Even though he was a biker, he still looked out of my league. Most of the bikers I had seen or even heard of, had tattoos, big beards, or were just plain mean, but not him. Not the guy who I could feel trying to crack down my walls.

Pushing open the door, I braced myself and walked toward him.

His head lifted, his eyes burning into mine behind his sunglasses. He pulled them off, his gaze searing into the deepest parts of my soul. A part of me I had never shared with anyone else. A part that I had assumed was no longer there. But it was and I could feel it slowly revealing itself once again.

"You look…" He swallowed, his eyes roaming down the length of me. "I have no words."

My face heated, a slow smile creeping along my lips. Pulling the strap of my purse higher up my shoulder, I stopped about a foot away from him. *I could say the same for you.*

He grinned, the smile reaching his eyes and creasing the corners. *I am honored to be taking you out for dinner, Ainsley. Thank you for this gift.*

My stomach tumbled. I had never met a man who spoke like him but even though that was the case, I vowed to never take his kind words for granted.

Cyrus winked and opened the passenger door.

I stepped around him, my gaze falling to a single white rose sitting on the seat.

"It means friendship," Cyrus explained, coming up behind me. "Or it does according to Google anyway."

I smiled up at him. *Thank you.*

"Of course, pet."

I picked up the rose and sat, lifting the pretty flower to my nose.

Cyrus closed the door behind me before joining me on the driver's side. "Do you like Italian?"

I nodded, assuming I did. Truth was, I didn't really get out much and wasn't normally prone to trying new things, but I didn't want him to think I was a hermit either. I just didn't like going out by myself.

"What is it?"

My head whipped around, finding him staring back at me.

"Is something wrong? We don't have to go for Italian. We can get anything you want."

I shook my head, opening my mouth but of course, the words I wanted to say never left. I looked away, my stomach twisting over the fact that I wanted to speak to him. I wanted him to hear my voice and give it to him in return. Hugging my arms around myself, I suddenly felt exposed. I shouldn't have worn this dress.

"I like your dress. It's easy access to the sweetness beneath it."

A shuddered breath left me at the memory. This was a bad idea. I couldn't do this. Cyrus deserved someone who wasn't so damn broken. Someone who didn't jump at every little sound. Someone who didn't live at a place that was locked up tighter than Fort Knox. Someone who could actually fucking speak.

"Ainsley," Cyrus said, his voice firm. "Look at me, pet."

I swallowed hard, wringing my hands together in my lap.

A big hand suddenly engulfed mine.

"Take a deep breath."

I inhaled as instructed.

"Now let it out."

I blew it out slowly.

"Again."

We repeated it a couple more times, his words instructing my breathing pattern. It was like some lame blonde joke. Him teaching me how to breathe.

Unclasping my hands, I linked my fingers between his.

"I got you, pet," he told me, his voice gentle.

I held his hand with both of mine, needing his rough touch. He had callouses, and I found as I ran my thumb over each of them, I wanted to know what they felt like against my naked skin.

"Are you allergic to anything?" he asked, his voice low.

Shaking my head, I stared out the window, but I couldn't meet his gaze. I didn't want to see the pity in his eyes or the look of concern and regret.

"Ainsley."

I chewed my bottom lip.

Cyrus cupped my jaw, turning my head to meet his intense stare. "Whatever you are thinking, I am not going to hurt you. I'm just going to take you out for some food and that's it. Nothing more. Understand me?"

I nodded, munching on my damn lip.

His eyes dropped to the movement, his nostrils flaring. "You're beautiful," he murmured, leaning toward me.

The air crackled around us and just when I thought he was going to kiss me, he cleared his throat and released me instead. A sense of loss washed over me that his hand was no longer cupping my jaw but at the same time, I appreciated it just the same.

Cyrus pulled the car out of the parking lot and drove us to our location. I didn't know where we were going. A restaurant, I presumed, but I wasn't sure which one.

Much to my surprise, we ended up at the same deli the first time Cyrus kissed me. I looked up at him then, wondering what he was thinking and why we were there when he had asked me if I liked Italian in the first place.

He caught my gaze, giving me a wink. "This place is actually slow at this time, even though it's a Friday night. They also have the best milkshakes in the area and a friend of Piper's makes the yummiest cherry pie."

My mouth watered at the thought.

"Does that sound okay with you?" he asked, running his thumb along the side of my hand.

I nodded. It did. It sounded perfect actually. Cyrus would quickly learn that I didn't need fancy meals. My apartment was in a richer part of town but that was only because it was safer.

"I know we're dressed up, but I want you comfortable, Ainsley. The Italian restaurant I was going to take you to might have been too busy for you."

My heart warmed at the thoughtfulness coming from him. I gave him a small smile, tightening my hold on his hand that was resting on my lap. The fact that Cyrus focused solely on me and my comfort alone, spoke volumes.

"Alright, pet." He brought my hand up to his mouth, placing a soft peck on the back of my knuckles. "Let's get you some of that pie."

We left the car and walked hand in hand toward the diner. Until we reached the door, Cyrus kept my fingers locked tightly between his. Even though it was something small, it forced a piece of my outer shell to shatter away. He told me to trust him before I even knew him and now, I found that I could. Maybe not completely yet, but I had a feeling that he could knock down all of my walls I had built, over time.

"After you, pet," Cyrus said, holding the door open for me.

I walked into the establishment, waiting for him to follow.

All eyes turned toward us, probably wondering why we were dressed the way we were at a deli.

Cyrus came up to my side, placed his hand at the small of my back, and led me to a nearby table.

"Well, don't you two look nice," a waitress said, coming up to us as we sat. She placed two menus on the table. "Going somewhere fancy?"

"Nope." Cyrus winked at me. "Just staying here. We dressed up for the milkshakes and pie."

The waitress laughed. "I love it. First date?"

"Yes." Cyrus reached across the table, finding my hand. "And hopefully the first of many."

My cheeks burned, a wide smile spreading on my face.

"I remember the first date my husband took me on. Was to a place similar to this and then we went roller skating after." She sighed. "It was perfect." She shook herself. "Anyway, what can I get for you both?"

"Two strawberry milkshakes and a cherry pie, please," Cyrus told her.

"A whole pie?" The waitress raised an eyebrow. "We usually only sell it by the piece."

"We'd like the whole pie," Cyrus told her. "I'll pay extra if needed."

"No need." The waitress grinned, looking between us. "I'll put your order in." She rushed off, leaving me alone with Cyrus.

"I hope you're fine with what I ordered us," he said, his eyes dropping to our joined hands. His calloused thumb brushed back and forth over the base of my palm.

Pulling my phone out of my small clutch, I placed it on the table and began typing with my free hand.

Me: Thank you for taking me out. I'm having a very good time. I can't ever repay you for this.

His phone dinged as soon as I hit send. He pulled it out of his inner pocket and placed it on the table between us. "You don't have to thank me, pet."

Me: I do. Most guys wouldn't do this.

"What?" He frowned. "Take you out on a date?"
I nodded.

"I'm not a romantic kind of guy but for you, Ainsley, I will be." His eyes burned into mine at his confession.

Me: Why?

"I'm not sure yet but when I figure it out, you'll be the first to know." He pulled his hand from mine and sat back in the booth. *I like you but I also know you're guarded to protect yourself,* he signed.

I want to be less guarded. I met his gaze. *With you.*

"It'll happen. We're only just getting to know each other, babe. Can't expect to spill all of our dirty secrets just yet."

I laughed lightly.

"Tell me one thing about yourself. One thing you wouldn't normally tell someone on the first date. I'll go first." He thought a moment.

Wouldn't this be our second date since we had breakfast together already? And you also spent the night at my place...

A slow grin spread on his face. "That's true actually. Okay, pretend this is our first date then." He chuckled. "I enjoy getting into fights."

I already knew that.

His chuckle deepened. "I couldn't think of anything else."

I kneed a guy in the balls once because he backed me into a corner, and I didn't know what else to do. Why the hell did I just tell him that?

The smile fell from Cyrus's face. "You should have kicked him in the knees, pet. He would have gone down much quicker. Surprisingly, a lot of guys can handle the pain of being kneed in the groin."

I swallowed hard at the intensity rolling off of him. Pulling the paper napkin off the table, I started picking it apart piece by piece. The little bits of the soft paper, rained down over my dress and fell to the floor beneath me.

The spot beside me dipped suddenly.

My head snapped up, finding Cyrus sitting directly beside me. His body was turned toward me, almost like he was insisting on giving me his full attention.

I'm sorry, he signed, his long fingers moving with each word he spoke. *I didn't mean to upset you.*

I placed the napkin on the table and brushed off my lap before grabbing his hands. I brought them to my mouth, kissing his fingers. It was a bold move on my part, one that I never expected to do, but I wanted him to know that he never needed to apologize. Not for the noise in my head, not for the anxiety rushing through me. None of it was his fault. At all.

His eyes darkened.

I was vaguely aware of the waitress bringing over our milkshakes and pie.

Cyrus murmured his thanks but never took his eyes off of me.

Clearing my throat, I dropped his hands and dished us a piece of pie each.

He inched closer, his hot breath fanning the side of my face. "I know there's a passionate little sex kitten inside of you, pet, and I don't care how long it takes either. I *will* find her."

Quickly grabbing my milkshake, I stuck the straw between my lips and sucked in hard pulls. I needed the drink to cool me off because as shy and timid as I was, he was right. She was inside me. Somewhere. I had hidden her to keep her safe until she found the right person to bring her out safely again. I longed for that part of myself. The part that didn't care. The part that went through life with my head held high. I missed the confidence I once felt before it was stolen from me. She was strong, carefree, and knew what she liked in bed. I had always enjoyed being controlled but when that little known fact got into the wrong hands, it was used against me.

Cyrus's eyes burned into the side of my head as he drank his own milkshake.

The longer time went on where he didn't say anything, it was like his eyes seared into me even more.

I eventually couldn't take it anymore and a huff left me. *What?*

Cyrus smirked but didn't say anything and continued sipping his milkshake.

I rolled my eyes, shaking my head but I couldn't help the smile tugging at my lips. I never had this before. This flirting back and forth. This need to be around someone. Cyrus calmed me in ways I wasn't sure I would ever be able to explain to him.

Taking a bite of the pie, the cherry flavor exploded on my tongue, forcing an unexpected moan from the back of my throat.

"Fuck," Cyrus whispered.

My eyes widened at my slip up. I coughed, going back to eating and trying to distract myself.

"Ainsley."

My head whipped around at the barked command of my name.

"Do not be embarrassed over getting any sort of reaction from me. One, it's been a while. Two, you're beyond beautiful. Stunning in fact. And three?" A cheeky grin spread on his handsome face. "You're such a good girl, that I wouldn't want to do anything to taint that part of you, but I also know that there's another part who wants to come out and play." He tilted his head. "Isn't there?"

I swallowed hard at the power rolling off of him and slowly nodded.

"It's been a while for you too," he said gently, the humor no longer there.

I looked away, shoveling another forkful of pie into my mouth. But this time, the sweet flavor was no longer there. It tasted bitter, much like the emotions rushing through me.

We ate the rest of the pie in silence, but I could feel Cyrus looking at me every so often. When I was done my piece along with my milkshake, I picked up my phone.

Me: It has been a long while for me, Cyrus, but I want to start over. I need a fresh start. I've been living in the past for a few years now and I need to change that. But I don't know how to make that happen.

Taking a deep breath, I pressed send and waited.

Cyrus's phone chimed. He pulled it out of his pocket, reading the text I sent him. When he was done, he placed it back in his pocket and signaled for the check.

My stomach tumbled. He was obviously done with me. Maybe he realized that I was too broken for him. He deserved more anyway but I had hoped that he wouldn't have been like the other guys I had come across prior to my time in captivity. Not that I had much experience in that area, but I still thought he could be different.

Maybe *they* were right. Maybe *they* had been right all along. I would forever be alone, no matter how much I didn't want to be.

Once the waitress came over, Cyrus paid for our food and drinks. When she left, he slid out of the booth and reached out a hand.

I looked up at him then, but he never met my gaze. A shaky breath left me as I slipped my fingers in his. I would not cry. I refused to cry. So many tears had been shed already over the years, there would be no point in crying over this anyway. It wasn't like Cyrus and I knew each other really. But I liked him. God did I ever like him.

He helped me out of the booth, only because he was a gentleman and didn't want to cause a scene, I was sure.

We left the restaurant, hand in hand.

When we stepped outside, I pulled my hand from his and hugged my arms around myself. I just wanted to go home, take a long hot bath, and forget this night. Cyrus clearly didn't want anything to do with me anymore, since he never responded to my text.

We walked to his car, the wind whipping around me, sending a shiver down my spine.

Once we reached his car, he opened the passenger door for me. I slipped into the vehicle and waited for him to join me.

When he sat in the driver's seat, we still didn't say anything to each other. Was he mad that I didn't talk? He knew after a few short minutes of meeting me that I didn't speak. Was that finally bothering him now? Did he think at first that he could handle it but realized now that he actually couldn't?

When my building came into view, my eyes welled. I just wanted a normal life. I didn't want to look over my shoulder constantly. I didn't want to live in fear. But knowing *he* still existed made it hard not to. It had been why I lived where I did. The security was top notch and made me feel safer than if I lived at a regular apartment. But the fact that Cyrus no longer wanted anything to do with me bothered me more than if I spent the rest of my life alone.

Cyrus pulled the car into the parking lot, found an empty space, and parked. He shut off the vehicle and much to my surprise, slid out of the driver's seat.

Instead of waiting for him, I opened the door and left the car just the same.

"I'll walk you to your door," he murmured.

I bit back a sigh but never argued with him. When we were on my floor outside my door, I stuck my key into the doorknob. As soon as I opened the door, Cyrus spun me around and pushed me up against the doorjamb before crushing his mouth to mine.

I gasped, my purse and keys falling from my hand at the rough unexpected contact. Snaking my arms around his shoulders, I pulled him closer.

Cyrus grabbed my hands from around his neck and pushed them above my head. Holding them in one hand, he let the other trail down the side of my body as he stepped closer. So close that I could feel him everywhere. Every hard line, every inch, every throbbing muscle. But it wasn't enough. My body suddenly burned, aching for more. It was a feeling I hadn't felt in a long time.

Cyrus ran his free hand back up the side of my body, cupping the side of my neck. He pushed his thumb beneath my jaw and tilted my head back. He took control of the kiss, igniting this desire and passion within me.

If his hands weren't holding me, I would have fallen to my knees just from his lips being on mine once again.

His hold tightened on my hands above my head. Being restrained by him, not being able to touch him, ignited this burn. This need. This want and desire for more. For *everything*.

Breaking the kiss, he tilted my head back even more. "I'll be your fresh start, pet," he said, his voice low and husky.

My stomach tumbled.

"I'll be everything you need." He kissed my forehead, letting go of my hands. "I know you need me to be patient, and I promise you that I will, but I want you to know that if you need something, anything, I'm here. If you wake up during the night from a nightmare, text me and I'll be right over. Never think you're being a pain in my ass because I promise you, baby, you are the fresh start I need too."

My heart jumped, feeling like it was about to bound out of my chest. *I thought you wanted this to end when you didn't respond to my text.*

Cyrus kissed my nose. "I'm sorry for making you think that but no, I do not want this end. Not at all. Not when it's only begun. Your text opened up something in me." His mouth brushed over mine. "It took everything I had not to kiss you at the deli. Another reason I brought you there was because it was the first place I felt your lips on mine. The first place I tasted your mouth." He gave my bottom lip a gentle bite. "The first place I swallowed your breath."

I'm broken. So, I understand if you do want this to end, Cyrus. I don't know how long it'll take for me to give you all of me, I signed slowly for him, wishing I could voice how I felt.

His lips pulled up in the corner, giving me a sexy smirk. "Trust me, pet." He leaned down to my ear. "With the way you kiss me back and with how you rub your body against mine, neither of us will have to wait long."

My face heated.

He chuckled, stepping away from me. "I'd like to take you out again. Say, next Friday?"

I nodded quickly. *I would love that and thank you for everything and for tonight.*

"You never have to thank me, babe." He kissed me one last time before backing up. "I want to see you before next Friday though. But we'll make our dates be a weekly thing."

You can spend the night.

"Hmm…" He ran his fingers along his mouth. "As much as I like that idea, we need to take this slow. Sleep well, pet." He turned and started walking down the hall away from me.

Before he could disappear around the corner that led to the elevators, I ran toward him.

Cyrus looked over his shoulder, raising an eyebrow. "What's wrong?"

I jumped into his arms, slamming my mouth down hard on his.

He groaned, the kiss fast and deep. "Fuck, baby." He broke the kiss before we could take it further. "What the hell was that for?" he asked, placing me back on my feet and hugging me to his hard body.

I wiggled out of his grip and began backing up.

Just wanted to give you something to remind you for later. I blew him a kiss and rushed back down the hall toward my apartment but not before I caught the grin on his face.

ELEVEN

CYRUS

IT HAD BEEN A few days since my date with Ainsley. We texted constantly and I found that it was the highlight of my day. I would wish her a good morning and a good night, and she would do the same. She would tell me her favorite quote from whatever book she was reading or a favorite line from a new song she heard. She would ask me how my brother was, and I would tell her that he was his same grumpy self. The fact that she cared enough to ask, did something funny to me. Even though Sammy was being a jerk to her, she still inquired as to how he was doing. It meant a lot to me that she still asked about him no matter how he treated her.

Both of us had been busy since our date the Friday before but no matter how many hours and days had passed, I couldn't get that last kiss out of my head. Her running toward me and jumping in my arms. Her crushing her mouth to mine and slipping her tongue between my lips, giving me a small taste of what to expect as we took things between us further.

I knew there was a passionate woman somewhere inside of her. I just had to get her to trust me enough to unleash her. She had been right though when she told me she wanted me to remember her later that night. I did remember her. And that kiss. I couldn't get it out of my damn head.

After I got home from dropping her off, I quickly headed to the bathroom, took a shower, and jerked off twice before my cock went down enough for me to sleep. But my dreams still consisted of her. Her on all fours, crawling toward me, wearing my collar while I held a leash. I had been looking for a submissive for so long, I was at the point of giving up when Ainsley unexpectedly came into my life.

I woke up the following morning only for it to start all over again. My hand had wrapped around my thick shaft while I was still half asleep, dreaming of her crawling toward me. I had tugged at the piercings lining my cock, the delicious pain forcing me awake. I felt like a boy who had just hit puberty and saw a naked woman for the first time.

Ainsley was something else, knowing my body had never reacted this way toward a woman before. It usually took a bit for me to get hard enough for sex. I eventually got bored of it and cut off sex completely and worked out or fought at The Ring to work off my frustrations. But with Ainsley, my cock was hard. All the fucking time. For her. Add to the fact that I had to be patient for her, it made this need grow and intensify into a raging inferno that I knew would eventually burn us both.

One night, it was late, pushing almost two in the morning in fact, and I couldn't sleep. I had only texted Ainsley an hour before, wishing her sweet dreams, but something was wrong. We spent the past couple of days video chatting because she suddenly got a cold from someone at the center and didn't want me to get sick. She was finally feeling better, and I still offered to make her soup, but I ended up getting called into work after a pipe burst. That ruined my plans of seeing her again. Finally getting home not too long ago, I still texted her even though it was late. While we hadn't seen each other in person in a while, I needed her to know that I wasn't going anywhere. But I couldn't figure out what this sudden feeling was.

Pushing out of bed, I trudged out into the hall and was about to head to the kitchen to get a bottle of water when the front door opened. "You're home late," I called out.

"Was out but came home to get changed," Sammy said, shutting the door.

"And you missed my pretty face." Things had been weird between us. I wasn't sure if it was because of Ainsley or not, but I tried not bringing her up. Especially when I didn't even know what was going on between us. I took it one day at a time because it was all we could do.

I stepped out into the hall, handing my brother a bottle of water. "Everything okay?"

"Yeah." He rubbed the back of his neck, heading to the couch. I noticed then how he was walking slowly. As he lowered to sit, he winced.

"What's wrong?" I asked, taking a swig from the water bottle.

"I broke a table," was all he said.

"Really?"

He only chuckled, running his fingers along his mouth.

I sighed, shaking my head. "Just make sure she has a safeword. I don't need to find out that you got charged with—"

"Don't worry about me, Cyrus. I know that communication is key."

"Good." I went to ask him if Amber was finally giving him the time of day but his next words stopped me.

"I heard that Price is causing a ripple. Someone from another chapter saw him and before they could take him down, he disappeared again. I don't like not knowing where he is."

My back stiffened. "I'm assuming this was in another city and that Piper's okay?" Jaron had asked us to watch out for her and their daughter but since Price Davies had disappeared, we didn't need to as much anymore.

"Yeah, he made his way north it seems. I don't know what his deal is. It's not like people won't recognize him. His face was splashed on the news for years. Fucking fucker is making me itchy but Piper's fine. Thank fuck she's fine." Sammy drank half of the bottle before continuing. "Jaron's adding a new security system at their house thanks to Lucas. You know, all the years he's helped the club, I've never actually met him."

"He stays away." I had been friends with Lucas Crane's son, Rowan, but we only contacted each other lately when we needed something.

"Right." Sammy finished off his water, rose from the couch, and went to the kitchen. "Why are you up still?" he asked, throwing the bottle into the recycling bin.

"Couldn't sleep," I mumbled, needing something stronger than water.

"Everything okay?"

I looked at him then. He was smaller than me, but it still felt like I was looking in a mirror. "I don't know. I'm feeling off tonight. I guess I—" My phone suddenly rang off in the distance. We both knew that if someone was calling this late, something was wrong. We learned that from experience.

Heading back to my bedroom, I picked my phone up off the nightstand. My eyes widened when I saw Ainsley's name flashing across the screen.

"Who is it?" Sammy asked from the doorway.

"It's Ainsley," I told him.

"Really? The quiet girl?"

Ignoring him, I answered the phone. "Hello?" When no response came, I frowned. "Ainsley?" My heart skipped a beat that something was wrong with her. She shouldn't have been calling me, a text or a video chat yes, but I hadn't earned her trust enough yet for her to actually speak to me. This didn't make sense. "Are you there, pet?"

I sensed Sammy behind me. He was probably wondering why I called her pet. As much as I loved him, she would be the first one to know. If she ever asked, of course.

"Ainsley," I repeated when suddenly, a click sounded in my ear. I pulled the phone from my ear and stared at the small screen. She hung up.

"What is it?"

"I don't know but I'm going to find out." I threw on a t-shirt, followed by a hoodie, and went to the door, when I realized that Sammy was still standing there. "What?"

"You're going over to her place?" he asked, something I couldn't quite put a finger on, flashing behind his eyes. "Now? At this time?"

"Yes, because something's wrong. Not that I have to explain anything to you, brother." I went to walk past him when he stepped in front of me. "I don't recommend trying to stop me."

"I'm not stopping you," he bit out. "But I want you to be sure about this."

"Just like you are? Come on, Sammy. Get your fucking head out of your ass and tell Amber that you're in love with her." Not waiting for a response from him, I rushed out of the apartment and headed to Ainsley's place.

I tried calling her again, hoping that maybe she would pick up and talk to me. But the phone only rang and rang. She didn't even have her voicemail set up.

As soon as I sat my ass in the SUV, I sent her a text.

Me: Pet, I'm on my way. Whatever you need, I'll give it to you.

I threw the phone on the passenger seat and went to put the vehicle into drive when my phone dinged.

Pet: I'm sorry for bothering you. You said I could text you if I had a nightmare. I didn't mean to call. I shouldn't have done that, but I wanted to talk. I tried to talk. I'm sorry.

My stomach twisted.

Me: Don't you dare apologize to me or to anyone for not speaking. You'll give me your voice when you're ready. Now stop texting me, so I can drive over and comfort my girl.

Pet: Thank you.

Taking a deep breath, I pulled out of the parking lot and sped across town to Ainsley's place. Maybe my brother was right. Did I even know what I was doing? No. I didn't. But I didn't give a shit about that because I knew that no matter what, I wanted to do it with Ainsley.

(Ainsley)

The nightmare had my nerves on edge, my first instinct was to call Cyrus. I should have just texted him, but my fingers got away from me and the next thing I knew, his deep voice sounded on the other end of the phone. The words asking for him to come over were on the tip of my tongue, but I still couldn't get them out. He was right. I didn't trust him enough yet. I wanted to, God did I ever want to. I also knew that I couldn't force it. No matter how much I tried.

A buzz sounded throughout the living room, indicating Cyrus's arrival. I rushed to the panel on the wall with the security system and buzzers and pressed a button.

"I'm here, pet. Let me in."

A breath I didn't realize I had been holding, left me. I stabbed the button that would let him in, needing Cyrus to comfort me like he promised.

I unlocked the door and stepped out into the hall.

Cyrus came around the corner a few minutes later, sucking all of the air from my lungs. He was wearing gray sweatpants along with a navy blue hoodie. His head lifted, his dark eyes meeting mine. He picked up his pace.

I took a couple of steps toward him when he stopped a few feet away.

He didn't say anything. He just waited. Maybe for me to make the first move. Maybe for me to finally say something. I wasn't sure. But I did know I needed him to distract me from the nightmares rushing through my mind.

Closing the distance between us, I fisted his hoodie and pulled him closer.

He took the hint, wrapping his big body around mine and lifting me into his arms. "I got you, baby." His lips found the side of my throat, sending a hot shiver racing down my spine.

I hugged myself around him, his powerful body between my thighs.

He walked us into my apartment, kicking the door closed. "Put in your code." He moved me, so I could enter the security number into the panel. He clicked the lock into place and carried me toward the hall that led to my bedroom.

Once we were in my room, he placed me gently on my bed and released me completely. "Why did you call instead of text me?"

I swallowed hard. *I don't know. It was like my fingers had a mind of their own.*

He gave me a small smile and placed a kiss on top of my head. "Get in bed, babe."

I did as I was told, watching him move around my room. It was nothing fancy. It didn't even hold much that could remind anyone of me. But what it did have, and it was something I would never get rid of, were my books. Two bookcases sat near the farthest wall, and they were stacked with layers upon layers of all different types of books. The only genre I didn't have on the shelves currently was romance. I never thought it could happen to me when parts of me were stripped away so easily but after meeting Cyrus, I found that I wanted to venture into that genre.

Cyrus stopped in front of one of the shelves and pulled a book off of a shelf.

When he turned toward me, my stomach did a flip. *Did I ruin your night?*

"Not at all. I couldn't sleep anyway. Not that I sleep much as it is. But I had a feeling something was wrong." He joined me on the bed, sitting on the edge and placing the book he chose in front of me. "This one okay?" he asked, pulling off his hoodie.

When his t-shirt had lifted with the movement, I saw the scars lining his back. Before I could stop myself, I reached over and traced my fingers along the light pink bumpy edges.

His body stiffened, his head turning. "They're just from fighting." He moved to the spot beside me, pulling me into his arms. "I promise that they're not from anything else."

I must have looked concerned because he chuckled.

"Thank you for worrying about me." He pulled me against him, his front to my back. "Not used to having a beautiful woman concerned for my health." He reached over and picked up the book. "I haven't read this one."

It was a classic, *Jane Eyre* by Charlotte Brontë. I've read it so many times that I had to tape the pages to keep them from falling out.

I sat forward, turning toward him. *It's really good.*

Cyrus smiled. "Good, then come here and I'll read it to you."

My eyes widened.

"Here. In my arms, pet. You had a nightmare. I'm going to read you a bedtime story to help you fall back asleep and then I'll cook you breakfast later."

I searched his face for a sign. Of what I wasn't sure. That he would hint for more? That he would take something without me willingly giving it to him? No, he wouldn't do any of that. It wasn't like he hadn't had chances already.

Cyrus frowned, his brows narrowing in the middle. Something flashed behind his dark eyes, something dark and sinister.

Before I could look away, his hand was at the back of my neck.

"I want you to know something, Ainsley," he growled, the deep rumble of his voice sending tingles racing all over my body. "I am not them. I am not the people who hurt you. I am the monster in your darkest shadows, protecting you, taking care of you, making sure that you're safe. I am patient. Some could say that I'm too patient. Who the fuck knows, but you know what? I don't give a shit. Not about them. Not about anyone. The only one I care about and who I hope appreciates my patience, is you." He tugged me forward, our mouths only an inch away from each other. "You hear me?"

I nodded quickly, unable to take my eyes off of his handsome, rugged face.

"Good girl." He placed a soft peck on my mouth before releasing me. Sitting back, he opened the book and cleared his throat. "I'm waiting," he said, raising an eyebrow.

A laugh escaped me. I moved to the spot beside him, pulled the blankets up and over us, and rested my head on his chest.

"Much better." He kissed the top of my head, circled an arm around my waist, and began reading.

TWELVE

Ainsley

I WOKE SOMETIME DURING the night, vaguely aware of Cyrus lying beside me. I was in between being awake and not awake. His deep voice rumbled through me. He was talking to someone. Was he on the phone?

Before I could ask who he was talking to so late, I fell back asleep. When I awoke later that morning, I was met by sunshine. The beams of light heated my face. For the first time in years, I actually had a good sleep. I felt at peace. Not completely but at least enough to wake up with a smile on my face.

I sighed, stretching my arms out under my pillow.

The bed suddenly dipped beside me, a heavy arm wrapping around my middle.

The small smile I woke up with, grew at feeling Cyrus lying beside me. Rolling onto my back, I stared up into the blackest eyes I had ever seen. My heart started racing, my chest feeling so damn tight, it felt like someone was sitting on top of me.

The man staring down at me, sneered. "I told you, you'll never forget me."

A scream fell from my lips.

The door suddenly banged open, startling me awake.

"Ainsley." Cyrus flicked on the light and rushed to my side, pulling me into his arms.

That was when I broke. Sobs wracked through me, tears streaming down my face as the remnants from the nightmare slid along my skin like millions of tiny little spiders.

Cyrus rocked me back and forth, holding me and running his hands in circles along my upper back.

The sobs had been so hard, I started hiccupping. I couldn't control my breathing, my chest ached as the cries trembled through me.

Cyrus ran his hand up and down my back, holding me tight. He never told me it was okay and that it was just a nightmare. He never told me to calm down. He just kept his arms around me.

My sobs eventually subsided, turning into soft whimpers. It had been a long time since I'd cried like that and somehow, it made me feel almost lighter in a way.

The sun was no longer streaming in through the window like my dream had implied. Glancing at the clock on my nightstand, I saw that it was only five in the morning.

"My brother was kidnapped when we were kids," Cyrus murmured, breaking the silence. He lifted me onto his lap and sat back against the headboard, hugging me close. He pulled the blankets up and over us before he continued, "My dad came in and didn't see Sammy anywhere. We had already lost our mom, so it hit a little too close to home for our father."

My whimpers turned to sniffles, but the tears wouldn't stop. My heart suddenly ached for two little boys who had lost so much at such a young age.

Cyrus ran his hand down my back, his fingers finding the hem of my oversized t-shirt. He slid them beneath the fabric, a shudder rippling through me when his hand came into contact with my skin. Anyone else and I would have pushed them away but with Cyrus, he could never get close enough. Not anymore.

"We lost our dad shortly after that," Cyrus muttered, his voice thick.

I lifted my head, finding him staring back at me. Placing a soft peck on his mouth, I tried giving him the strength the little boy inside of him needed. The one who longed for his parents. I couldn't say I blamed him.

I'm so sorry.

"I like to think that Sammy and I became stronger because of it. It's not like we had a bad childhood or anything after that. It's just been hard without them. I took my first drink at the age of eleven. The anniversaries of their deaths were coming up and I wanted to forget. I got in trouble, but with the alcohol burning through me at the time, I didn't give a shit. About anything. My brother…" A dark shadow passed over Cyrus's face. "He's more closed up than I am. I think he refuses to find happiness because he's scared it'll be taken away from him."

That's so sad. For both of you.

Do you feel better? he signed to me.

My stomach tumbled like it always did whenever Cyrus used sign language. I nodded slowly.

He sighed, his shoulders slumping. "Good."

I went to slide off his lap when his hold tightened on me.

"Where do you think you're going?" he asked, his hands moving to my waist.

I swallowed hard. *I was going to lay down, so you're more comfortable. I'm sure I'm heavy.*

"You are not heavy." He pulled me even closer, a part of him jumping beneath me. "At all."

My breath caught in my throat.

"I just need you close," he murmured, running his hands up my back. "But if you need space, let me know."

I nodded.

He cupped the back of my neck. "Good girl."

Before I could respond, his lips were on mine.

I sighed, breathing him in. Needing a little more, I parted my lips just enough for him to get the hint.

His hold on the back of my neck tightened, his tongue slowly sliding against mine.

The kiss became fast, hard, deep. It ignited this yearning for more. That little voice inside of me warned me to take it slow, but as slow as we were, I could still have a taste. Couldn't I? Were there rules? No matter how much therapy I'd had, no one told me how soon before I could have sex again. I had tried asking but no one gave me a straight answer. They only said that I could do it whenever I was ready. I hadn't been ready to get physical with anyone yet, until now.

I could feel Cyrus everywhere. My senses were on overload, my body completely aware of the man beneath me. My emotions were raw, but I found that I needed this. I needed him. To help me forget. To help me feel like a woman instead of this terrified little girl who jumped at every single thing that went bump in the night.

Wrapping my arms around his broad shoulders, I ran my fingers through his hair and deepened the kiss.

He groaned, pushing me onto my back. Breaking the kiss, he ran his thumb along the edge of my jaw. "Do you want me to stop?" he asked, his voice low, his eyes holding lust I had never seen directed at me before.

I shook my head, swallowing hard.

"We don't have to take this any further than you want." He sat back on his heels, placing his hands on my bent knees. "Okay?"

I nodded quickly, my chest rising and falling with rapid breaths.

Cyrus reached behind him, pulling his t-shirt up and over his head before tossing the fabric to the floor.

My eyes roamed down the length of his torso. I knew he was big but seeing him shirtless made him almost appear bigger. A tattoo sat on his ribs with the words 'Mom and Dad' in fancy script along with two dates.

"My brother has the same tattoo," he murmured.

He had a gold barbell in each nipple and one in his belly button. I had never seen a guy with a belly button piercing before.

"Ainsley."

My gaze snapped to his, my face heating at being caught staring.

He chuckled. "I got the belly button piercing on a dare. Figured since I went through the pain of getting it done, I would leave it in."

I think it's sexy, I told him, thankful for the use of sign language at the moment because I wasn't sure if my voice would have worked otherwise.

A sly smirk spread on his face. "Just wait until you see the rest of my piercings."

My gaze fell to his waist, my eyes widening at the image he put in my head.

A laugh boomed through him. "You're a naughty girl, pet."

Getting a sense of bravery, I crooked a finger, indicating for him to come closer.

Cyrus towered over me. "Something you want?"

I nodded, tilting my head back, needing his mouth on mine before fear took over. *I don't know how far I can go but I'm willing to try to do a little more than we have. I just need you. I need to forget.*

His mouth landed down hard on mine, pulling every dark thought from my mind.

(Cyrus)

Ainsley ran her hands down my back, her nails digging into my skin the deeper she kissed me. I never expected this to go any further than it already had but I also knew she needed a push. Even if it was just a little one. Her emotions were all over the place since her nightmare, so I wasn't sure how far this would go but I would help her forget. Even if it was just for a moment.

Her fingers moved around to my waist, her knuckles brushing over my abs. A shiver raced down my back at the soft touch coming from her. This woman who consumed my every thought.

Earlier when I had heard her scream, a part of me shattered. I had been there. Waking up in a cold sweat, fearing that the demons from your dreams were still lingering around. I had my brother to talk me through it while I did the same for him. But who did Ainsley have?

Me. She had me.

Her fingers hooked into the waist of my pants, pulling me even closer. She may have been shy and timid, but I was right when I told her that there was a fierce woman inside of her too. I couldn't wait to meet her, but for now we had to take this slow. I didn't want Ainsley to regret anything.

I broke the kiss, leaning my forehead against hers and just breathed her in. The sweet scent of her shampoo tickled my nose. Before I could tell her we should stop, I felt a hand push into the waist of my sweats. "Babe." My eyes widened. "You don't—" A groan escaped me when her fingers wrapped around my dick. "*Fuck.*"

Ainsley was staring up at me with a look of surprise and a dark hint of lust in her beautiful gaze.

"It's called a Jacob's Ladder," I muttered, trying to control the urge to pump my cock into her hand.

Her eyes twinkled when her hand lifted up the length of my dick only for it to travel back down the pierced shaft.

"Ainsley." I shook my head. "You don't have to do this."

When her hand picked up speed, her eyes never left mine. Besides my dick being in her hand, no other part of me touched her. My hands were gripping the blankets on the bed at either side of her head. Her legs were spread wide. If she closed them just a bit, her thighs would be wrapped around me, but this was almost…better.

It had been the first time I truly gave a woman full control. I liked to let them think they ran the show when it came to having sex with me, but it never lasted long. Yet with Ainsley, she could take all the control she wanted and I would always willingly comply.

THIRTEEN

Ainsley

SEX HAD NO LONGER been of interest to me. Not when it was taken without my consent for years. But with Cyrus I wanted it, and more. I wanted to take command of his body but offer him my submission as well. I wanted us to control each other and bask in the glow of being connected as two people should be.

Pushing him back until he sat on his heels, I knelt in front of him and pulled his cock free from his pants. I didn't get a chance to actually look at him when his hand caught the back of my head, and he crushed his mouth to mine.

My hand picked up speed, pumping up and down his thick length. I didn't have to see to know that he was big. As my palm moved over the barbells, I wondered what they would feel like inside of me.

No, it was too soon. We couldn't take it that far yet. I wasn't even sure if he would even want to have sex with me after he saw my scars. Maybe I needed to stop.

I broke the kiss, my hand slowing.

"What is it?" Cyrus asked, his eyes searching my face.

I swallowed hard, images wracking through my mind of what had happened to me. It felt like just yesterday that I had been taken from that café.

"Baby." Cyrus covered my hand, pulling it from around his length. "Hey."

A sigh trembled through me. I pushed away from him and slid off the bed.

"Ainsley." He was faster than I expected and caught my arm before I could get too far. "I told you to tell me or at least give me some sort of sign that we were moving too fast."

I pulled away from him, letting out a huff. *But I want you,* I signed before I could stop myself.

He sighed, righting his pants and running a hand through his hair. "Listen, I like you. A lot. I wouldn't be here if I didn't, but this is new for me too. I've never gone to a woman's home before because she woke up from a nightmare. I've never taken a woman out on a date only to drop her off right after." He came toward me. "I've never played video games with a woman either," he said gently, cupping my face. "And I've never drank wine for a woman either."

I frowned, staring up at him.

He chuckled, placing a soft peck on my forehead. "I don't like wine, but I didn't want you to go through the trouble of getting me a different drink."

I pushed out of his hold. *So you drank almost two bottles with me, just so you wouldn't bother me?*

Cyrus shrugged. "I was trying to get to know you and to not be difficult."

What do you like to drink?

He grabbed my hands, kissing my fingertips. "Dark rum is my drink of choice, but I'll settle for a cold beer too."

I made a mental note to grab a bottle of dark rum, so he could have some the next time he was over.

Pulling my hands from his, I took a step closer to him. I reached a hand out, running my fingers along the light scars scattered across his hard torso.

When my fingers touched his tattoo, my throat closed over a hard lump. I wish I'd loved my parents enough to miss them like he did. Or maybe it was a good thing I didn't, seeing as what I had already been through. Dealing with the loss of parents I had never been close with, plus my trauma, might not be a good mix. But I would always wish I could tell them I loved them. So maybe I did miss them more than I thought I had.

"They would have liked you," Cyrus said, kissing the top of my head.

My parents would have liked him too. Even though I had a hard time getting along with them, they were good people. I just didn't like their strict ways even though I definitely could have had it worse.

Now that our moment was over, I gave Cyrus a small smile, a hard sigh leaving me that I couldn't give him what I wanted to yet. Could we ever get to that? The physical touch? Sex? I had sworn it off ever since I was rescued from hell, literally, but now that I'd met Cyrus, I wondered if I could give him enough of me that we could get to that point.

Cyrus tilted my head back, placing a soft peck on my mouth. "Thank you for giving me a piece of you, pet. I promise to protect it and to never take these pieces you share, for granted."

I threw my arms around his shoulders, my eyes welling at his sweet words.

"Why the tears, baby?" he murmured, kissing the side of my throat.

Before I knew what I was doing, I cupped his nape and pulled him down to meet my mouth. The rough impact forced a growl from somewhere deep inside of him and it only intensified this burn I felt for him.

"Ainsley," he whispered, but he never stopped me.

He had said that there was a passionate woman inside of me. A sex kitten. He was right. She was there, waiting until I was ready for her. Maybe I already was, and I just didn't know it. Looked like there was only one way to find out.

Lowering to my knees, I took a deep breath and then another before I met his beautiful dark eyes.

"You don't…what are you…Ainsley." He petted a hand over my head. "You don't have to do anything."

I know but I want to try. Please let me try. I needed some sort of control in my life. I needed to know what it felt like to be in control of someone else. As long as Cyrus gave me his consent, it was all I needed to satisfy this ache, this need to be powerful. I wasn't a dominant person by any means, but I needed this.

"What do you need?" he asked me, staring down at me with lust written all over his handsome face.

Control.

He backed up and went to the bed. "I'll give that to you, Ainsley. Whatever you need," he said, lying down.

My stomach flipped.

Rising to my feet, I went to the bed. His cock was still semi-erect beneath his pants, the bulge making my mouth water. Was this normal? Should I even be reacting this way? Was it too soon?

"What are you thinking?"

My eyes snapped to his. Lifting my hands, I reminded myself to sign slowly for him. *I keep asking myself if this is too soon. Should I be attracted to you like this? Is this normal? I went through hell, Cyrus. Pieces of me were stolen without my permission and I don't know how to get them back.*

I dropped my arms to my side, waiting for him to freak out and leave.

He sat up, stretching out his arms. "Come here."

I did as I was told and crawled onto the bed and right into his arms.

"I'll help you find those pieces, Ainsley. Even if it takes years. I'm not going anywhere."

Why are you so damn patient?

He chuckled, giving his shoulders a small shrug. "I honestly don't know. I'm not a virgin by any means but sex isn't everything. Sure, it can feel great with the right person, but I haven't found the right person. Not until now. I'm not saying that we'll be together forever, but I do like you, I meant that, and I would like to see where this goes."

It felt like a weight had been lifted off my shoulders. I had never met a guy like him. Most would have wanted sex right away but with Cyrus, he wanted to make sure I was comfortable and ready first. I wasn't sure how I could ever repay him for that.

I like you too. And even though that was the case, I still needed a little something more. Lowering my mouth to his, I grazed my hand down his stomach before dipping it back into his pants.

He jumped. "Pet."

"Shhh…" I whispered against his lips, wrapping my fingers around his thick shaft.

"Fuck." Cyrus cupped the back of my head, deepening the kiss.

My hand slid up and down his length, pumping hard and fast. I craved his control, his need to dominate. I had been trained to be a submissive and that would forever be engrained in my soul, but this was different. The fact that Cyrus gave me a tiny bit of his dominance, made me feel powerful and feel like I could finally conquer the demons from my past.

Cyrus laid back onto the bed, pulling me down with him. My hand picked up speed, needing his release.

"Faster," he panted, his tongue controlling mine.

Breaking the kiss, I lowered his pants and watched my hand pump up and down his hard, pierced shaft.

A harsh groan left him as hot jets of his cum coated his stomach.

When he calmed down, I fixed his pants and ran a thumb through a drop of his release before bringing it up to my mouth.

His dark eyes watched me the entire time, his jaw clenching.

When the tip of my thumb touched my tongue, Cyrus was on me.

FOURTEEN

CYRUS

I WASN'T EXPECTING AINSLEY to give me a damn hand job. Best hand job ever in fact. But when she stuck her thumb between her lips, the fact that my cum was now on her tongue, made me lose it.

I had her back pinned to the bed as my mouth attacked hers. Part of me thought she would push me away, knowing she had gone through some sort of trauma, but when she only moaned and wrapped her legs around my waist, I continued.

If we only spent the night kissing, it would still be the best experience I'd ever had with a woman.

Ainsley may have been withdrawn, but I was determined to show her that I meant every single thing that left my mouth. I was too old for games. I had seen friends go through that shit. While it was none of my business, I was ready to bash their heads together, but refrained since it had nothing to do with me.

Ainsley ran her hands down my back, dipping them into my sweatpants and pushing them lower.

A shiver trembled through me at feeling her hands on my skin. Breaking the kiss, I rested my arms on either side of her head and stared down at her. "If you want this to continue and go further than it already has, show me, pet. This is your move." I kissed her nose. "You are in control, Ainsley."

She nodded, chewing her bottom lip. *I have scars. A lot of scars. I don't like being naked. But I feel comfortable with you and want...*

My chest tightened as her hands moved over words I understood but didn't like just the same. I pushed away from her, sitting back on my heels, not caring in the least that I was now completely exposed to her. "Show me."

She took a breath, looking up at the ceiling. With some maneuvering, she pulled her t-shirt up her torso and over her head before throwing it to the floor behind her.

Her breasts were full, her nipples hard. She was small around the middle with a slender figure.

Reaching out, I brushed my thumb over her nipple.

Her breath caught, her teeth sinking into her bottom lip.

I just need a second, she signed, her fingers moving over the words slowly, almost like she was hesitating or didn't want me to actually see her completely.

"I'll sit here and look away. You let me know when you're ready for me to see you." I kept my head turned, waiting for her permission to look at her.

Ainsley shifted on the bed, her bottoms coming into my line of sight. They landed on the floor in front of me, forcing all air from my lungs.

Before I could look at her, I slid out of my pants and waited.

(Ainsley)

Cyrus sat on the edge of the bed, completely naked, and waited.

The fact that as soon as I stripped for him and he never looked like I assumed he would, made this respect I had for him grow even more.

I moved to my knees, shuffling closer to him. When my front pressed up against the side of his arm, I leaned forward and placed a soft peck on his shoulder.

Cupping his jaw, I turned his head to face me. To look at me. To see me for me. In all of my broken, scarred beauty.

His dark eyes roamed down the length of me, his jaw clenching the lower his gaze went. "What happened?" he bit out.

I knew he was seeing things I had never shown anyone. He was seeing parts of me that had been hidden ever since I woke up in that hospital bed nearly two years ago.

My throat went dry, unable to figure out how to tell him what happened to me. *I haven't always worked at The Dove Project. I was first brought there nearly two years ago as a survivor.*

"Did they get theirs?" Cyrus all but growled.

My eyes widened at the rage seeping off of him. I shook my head. *Not all of them. Some escaped. Some were caught and ended up in jail. Some were shot and killed on the spot. Some played it off like they were victims too. I want to tell you more. I want to tell you everything. But right now, I just want to feel you. I want to feel normal, Cyrus. Just for a little bit at least. But I also want you to know that I can't feel much anymore. Not physically.*

Cyrus's eyes popped to mine. *I'll make it so you can feel me. No matter what we have to do. We can get toys if we need to.*

I gave him a small smile. *I haven't had sex since, so I don't—*

"Ainsley." Cyrus grabbed my hands, kissing the tips of my fingers. "We'll take this slow. Stay kneeling and spread your legs, baby."

I swallowed hard and did as I was told.

Cyrus knelt in front of me, placing a soft peck on my mouth. "We're not fucking tonight but I want to test something. If it gets to be too much for you, just tap my shoulder, okay?"

I nodded quickly, grabbed onto the blankets beneath me, and waited.

"Good girl." His mouth trailed down the length of my jaw. "Thank you for the orgasm earlier. Even my own hands don't feel that good."

A husky laugh left me.

He chuckled, the growly sound rumbling through me.

Cyrus placed a peck between my breasts before taking a nipple between his lips.

An explosion of desire rushed through me.

While his tongue teased and licked the budding peak, I was very aware of his hand inching between my legs. When they slowly grazed higher up my thigh, I squeezed my eyes shut. I wished, no, I prayed, that I could feel any spark of pleasure from them.

Once his fingers touched the spot I wanted, I jumped.

He lifted his head. "Tell me."

I lifted my hands, my fingers flying over words I hoped he could understand.

(Cyrus)

Trafficking.
  Victim.
  Survival.
  Sex.
  A whole fucking lot of sex.
  Slave.
  Submission.
  Castration.

As I watched Ainsley's fingers and hands move over words that would forever taint her soul, it took everything in me not to wrap her up in my arms and tuck her safely in my hold. I wanted to protect her from the terrors of the world. I wanted to keep her safe. I wanted her to be mine. In every sense of the damn word.

When she was done, I learned that she had been kidnapped on the way to her favorite café when she was twenty, only to be rescued five years later. She was partially castrated at the same time to prevent her from being sexually aroused. It didn't make sense, but it was what happened.

Leaving the bed, I turned off the light and took a breath. I knew she had past trauma, but I never knew just how bad it was. No wonder she didn't speak anymore.

When I joined her back on the bed, I leaned against the headboard and held out my arms. "Come here."

She searched my face, probably waiting for me to bolt but I wouldn't. She never had to worry about that.

"Please, Ainsley," I said gently.

She tentatively slipped into my arms and straddled my lap.

I pulled the blankets up and over us, her scars now hidden by the shadows. I grazed the back of my hand from the spot between her breasts, down to her belly button.

Her breath caught.

"I'm sorry for what you went through, pet, but I want you to know that I am honored you shared that bit of yourself with me. I could go on to tell you how much I hope those people who hurt all of you suffer, but I won't. I *will* tell you that I will do what I can to show you a gentle touch. To show you that not all men are evil. If I have to spend the rest of my life waiting for you to give me every piece of yourself, I will. Because I know that when I have you in your entirety, it will be the greatest gift I have ever received."

Ainsley placed her hands on my shoulders, her gaze burning into mine.

The sun was just starting to come up, but the room was still dark enough that I could only see a silhouette of her.

I could see the tears on her cheeks. I sat up, pulling her closer. I brushed my thumb along her cheek, wiping away the tears.

I slipped my other hand up her inner thigh and when I reached her center, a growl left me at the sudden wetness coating the tips.

She trembled against me, her nails digging into my shoulders and waited.

I wasn't sure how much she could feel but as I slipped a finger into her body, a soft sigh left her. Her head fell back, exposing her slender throat.

Moving my hand from her cheek to her hair, I fisted the long locks and licked up the length of her throat, all the while pumping my other hand against her.

She whimpered, squeezing her fingers into my shoulders. She rocked her hips back and forth, clearly hinting for more. But I wouldn't. Not yet. Not completely. Not when she'd just told me things I was sure she'd never told anyone outside of a therapist, if that. She was too emotionally raw, but I wanted to give her a little something in return.

Pulling my finger out of her, I slowly inserted a second one, reveling in the way she arched into my touch.

Her nails dug into my muscles even more, her hips rocked harder against me and sounds of pleasure left her lips. She moaned, whimpered, damn near cried for a release.

My dick throbbed, thankful that she could feel something.

Sliding my mouth up to her ear, I gave the lobe a gentle bite. "Whenever you're ready, I want you to come all over my fingers, baby."

She turned her head, her mouth meeting mine.

"Can you do that for me?" I murmured against her lips.

She nodded, a low moan leaving her.

"Good girl." I fisted her hair and deepened the kiss, pumping my hand harder against her center.

She cried out.

Before she could come like I knew she wanted to, I quickly inserted a third finger into her.

She rode my hand for a couple more seconds, until she was finally falling apart in my arms. A rough scream left her as the release slammed into her.

"Fucking hell, pet. You're beautiful." I nipped her bottom lip, pulling my fingers from her body and bringing them up to my mouth. Sucking her juices off of them, I swallowed the sweet acidic desire coating them.

She shivered, sliding off my lap before lying down.

I moved in behind her, wrapping my arms around her middle. "Thank you, Ainsley," I murmured.

She turned around, facing me and kissing me softly. "Thank you," she whispered.

My eyes widened. I lifted my head, unsure if I heard her correctly or not. Even if it was just a whisper like I thought, the fact that she actually spoke, made me feel like the mother fucking king of the damn world.

FIFTEEN

Ainsley

CYRUS: WEAR SOMETHING COMFORTABLE. We're going to take a little drive for our date this evening.

Me: Okay, I'm looking forward to it.

Cyrus: Me too, pet.

Me: Have a good day.

Cyrus: You too.

I sighed, put my phone away, and went back to listening to Cheesy instruct the current class learning American Sign Language. While they did actually speak well, I knew that they appreciated having other options when they didn't feel like using their words.

As much as I tried paying attention though, I couldn't help but think back to that delicious night a few weeks ago. We hadn't gone on another date outside of hanging out at my apartment. Cyrus didn't want to overwhelm me and would bring flowers and dinner over every Friday evening since. Sex was still off the table, but we kissed, touched, shared a few more orgasms between us and just spent time together. Foreplay with him left me aching for more but we both knew that I hadn't been ready to go all the way. Not until recently. I just didn't know how to let it be known that I wanted him to fuck me.

Cyrus and I had spent many hours kissing, cuddling, touching. I had wanted to have sex with him but was thankful when he told me that we wouldn't. Not yet. I often wondered if a part of me didn't expect to just do it because that seemed to be the normal thing. But when he turned it down, it was like a sense of relief washed over me instead.

I already knew it was going to happen. For whatever reason, I had never even considered it with any other guy. Even a couple guys I had dated as a teen wanted sex. Instantly.

I scoffed.

"Ainsley?"

My head snapped up, finding Cheesy and a couple of the students looking my way.

My cheeks flamed. *Sorry.*

Continue practicing with each other, Cheesy instructed before heading toward me. He sat on the couch beside me, stretching out his long legs in front of him.

"How was your date with Cyrus?"

My head whipped around. *You know about that?*

He chuckled. "Word travels fast. Cyrus doesn't date. Neither does Sammy. So when a woman catches their eye, people notice."

Interesting.

"He likes you. He's hardly at the clubhouse anymore."

Cheesy didn't have to tell me that. I already knew Cyrus liked me. I liked him too. If I didn't, I wouldn't have asked him to come over and I definitely wouldn't be spending as much time with him as I did.

My body heated. I could still feel his hands on me. His tongue deep in my mouth. His fingers in a part of my body that hadn't been given to someone consensually in years. The fact that he had given me control when I knew that he needed it himself, said more than words ever could.

Do you like being a biker? I asked Cheesy, wanting to get the conversation off of Cyrus and me. Even though we had been dating for a few weeks, our relationship was still new, and I didn't want to do anything to mess it up.

"I do. Which is funny because my dad is a cop, but he knows what I do and what club I'm trying to patch into." Cheesy gave me a small smile. "Hell's Harlem are good men. This chapter is anyway. Greyson spent years trying to clean it up and while Jaron isn't as into it as his dad was, I know he wouldn't do anything to screw up his father's work. As long as his loved ones are safe at least."

I nodded in understanding.

Piper took that moment to come into the large room. When her gaze found mine, she smiled. "Cyrus is here."

My skin flushed at the thought of seeing him again.

I gave Cheesy a wave and followed Piper out of the room.

She stopped before we could head out into the reception area.

I frowned, wondering what kind of warning she was about to give me.

"I like you for him," she said softly. "He smiles more. Even Jaron noticed it."

I like him, I signed slowly for her. She was learning ASL but hadn't kept up on practicing it like a few others had. But she still knew a bit, so I appreciated her trying.

"I know you do." She hesitated, chewing her bottom lip. "I'm going to be honest with you. I warned him against seeing you originally."

My eyes widened a bit.

"I know." She sighed. "Cyrus is a big boy and can handle his own shit, but I know you've been through a lot." She shook her head. "It doesn't matter. I don't know your story, not all of it anyway, but I know you'll tell Cyrus when you're ready, if you haven't yet. Anyway, I just want you to know that I think you're good for him." Before I could stop her, she pulled me into a hug. "I also know that you don't like touching or hugs but I'm hugging you anyway."

I returned the embrace, not used to having female friends.

Her body stiffened before she gave me a final squeeze. "Be good to each other and talk. Not like Jaron and me. We struggled in the beginning. I don't want that for you." She released me and hooked her arm in mine. "I heard you're going on another date tonight. Outside of your apartment anyway."

I nodded, a smile spreading on my face.

"Good because I'd kick his ass if it was with another woman."

A laugh escaped me.

She gently nudged me in the shoulder. "He's outside. He picked me up and dropped me off, so we didn't have to pack up Brynlee. Jaron has a playdate with her and a couple of the other fathers we know. Is it weird that I find that hot as hell?"

The thought of Cyrus playing with children, warmed my heart, so I understood.

Piper stopped when we reached the door and unlinked her arm from mine. "Anyway, enough of my random rambling. I just wanted to let you know that I like you together." *I like you with him. A lot.*

I smiled as her hands stumbled over the words but was still able to make out what she was trying to say. *You've been practicing.*

"I'm trying to." She grinned, nodding. *I've been teaching Jaron and Brynlee too.* She started backing up. "Go see him before he comes in here and tears the walls down to get to you." She waggled her eyebrows.

I laughed, shaking my head. Taking a deep breath, I headed outside only to be met by Cyrus leaning against his large black SUV. He was puffing on a smoke, a faraway look on his face. When he caught me standing there, he pulled the cigarette from between his lips, blew out a gray cloud, and dropped the cigarette on the ground before stepping on it with his Shit-Kicker.

My breath caught at the mere sight of him.

He was wearing a black hoodie, his leather cut, and ripped blue jeans. The scruff on his jaw had grown in some but God, he was beautiful.

He crooked a finger, indicating for me to go to him.

My feet took me forward, carrying me to him. My sudden safety.

When I stood less than a foot away, I smiled up at him.

"Hi." He cupped my jaw, tilting my head back and placing a firm peck on my mouth.

I sighed, breathing him in. The menthol had a sweet lingering taste.

"How are you?" he asked against my lips.

I leaned back. *Not too bad. You?*

"Better now," he murmured, running his thumb back and forth over my jaw. "Spend the day with me?"

I thought we weren't meeting until tonight?

"Oh, I'm still taking you on our date, but I want to spend the afternoon with you too. If you want to that is."

I do.

A cheeky grin spread on his handsome face. "Good. Do you need to tell anyone you're leaving?"

I nodded, pulling away from him. I rushed back into the building to grab my bag and let Jay know that I'd be leaving early for the day. She was good about it, since I never had a set schedule. I just had to work a certain amount of hours each week. She and the other owners were good with whatever I set my schedule as.

When I ran back outside, Cyrus was sitting in the driver's seat. I joined him but as I shut the door and turned back around to ask him what we were doing, he captured my mouth in a hard bruising kiss.

My hands cupped the back of his head of their own accord, pulling him harder against me. I almost forgot where we were when a husky chuckle left him.

"I knew there was a little sex kitten inside of you."

I laughed, lightly punching him in the shoulder.

He winked, kissing my nose and pulling away from me. "Don't worry, babe. You can hide her from me for as long as you want but I promise you, I will eventually get to meet her."

Today. He was going to meet her today.

Cyrus smiled at me every so often while he drove us to my apartment. "We'll head to your place and hang out there for a little bit."

I nodded but he couldn't see me. Damn words. I needed to speak to him, but I didn't know how. Maybe I never would. Could I give him my voice? Could I trust him enough to give him that part of me I hadn't given to anyone since before I was taken?

My thoughts traveled to those five years where I was missing. I wasn't even sure if anyone had looked for me. Did my parents demand for me to be found? Did they think that I just upped and left without saying so? Did they cry, shed a tear for our estranged relationship before they died?

So many questions bounced around in my head. Questions I would never get the answers to.

Even though I was now safe, a part of me would be missing forever.

"Hey." Cyrus cupped my hands that were resting on my lap. "Whatever you're thinking, it's over. You're safe, baby, and I promise to protect you."

I looked at him then, leaning my head against the back of the seat. I gave him a slight nod.

While he stared out at the road ahead of us, I couldn't help but watch him. Really look at him then. He was beautiful. But it was more than that. He had an air about him that indicated how he would protect those he loved first before even considering himself. He had a big heart and I prayed that one day, we could give our hearts to each other.

No matter what came of this, he had already helped me so much that I could never repay him.

When my building came into view, my stomach tumbled a bit knowing that we would once again be alone. I remembered everything we had done already. How his hands felt. How he looked. How he made me feel. How he held me after I fell apart in his arms. How he consoled me after I woke from nightmares. I remembered everything about him, and I was greedy for more.

"I can feel you staring, pet," he said, laughing.

My cheeks burned, like they always did whenever he caught me doing something I shouldn't have been.

He glanced my way. "I like that blush on your cheeks. Makes me wonder what the rest of you looks like with that pink on your skin." He waggled his eyebrows.

I laughed, shaking my head.

Cyrus brought my hand up to his mouth, running his lips back and forth over my knuckles.

Once we pulled into the parking lot, he found an empty space and killed the engine before turning to me. "I'm going to be honest with you, Ainsley. I haven't stopped thinking about you and these past weeks together. But as much as I've enjoyed myself, I want to make sure that you're okay."

I undid my seat belt and slid a little closer to him before cupping his face. I only nodded, hoping, no, praying that he could sense how much he meant to me. How our time together, had given me a strength I never thought I would ever feel again.

I could never repay him for helping me put some pieces of my soul back together.

He glanced down at my mouth, licking along his bottom lip.

The air crackled around us, testing our limits.

"Let's go before we get caught doing something in public that could get us in trouble." He winked, kissed my forehead, and left the vehicle.

A breath left me on a whoosh. Sliding from the SUV, I closed the door.

Cyrus came up to my side, locked the vehicle, and held out his hand.

Slipping my fingers between his, I led us to my apartment building.

When we finally entered my place, Cyrus closed the door. "Don't forget the code, baby."

I entered it into the security panel as Cyrus clicked the lock into place.

As soon as I turned, Cyrus grabbed my hand and pulled me against him. I never even had a chance to take a breath as his mouth came down hard on mine.

"I missed you," he murmured against my lips, pushing me up against the wall. "I know I saw you yesterday but fuck, pet, I missed you."

Snaking my arms around his neck, I pulled him closer. I wanted to tell him how I missed him too but instead, I decided to show him.

Lifting my leg, I wrapped it around his waist and tugged him even closer.

He groaned, a soft curse leaving him. "Fuck, Ainsley." He broke the kiss, trailing soft pecks down the length of my jaw. "You're so damn passionate, I can feel you. I can feel all of you. Thank you."

He thanked me often, knowing he had been the only person I gave any part of myself to.

His teeth found the side of my throat, igniting a low moan from the back of my throat.

"Geezus, that's a sexy sound."

Turning my head at the same time he lifted his, our mouths met in the middle. I grabbed onto his waist, unbuckling his belt.

He stiffened, grabbing my hands. "We can just kiss."

I shook my head. I had every intention of waiting until tonight before I gave him all of me, but I couldn't wait anymore. I needed him to help me feel normal. Even if it was a little bit.

"Ainsley." He lifted his head, staring down at me. "We don't have to."

I pulled my hands from his. *I need to feel normal. I need you to help me. I need...God, I need you, Cyrus.*

"You have me, always. But we don't have to have sex until you're ready."

I pushed him back, dropping both feet to the floor. *I am ready now.*

His eyes darkened. "You are fucking sexy when you're frustrated."

I huffed, pushing past him when he caught me around the middle.

"I don't want you to regret anything we do," he murmured against my ear. "I like you a lot, pet, and I don't want to jeopardize that."

I turned in his arms, my hands going back to his belt. I stared at him, waiting for a sign that he would push me away again.

"You want to use me?" he asked, his voice husky and deep.

I nodded.

"You need to use me?"

I nodded again.

"Then lead the way, pet. Show me what you want." He kissed my cheek. "Take control. But I want to warn you." His mouth brushed over the shell of my ear. "I will give you control for now, but I will eventually take it back."

A breath left me at what he was offering.

Tugging on his belt, I walked backwards, leading him to my bedroom.

Along the way, Cyrus shrugged out of his leather cut. He threw it over the arm of the couch, followed by his hoodie and t-shirt.

The closer we got to my room, the harder my heart raced. Once we stepped into my bedroom, his belt was undone along with the zipper of his jeans.

"Keep going, pet," he growled.

I spun us around, pushing him back onto the bed. A part of me knew that he only complied because he knew I needed this. That I needed to be in control even if it was just for a moment. He let me run the show, even if it was only the one time, it didn't matter. The fact that he did so, forced this sense of awareness in me.

I had never been in control before and now that I had it, it was on a whole other level of power I thought I would never feel.

Cyrus kept his hands at his sides, keeping them to himself. "Your show, babe. Remember that."

I nodded, bending at the waist and placing a kiss on his hip bone.

I tugged on his jeans, slipping them down his legs and off of him before tossing them to the side.

When he was naked, I stripped out of my own clothes, leaving me completely bare to his hungry eyes. No matter how many scars I had and how deformed the apex between my thighs was, the way he looked at me made me feel like I was the most beautiful thing he had ever seen.

"There's a condom in my wallet," he told me. "Before you ask, I didn't put it there thinking I would get that part of you, but I put it there to be safe."

I nodded. *Thank you but you don't have to explain.*

"I didn't want you thinking I assumed you would let me fuck you, pet."

I stepped between his legs, placing a finger against his mouth. "Shhh..."

Cyrus's eyes darkened.

Stepping away from him, I picked up his jeans and grabbed the wallet out of his pocket. Pulling the condom out of it, I turned toward him.

He was staring back at me, his hands still at his sides.

I let my eyes roam down the length of his hard, long body. His cock hit just below his belly button. It was fully erect, ready and waiting for me. My core clenched, aching to be filled by every pierced inch of him.

Dropping the wallet and jeans, I stepped back between his thighs. I opened the condom wrapper, slipping the rubber down the length of him.

Cyrus slid further up the bed, his feet dangling over the edge.

I slid onto the bed and straddled his waist. Rising to my knees, I wrapped my fingers around his cock, stroking from base to tip.

His breath caught, his dark eyes watched me, but he still never touched me. I wanted him to but not yet. He knew I needed this, before I even knew that I did.

Running the tip of him over my slit, I shivered. It had been a long time for me and I knew this was going to hurt but feel so damn good just the same.

I slowly lowered a little, the head of his cock now inside of me. Blowing out a slow breath, the slight burn from him stretching me forced all air from my lungs.

Cyrus's jaw clenched but he still never touched me.

Placing my hands on his chest, I took a deep breath and dropped my body onto him in a single hard move.

He shouted out, his eyes rolling into the back of his head while a cry left my own mouth.

"Fuck, Ainsley." He fisted the blankets beneath us. "So tight," he panted.

The hairs on my body tingled, my eyes welling at the burn of something foreign being inside of my body. Lifting my body up a few inches, I slowly lowered back down and began riding him.

A groan fell between us, I couldn't even be sure who made the noise.

Digging my nails into his chest, I used him as leverage and thrust my hips back and forth in hard, rough moves. I could feel the piercings lining his length, rubbing against the walls of my pussy. Knowing I was in full control made my body wetter and open to him even more.

"That's it, baby. Take that control. It's all yours."

I took it, claimed it, and I made it fucking mine.

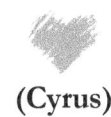

(Cyrus)

I had meant what I said when I told her that I didn't put the condom in my wallet because I assumed we were going to have sex today. Sure, it would be nice, but it wasn't something I needed or would even consider hinting at until she was good and ready.

But now that she was riding me, I was thankful for that condom. While I was clean, and I knew that she was as well when Piper told me they did regular tests at the center, I didn't want to take any chances.

Ainsley whimpered, her body bouncing up and down on my cock.

She was a sight to watch. Her breasts swayed with the movements; her nails dug into my chest. Her long blonde locks fell down around her shoulders. A glow hit her cheeks and I vowed to keep that glow there if she let me.

"Harder, pet," I told her.

She cried out, circling her hips back and forth.

"Harder," I barked, knowing she needed to let herself go. "You won't hurt me, so fuck me harder."

Ainsley lifted her knees, crouched above my waist, and began slamming her body up and down onto my cock.

"Yes," I panted. "Fucking hell, baby."

For someone who hadn't had sex in a while, she sure as hell knew what she wanted.

My eyes dropped to my waist, watching my cock slip in and out of her soaked body. That sight alone had my balls tighten. Just when I thought I was going to explode, a hard scream left her.

Before she could stop riding me, I sat up and grabbed her shoulders, taking over.

I fisted her hair, covered her mouth with mine, and swallowed the rest of her screams.

My release followed soon after, spilling into the condom. It had been so hard, it took the very breath out of me.

When we both finally calmed down, I was still inside of her with my mouth fused to hers.

"Thank you, pet. Thank you for that gift," I whispered.

Ainsley broke the kiss, throwing her arms around my shoulders and hugging me.

"I got you, baby." I wrapped my arms around her and slid off the bed. I carried her to the bathroom and into the shower before turning on the water.

Placing her gently on her feet, I removed the condom, tied it off, and dropped it in the garbage.

We spent the next hour washing each other, touching, and kissing. I realized then that I could easily fall for her. Maybe I already had. I wasn't sure. Could it happen this fast? I didn't have much experience with love, never being in love before, but I had seen friends fall in love or reclaim their love. I wished there was a book on this. It would help. But there wasn't, so for now, I would consider the possibility and just continue dating Ainsley.

RESCUE US

My next goal was to get her to trust me enough to share her voice with me. Even if it was a few words at a time, hearing her speak was all I wanted.

SIXTEEN

Ainsley

AFTER OUR SHOWER, CYRUS dried me off, keeping me close. It was like as soon as we had sex, something switched between us. He constantly touched me. Even hours later when we were driving to wherever it was that he was taking me for our date. His hand was currently cupping my inner thigh. It was a firm hold but not too tight. It made me feel safe and secure, knowing that he wouldn't hurt me. I wasn't sure how I knew that, but I could feel a part of him reaching out to me. It was a part I needed. A part I was sure he didn't share with too many people, if anyone at all. I knew because I felt it too. I had that same part and kept it close and hidden.

Cyrus's hand moved higher up my thigh, reminding me of what we had done earlier that day. We didn't have sex again, but I hoped we would again and soon.

"You're thinking about something, babe."

I slowly turned my head to face him, hugging his arm.

His gaze flicked to mine. "You good?"

I nodded, giving him a small smile.

"You sure?"

I nodded again.

"Good." He looked back out at the road ahead of us. "I meant what I said. Thank you for what you gave me."

My heart stuttered. Cyrus wasn't your typical guy. I never met one who thanked someone for sex.

"You're probably wondering why I thanked you." He glanced at me. "Aren't you?"

I shrugged.

"I know you've been through hell and that sex was off the table for you for a while. So the fact that you trust me enough to give me your body, means something to me, Ainsley."

I sighed.

"You know it's true."

Maybe it was.

Cyrus never said anything more on the subject and turned on the music instead. "Choose whatever you want to listen to, pet."

I put on something that spoke volumes to me. It hit somewhere deep in my soul, add to the fact that even though it wasn't Cyrus's type of music he usually listened to, he never said a word about it.

"Here's To Starting Over" by Asking Alexandria pumped through the speakers. While it was milder than what I usually listened to, it was a favorite song and one I listened to regularly.

"And here I thought you only liked that black metal stuff," Cyrus teased.

I laughed, shaking my head. I tapped his arm, getting his attention and leaned against the door. *I like all music, but metal is my favorite. It speaks to me more than others do.*

He nodded. "Do you understand everything they say too?"

I do. I leaned forward. The movement made his hand fall off my thigh and hit my center. *I prefer when it's hard though.*

"Fuck," he whispered.

I giggled.

"You're a naughty girl, my little sex kitten." He chuckled, shaking his head.

I blew him a kiss.

I enjoyed this side of us. The flirting. The touching. Now that we didn't have to skirt around the subject of sex, it was like we were more comfortable with each other. Even though Cyrus never acted differently and would have been patient if I needed to wait longer to have sex with him, I was happy that I trusted him enough to give him that part of me.

"We're almost there," Cyrus told me, breaking the silence.

We were in the next city over, about an hour from the one I currently lived in. I never met a guy who was willing to drive a longer than normal distance just to show his girl a good time.

"We're going to stop somewhere first and then we'll grab some food."

I could only nod as I watched the city pass us by. We were heading into what looked like the downtown of the urban area.

"You've always been a reader," he pointed out.

I glanced at him then, nodding slightly. *It keeps me out of trouble.*

Cyrus winked, that single movement sending a flutter rushing through me.

We ended up pulling into a parking lot by a large building. I didn't know where we were, never being in this city before. I wasn't even from this part of the country but after everything that had happened, I picked everything up and started over. Literally.

"We're here, pet." Cyrus killed the engine and left the SUV, making his way around to my side. When he opened the door, he leaned in, placing a soft peck on my mouth. "Ready?"

I breathed him in, my tongue peeking out to lick along his bottom lip.

A low growl left him. "Careful, pet."

I cupped his cheek, giving him a small smile.

He shook his head, kissed my nose, and helped me out of the vehicle. "When I went over to your apartment that first night and saw the stack of books on your shelves, I knew what kind of date I had to take you on."

I frowned, staring up at him as he closed the door behind me.

He grabbed my hand, linked our fingers, and led me through the parking lot toward the larger brick building. "Greyson, Jaron's dad, raised my brother and me. Along with his wife of course, and every other member who stayed at the clubhouse. Grey's a reader. He'll read anything. From romance books to horror, as long as it's filled with words, he'll read it."

I soaked up the information Cyrus was telling me. I had only seen Greyson Mercer a handful of times whenever he showed up at the center, but I never pegged him for a guy who read romance books.

"I'm not as much of an avid reader like he is but I can appreciate the love for it. To slip into another world and escape your own for a couple of hours. It's therapeutic."

I nodded before I could stop myself. I had always been a reader but after being kidnapped and rescued, I fell into reading more. The center had a beautiful library that I lost myself in many times.

When we stepped in front of the building, I looked up and up.

"Come," Cyrus said, tugging my hand gently, a wide grin spreading on his face.

He seemed to be almost as excited as I was with whatever this surprise was he had for me.

We walked up the steps. Cyrus let go of my hand to grab the doors for me and waited for me to pass.

As I stepped into the building, a gasp left me. It was a library. And not just any library. But an older one that you saw in movies. One I had always dreamed of going to but never thought I would.

Cyrus came up behind me, a single red rose coming into my vision.

My heart thumped, my eyes welling that he would do this for me. Me, a broken mess of a woman who never thought she would find any amount of happiness ever again. Especially not from someone like Cyrus.

I took the rose and brought it up to my nose, inhaling the sweet scent.

"My goal is to keep that smile on your face, Ainsley," Cyrus murmured in my ear. "No matter what I have to do. Even if we fight, that smile is mine."

I shivered as his deep voice washed over me. Turning toward him, I stood on tiptoes and placed a soft peck on his cheek. *I can't thank you enough for this.*

"I can think of ways you can thank me later," he offered, a sly grin spreading on his handsome face.

I laughed, shaking my head. He didn't have to worry about that though. I already made it a goal to have him back in my bed. Now that we'd had sex already, we got that first moment of awkwardness out of the way. We could start enjoying each other more, getting to know what we liked and didn't like. Cyrus had been gentle with me, but I found that it wasn't something I wanted. Not always anyway. I would have to be patient, knowing that because of what I told him, he wouldn't do anything to put me back in that place. To trigger a memory accidentally. But I wanted him to show me how he was and what he liked, so I could learn from him.

As we walked hand in hand through the library, I kept the rose at my nose and realized then that my feelings for Cyrus were blooming. Much like the flower in my hand.

(Cyrus)

The smile on Ainsley's face was something I vowed to always keep there. She was beautiful already, but she was absolutely stunning when her face lit up. I hadn't seen her smile much and based on the little bit I got from Piper, she wasn't a happy person. Understandably so with the shit she had told me.

I made a mental note to contact someone regarding what happened to Ainsley. She had said that some of the bastards running the trafficking ring had been killed, caught, or escaped. The ones who escaped were the ones I wanted to go after. But I wouldn't. Not yet. Not until I knew that Ainsley trusted me enough to take her to the clubhouse and keep her there while I went after the fuckers who hurt her and everyone else they kept locked up.

I also needed her to trust me enough to give me her voice. I craved her words but most of all, I just wanted to hear her say my name. At least once. I wanted to know what it sounded like on her tongue. I wanted her to taste each syllable as my name fell from her sweet lips. I wanted her to want me like I wanted her.

As we walked through the library, she let go of my hand and went a couple of steps ahead of me. My eyes fell to her ass. She was wearing dark blue jeans that hugged her curves. A white oversized sweater was tucked into the waist and even though she was completely covered, I remembered exactly what she looked like beneath those layers.

I also remembered how she reacted when I saw her scars. She tried hiding them from me, but it didn't work. Every inch of her was in my mind's eye as I attempted to remain calm, knowing what those bastards had done to her.

It was beyond sick and twisted to think that they could remove a part of her and that would prevent her from having any sexual gratification. I had spent hours on Google trying to get some answers, but the main internet only did so much. I would have to contact a friend and dig deeper. But for now, I was going to spend the day with Ainsley and attempt to keep that smile on her face and that brightness in her eyes.

She stopped every couple of rows, keeping the rose at her nose and brushing a finger over the spine of a book.

When she stopped and pulled a book from a shelf, I looked around us. The library wasn't overly busy. A few people sat at tables, hunched over books or taking down notes. Several of the computers were being used. Nothing seemed out of the ordinary. Not until I saw a man looking back at me. From where I was standing, I could see that he was heavily tattooed. He was sitting at a table, with a book spread out in front of him but he was staring directly at me.

He looked familiar but I couldn't place where I had seen him before.

A throat clearing pulled my head around.

Ainsley came up to me. *You okay?*

I looked back out at the strange man who was staring at me but found his table completely empty. Scanning the large room, I didn't see him anywhere. I had no idea who he was, but I knew that I had seen him before. I just couldn't figure out where.

"I am." I gave Ainsley a quick peck on the mouth. "Go play."

She laughed, heading back to the books.

Ainsley looked back at me every so often. A small smile would spread on her face, her cheeks would turn a light shade of red, and her eyes would flash with something I had never seen before. Not directed at me anyway.

I liked her. I really liked her. I found that ever since I first met her, there was a part of me that wanted to take things slow. So I appreciated the fact that it took a bit for us to actually have sex. It wasn't something I was used to. Most of the women I had been with would give it up right away and I found that it no longer did anything for me.

My phone took that moment to buzz. I fished it out of my pocket, saw that it was Sammy, and unlocked the screen.

Sam: You down for drinks tonight?

Me: Can't. On a date.

Sam: With Mouse?

I frowned.

Me: I thought she was Quiet Girl.

Sam: Mouse sounds better. Enjoy, brother.

I could almost see his eye roll from here.

Ainsley glanced at me over her shoulder, her brows furrowing in the middle.

I went up to her and kissed her cheek. "I have to make a call," I told her, keeping my mouth against her skin. "Take all the time you need. I'll just be over here."

175

She nodded, turned her head, and placed a soft peck on my lips.

That single movement, although small, did something funny to me. It made me realize that I would do anything for this woman. Even if it meant putting my relationship with my own brother on the line.

(Ainsley)

I sensed that something was wrong with Cyrus, but I couldn't place what it was. He was only a few feet away, but I could almost see the stiffness in his muscles. Did someone call him and piss him off?

My thoughts went to his brother. Maybe Sammy didn't approve of whatever it was that Cyrus and me were doing. Not that it was any of his business of course but I also didn't want to come between them at all.

Cyrus went on like he didn't care what his brother thought, but I knew he did. How could he not? They were close and had already been through so much. Maybe I could try and reach out to Sammy, write him a letter and see what the hell his problem was.

Cyrus had his cell up to his ear, a deep scowl on his face. Whoever he was talking to had changed his mood completely. Just when I thought the night was ruined, Cyrus caught my gaze and winked.

My stomach fluttered.

He came toward me, pulling the phone from his ear. "My brother says hi."

I raised an eyebrow.

"I don't know why either." He shook his head. "He won't tell me what his deal is." He reached out, cupping my cheek. "We'll spend a little longer here and then I'll take you out for food."

I nodded, the air rolling off of him making me uneasy. *We can head back if Sammy needs you.*

"No." Cyrus's brows narrowed. "*I* need you. He's moping about something, and I honestly don't give a shit at the moment."

He did but I wasn't going to call him out on it. I didn't know much about his relationship with his brother. I assumed they were close but maybe they weren't as close as I thought they were.

"You're staring, pet." Cyrus leaned down to my ear. "As much as I like your eyes on me, the sooner we finish here and get food, the sooner I can take you home and we can have dessert."

A husky laugh left me, my body heating at the idea of him being inside me again.

"Hmm..." He linked his fingers with mine. "My girl likes that idea."

I nodded even though he already knew the answer.

"She likes that idea a lot." He kissed the spot by my ear. "Your man likes that idea too."

My man. God, I loved the sound of that. I leaned back, staring up at him. *My man? Really?*

He shrugged, the movement almost strange coming from him, seeing as how big he was. "If you want of course. I won't pressure you, but I like you, Ainsley. I like you a lot. This is our second date or third if you count the first night I slept at your place."

We've had many dates at my place. I smiled. *And I like you too, Cyrus, and I would like to continue this. If you want.*

He grinned, placing a hard peck on my mouth. "I want. You have no idea how much I want."

I giggled, cupping his jaw.

Cyrus pulled away, giving me another wink and slipping his fingers in mine. "Let's get you some books."

Once I chose which ones I wanted, Cyrus helped me by carrying my bag of books. Even though they were purchased, he still helped me get a library card for whenever I was in the area. Even if I never used the card, I still stared at it in awe that I actually had one.

"You've never had a library card before, have you?" he asked, as if he could read my thoughts.

I shook my head, wishing I could have been more normal for him.

"Hey, it's not a big deal."

But it was. Maybe not for him but it definitely was a big deal for me. There were a lot of things I had never done before, but I hoped that with Cyrus's help, that maybe one day I could.

We had quickly gone for a bite to eat but both of us were suddenly on edge, so much so that I couldn't even taste the food once it hit my tongue. We ended up getting most of our meal to go and ate in the SUV on the way home.

Once we stood outside my apartment door, I expected Cyrus to kiss me goodnight and leave like he did after the first date we went on. But this time, he stared down at me. Waiting.

I took a deep breath, unlocked the door and stepped into my apartment. I figured he would follow me but when I turned and saw that he was still standing at the door, I realized then that he was waiting for an invitation.

His dark eyes were locked with mine, his body rigid and stiff. He was waiting. For my permission. For my words. For me to tell him that I needed him. I did. I needed him more than I had earlier that day.

Placing my bag on the floor by the wall, I pulled off my sweater. Keeping my eyes on Cyrus the whole time, I hoped that with me removing my clothing, he would get the hint.

Letting the sweater drop to the floor, I backed up and started unbuttoning my jeans.

His eyes darkened, his tongue peeking out to lick along his bottom lip. He stepped over the threshold, closed the door behind him, and clicked the lock into place.

I took a step to the right and began backing up down the hallway leading to my bedroom.

Cyrus followed, his steps slow and powerful. I could feel the anticipation the closer he got to me.

By the time I reached my room, I was completely naked while he was still fully clothed.

The backs of my knees hit the edge of my bed, forcing my heart to jump to my throat.

No words slid between us the closer we came to giving each other what we both wanted.

Sitting on the bed, I slid back as he crawled onto the bed between my knees. Our mouths were the first to touch. The kiss turned hard and frantic quickly. My body burned with need for him. He ignored my scars and replaced them with happy memories. Memories I could never thank him enough for.

Reaching between us, I undid his belt and lowered the zipper to his jeans. I didn't care that he wasn't naked. I just needed him inside of me. So deep inside me that all I could feel was him. That was what I wanted.

I slipped my hand into his jeans and pulled out his thick cock. He groaned, deepened the kiss, and fisted the blankets at either side of my head.

Spreading my legs, I lined the tip of him up to my center when he thrust forward, filling me to the hilt.

I cried out, arching beneath him.

Cyrus cupped my inner thigh, pulled my leg out to the side, and picked up speed with his hips. The first time we had sex, I was in full control but now, this was all Cyrus. He took, he gave, and he completely devoured me.

His powerful thrusts forced me over the edge in a matter of minutes, my screams becoming louder and louder.

He never said anything the whole time. He only touched me, kissed me, and made love to me until all I could feel was him.

I came a second time when Cyrus pulled out of me and slid off the bed. He grabbed my hips and pulled me to the edge before flipping me onto my stomach.

My heart leapt to my throat.

"You need me to stop, you tell me," he whispered, slowly slipping back inside me. He kissed my shoulder, linking his fingers with mine above my head.

Spreading my legs, a hard moan left me.

"Fuck," he growled, his teeth sinking into my shoulder. "I forgot a condom, baby."

I shook my head, not caring in the least about that.

"I'm clean." He pushed forward. "Fucking hell, you feel good. But I'm clean. Shit, pet. I can't even concentrate with your hot pussy wrapped around me."

A breathless laugh left me.

He pulled his arm back, his phone coming into my line of sight a moment later. The screen was open to his notepad app. I took the hint and began typing.

I'm clean too. I promise I'm clean. Just please don't stop.

I threw the phone on the bed.

"I'm not stopping." He leaned back, grabbed my hips, and pulled me to all fours.

When his hips picked up speed, a shattered scream left me as the new angle forced him to go even deeper inside of me.

"That's it, Ainsley," he groaned. "Scream for your man. Scream hard and come all over my cock."

My thighs shook, trembling around him. The powerful release vibrated through me, forcing all air from my lungs.

I never thought since everything that had happened, I would actually get to enjoy sex again. But with Cyrus's patience, I did. Because of him, I embraced the powerful woman inside of me and gave it back to him tenfold.

SEVENTEEN

CYRUS

WHILE AINSLEY SLEPT PEACEFULLY beside me, I couldn't help but watch her. Her ass was pushed up against my crotch. The blankets had ridden low enough that I could see the curves of her body. Freckles and scars marked her pale skin but while she thought they were imperfections, I thought they were perfect. Because they meant she was a survivor. She had been through hell. Literally. Most wouldn't have come out of that swinging but she had. While she still didn't have her voice, she trusted me enough to give me her body. That was saying something when the fuckers took that part of her away in the first place.

A sudden whimper left her, making my stomach clench.

Before the nightmares in her mind could take over, I wrapped myself around her and pulled the blankets up and over us.

"Shhh, baby. I'm here," I murmured in her ear. "I'm always here." I ran my hand up and down her arm, trying to do everything I could to save her from her demons.

Ainsley sighed, her tense body finally relaxing at my touch.

I kissed her temple, breathing her in. She smelled like sex, a sweet perfume, and me. It was a scent that I vowed to keep on her skin for as long as possible.

My phone rang off in the distance, but I ignored it. I was sure it was my brother. He probably woke from having a nightmare himself and while he was going to give me shit for not taking his call, taking care of Ainsley was more important at the moment. He would have to get over it and find another way to cope.

Ainsley shifted beside me, another whimper leaving her. The sound stabbed me right in the heart. I didn't know what her nightmare was about, but I could only imagine.

"Cyrus," she whispered.

My eyes widened. This whole time. This whole mother fucking time, I had never heard her voice. Even though it was just a whisper, I would take it, but I wondered. Was I dreaming? Did I imagine it?

Reaching over, I turned on the lamp sitting on her nightstand and looked back down at her. Her eyes were squeezed shut, her jaw clenching. She was still sleeping, so there was no way she could have said my name. Was there? I had wanted to hear her voice for so long, maybe my mind made me think she said it. I didn't know.

"Baby." I kissed her head. "Wake up. You're having a nightmare." I gently nudged her, needing to help her escape her mind.

She suddenly jumped, lifting her head. Her back rose and fell with ragged breaths, a light sheen of sweat coating her skin. She shook her head, probably trying to ward off the evil threatening to take over.

"Hey." I pulled her into my arms and on top of me.

Ainsley straddled my waist, wrapped herself around me, and let out a soft sigh.

Shifting my weight, I leaned against the headboard and pulled the blankets up and around us. I turned off the lamp and held her close. If she needed to sleep on me to get a good night's rest, I would forever be willing to help her with that.

My phone buzzed again.

Since I was wide awake and Ainsley fell back asleep, I checked my phone.

Sammy: You don't answer your phone anymore?

I ground my teeth together, a sharp pain shooting up the side of my face. I loved my brother, but his mood swings were starting to piss me off. I hoped Red kicked his ass and made him beg for whatever it was he wanted from her.

Me: I was in the middle of something.

Sammy: It's called sex, C.

I rolled my eyes.

Me: It wasn't sex. Helping my girl through her nightmare.

I didn't have to explain myself to him, but I knew that he wouldn't let it go if I didn't give him some sort of an answer.

Sammy: Huh.

Not wanting to disturb Ainsley now that she had fallen back asleep, I wasn't going to call my brother but that single-worded text he just sent, annoyed the fuck out of me. Dialing him up, I waited for him to answer.

"Now you call me," he said, his voice curt.

"What the hell is your problem, Sammy?" I demanded, keeping my voice as quiet as possible, so I wouldn't disturb Ainsley.

She shifted on top of me.

Running my hand up and down her back, I waited for her to settle.

"Did you not have a nightmare?" Sam asked.

I almost forgot I was on the phone with him, Ainsley had me so wrapped up in her, I lost focus on what I was doing.

"No," I told him as she shifted her weight until my cock was snug against her hot center.

Her body relaxed then, and I realized that feeling me, helped calm her. It made the alpha in me roar and the Dom in me stir. If my cock was what she needed, she had it. Always.

"I was awake already," I told Sammy before he could respond.

"I'm sick of this shit," he muttered, and I wondered if he was referring to the nightmares or the fact that I now had someone else in my life besides him.

"Call up Red," I suggested.

"Yeah, right. She has her own shit to deal with," he grunted. "I gotta go. I'll see you around, Cyrus."

The click in my ear reverberated through me.

It dawned on me that the closer I got to Ainsley, the farther apart I was getting from my brother. It shouldn't be that way. We should want each other to find the happiness I knew we both deserved, but Sammy was so wrapped up in his head, I wasn't sure how any woman, including Red, would help him unravel those thoughts.

Bottom line, he was scared. Of something. I just didn't know what.

(Ainsley)

I could still feel the remnants of the nightmare rushing through me. It left my stomach aching and a sheen of sweat on my skin. I vaguely remembered Cyrus pulling me into his arms some time during the night. I must have fallen asleep like that because when I woke once again, we were in the same position.

Sitting up, I scrubbed a hand down my face.

"Good morning, pet," he said, his voice deep and gravely.

Morning. Did you not sleep at all?

He gave me a small smile. "Not really. Did I wake you?"

I shook my head, my stomach sinking a little that he hadn't slept much and took care of me instead. I had never been one to be doted on. I found that the only person I could truly trust was myself, but a part of me was learning to trust Cyrus too. I just wished this trust would happen faster, so I could finally give him my voice.

"What is it?" he asked, running a hand down my bare arm.

I looked down, realizing then that we were both still naked. His cock, although soft, twitched under my scrutiny. It rested against my inner thigh. A shiver raced down my spine, suddenly needing him back inside of me.

"Ainsley."

My eyes snapped up, locking with Cyrus's intense stare.

"If you want it, you know what to do but I wasn't overly gentle last night, so I'm sure you're sore."

I shrugged, not really caring in the least if I was sore or not.

"Are you?" Cyrus sat forward, his mouth mere inches from mine.

I swallowed hard, still not used to the fact that I had this beautiful man beneath me.

"Tell me," he whispered, his lips brushing along the line of my jaw.

I shook my head again.

"No." He cupped my shoulders, sliding his hands slowly down my arms. "*Tell* me."

My heart jumped. He had never asked me to speak. Not until now. Not until we became closer. Not until our feelings for each other grew.

I swallowed hard but the words wouldn't leave my mouth.

"Tell me if in fact you are sore or not, pet." His voice was low, hitting somewhere deep inside of me. Somewhere that had remained hidden for years.

My mouth fell open but still, the words wouldn't escape past my lips.

"You said my name earlier," he murmured, his mouth pressed against my ear.

My eyes widened.

"You were having a nightmare, but I was able to calm you down and then you said my name," he explained. "I pulled you into my arms and having my cock rubbing up against you, settled you down."

My body heated, not realizing the physical touch could calm me down like he said.

"Say it again, Ainsley. Say my name."

As much as I wanted to, I couldn't. Not yet. Not until I knew for sure that he wasn't going to break me. But he hadn't given me any reason to think he would. Maybe I needed to talk to someone. Maybe I needed to find out when it was okay to open myself up completely to him. To anyone for that matter.

"Say it," he growled, nipping my jaw.

I went to pull away from him when his hold on me tightened.

"No, you're not getting away from me. Not this time."

Pushing against him, I could feel myself closing in. I needed away. Out of his touch. Off of this bed. I needed a damn moment.

"Ainsley." Cyrus shoved me onto my back. "Stop fighting me."

I suddenly felt backed into a corner. My heart pounded in my ears, my stomach clenching to the point of painful. Bile rose to my throat as memories came rushing back.

So much agony. So many tears.

"Look at me." Cyrus's voice sounded so far away.

I couldn't focus. I couldn't concentrate on anything but the demons of my past.

Suddenly, a firm mouth captured mine in a deep, bruising kiss.

I gasped at the contact.

Cyrus slipped his tongue between my lips, the kiss becoming deeper. He grabbed my hands that were still pressed against his chest and shoved my arms above my head.

A part of me wanted to fight him, while the other wanted him to fuck me. Lifting my hips, I shivered as my body slid along his cock.

He growled, nipping my bottom lip. "Stop. I'm not fucking you like this."

I whimpered, lifting my hips once again.

"Ainsley." He pinned me down with his body, stopping me from teasing us both. "What did I just say?"

Please was on the tip of my tongue but I couldn't say it. I knew that if I would just say his name, this could end and I could get what I wanted, but I feared that in that moment, he would laugh and leave.

"Tell me what you're thinking right now," he demanded, his dark eyes staring down into my soul.

Shaking my head, I squeezed my eyes shut.

"I will get your voice, pet," he murmured in my ear. "If it's the last thing I fucking do, I will make it so you trust me enough to speak to me."

Cyrus lifted off of me and left the bed.

I sat up, swung my legs over the side, and waited for him to look at me. When he only pulled on his clothes and never met my gaze, I huffed. His eyes finally met mine.

"What?"

I do trust you, I told him.

Much to my surprise, he laughed. "Right." *You do not trust me. Not enough to give me your damn voice, pet.*

Shoving from the bed, I stomped up to him. *I wouldn't have let you fuck me if I didn't trust you.*

Once he finished getting dressed instead of responding, I pushed him.

His gaze snapped to mine, his eyes cold and angry. "I'm a patient man, pet. A very patient man. I know you need a push but at the same time, I won't push you to the point of hurting you. I can be an asshole, but I know when not to overstep. However, I do not appreciate being lied to."

I'm not lying.

In a quick move, his hand wrapped around my throat.

A sharp gasp escaped me at the sudden change in him. But this change, this dominant side of him, a side that I didn't see often because he had always been gentle with me, was a side I suddenly realized that I needed. It called out to the submissive in me. Even though I had been trained and conditioned to comply, with Cyrus, I found that I actually wanted to submit to him.

With his hand around my throat, he pulled me toward him. "Want to try that again, pet?" His voice took on a raspy tone that made the tiny hairs on my body tingle.

I am not lying, I signed slowly.

In a quick move, his free hand landed against my ass.

I whimpered, the slight tinge of pain erupting through me.

His brows narrowed, pushing me back until I hit the edge of the bed. "Are you sure about that?"

I trust you. Even though I signed those words to him, I knew that I wasn't being completely truthful.

His hand landed against my ass again. "What the fuck did I say?"

I shoved out of his grip, geared my hand back, and landed my palm against his cheek.

Cyrus stared at me. He didn't flinch. He didn't say anything. The muscle in his strong jaw ticked. The spot turned red from where my hand had connected with his cheek.

My chest rose and fell, my palm tingled at the impact. I regretted slapping him the moment I did it, but I couldn't stop myself. He pushed me and I didn't like it. Not one fucking bit.

Much to my surprise, he spun on his heel and left the room. The sound of the door to my apartment closing a moment later, sucked all air from my lungs.

I should have gone after him. I should have stopped him from leaving. I should have done a lot of things, but I didn't.

Instead, I fell to my knees and let the shame of what I had just done, rip through me.

EIGHTEEN

CYRUS

I SHOULDN'T HAVE PUSHED her. Not like that. But when Ainsley had continuously given me her body, I only assumed that the trust was there. It wasn't. Not enough. I didn't know how to crack that final wall between us. I didn't need to break it down. Not at first. I just needed it to crumble enough that I could get her voice. It was the only thing I wanted. I could have waited for sex. I often wondered why she would be with me psychically but not emotionally,

When I demanded she actually speak to me, that little voice in my head warned me she wouldn't like it and would close up on me. But of course, I didn't listen and only kept demanding for her to say something.

It had been a couple of days since we had seen each other. I texted her, asking if she would be willing to go on another date this coming Friday and all I got back was a *sure*.

My body vibrated with the need to see her, but I didn't want to overstep and lose the progress I had made these past couple of months. As much as I didn't like it, I would have to wait.

It didn't sit well with me at how quiet she was being. Maybe this was over before it even began.

When Friday finally came, I got a text from her that I wasn't prepared for.

Pet: I can't meet up tonight.

I responded, asking her why but I never got a reply. I clearly fucked up.

Friday came and went and so did the good mood I was in earlier in the week. With Ainsley, I was at my happiest but now that there was this issue between us, I couldn't figure out how to make things right.

Everything and everyone was pissing me off. So before I did or said something I regretted, I decided I needed to fight off the aggression. When I was leaving the clubhouse, the hairs on the back of my neck tingled. I looked around me, finding Sammy leaning against the brick wall, puffing on a smoke.

"Where are you going?" he asked.

"Out," was all I said.

"Figured that much, brother."

My jaw clenched.

Things hadn't been well between us either ever since I ignored his phone call the last time I was at Ainsley's. Apparently, taking care of a woman who had a nightmare wasn't a good enough a reason for him.

"You going to see Mouse?" he asked, flicking the smoke to the ground.

"No. I'm going to The Ring." I needed a good fight. Although, it probably wouldn't help my mood, I just needed to hurt while I figured out how to fix things with Ainsley. Especially since I hadn't heard from her since the Friday before.

"Trouble in paradise already?" Sammy chuckled.

My head whipped around. "Careful, brother. You're treading on very dangerous ground at the moment."

He pushed away from the wall and stalked toward me. "Am I really? You told me to get my head out of my ass when it comes to Red. Seems to me like you should do the same when it comes to Ainsley."

"I have no idea what you're talking about." I spun on my heel, heading toward my bike.

"No?" Sammy followed me, much to my dismay of course. "You've been moping around here for the past week. What happened?"

"None of your business," I grumbled, not liking the fact that he was pushing me.

"None of my business," he repeated, chuckling. "You know, Cyrus, if you like this woman as much as I think you do, you should fight for her."

I stopped, slowly looking over my shoulder at my twin. "Thought you didn't like her?"

He scowled. "I never once said that."

I grunted. "Could have fooled me. Even she thinks you don't like her, Sammy."

"I don't give a shit if she thinks that or not. I'm not the one fucking her."

"Why are you an asshole?"

"Because." He shrugged. "It turns my girl on."

Shaking my head, I continued heading to my bike when his next words stopped me.

"You sure you want someone as broken as her?" Sammy pulled a pack of smokes out of the inner pocket of his leather cut. "Piper said she's pretty messed up."

"Piper wouldn't say that and also, you're just as fucking broken. Just in a different way," I told him.

"I'm fine." And with that, he walked back toward the large house.

He was fine. Yeah, right.

Sammy *was* in fact broken. You didn't need to be tortured, raped, and abused to be emotionally shattered. Something was up with my brother, but I could never get it out of him. Not even sure if Red could.

Straddling my bike, I pulled out my phone to send Ainsley a text. I was sick of this shit.

Me: I'm stopping by your place later. We need to talk.

Putting my phone away, a hard sigh left me when I felt it vibrate. I didn't care if she didn't want to see me. I was going over after heading to The Ring. She was going to listen to what I had to say because I couldn't go on with the way things currently were.

These feelings I had for Ainsley weren't superficial. They went deeper than that. And she was going to hear me tell her how I felt. Whether she liked it or not.

(Ainsley)

I shouldn't have canceled the date, but truth was, I was scared. Scared of my feelings for Cyrus. Scared that he didn't feel the same way. Scared that this would end before it even began. I knew that if it did in fact end, it would probably fall on me. Cyrus had taken this seriously since the beginning. I did as well but for whatever reason, I couldn't open up completely to him.

When he texted that he was coming over later, I responded instantly, telling him that he didn't have to. But even though I had texted him that, I still couldn't help the happiness rushing through me. A jittery feeling settled in my stomach as I spent the evening cleaning and trying to distract myself from thoughts of the man who had barreled his way into my life.

It was pushing midnight and there was still no sign of Cyrus. Maybe he changed his mind about coming over. Or he moved on to someone better and less broken than I was. I scowled, ashamed at myself for thinking such things. Cyrus would never do something like that, and he was a gentleman. Until you got him into bed anyway.

My body still burned with memories of the few times we slept together. I could feel him all over me, throughout every inch of me. In the deepest parts of my soul.

With a glass of wine in hand, I decided to play one of my games when a hard bang sounded on the door. I jumped, almost spilling my wine.

Placing the glass on the end table, I went to the door and checked the peep hole. My eyes widened.

Unlocking the door, I opened it and found a disheveled and bloody Cyrus standing there.

"I'm sorry I'm late," he mumbled, pushing his way into my apartment. He closed the door and clicked the lock into place.

What happened to you? I typed in the security code while I waited for his answer.

He wobbled on his feet, pinching the bridge of his nose. Was he drunk?

"I think I got hit too hard." He dropped his arm, his dark eyes landing on me. "I missed you."

My stomach tumbled, taking him in. A dark bruise sat on his cheek, his lip was split and there was blood on his white t-shirt that was under his zip-up hoodie.

I took his hand, leading him to the dining room table.

"I went to The Ring tonight and wasn't focused." He pulled me against him as he sat. "I don't like how we left things the last time."

My body heated at being this close to him again. Brushing my fingers through his hair, I kissed his forehead. Sliding from his lap, I went to the kitchen and grabbed the First Aid kit that I kept under the sink.

Pulling up a chair in front of him, I started rummaging through the items in the kit.

"Hey." He covered my hands that I only just realized were shaking. He brought them to his mouth, kissing the tips of my fingers. "I *am* sorry. I'm sorry for pushing you and I'm sorry for not being patient."

I pulled my hands from his grasp. *But you are patient, Cyrus. More patient than anyone I know. And I'm sorry for slapping you. I know that sometimes I need to be pushed. I do know that. And I do trust you. I do. Maybe not completely. Not yet. But over time, I know it'll happen where I trust you completely.*

He gave me a small smile. *Do you forgive me?*

My stomach tumbled like it always did whenever he signed. I nodded. *Do you forgive me?*

"No forgiveness needed, pet, but if you need to hear the words, yes, I forgive you." He grabbed my hands again, leaning his forehead against mine. "I care about you, Ainsley. I care about you a lot."

My heart stuttered, my eyes fluttering closed.

"I was worried you canceled our date because you didn't want anything to do with me ever again."

I leaned back, staring at him. *Never, and I care about you too, Cyrus. A lot. I've told you things no one else knows. Not even all the therapists I've seen over the past few years know half the shit I've told you.*

"Good. Let's keep it that way." He moved to kiss me when my hands landed against his chest. "Baby, let me kiss you."

A breathless gasp escaped me at the desperation rolling off of him. *Let me tend to your wounds first.*

"Fine," he grumbled, sitting back.

I laughed, rising from my chair. *I'll take care of you, Cyrus.*

"You already have."

My smile was so damn wide, my cheeks hurt. While I took care of him and cleaned up his cuts, he stared at me. Before him, I hated being the center of attention. I hated being touched and even looked at. I wore clothes bigger than needed, so I could hide behind the oversized fabric. But now, with Cyrus, with this beautiful man sitting across from me, I wanted to strip myself bare and let him see everything. Every inch. Every shattered and messy piece of me.

"Ainsley," he growled.

My eyes snapped to his.

"You need to stop thinking whatever is going on in that beautiful head of yours. And you especially need to stop biting your lip." He pinched my chin, pulling my lip from the onslaught of my teeth. "It's my lip to bite." He tugged me forward, crushing his mouth to mine.

The bandages fell from my hands, landing on the floor beneath us with a soft thud. Snaking my arms around his shoulders, I deepened the kiss.

He growled, nipping my bottom lip until it throbbed. "My lip. My body. My pet."

I whimpered. *Yes, yes, I am all of yours.* The words screamed in my head but wouldn't leave my lips.

"Say it," he demanded, keeping his mouth locked on mine.

Make me, please make me.

"Say. It," he repeated, moving his hand to my throat.

"Yes," I whispered.

A snarl left him as he attacked my mouth.

It wasn't a full sentence, but it was a start. A single word that held so much weight behind it. That hinted for everything I knew he could give me and more.

NINETEEN

CYRUS

"YES."

That word. One syllable. So many different meanings.

Ainsley shook against me, her small body trembling with what I could only imagine was a need for more. I pulled her into my arms, needing to feel her against me. I craved her moans and her silent pleas for everything I had to offer her.

Tonight had been one hell of a night. I went to The Ring with every intention of having one fight and leaving but some fucker started provoking me and the rest of the night ended up in a blur. I could usually keep my temper in check, but he was going on about my brother. Sammy didn't fight often. He liked fighting with me or Jaron instead, never a stranger because he didn't trust them. His words. Add to the fact I hadn't seen Ainsley and we didn't leave things the way I would have liked, and it all went downhill from there.

Ainsley's soft whimper pulled me back to the present. She broke the kiss, her eyes shining bright with lust. Her lips pulled up into a small smile.

"You're beautiful," I told her. "Thank you for giving me another piece of you." As much as I appreciated her giving me the single word, I needed something else. Something more. Something we hadn't done yet.

Her smile widened.

I kissed her jaw. "So fucking beautiful." My feelings grew for her every time I saw her, every time I hung out with her. Every damn time I thought of her.

A shudder rippled through her.

"I want to try something," I murmured against her jaw.

She leaned back, confusion pulling her brows to the middle of her forehead.

I winked, wrapping my arms around her and lifting her onto the table.

She gasped, her eyes widening.

"Shhh..." I kissed her softly. "Trust me, pet. Now lay back." I sat back down, pulling her ass to the edge of the table.

Ainsley leaned on her elbows, watching me.

"Lay back," I instructed gently.

She chewed her bottom lip but finally did as I said and laid back on the table.

Cupping her knees, I slid my hands slowly up her legs. I wasn't sure how much she would feel since she didn't have complete sensation in her clit but I sure as hell wanted to try. I would spend hours feasting on her if I had to.

Hooking my fingers into her pajama pants, I pulled them off her waist and down her legs.

Her chest rose and fell, her eyes locking with mine.

I winked, pulling the pants off her feet and tossing them to the floor. "I'm probably going to enjoy this more than you."

She lifted her hands, pausing.

"What?" I asked, tugging her closer to me.

I've never done this. I mean, no man has ever done this. To me.

My cock twitched at that confession. "Oh I'm definitely going to enjoy this more then."

A breathless laugh left her.

As much as I wanted to just dive into her heat and never come up for air, with her, I had to go slow. I already got more from her than I was sure she gave most people. So I didn't want to take advantage of that and have it backfire on me either.

"Just relax, pet." I placed a soft peck on her knee. "I got you."

She nodded.

"Put your feet on the edge of the table."

She did as she was told and let her knees fall to the sides.

A low growl left me as the movement caused her body to open for me.

Her breath caught, her knees slamming closed.

"No." I cupped her thighs. "I'm sorry, baby. You're just fucking perfect."

I'm not. I have scars. I have—

I grabbed her hands, stopping her from putting herself down even more. "You are a survivor. I wouldn't give a shit if you had scars from head to toe, I would still be attracted to you. I would still be falling for you. I would still want to make love to you, date you, be your boyfriend and eat the fuck out of your pussy. Not all in that order of course."

Her eyes welled, her throat working over a hard swallow.

"Ainsley." I stood from the chair and gently pried her knees apart so I could move between them. "I will spend the rest of my days apologizing for pushing you, but I want you to know, that I don't regret you slapping me. I know I left after, but it was because..."

Her eyes met mine when my words trailed off.

I sighed, pushing her hair off her forehead. "I was proud of you for that reaction and wanted to fuck you. But I didn't want you to see me like that. So I left. I'm sorry if I made you think I didn't want more out of this."

You wanted sex?

"I did because when I pushed you, it forced this passionate woman to reveal herself." I gave her a small smirk. "And besides, I always want sex with you but it's not a requirement. Like I keep telling you, I'm a patient guy. But I also meant what I said. I don't like being lied to."

I'm sorry for lying and I... She reached out to brush her thumb along my bottom lip. *I'm falling for you too.*

My grin grew. "We should celebrate." I sat back down on the chair and slid even closer to her.

Ainsley spread her knees apart and gave me another piece of her.

Hooking my arms around her, I pulled her closer and leaned down toward the apex between her thighs. Brushing my nose from her center to her scarred clit, I inhaled. A low groan left me, the sweet acidic scent of her body wafting into my nose. "Fuck me, you smell like heaven."

She whimpered.

I had to rein in on that beast who wanted to devour her whole. In time, I would show her the true nature of my ways and I knew she would enjoy it, but I didn't want to scare her.

Running my nose along her clit, I kept breathing her in. It was a scent I could bottle. She was as turned on as I was, but this was all for her. I wouldn't fuck her. Maybe later or tomorrow or a few days from now. I needed her to know that I never expected anything in return from her. She could trust me.

Sounds left her. Soft whimpers and mewls.

"You can feel that, baby." I looked up the length of her body. "Can't you?"

She nodded quickly.

"Good. I'm glad." So I kept doing it again and again.

She sighed. "Please," she whispered.

That single word controlled my next move. Covering her with my mouth, I shoved my tongue into her.

She cried out, latching on to my hair and lifting her hips.

I had every intention of being gentle, but her voice, although a whisper, prevented me from doing so. It was the driving force I needed to give her everything she wanted and could ever ask for.

Cupping the backs of her legs, I pushed her knees to her chest and shoved my mouth harder against her.

My eyes rolled into the back of my head as her sweet nectar slid down the back of my tongue.

Her cries became louder, her body shaking beneath me. *Come for me, baby. Come for your man and let him drink up your orgasm.*

Opening my eyes, they locked with hers.

I growled, thrusting my tongue in and out of her.

Her hips lifted and dropped, lifted again and lowered back to the table.

I shook my head, snarling as she fucked herself on my tongue.

Ainsley's fingers tightened in my hair, pulling and ripping at my scalp until a shattered scream left her. She threw her head back, her body bowing on the table. A gush of liquid sprayed into my mouth and it only made the groans and growls leaving me that more pronounced.

Not wanting this moment to end, I shoved to my feet, pushing her knees higher toward her chest.

She cried out, her thighs trying to close around my head. But I wouldn't let them. I wasn't stopping until she came again for me.

Until then, I was going to enjoy every single inch of her pussy.

(Ainsley)

The second orgasm slammed into me. I had never felt anything like it. Not even when Cyrus had fucked me the handful of times before. This was more. It was intense, leaving my lips on a harsh scream for the second time that night.

I never expected that I could have a release that way. Not after part of me had been mutilated.

So many different emotions suddenly hit me. They weighed me down and sat on my shoulders until a sob left me.

I covered my face, the impact of the release forcing tears from the corners of my eyes.

Heavy arms wrapped around me, lifting me off the table.

I was vaguely aware that I was being moved but I couldn't concentrate on anything other than the sobs wracking through me.

"I got you, pet," Cyrus said gently, running his hands in circles over my upper back.

The cries subsided. Now I just felt exhausted. I was confused as to why I could cry when the orgasms had been nothing but amazing.

Sitting up, I wiped my face and saw that we were sitting on the couch. "I'm sorry," I whispered.

"That's the third time you spoke to me tonight," he pointed out.

I gave him a small smile, shrugging. *Are you going to ask me why I cried?*

"Nope." He shook his head. "You can tell me if you want but you don't have to."

I stared at him. *Who the hell are you and where did you come from?*

Cyrus chuckled, his body shaking beneath me. "I'm just a man who knows a thing or two about a woman's emotional release after an orgasm. Especially if they've been through a trauma like you have. But again, I'm not asking because it's not my place. If you have questions, I'll answer them to the best of my ability. But not until then."

He was a whole other level of man. Not that I was experienced in that department but just from the movies I had seen and people I had met in life, Cyrus was something else.

Do you know why I cried?

"I have an idea. In BDSM, it's called sub drop. You could have gone through several different emotions before your orgasms. Also, you gave a part of yourself to me that people tried taking from you. You trusted me enough to know that I would never hurt you. Ever. Sure, I'm down for spanking and biting but that's it."

I laughed lightly, a fresh tear rolling down my cheek.

Cyrus gently pushed me off his lap and kissed the top of my head. "I have an idea. Where's your linen closet?"

In the bathroom, I signed but unsure as to why he would need to know where the closet was.

"Stay here." He kissed my cheek. "But I do suggest getting dressed. Unless you want to spend the rest of the night naked."

I looked down at myself, my cheeks burning when I realized I was only in a shirt nd nothing else.

He chuckled.

I playfully punched his arm, laughing.

While he went to the closet for whatever reason, I got dressed and grabbed us some snacks and a couple of beers from the fridge. When I went back out into the living room, I found Cyrus laying blankets down on the floor by the couch after the coffee table was moved out of the way.

He caught my gaze, a wide grin spreading on his face. "We're camping out." He nodded to the items in my hand. "It's like you read my mind."

I placed the items on the end table and helped him.

"We'll play your video games too, watch movies and..."

More? I asked, hinting for everything else he had to give me.

"Maybe." He winked. "If you're a good girl."

I giggled, shaking my head.

When the blankets were laid and pillows were sitting against the bottom of the couch, I grabbed the beer and snacks.

Cyrus sat down, helping me spread out the items on the blankets in front of us.

He leaned over, placing a soft peck on my temple. "Thank you, pet."

A thought came to me, forcing me to turn toward him.

"What's wrong?" he asked, raising an eyebrow.

You didn't hint for more. After you gave me two orgasms, you didn't hint for sex.

"No, why would I? One, you started crying and two, that wasn't my intention. Sure, I look forward to it later but in that moment, all I wanted was to earn more of your trust and it worked."

I stared at him.

He took a swig of his beer, glancing my way. "What?"

I opened my mouth, but no words came out.

"If you start talking now, we won't be spending the rest of the night playing video games."

My cheeks burned.

He reached out, brushing the back of his knuckles down my cheek. "I like this blush." He grabbed my hand, tugging me into his side and wrapping his arm around my shoulders. "When you talk to me and you will talk to me, Ainsley, I'm going to have so much fun getting you to say all the nasty things I can think of."

I laughed, snuggling into him.

He kissed the top of my head. "Now, what kind of snacks do we have?"

TWENTY

Ainsley

I WOKE SOME TIME later that morning and rolled onto my back.

Cyrus was lying beside me, his breaths were deep and even. His heavy arm was wrapped around my middle, holding me tightly against him.

I sighed, thinking back to earlier that morning. Cyrus's mouth on me. His tongue deep inside of me. His words promising pleasure, only for his body to comply.

We played a few rounds of *Grand Theft Auto*, drank some beers, and pigged out on Cheetos and popcorn. We did that until around five in the morning, when I had started yawning.

I pulled out from under his arm which earned me a grunt of protest, but he never opened his eyes. God, he was beautiful. The fact that he made us camp out in my living room on a Friday night, when he could have gone to a bar or hung out with his brother and friends, stirred something in me. Add to the fact that he was falling for me. My heart stuttered.

I leaned down, placing a soft peck on his cheek. "Thank you," I whispered. I had been thanking him a lot and I would probably continue doing so for the rest of my life.

Using the bathroom, I went about my business when I heard a phone ring off in the distance. I knew it wasn't mine since I kept it on silent.

When I was done using the facilities, I stepped out into the hall when I heard Cyrus's gruff voice.

"I'm not home, Sammy." Cyrus grunted. "Listen, I don't know what you're fucking deal—I didn't hear my phone when you called earlier. No, you know that's not true. Sam...yes, I know. I love you too."

My stomach sunk. I didn't know what Sammy's problem was with me. It wasn't like I had ever actually talked to the guy. Maybe he didn't like that I was getting close with Cyrus because he was scared that I would come between them. I didn't know. I didn't have any siblings of my own, so I wasn't sure if that was a reasonable response.

Bracing myself, I joined Cyrus back in the living room. He was sitting on the couch with his head bowed, his hand running through his hair.

I cleared my throat, tentatively taking a step toward him.

His head snapped up, the hard lines of his face softening when he noticed me approaching him. "Morning, pet."

I knelt in front of him and wrapped myself around him, just hugging him.

I must have caught him off guard because his body stiffened, but after a moment he relaxed and pulled me into his arms.

"Thank you," he murmured against the side of my throat.

Giving him a squeeze, I leaned back and straddled his lap. *Everything okay?*

He gave me one of his signature sexy smirks, but I noticed how the smile never reached his eyes. *Everything is always okay when you're around.*

God, this man. I realized then that I could fall in love with him. Actually, I could fall deeper than that.

I heard you talking to your brother.

Cyrus's face fell. "Yeah, he's being an ass. He doesn't like when he can't get a hold of me after having a nightmare."

It's my fault. You've been focused on helping me through my own. I'm sorry.

"Don't be." Cyrus pulled me closer. "But I don't want to talk about that anymore. I'll deal with him." He nipped my chin, a part of him growing beneath my ass.

I shivered but as much as I wanted this to continue, I needed to know something. Pushing against him, I lifted my hands to run my fingers along his face. Whatever happened between us, I thanked God for giving me him. Even if this didn't last.

"Spend the rest of the weekend with me," Cyrus said, kissing my fingers as they passed along his mouth. "I don't want to see my brother because if I do, I'll kick his ass."

A sour taste filled my mouth, the moment lost. Pushing out of his hold, I rose to my full height.

"Pet."

Spinning on him, I huffed. *I refuse to come between you two.*

You won't come between us. Whatever happens is because of him and his moods.

I stared at him. When Cyrus usually used ASL, it was shortened to a few words and not several sentences. *You've been practicing.*

He smiled, nodding. Pushing to his full height, he took a step toward me but still remained at a distance. "I've never felt this way about anyone. Sammy knows that. We've been through a lot together. Grew up together too even though we had others helping us. It didn't matter. There were times where we still felt like it was just us against the world. The first time I felt like I belonged was when Jaron asked us to look after Piper and their daughter while he was in jail. I know my brother feels the same way. They are our family, my family, but you..." He took a step toward me. "The things you have given me. The things you have opened up," he tapped his chest, "in me. I can never thank you enough for that." He took another step closer. "Losing our parents have messed both of us up. And then the shit that happened with Piper and Jaron...their daughter was almost taken from them for good and it..." He sighed, shaking his head. "It doesn't matter. They're fine now. And I'm rambling."

I laughed lightly.

"I don't expect you to give me all of you. Not completely but I want you to know..." Cyrus paused, tilting his head, his dark eyes locking with mine. "I'm falling in love with you."

My eyes widened at his confession.

"Maybe it's too soon. I don't know. It's not like there are rules for this sort of thing. And I don't expect you to return those feelings, but I will spend this time we have together, however long that may be, earning your trust and making you realize that you can love me back without getting hurt in the process."

I opened my mouth, begging the words to come out.

Cyrus closed the last few steps between us, cupping the back of my head and kissing my cheek. "You don't have to say anything, pet."

Grabbing his shirt in my fist, I pulled him closer. "I love you, too," I whispered.

His eyes widened. "What did you just say?"

A breath left me on a whoosh. "I love you." And I did. God, did I ever love him. It all made sense now. This need for him. This sadness when he wasn't near. This flutter in my stomach every time he was. He pushed me and challenged me, and I loved him even more for that.

The sound that left his mouth, a low deep raspy growl, set my body on fire.

"Say that again," he demanded, cupping my ass and lifting me in his arms.

"I love you," I repeated.

He carried me to the couch. "Again. Louder."

"I love you." I had said more words because of him in the time we had been together, than I had in years.

"Fuck, pet." He covered my mouth with his, licking and sucking at my tongue.

Heat seared through me at the intensity rolling off of him. It was like as soon as I said those words, something inside of him snapped. Add to the fact that I actually spoke and not signed, he became unhinged.

In a quick move, he had my pajama bottoms off and his mouth between my legs.

A harsh cry left me.

Saying those three little words switched something inside of him. He was usually gentle in the way he handled me. Knowing what I had been through with my previous aversion to sex. But now that I was finally able to get a few words out, he became another person. Another person I craved. Wanted. Needed.

Cyrus was brutal in the way he attacked my center with his mouth. Although the damaged nerve endings prohibited me from feeling everything, I could still feel enough.

His hair tickling my inner thighs.

The scruff of his beard scratching at my hot flesh.

His tongue thrusting in and out of me.

Because of him, I had gotten used to the idea of sex. I thought him going down on me would give me anxiety, but instead it helped me feel connected to him on a whole other level. It was far more intimate than intercourse. Knowing he was in full control the whole time; I wasn't on the verge of a breakdown.

Cyrus licked at my very soul. The happy wet noises coming from him, sparking this incessant urge to beg. For more. For him to stop. It wasn't enough. It was too much.

With his calloused fingers pushing against my inner thighs, he looked up the length of my body until our eyes connected. Something flashed in the dark orbs. My skin flushed. My hips thrusted up and down of their own accord.

I needed more.

"P-Please," I heard myself say.

He growled, shaking his head against me.

As much as I wanted him inside me, I didn't beg and instead, gave him my complete and utter submission.

(Cyrus)

She loved me. I wasn't expecting to fall for her so quickly but as much as I was opposed to love at first sight, even I knew that love could happen when you least expected it.

After I had given Ainsley two orgasms back to back, I was finally seated inside of her. I took things slow, making love to her like she deserved. But that sweet little sex kitten in her tried convincing me to go faster and harder. I didn't. As much as she protested.

"Are you good?" I asked her an hour later. We were still on the couch but now completely dressed. I had helped her put the linen away and put the living room back to the way it was before our campout.

She nodded. "I..." She cleared her throat. "Am."

Feelings I had never felt before rushed through me. My chest was tight, and a damn lump was in my throat. I didn't know why. Maybe I never would. But what I did know was that I would spend the rest of my life, thanking her for finally giving me her voice.

"Why are you looking at me like that?" she asked, staring up at me with her beautiful eyes.

"I'm still not using to hearing you." Her voice was soft and husky, maybe from years of not using it. I couldn't be sure. But it was the sexiest sound I had ever heard.

"I'm sorry." She turned toward me, linking her fingers in mine.

"Don't be sorry." I placed a soft peck on her forehead. "Just not used to it, pet."

"Thank you."

I lifted my head, frowning. "For what?"

"For being patient with me. For...for just...for loving me." Her eyes shone.

"I do love you. I love you so fucking much. I didn't know it could feel this way and even though I was looking for it, I still wasn't expecting to find it. But you, Ainsley, are something else."

She snuggled into my side, resting her head against my shoulder.

"So, I take it you do want to spend the rest of the weekend together?"

She laughed, lifting her head. "Yes."

"Good." I kissed her nose. "Can I ask you something?"

She nodded.

"Did you ever see that guy again? The one who followed you to the deli or are you thinking he was just some random stranger?" I knew through experience that things weren't just random usually. Especially not with the trauma she endured. I was sure the people who survived the raid wanted to make sure there was no one left who could rat them out.

Ainsley shook her head. "No." She cleared her throat. *But I've spent a lot of time with you. I don't get out much if you haven't noticed.*

"What about the bastards who got away? Have you had any issues?"

"No." She chewed her bottom lip. "Why?"

"Because I want to know if I have to go after—"

"No." She jumped to her feet.

"Baby." I went to her, but she lifted her hands, warding me off. That single act didn't sit well with me. It was like the wall that I had already broken down, grew between us. Well fuck that. I went to her anyway, bracing myself for her wrath. Tugging her against me, I wrapped her up in my arms.

"Cyrus." She struggled against me.

"Shut the fuck up." I fisted her hair, tugged her head back, and forced her to look up at me. "Don't you dare close up on me."

I don't want you going after them, she signed, her fingers flying over the words. Her hands pushed against my chest. "Please. You can't. I've spent a long time trying to forget that shit and to forget *them*. I can't...you can't..." Her chin wobbled.

Shit. I crushed my mouth to hers, drinking up her soft cries. Her tears coated my tongue, making my taste buds tingle.

"Cyrus," she whispered.

A shiver rippled down the length of my dick. Fucking hell, I loved when she said my name.

Ainsley latched on to my shirt. It was like she was trying to get closer.

"What do you want, pet?" I asked, sucking her bottom lip between my teeth.

A notable shiver trembled through her. "I want you to stay here. With me. Not go after them."

"I wasn't going to leave now, Ainsley." I tugged her head back even more, staring into her eyes. "I just wanted to know. I was asking because..."

"You want to go after them," she answered for me. "Even if it's not now. Tomorrow. Next week. You *are* going to go after them."

Fuck me. For someone who spent years not talking, she sure as hell had a lot to say about the matter.

"I'm right, Cyrus. I know I'm right." She took a step back, pulling me with her. "Tell me I'm right."

"You're right," I said, cupping her ass and lifting her into my arms. "You want to know why though? Because I fell in love with a woman who had some serious shit happen to her and I won't rest until those bastards are taken care of. If I can't find them all, I will take you out of here and shack up somewhere no one knows about. I will do this to protect you." I carried her into the kitchen, sitting her ass on the counter.

"You can't take me out of here, Cyrus. Out of my life. My job."

"Nope. I can't." I was being unreasonable. I knew that. But it still didn't mean I wouldn't try. "But I will do everything I can to protect you. Okay?"

She nodded. "Okay."

"Good girl. Now sit your sexy ass there while I cook you breakfast."

"Really?"

I stepped between her knees and cupped her jaw, pulling her forward until our mouths met in the middle. "Really."

(Ainsley)

I remained seated on the counter while Cyrus cooked for us. He ended up deciding on omelets. He cut up some veggies to throw in with the eggs. While doing so, he kept looking my way. He wouldn't accept my help when I offered to assist him, so I just sat there and watched him instead.

I meant what I had told him. I didn't want him going after the people who took me and the other girls and even guys. It was done and over with. I hadn't seen anyone out of the ordinary since the time I ended up at the deli. My lips tingled, remembering how that had been the first time Cyrus kissed me. I should have known even from that point that I could fall in love with him. He said what was on his mind, looked at me like I was the only one who existed in his world, and even fought his brother over me.

My stomach twisted, hoping that Sammy and I could at least be civil one day. I didn't know what I had done but I knew that I wanted to make things right with him.

For Cyrus.

Now that I was actually talking to Cyrus, it made communicating with him so much easier. But I found that there were still times where I wanted to close up and use my hands. It almost felt safer that way. Like when I used ASL, a protective barrier wrapped itself around my body, shielding me from the many demons I had lurking in the darkest corners of my mind.

"Are you sure you don't want my help?" I asked him, kicking my feet back and forth.

"I'm sure." He gave me a small smile and went back to cooking.

"I've never done this before," I told him.

"Trust me, pet. Neither have I."

"What, you mean that you don't have a secret wife and kids I don't know about that you've practiced this with?"

He shot me a look. "Ha. You're funny."

"It happens." I meant it to be funny, but it did actually happen. Especially in the hell I spent years in.

Cyrus paused in cooking. "You're not kidding."

I shook my head. "There were men who had wives and families at home that would come to the brothel I was in. It was like they lived some secret life that no one knew about. They were the worst of them all." My mouth snapped shut. Weeks ago, I told Cyrus what had happened to me, and we hadn't talked about it since. I shouldn't have said anything about it. Especially not when he already threatened to go after the bastards who took me. "I'm sorry."

"Stop," he said, his voice raising.

I cowered into myself, needing to get away. To a safe place. To a spot that I could be by myself in.

"Shit, baby." Cyrus rushed to me and pulled me against him. "I'm sorry. I'm so fucking sorry. I didn't mean to snap at you." He rained kisses on my face. "I promise. That wasn't geared at you. It just pisses me off that there are people out there like this. I had a moment and took it out on you. I'm sorry."

I wrapped myself around him.

"You shouldn't be sorry though. Never be sorry for telling me what you went through. Never be sorry for voicing your thoughts and feelings." He cupped my face, covering my mouth with his. "You hear me?" he asked gently.

I nodded, pouting.

His lips twitched. Giving me another kiss, his mouth lingered. "The things I want to do to this lip." He gave it a gentle bite.

A breathless laugh left me. "Thank you."

"Always, pet. Always. I'll try to rein in control of my anger. I just hate..."

I stared up at him. "What?"

"I wish I could have been there to protect you. I know it doesn't make sense when we didn't know each other then but it's how I feel."

"I considered looking for the ones who escaped. But it's not like it was a single brothel. There were a bunch of them. And that was only the beginning. There was an actual compound that held far worse things than I ever experienced and I...I went..." I lifted my hands, my mouth going dry as the memories slid into me. *I went through a lot,* I finished.

"I could say I know you did, but I don't really know. You've told me things, but I don't think anyone could actually know what you went through unless they were right there alongside you." Cyrus kissed me one last time before going back to the stove. "But no matter what, I'm here. Even if you don't want to talk about it or anything at all, I'll sit there with you."

"Isn't that boring?" I asked softly.

"No, not at all. If it helps you get through each day, I'll sit in the fucking dark with you, pet. I promise."

"God." My breath hitched. "I think I fell in love with you even more just now."

A cocky grin spread on his face. "I am pretty awesome." His smile fell. "Now I sound like Sammy." He scowled.

My heart dropped, wishing there was something I could do for him.

I made a mental note to try and talk to Sammy. Even if I had to type up a damn letter and send it to him, he was going to listen to me, some way, some how.

"Have you tried talking to your brother?" I asked Cyrus while he was preparing our plates of food.

"Talking to Sammy is like talking to a wall. And if he's cornered, he's like a cat. He'll spit, and hiss, and raise fucking hell before you have a chance to ask him how he feels."

"I didn't realize it was that bad."

"It's not as bad as I'm making it out to be." Cyrus helped me set the rest of the table, but I couldn't help but wonder if he was trying to downplay what was really going on between him and Sammy. I didn't want to assume it had something to do with me, but I was definitely a part of it. Whether it be small or big, I knew there was a reason that Sammy didn't like me.

I didn't respond because I wasn't even sure what to say. I didn't want to start anything, but it bothered me that Sammy automatically didn't like me while Cyrus had been nothing but kind.

"What did you want to drink?" I asked, figuring that would be a safe question and then I wouldn't say something I would regret. I looked out at the spread we had laid out on the table and smiled to myself. When I went to head into the kitchen, I found Cyrus staring at me. "What?"

Instead of responding, he came toward me.

Before I could ask what was going on, he had me in his arms and his mouth on mine in a firm kiss.

I sighed, snaking my arms around his neck.

He broke the kiss, leaning his forehead against mine. "I know you're worried about my issues with my brother."

"How did you know?" I asked, reaching up to run my fingers along his cheek.

"Because I can tell. Whenever I talk about how much of a dick he's being, you get this look on your face."

"What kind of look?" I asked, staring up at the man who had suddenly captured every piece of my soul without even trying.

"You look sad, but I can also see a longing," Cyrus murmured.

"I would give anything to have a sibling of my own. It's like you have an automatic best friend."

He grunted. "Sammy and I are twins and sure, we're close, and he is my best friend, but we still fight. And it's not pretty fighting either. It's downright filthy and nasty with the shit he likes to pull. He's a dirty fighter, baby. But I promise, we're fine. And if we're not fine now, we will be because that's how it is with us." He crouched until he was eye level with me. "Okay?"

I nodded. "Okay."

"Good." He kissed my forehead. "Now let's eat before it gets cold."

(Cyrus)

"I seriously can't believe how good you are at this game," I said in awe at Ainsley's racing skills.

She giggled, gently nudging me in the shoulder. "I have a lot of time on my hands."

"I'd like to have my hands on you," I growled in her ear.

Her laugh deepened. "Stop, you're going to make me crash."

I chuckled, placing the controller down on the floor beside us. She was sitting between my legs with her back to my front.

"You don't want to play anymore?" she asked, a frown settling between her brows when one of the other racers crashed into her.

"Nah." I brushed her hair off the back of her neck. "I'm enjoying watching you." And I wasn't lying either. She chewed her bottom lip, her gaze hard and determined as she kicked the opponent's asses she was playing against.

After breakfast, we cleaned and washed the dishes, took a shower together and spent the day doing nothing. It was now late that night and we were enjoying each other's company.

A few minutes later and she cheered. "I said I would kick their ass."

"You did, baby." I pulled her back against my chest, running my hands through her hair.

"I can't play like this," she said, a soft sigh leaving her.

"I know." I fisted her hair and turned her head to meet the hard impact of my mouth. "Just need my hands on you, pet."

Slipping my tongue between her lips, I controlled the kiss, but she was in control of everything else. As much as I craved her submission, I had to earn it. Didn't matter that I was already in love with her and had her trusting me enough where she could now talk to me. Everything else would come over time.

"Cyrus," she whispered, shivering against me.

I cupped her jaw and deepened the kiss. I kept my other hand locked around her throat. A power play slid between us. While I dominated her, she still had the upper hand and always would.

A moan escaped her as my fingers traveled over her jugular.

Breaking the kiss, I lifted my head and stared down at her.

Her eyes were glassy, and her lips were swollen from my rough kiss.

"I love you, Ainsley. I know we're still learning things about each other and we'll continue to learn, but I promise to never let us go to bed angry. I promise to take care of you and protect you but also push you just the same. I promise to be yours and only yours."

She nodded, her breath catching. She sat up, turned toward me, and lifted her hands. *I love you too, Cyrus.*

I turned off the TV and pulled her back into my arms. Standing with her wrapped around me, I headed to the wall where the light switch sat and flicked it off. I made my way down the hall with her in my arms where she was safe. I sat her on her bed and helped her undress, no words passed between us.

"Make love to me," she murmured, a yawn trembling through her.

I smirked, placing a soft peck on her nose. "You need rest."

She pouted but never argued and slid beneath the covers.

I joined her and pulled her into my arms. She fell asleep rather quickly, her breathing becoming even. I never realized how much I could love another person until meeting Ainsley. I loved the club, my family, my job, but with her, it was a different kind of love. It went deeper than that.

My phone buzzed, bouncing on the nightstand. I took a breath and braced myself, knowing it was probably Sammy.

Sammy: You coming home tonight?

Me: No.

Sammy: Do you love her?

My heart stuttered. He had never questioned my feelings for a woman before. Never asked what my intentions were or how I felt about them. So why now?

Me: Why?

When no response came, I kissed Ainsley's cheek and left her warmth. Quickly slipping into my jeans, I left her bedroom and quietly shut the door behind me.

Heading back to the living room, I called my brother.

"Yeah," he grunted.

"What's going on?"

"Nothing."

"Sam, you've been off ever since I met Ainsley. What's your—"

"We are not doing this over the fucking phone, Cyrus."

My back stiffened. "You are the one who texted me shit, so yeah, we are doing this over the fucking phone."

The click sounded in my ear faster than I expected.

"Asshole," I mumbled, looking back down the hall to where Ainsley was currently sleeping. I toyed with the idea of leaving and going to confront my brother, but I knew that when he got like this, our fists would fly first before I got any words out of him.

Instead, I would spend the rest of the weekend with Ainsley, like I promised her, and then I would call my brother out on his shit later. Whether he liked it or not, this would end. Either he supported us or I had no idea what I would do.

TWENTY-ONE

Ainsley

EVER SINCE CYRUS AND I spent the weekend together, I couldn't help but think of him. Our feelings for each other were revealed and I was shocked but proud of myself at how he got me to open up so damn quickly.

It was a few weeks later and I hadn't seen him a whole lot since, but we texted every day and every chance we could. I found out that he was helping his aunt at her auto shop while she had been on vacation, but now that she was home the shop had been busy. I didn't know he was handy with cars. He was a man of many talents it seemed.

One afternoon, I had a huge grin on my face after reading a text from Cyrus stating how much he missed me and that he was going to pick me up after work. I sighed and told him I couldn't wait to see him.

The weekend we spent together had been nothing short of amazing. He never pushed for sex. I initiated it before he left Sunday night and while he had been gentle, I had a feeling that there was something in him that was downright filthy. I would find it. The part of him he was holding back. He told me there was a sex kitten in me. Well I knew there was something deeper in him than just him being dominant in bed. I wanted to find that part of him and curl up in his passionate embrace.

"Ainsley."

I jumped, finding Piper standing a few feet away.

She laughed. "Sorry, I didn't mean to scare you."

I only smiled.

"I know you've been spending a lot of time with Cyrus."

My heart skipped a beat. I expected her to jump to accusations or demand to know what it was that Cyrus and I had, but when she didn't, I only nodded.

"I haven't seen him in a couple days because he's been working a lot, but I talked to him this morning on the phone and..." Her smile widened. "God, Ainsley, he sounds so happy." She came toward me. "I don't know what you did but thank you. I love him and Sammy like brothers. They did so much for me and Brynlee while Jaron wasn't home. I always felt guilty and as though I was preventing them from finding a love of their own." She sighed, rubbing her swollen stomach. "I don't expect you to tell me anything about what you and Cyrus are doing but I just wanted to thank you. That's all."

"You're welcome," I blurted, my eyes widening.

Her mouth dropped. "You...you just spoke to me."

It's no big deal, I signed slowly for her.

Before I could stop her, she pulled me into a hug. "I know you hate hugs, but I need to hug you and yes, Ainsley, it is a big deal. A very big deal."

A lump formed in my throat. I wrapped my arms around her, returning the embrace.

A shuddered breath left her. As she released me, I saw a car pull into the parking lot out of the corner of my eye.

When the car stopped, Jaron got out of the driver's side and Sammy got out of the passenger's side.

I hadn't seen Sammy in a while, but I knew the situation between him and his brother was getting under Cyrus's skin. Even though he tried hiding it, I could sense that he was bothered by something. I just never knew what. I asked but he told me not to worry about it.

Jaron came into the building followed by Sammy. "Hi, beautiful, it's almost time."

She laughed. "It is time, but he doesn't want to come out."

"He's safe." Jaron wrapped Piper up in a hug and kissed her. The kiss bordered on inappropriate but before it could get very far, Piper pushed him back.

"God, Jaron." She laughed, her cheeks flushed.

He chuckled, cupping her stomach. "How's my boy?"

"Good." She covered his hands and stared up at him with so much love, it took my breath away. "I think he wants to stay in there forever."

"He'll come when he's ready but he's safe and you're safe, so that's all that matters." He kissed her forehead. "Both of you are safe."

The hairs on the back of my neck tingled.

A throat cleared.

I ignored it and sat at the desk, pulling up my schedule for the next week. When the throat cleared again, my eyes shot to Sammy.

He smirked. "Nothing to say?"

My jaw clenched. I wondered how much Cyrus would get mad at me if I punched that smirk off his brother's face.

I could feel Piper and Jaron looking our way, but I didn't care. I wasn't going to play into Sammy's games because I didn't want it to ruin what I had with his brother.

Sammy came around the desk and crouched beside me. "Look at me."

I huffed but met his gaze.

"I don't know what you have going on with my brother but if you hurt him in any way, whether it be big or small, I will find every single member of your family and kill them."

I rolled my eyes. "You know that I will tell Cyrus about your silly little threats, right?"

Sammy's eyes widened a bit over the fact that I actually spoke to him.

"They're already dead, so I have no one left for you to kill but thank you for the not-so-subtle reminder. And why don't you go crawl back to your hole or man up and grow a pair. When you finally get your head out of your ass and tell the woman you love that you're actually in love with her, then we can talk." I turned back around in the desk, attempting to ignore him.

"You have no idea what the fuck you're talking about."

"I don't?" I laughed. "Trust me, Sammy, I know enough."

"Do you give my brother this much sass?"

I glared at him. "No, because your brother actually loves me, and I love him." I wasn't opposed to being a brat for Cyrus but that was a whole other story I would discuss with only him.

"Love." Sammy scoffed, rising to his full height. "Right." He left the building, the door slamming shut behind him.

"Ainsley."

I looked at both Piper and Jaron who were still standing there and who clearly had watched the whole exchange.

"I'm sorry but I've had enough," I told them, jumping up from the chair and following Sammy out of the building.

He was walking across the parking lot, a cloud of smoke following his trail.

"Sammy," I yelled, catching up with him.

He stopped, looking at me over his shoulder. "Why are you talking to me, Mouse? This whole time, you haven't said fucking boo."

"Mouse?"

"It's your nickname." He said it like it was the most obvious reason.

I shook my head, finding that while I liked the nickname, I would dwell on that later. "Why do you hate me? I've never once given you any reason to not like me or at least put up with me. But this...this is..."

"I don't like that you're taking him away from me." Sammy stuck the smoke back between his lips, puffing hard.

"I'm not—"

A black SUV suddenly pulled into the parking lot. It drove into an empty spot, the engine cutting shortly after. Cyrus stepped out of the vehicle and came toward us.

"What's going on?" he asked, coming up to me. He kissed the top of my head. "I missed you," he whispered.

"I missed you too," I mumbled.

"Mouse and I were just having a conversation," Sammy told him.

Cyrus looked between us. "You were?"

I ground my teeth together.

Sammy chuckled.

That sound, that single sound grated on my very last nerve. Pushing away from Cyrus, I stomped toward Sammy and shoved him. He was much bigger than I was so the impact didn't make him move much, but it definitely got his attention.

"I don't know what your problem is, but you don't scare me. Trust me, Sammy, I've dealt with far worse people than you could ever imagine. You're a pussy cat compared to them. I love your brother and if you can't accept it, that's your problem. Not mine. And not your brother's." I turned back around and went back up to Cyrus.

He hooked his arm around my shoulders, staring at his brother. "What's your deal?"

"This is it?" Sammy asked. "You choose pussy over your own sibling?"

Faster than I ever thought possible, Cyrus stepped around me and charged for his brother.

(Cyrus)

I had never been as furious at my brother as I was in that single moment. When I charged for him, he stood taller and waited for the impact. It was like he was intentionally pissing me off just to get into a fight. *Well, fucker, you got your damn wish.*

My fist connected with his jaw before I could stop myself.

Gasps sounded from somewhere, demands and pleas for us to stop.

"Leave them." That was Jaron.

We shouldn't be fighting here. I knew that. But I couldn't stop myself. I'd had enough. If he would just tell me what the hell his problem was, we could deal with it and move on.

"Come on, Cyrus," he sneered. "You can hit harder than that."

I got in his face, grabbing the collar of his leather cut. "Tell me what your issue is with my girlfriend."

His jaw clenched but his gaze never wavered from mine.

Releasing him roughly, I headed back to where Ainsley was now standing with Piper and Jaron. "I'm moving out," I told my brother.

"What? Why the hell are you doing that?" Sammy bit out. "Is it because of her?"

I cupped Ainsley's face, taking a deep breath. "Will you still love me if I kill my brother?"

She covered my hand. "He feels like I'm taking you from him," she murmured softly.

I was taken aback by her words. Looking at Sammy over my shoulder, I wondered if that was the case, but I could use that. "Meet me at your place. I need some time with him."

"Of course. Take all the time you need." She reached into her bag and pulled out a key before slipping it into my jeans pocket. "Now you can come and go as you please."

"I'll never go, pet." I kissed her forehead. "Will you make sure she gets home and into her apartment safely?" I asked Jaron.

He nodded. "Of course."

Before they could ask what was going on between Sammy and me, I kissed Ainsley one last time and went up to my brother.

"We're taking a walk," I told him, heading past him and not waiting for him to catch up. I knew he would because I was sure he was as sick of this as I was. Being so damn negative all the time was too much work. It needed to stop. Both of us deserved happiness. We fucking earned it.

Just like I thought, Sammy fell in line with me. His hands were shoved in his pockets but I knew he was itching for a smoke.

"Smoke, Sam. It'll calm you down."

He lit one up before I could even finish the sentence. "I like her for you," he said, inhaling the spicy sustenance.

I grunted. "You don't have to say that just to humor me."

"I'm not. She's got some sass in her. I know it's what you need."

"She's a good girl. *That's* what I need," I corrected him.

"You love her."

It wasn't a question, but I ended up nodding anyway. "And she loves me."

"I was shocked when she spoke to me."

"Me too but I know why she did." I shoved my hands in my pockets, fingering the key she had given me.

"Why's that?"

"She respects you." It was the only thing that made sense.

"Why? I haven't been overly nice to her."

I looked at him then. "Nope, you haven't but I also know that if something were to happen, you would do what you could to protect her because that's how you are. I don't know what's going on with you and Red. Maybe that's part of the reason for your mood swings but I know you love her. You don't have to admit it, but love is definitely there, among other things."

"Among other things," he repeated, stopping. "I'm sorry."

I stepped in front of him. "For what?"

He threw the smoke to the ground, butting it out with his Shit-Kicker. "Red has me unraveled. I'm not used to a woman making me react this way. They need a handbook on this shit."

I chuckled. "If that were the case, Jaron and Piper would have talked right away."

Sammy grunted. "Red and I may not be serious but at least she knows where she stands with me."

"Does she really?" I asked, not used to the fact that we were having a conversation about the one and only woman who had gotten under Sam's skin.

"I gave her my number and told her to text me whenever she wants to fuck. I've also punched a few fuckers out who hit on her." He shrugged. "Can't really get clearer than that." He lit up another smoke. "I'm sorry, brother. I'm sorry for being an ass.

I'm sorry for the way I've treated your girl. I can see that you love her. But I...I just..." He swallowed hard, looking away.

Going up to him, I pulled him into my arms. "I'm not going anywhere. This isn't changing shit."

"But it is." His voice wavered. "It's always been you and me. When Mom died, and then Dad..."

"You can't expect me to remain single for the rest of my life, Sammy."

"Fuck." He shoved away. "No, I don't expect that."

"Then what the hell is going on?"

"I can't lose you too," he yelled.

"You won't lose me. Ever." I went up to him and pulled him back into a hug. "My promise stands."

"It can't when you've fallen in love. You're going to get married, have kids of your own and shit. I—."

"Stop. I told you that no matter what happens, you and I will always be best friends and that we come first before any woman. Ainsley pushed me to talk to you, but I said that everything was fine. Obviously, it wasn't and that's on me. Not her." I leaned my forehead against his. "Okay?"

He nodded. "I guess I should apologize to her."

"You can but later. We're going to The Ring."

(Ainsley)

Jaron and Piper dropped me off at home. They were walking me to the front door of the building when the hairs on the back of my neck tingled. I faltered in my tracks, looking around me.

"Ainsley?" Piper frowned. "You okay?"

I opened my mouth, but no sound came out. My words were failing me as my eyes scanned the area. Nothing was out of the ordinary. I lived in a safer part of town, but that didn't mean anything. Not when I knew there was still a possibility that people from my past could find me.

"Did you want me to call Cyrus?" Jaron asked, pulling me from my thoughts.

I shook my head, walking past them and into the building. They walked me to my door like Cyrus asked of them and made sure I was safe inside.

Just when I thought they were going to leave, Jaron came into the apartment.

I raised an eyebrow.

"Not leaving you alone unless I know for sure you're safe." He headed down the hall toward the bathroom and my bedroom.

I looked at Piper.

She only shrugged.

Jaron came back a moment later. "You're good."

"What were you looking for?" Piper asked, taking the question right out of my head.

"I was making sure there was no one here who shouldn't be," Jaron said like he was talking about the weather and not the fact that there could have been someone in my apartment.

Piper gasped. "Oh my."

Jaron grabbed her hand. "Cyrus would kill me if we left, and something happened to her." He looked at me then. "He loves you. I haven't seen much of him lately but that's because he's been spending time with you and working when he isn't. I'm right, aren't I?"

I nodded.

"He's happy," Piper told Jaron. She came up to me and pulled me into a hug.

My body stiffened but that familiar anxiety was soon replaced with a sense of peace. I returned Piper's embrace, hugging her back. Hard.

"Thank you," she whispered.

"We'll leave you alone now but if you need anything, don't hesitate to call either of us," Jaron instructed. "You're Cyrus's girl, so now you're automatically family."

My eyes welled, a lump forming in my throat.

Piper released me, a wide smile on her face. "It's true."

I've never had a family before.

Jaron frowned.

Piper sniffed. "She said she's never had a family before."

"Now you do," Jaron said gently. "Let's go, baby," he said to Piper.

She nodded, giving me one final hug before they slipped out of the apartment.

As soon as they left and I was alone, I let out a harsh sigh. Locking up, I entered the security code into the panel. Leaning against the wall, I slid down until I landed on the floor with a soft thud.

A family. I have a family.

If what Cyrus and I had turned into something even more serious, I knew that Sammy would be my brother in-law, but I never even clued in that it would include more people. I mentally smacked myself. Of course it would come with more people. Sammy wasn't Cyrus's only family. He had the club and the people he grew up with. That fact alone, forced a smile to spread on my face. My body felt lighter, and this sense of calm washed over me.

"You'll never amount to anything, you dirty little slut." The dark eyes peered down at me, the voice cold and deep.

As broken as he left me, I still lifted my chin defiantly. It was all I had for fear of losing myself completely.

The man chuckled, his fist landing against the side of my head while another man brutally violated my body.

A gasp left me as the memory hit me. I tried forgetting. I tried to forget *him*. But every now and again, the memories slipped through the cracks when I least expected it.

Ever since meeting Cyrus, the disturbing memories were few and far between. But when they came, they came out of nowhere and usually took my breath away.

As I rose to my feet, a hard bang sounded on the door. I jumped, almost falling back on my ass. My skin became clammy. It couldn't have been Cyrus. Not when I slipped a key into his pocket.

I checked my phone anyway but when I didn't see a text from him, that didn't leave me feeling any better.

The hard knock sounded again.

I wanted to ask who was there, but I had seen enough horror movies to know that you shouldn't do that.

Slowly making my way to the door, I took a deep breath and looked out the peep hole. My stomach dropped when I didn't see anyone standing on the other side of it.

Someone had been watching too many horror movies and was clearly trying to scare me.

I made sure the door was locked and double-checked that the security system was armed.

I sent Cyrus a quick text that I hoped he and his brother were able to work out their issues and spent the rest of the evening cleaning, trying to get my mind off whoever it was that knocked on my door. It didn't make sense. This sudden feeling like someone had been watching me. I felt it when Jaron and Piper dropped me off but hadn't sensed anything out of the ordinary since I ended up at the deli. I wondered if Cyrus and I would still have ended up together if I hadn't gone into the restaurant that day.

Once I was done cleaning everything, I saw that it was now pushing eleven at night with no response from Cyrus. I just hoped that everything was okay and that he and Sammy were able to talk it out.

I decided to get ready for bed and read for a bit. Once I was settled beneath the covers, I opened my book. My eyes became heavy, but I tried fighting through it when suddenly, a heavy body wrapped around me.

A scream broke free, my hand landing against a cheek.

"Shit, baby. It's me."

I struggled against the heavy body, the deep voice forcing bile to my throat.

"Ainsley, wake the fuck up."

My eyes snapped open at the rough command, landing on Cyrus's handsome face. I must have fallen asleep while reading.

He stared down at me, his brows furrowed.

My chest rose and fell, my heart thundering in my ears.

"You were dreaming," he said gently, pushing my hair off my forehead.

My eyes welled, the remnants of the nightmare settling on my skin. "I'm...I'm..."

"Shhh..." He pulled me into his arms, hugging me against his chest as a sob broke free. He lifted me off the bed, holding me tight.

I was vaguely aware of us leaving my bedroom, but I couldn't focus. I didn't know what time it was. I didn't even remember falling asleep.

When I was placed on something hard, I looked around me. We were in the kitchen, and I was sitting on the counter. Roughly wiping under my eyes, I took a deep breath and then another, calming the racing of my heart.

Cyrus moved around the kitchen like he belonged. In fact, he did. He always belonged. From the first time he spent the night at my place to now, he wedged his way into my life without even realizing that either of us needed it.

He pulled milk from the fridge, grabbed honey from the cupboard and mixed the two together in a glass. He added a shot of rum from the bottle I had purchased weeks ago for whenever he was over. He put it in the microwave and waited the minute it took to heat before coming back toward me. "I usually put more rum in this." He stepped between my knees, handing me the glass.

I took the drink from him and sipped at it. The sweet taste hitting my tongue, easing some of the anxiety rushing through me.

Cyrus wrapped his arms around me, kissing the side of my head.

"Thank you," I whispered, finishing the drink and placing the glass on the counter beside me.

"Are you okay?" he asked gently, cupping my nape and running his fingers through my hair.

"I was reading and must have fallen asleep. I didn't know it was you in bed with me. I thought..." I looked down at my hands on my lap. "I was having a nightmare, but I don't remember what it was about. You scared me and I'm sorry."

"Hey." He pushed his thumb beneath my chin and tilted my head back. "You have nothing to be sorry about. I was about to join you when I heard you whimpering. I assumed you were having a nightmare and was trying to gently wake you up. That's my fault. I should have turned on the light or spoken to you. I'm sorry I didn't."

"Don't be sorry. I guess my mind still isn't used to having someone in bed with me."

"We probably should have eased you into this." Cyrus ran both hands through my hair, pulling my head back gently. "I love you, pet, but if you need me to sleep on the couch, I will."

"No." I shook my head. "I've felt out of sorts since earlier this afternoon when Jaron and Piper dropped me off."

"What do you mean?"

"I felt like someone was watching me and then when they left, someone knocked on my door but when I looked through the peephole, there was no one on the other side of it," I explained. "It creeped me out and I think my mind was just playing tricks on me."

"Have you noticed anything else off? I mean, since that man followed you to the deli. I know you said when I asked you last time, that everything was fine but..." Cyrus's grip on my head tightened. "I don't like this fear rolling off of you."

I swallowed hard. "I know. I don't like it either. But no, nothing else has happened. Not since today or..." I glanced at the clock on the microwave, seeing that it was now into the morning. "Yesterday, I should say."

Cyrus released me and began pacing. "I know you gave me a key to your place but if you need out of here, we can rent a hotel or go to the clubhouse. It's safe there. Greyson is constantly updating the security. Did you want to go there?"

I thought a moment. "Are you really moving out of your apartment with your brother?"

Cyrus stopped pacing. "Yeah."

"Where are you going to move to?" I asked softly.

He smirked. "Anywhere with you hopefully."

My heart jumped. "Your brother is okay with this?"

"Sammy and I talked and then we went to The Ring, and he fought off some frustration."

"But you didn't?" I asked, noticing that he didn't have any new bruises or cuts.

"Nope. I'm not frustrated anymore. Now that Sammy and I talked, and I have you, I'm good." He came back toward me, pushing his way between my knees.

A sigh left me, that submissive part of me liking how he touched me and took care of me before I could even register that I needed it.

"Tell me what you want, pet. You want me to take you out of here, I will." He kissed my cheek. "You want to stay, we can do that too. You want to travel the damn world, I'll make it happen."

A breathless laugh left me. "I think..." I looked up at him. How could I tell him that I wanted him to make love to me? To make both of us drown out the world and the noise in our heads and just be as one. "I want..."

"What, baby?" His mouth brushed along the shell of my ear. "Tell me."

But I didn't know how. I wasn't overly vocal when it came to sex and what I liked and disliked. Instead of saying what I was thinking, I pushed Cyrus back and jumped off the counter. Grabbing his hand, I led him to my bedroom, hoping he would get the hint.

As soon as we stepped into the room, I pulled away from him, turned around, and lowered to my knees.

Cyrus closed the distance between us, cupping my face. "We don't have to do any of that tonight."

"I know," I whispered. "I just need something to take me out of my head." I placed my hands on my thighs, palms up.

His eyes followed the movement, his nostrils flaring and his eyes darkening.

"I want you to help me see that submission isn't a bad thing. That if done right and with a person you trust and love, it can be beautiful." I turned my head and kissed his palm. "You've been nothing but patient with me, but I know there's a deeper, darker side of you that wants to come out and play. It wants to control me. It wants to bruise my knees and leave marks on my ass. I know because I can feel it. I can sense him, Cyrus. Let him out."

A low growl left him. "I can't."

"You can and then I'll pack a bag and we can leave. I just need this first. Please." I licked my lips. "*Sir.*"

TWENTY-TWO

CYRUS

"SIR."

When that single word left Ainsley's mouth, it took every single thing I was made of not to throw her down to the ground and kiss the hell out of her. I didn't, because she needed that part of me that had laid dormant for so long. I wasn't sure how I would ever keep this side in check, but I would try. For her.

"Keep your hands on your thighs and your eyes on me. Always on me," I instructed. "Understand?"

She nodded. "Yes."

"Good girl. I don't want your eyes moving from mine. I know you trust me, but our minds are a funny thing. I don't need your brain conjuring up images of your past."

She nodded again.

"I have a present for you but first..." I unbuckled my belt. "Tell me what you want."

"To taste you," she said, not missing a beat.

My cock twitched, begging for her hot mouth.

Lowering the zipper of my jeans, I reached into them and pulled out my cock. "Keep your hands on your thighs but if it gets to be too much, tap my hip twice." I would eventually give her a safeword but that would come over time. We had to take it slow, especially if she wanted me to dominate her like she said she did.

"Okay." She took a deep breath and then another, her eyes dropping to my pierced cock.

I stepped between her spread knees, running the tip of my dick along her lips. A hot shiver trembled down my spine at the gentle touch.

She moaned, inhaling deep.

"Open," I demanded.

Her lips parted, allowing me access to her throat.

Thrusting into her mouth gently, I pumped my hips slowly. Her tongue ran along my piercings, her throat swallowing around me. That single movement sent a throbbing ache in my balls.

"Fuck," I groaned, slipping my fingers into her hair. "You okay?" I asked between clenched teeth.

She nodded, lowering her mouth down the length of me even more without my guidance.

A low moan slipped from deep in my throat, forcing my eyes into the back of my head. "Baby, fuck I love you."

Her head bobbed, her mouth sucking in hard rough pulls.

"Ainsley, yes, that's it. Feels so good, pet. You're doing such a good job." My balls drew up into my body, a hot tingle racing down my spine. "I'm going to come if you don't stop doing that."

She sucked harder, pulling the release right out of my body.

I muttered a curse, my cum spilling down the back of her tongue.

She moaned, swallowing every drop.

When my heart stopped racing, I pulled from her lips and stuffed myself away. "I wasn't expecting that."

Ainsley laughed lightly. "I told you I wanted to taste you."

"I know." I crouched, lifting her into my arms and placing her on the bed. "But I never expected to come in your pretty mouth."

She grinned, her cheeks rosy.

"Now for your surprise. I bought this a while ago but we'd both been so busy that I actually forgot I had it." I slid out of my leather cut and laid it over the arm of the chair sitting in the corner of her room. Pulling the small item I was looking for from the inside pocket, I turned back to her. "I know you can feel a little bit in your clit but I would like to make it so you can feel more."

She stared at me, tilting her head. "What do you mean?"

I went back to where she laid on the bed and dumped the item from the small bag onto the bed. "Have you ever seen one of these?"

"No. What is it?"

I kissed her cheek. "This one is called a Lelo but there's all different types. It vibrates and sucks on your clit."

"But you can do that."

I chuckled. "I can but I want to give you more. My mouth can only do so much."

"Okay." She spread her legs. "I trust you."

"I know you do." I placed a soft peck on her mouth, a lingering taste of my release on her lips. "And I'll never be able to thank you enough for that." Moving down the length of her body, I slipped her out of her pajama bottoms and panties and threw them to the floor. "Take off your top," I said, lowering my nose to her center and taking a deep inhale. The sweet scent from her body, slid into my nose. "Fuck me, you always smell so good."

A husky laugh left her as she slipped out of her shirt, leaving her naked.

"Keep your knees spread." I grabbed the small toy and a package of lube. I opened it and squeezed some of the jelly between her legs.

She gasped. "That's cold."

"Don't worry, pet. You'll get hot. Very quickly." Turning the toy on, it started vibrating lightly in my hand. "Your safeword is now Friday. That's the day we first went on a date. If you use this word, everything stops. But if you don't feel comfortable speaking, just tap me twice wherever you can reach. Do you understand?" I asked her, knowing she wouldn't have been given a safeword when she was previously taken.

She nodded quickly. "Friday or tap you twice anywhere I can reach. Got it."

"Good girl." I kissed her knee, lowering the toy to her clit. As soon as it closed around the swollen nub, she jumped, a deep moan leaving her mouth.

I pressed the button a couple more times, turning up the power.

A cry left her, her back bowing on the bed. Her thighs shook, her hips lifting up and down as the pleasure tore through her.

I watched her tremble. I wanted to make her break, shatter her into a million pieces where all she felt was ecstasy. I wanted the orgasms she had to be violent and push her over the edge.

"Cyrus," she whimpered, her hands clenching the blankets. Her eyes were squeezed shut, a sheen of sweat coating her forehead.

"Let your body go for me, pet." Inserting a finger into her pussy, I ran the toy across her clit. I could feel her core clenching around me. It was a beautiful sight, watching her struggle and trying to chase that delicious release I knew she craved.

"More," she whispered.

"There she is." I turned the toy up even more, the sounds of the vibration along with her cries, filling my ears. Her body spasmed, her hips lifting up into the air as a violent scream left her. Liquid sprayed out of her pussy, coating my hand. I took that as my cue and slid a second finger into her and began slamming my hand against her body.

She cried out, lifting her hips up and down, fucking my fingers that were currently inside of her. Her thighs shook, another scream leaving her as a second orgasm ripped through her.

Pulling my fingers from her, I kept the toy locked on her clit. Tugging off my jeans, I pumped my hand up and down my cock. "Move to the edge of the bed," I demanded, my voice gruff.

Ainsley did as she was told, her chest rising and falling, no doubt still feeling the remnants from her orgasms.

"Safeword."

"Friday," she said as I thrust into her. She cried out, locking her thighs around my hips.

I lifted one of her legs onto my shoulder, getting my cock even deeper into her body.

She gasped, her eyes widening.

"Safeword," I demanded again.

"Friday but I don't need it." Her eyes rolled into the back of her head. "God, baby, I really don't need it."

I chuckled, slamming my cock in and out of her. My thrusts were deliberate and rough, bordering on violent. But I needed her to see that rough sex with the right person was safe. As long as it was consensual between all adult parties, it could be perfect and beautiful.

Reaching between us, I pushed the toy even harder against her clit.

She whimpered, her chest rising and falling with ragged breaths. When a third orgasm slowly trembled through her, I tossed the toy to the side and covered her body with mine. I made sure that her fourth orgasm would be because of me and only me.

(Ainsley)

"Are you good, pet?" Cyrus whispered in my ear, running his hand down the side of my body.

"Yeah." I sighed, pushing my ass into him.

His cock was soft between us, but I couldn't help but tease us both a bit.

He grunted, slipping his fingers back between my legs. "The handful of orgasms I gave you, not enough, my greedy girl?"

I laughed, a shiver racing over me as he slowly brushed his fingers along my swollen center. "Apparently not."

He chuckled, running his fingers along my throbbing clit. "I thought you were going to break my dick. This sweet little cunt has some strength behind it."

"I couldn't help it," I murmured, curling onto my side. "You felt really good."

"Good." Cyrus kissed my shoulder. "It's late. Did you still want to come to the clubhouse with me?" he asked, slowly slipping his fingers into me.

"Yes," I moaned.

"Come again for me first." His hand picked up speed, pumping between my legs. "I'm going to train you to come at my command, pet. Over time, it'll happen, and I can't wait." He kissed the spot behind my ear. "Let yourself go for me whenever you're ready."

I whimpered, a fast release trembling through me.

"Good girl." He kissed my shoulder one last time, pulling his hand from my body. "We're going to take a shower first and then I'll take you to my home."

I yawned. "Okay."

He looked down at me with a raised eyebrow. "You sure you don't want to sleep here?"

I nodded. "Thank you for taking my mind off of everything."

Cyrus placed a hard peck on my mouth. "You don't need to thank me, baby. That's my job." He kissed me one last time before pulling away from me. As he did, I couldn't help but watch him in all his naked glory. His muscles rippled over his bones, his dick, although flaccid, jumped under my scrutiny. His piercings glittered in the dim lighting of the room.

A throat cleared, forcing my eyes to meet his.

"Checking me out, pet?"

I nodded, rising to my knees and shuffling toward him. "You're beautiful," I told him softly. "With all of your metal and scars." I cupped the side of his neck and crushed my mouth to his. "I love you," I whispered against his lips.

"Hmm..." He gave my bottom lip a gentle bite. "I love you too. Now let's shower, so I can bring you home and put you in my bed."

As much as I wanted to draw out the shower, we didn't and ended up making it quick instead.

"We can go to your apartment," I told him as I finished getting dressed. "We don't have to go to the clubhouse."

Cyrus stiffened, his gaze slowly meeting mine. "I don't think going to the apartment is a good idea."

"Oh. How come? Sammy and I can be civil now that you talked."

"It's not that." Cyrus rubbed the back of his neck, clearly uncomfortable about something. "It's where we...I brought...I just don't want you there because it's not good enough for you."

I thought a moment. "Is that where you brought the other women?"

"I never brought them to the clubhouse and neither did Sammy. We consider it our actual home and the apartment is just...fuck, I'm not making this sound any better." He closed the distance between us. "I hadn't been with someone for a while before I met you. In fact, it was months. I had issues getting hard. I don't know why. I'll probably never know. But when I met you, both my dick and I knew that you were it. That you were what we needed."

A lump formed in my throat, followed by a laugh. "God, you say the sweetest but dirtiest things."

"Just being honest with you." He shrugged. "Life's too serious. You of all people should know that. If I can make you laugh at least once a day, then that's all that matters to me. Love and laughter, pet. It's life's perfect medicine."

I threw my arms around his middle. "Thank you, Cyrus. For everything. For being my friend first, for falling in love with me, for showing me that I can be passionate and fierce, and it won't backfire on me. That I can be with someone who loves me for me. Who can bring out the submissive in me. Who can—"

A warm mouth crushed against mine. "No, thank *you*, pet."

A shuddered breath left me.

"Pack a bag and then I'll take you out of here. Are you wanting to actually move out?"

"I do. I wanted to before I met you but then I got distracted." I cupped his cheek, the dark scruff on his strong jaw tickling my palm. "You distracted me, and I appreciate it because I've been so stuck in my head, that the words could never come out. You helped me get them out."

Cyrus kissed my palm. "Have you thought of subletting this place instead? You could pack up your clothes and personal items but leave the furniture. I know you just gave me a key..."

"I like that idea but..." I wasn't sure what he wanted out of this but if he taught me anything, it was to say how I felt and to speak my mind. "Would you want to move in together?"

A cheeky grin spread on his face. "I thought you'd never ask."

I laughed.

"We can live at the clubhouse until we find a place of our own." He leaned back, crouching until we were at eye level. "It's safe, so I'd like to stay there until we can figure out if someone is in fact stalking you or not."

A sour taste filled my mouth. I pulled away from him and went to the closet. Grabbing a large bag, I started pulling items off the hangers and shoving them into the bag. A warm body came up behind me, forcing a sigh from my mouth. "I don't know why all of a sudden they're stalking me, whoever it is. I don't know if the bastards who ended up in jail after the raid, are now free instead of being locked up for life like they should have been."

"I can do some digging." He cupped my shoulders, spinning me around. "I should have dug a while ago, but you asked me not to, so I didn't. But now..."

"You'll dig whether I ask you to or not," I finished for him.

Cyrus nodded.

I sighed, pulled away from him, and finished packing my bag. "I don't have a lot here. I'll talk to Jay when I go to work next Monday and see if anyone there wants to rent this apartment."

"This building is owned by the center?" Cyrus asked, helping me pull clothes from my dresser.

"Yeah, it's funded by the government but those who live here are from the center. If they aren't, it's for other victims. Like domestic violence victims. It's safe but now..." My thoughts went back to when someone knocked on my door earlier. I tried wracking my brain if there had been someone out of the ordinary I had seen in the building but I couldn't think of anyone.

"Let me contact a friend. He can find out who was released from jail, and he can find out who has come and gone from here."

I paused, meeting Cyrus's eyes in the reflection of the mirror. "That information is confidential."

He grunted. "You don't know my friend."

"I just don't want you going after them but I'm fine with you finding out whatever information you can." I could tell Cyrus how scary the people who had taken me were, but I wasn't sure if he would accept it. He knew why I was scared of them but when it came to him, I knew that he would do anything to avenge me.

"I won't go after them," Cyrus said but I felt like there was more to his promise than he let on.

We finished packing up my clothes and some of my personal items. I would have to make another trip or two, but this would work for now.

When we were leaving my apartment, I gave the space one final look before stepping out into the hall with him.

"You good?"

I nodded. "I need a fresh start."

"I get that." Pulling the strap of my bag up higher on his shoulder, he hooked his other arm around me, leading me down the hall.

Once we were leaving the building, I breathed in a scent of fresh air. It was still early in the morning or late at night, depending on how you looked at it. But it smelled like peace and serenity. Things I had never felt before whenever I left this place.

"I got you, babe," Cyrus murmured, kissing the top of my head.

I snuggled into his side as we walked toward his SUV. When we neared the large vehicle, someone came toward us and bumped into me. A sharp pain erupted through my shoulder and side, the impact almost knocking off my feet.

"Hey," Cyrus snapped, pulling me against him.

"It's okay," I reassured him. "I'm fine." I looked behind me, finding the person walking into the building. They stopped, glancing at me over their shoulder. My stomach flipped, a sense of dread washing over me.

"Asshole," Cyrus murmured, leading me to his vehicle.

As we neared the large black beast of an SUV, I became light-headed. The pain from being bumped into was more pronounced as time went on.

Cyrus opened the passenger door, waiting for me to enter the vehicle.

"I don't..." I wavered on my feet, spots dancing in my vision. "I suddenly don't feel well."

He came toward me, cupping my face. His eyes roamed over me, widening when they landed on a spot at my abdomen. "You're bleeding."

"What?" I looked down at myself. A red liquid was soaking through my white sweater. I lifted the fabric along with my tank top and saw blood profusely leaving a gaping wound in my side.

"Fuck, baby." Cyrus's eyes were wide. "You were stabbed. That bastard stabbed you."

That was the last thing I heard before everything went dark.

TWENTY-THREE

CYRUS

WHEN MY DAD HAD lost my mom, I never understood his anguish. Even now, I still didn't completely understand. Our father had fallen within himself. He took care of us as best he could, but it wasn't enough. It wasn't his fault. He was stuck in his head, probably wishing he could have burnt the world down to bring our mom back again.

As Ainsley bled out in my arms, I hadn't felt fear like that until now. The fear of losing someone. The fear of not knowing if you'll ever survive it. I had only just found her. There was no way I could move on if she didn't make it through this.

I didn't know who had stabbed her as I never got a good look at their face, but it was someone who must have known Ainsley, or at least knew who she was. Maybe they were paid off. Or it was random. No, I had learned rather quickly in life that nothing happened at random. Not with the people we knew.

I was in a trance as I dialed 9-1-1. I couldn't even recall the conversation I had with the dispatcher as I tried to stop the bleeding. I couldn't figure out if there were any other injuries but the one in her side.

Brushing her hair off her head, I kissed her over and over. "Please don't leave me," I whispered, my voice thick. "I can't handle it. I'm not strong enough. I've already lost so much. I can't lose you too."

Sirens sounded off in the distance. They got closer and closer but all I could focus on was how Ainsley had her eyes closed. How her breathing became shallow and uneven. How her skin became ashen and clammy.

"Please, God. Take me instead." I kissed her lips, my tears falling onto her beautiful face.

Movement sounded behind me, deep voices followed but I couldn't make out who was who and what was what. All I could see was Ainsley, dying in front of me.

"Please save her," I begged to no one.

"Son." An older man dressed in a police uniform placed a gentle hand on my shoulder. The touch was a contradiction. He looked to be around in his mid to late forties, with wrinkles at the corners of his eyes and pain in the deep black depths. He had seen shit. I knew because I had seen it in the eyes of the men who had raised my brother and me.

"I'm Officer Jaxon but you can call me Andy."

"Where are they taking her?" I demanded, when I realized that the EMTs were putting Ainsley onto a stretcher. I went to rush after them when Officer Jaxon stepped in front of me, blocking my path.

"I don't suggest doing that right now." He nodded toward the ambulance. "They'll take good care of her."

"Yeah, and I'm going to go with them." I sidestepped around him when he followed. Narrowing my eyes at him, it took everything in me not to charge past him. "Problem?"

"Yes. You see, I get a call that a woman has been stabbed and I find a man crouching over her covered in blood. There are no other witnesses around, so it's just your word against hers.

And I know we won't be getting any information from her anytime soon."

"I was the one who fucking called in the first place. If I wanted my girlfriend dead, the police would be the last people I'd contact." I took a step toward him, going to toe with him. "I also don't give a shit that you're a cop. You're probably paid off by Price Davies anyway."

The cop chuckled. "Listen, kid. You're funny. But no one pays me off. If I want to do shady shit, I will. If I don't want to do it, I won't. I've been around long enough and have been a cop for over fifteen years—"

"I'm done. I need to go—" The ambulance drove off with Ainsley inside of it, leaving me with Officer Jaxon. "You think I had something do with this, don't you?" I asked, my voice flat.

"Don't know. That's what I need to find out."

"We were leaving her apartment." I nodded to the bag on the ground. "She's moving in with me and we were going to come collect the rest of her stuff over the next few days." I continued explaining about the guy who bumped into her and how seconds later, she wasn't feeling well. "If she dies, I won't stop, and I will burn this fucking world down trying to figure out who the hell stabbed her."

"I don't doubt it." Officer Jaxon met my gaze then. "So let's get this shit on the road then."

As much as I didn't want to, I complied and answered his questions.

How was our relationship?

Did I have any reason to stab her myself?

Did I see anyone else?

Where did the fucker go who hurt my girl? I only stared at the cop when he asked this question using those exact words. He shrugged, pulling a pack of smokes from his pocket.

I took one from him, lit it up, and inhaled the substance I had depended on to make me feel better ever since I was a teenager.

"I'll make some calls. We'll find out who did this."

My eyes landed on the dark spot on the pavement a few feet away. I could still see the dark pool of blood. Ainsley's blood. My girl. The only woman who had ever dug herself beneath my skin and made me feel better just by being there.

"You can go but I don't suggest leaving town. I'll be in touch." Officer Jaxon went to his car. "We will find him, Cyrus. Leave it to me and I'll make sure he gets his."

I ignored him, grabbed Ainsley's bag and went to my SUV. Once I was sitting behind the steering wheel, my fist landed against it. I bellowed out a "fuck," the walls I had built up over the years to protect myself, crumbling down all around me.

Taking a deep breath, I headed to the hospital, sending up prayers along the way that Ainsley would make it out of this. Her mental health had already been through enough. Sure, she had been hurt physically and she had scars to prove it but the fact that she had stopped talking because of the trauma she endured, I was terrified that this would set her back. She had come so far, opening up to me, giving me pieces of herself she had never shared with anyone before. I took it for granted but now, I made a promise to myself, and I would promise her just the same, that it wouldn't happen again.

Once the large building of the hospital came into view, a breath left me. I pulled the SUV into the parking lot, created a random parking spot that would probably earn me a ticket, and ran into the building.

When I reached the reception desk, I was frantic with worry as I saw no one around. "Fucking hell." I rubbed the back of my neck, not sure what to do.

"Sir?"

I spun on my heel, finding a young woman dressed in colorful scrubs, coming toward me. "I'm here to see Ainsley Cloet. She was just brought in and I'm assuming she's in surgery. She was stabbed."

"Are you family?"

"She doesn't have...yes, yes, I'm her family." Her only family. The only family who mattered.

The woman nodded and went behind the desk, clicked a few keys on the computer. "Yes, she's still in surgery. You can sit in the waiting room and the doctor will be with you after."

"He can call me." I gave her my cell number and left the area, needing fresh air and to call my brother. When I stepped outside, I lifted my phone to my ear.

"Hey, C," Sammy answered a second later. "What's up?"

The words became stuck, unable to break free from my throat.

My knees shook, giving out on me when a sob finally broke free.

"Cyrus," Sammy barked. "What the fuck is going on?"

"Hospital," I was finally able to get out.

"On my way."

"Cyrus."

As soon as I heard my name, my head snapped up. I saw Sammy coming toward me and did the only thing I knew. I rushed to him.

"What's going on?" Sammy demanded.

I charged into him, throwing myself around my brother and needing his hug. Fuck, I needed him to tell me that I was losing it and that everything was going to be fine. I needed him to say that I was worrying for nothing, and that Ainsley would pull out of this.

"Cyrus," he murmured, hugging me back.

We weren't huggers. Not lately anyway. Sammy had walls up because he hated to let anyone get too close for fear of getting hurt. I almost expected him to push me away but when he didn't, it forced this ache in my chest to grow even more.

"What happened?" he demanded.

I pulled away from him and began pacing. "We were at Ainsley's apartment. She was coming to the clubhouse with me. We want to move in together." I looked at him then, waiting for some sort of reaction to what I just told him but when I got nothing, I took a breath and continued. "We think someone's been stalking her. It's just been small things but a few months ago, she ended up at a deli that I was at, and someone was following her." That had been so long ago. My lips still tingled with the memory of the first kiss we shared.

"And what happened tonight?" Sammy asked gently, lighting up a smoke. He handed it to me before lighting one up for himself.

"We were walking to the SUV and some fucker bumped into her. I thought he just hit her really hard but she...I..." I swallowed hard. "She suddenly wasn't feeling well and she...fuck, Sam, he stabbed her."

His eyes widened. "Fuck me."

"She's in surgery now but I...I can't lose her. Not when I just found her. I've spent years looking for someone like her." My knees shook, threatening to collapse beneath me.

Sammy clapped my shoulder. "Have you called anyone else?"

I shook my head. "Just you. I should call Jaron but I just...I didn't...I..." I felt like I was losing myself. The part I built walls around to protect for years.

"Where does she live? I can get Rowan to look into the security tapes."

I grunted, rising back to my full height and began pacing. "He's still pissed at you."

Sammy scoffed. "I didn't know she was his. Last time I saw him, he was with a guy anyway. I can't keep up with the things he's into or not into." He shook his head. "It doesn't matter. Give me his number and I'll call him anyway. I know he'll do it for you."

There was no point in arguing with him. Sammy had slept with someone Rowan was dating for half a second. It didn't end well for either of them. That was before Red from what I could tell, but I wasn't even sure anymore.

"Cyrus." Sammy held out his hand. "Give me your phone. I'll call him and make him actually get off his lazy ass for once and find this fucker who stabbed my future sister-in-law."

Handing him my phone, I looked behind me at the large hospital. "He's under RC. Ainsley lives at an apartment run by the center." I gave him the address and lit up another smoke.

Sammy nodded, holding the phone to his ear. "Hey, Rowan. It's your favorite person." He chuckled, walking away from me and leaving me to my thoughts. My prayers. My worries. My need to find this bastard and avenge Ainsley.

But for now, all I could do was wait.

(Ainsley)

I knew the possibility of something like this happening, was few and far between but the fact it happened to me, proved that life was cruel.

With my hands tied behind my back, I was hunched over. My knees hurt, the gravel beneath me, digging into my skin. Whatever was tied around my wrists, scratched and scraped at me every time I moved. My cheek was pressed against the cold ground, my hair matted to my forehead. I didn't know where I was. I didn't even bother asking after another girl tried and had her tongue cut out for even voicing such things.

I could still hear her screams and the noises leaving her as she gagged on her own blood. She threw up quickly after that, which I was sure didn't make the pain any less.

I didn't know who had taken us, but I watched movies and read enough books to know that we were taken for a purpose.

"Where are we? What are we doing here? What do you want?" another girl asked.

It was dark, so I couldn't make out her features, but I knew that she was close by. It was on the tip of my tongue to tell her to shut up for fear that the same thing would happen to her that happened to the other girl.

"Please let me go," she sobbed. "I have a family. I have parents. I have a son. He's two. Please."

My eyes welled, my chest tightening over what she was saying.

"I promise I won't tell anyone," she pleaded, begging for her life so she could get home to her boy.

Just when I was about to tell her to be quiet, she gagged. The sound was followed by whimpers and other noises that I didn't want to know the cause of.

Squeezing my eyes shut, I tried ignoring the sounds, but I couldn't. The more I tried, it was like the louder they became. Her sobs were muffled. The sound of a moan filling the room, forced a deep chuckle from somewhere nearby. The sobs hardened, her body clearly betraying her.

Taking a deep breath, I willed my brain to let me fall into it. To disappear and find a safe place within. But when a hand grabbed my hair and pulled me upright, I knew. I no longer had a safe place. Not now. Not tomorrow. Maybe not ever.

Light burned into my eyes, making them water. I was vaguely aware of the deep voices coming from somewhere in the room I was in. Wherever that may be.

Blinking a couple of times, my vision finally cleared. I looked around me, realizing that I was in a large white room. It was so damn bright, even the sight of it, hurt my eyes.

"Cyrus," I whispered, trying to wrack my brain over what had happened tonight.

"Call him," a deep voice said. "Tell him she's awake."

Squeezing my eyes shut, I blew out a slow breath, the sudden anxiety rushing through me, making my head pound.

"Ainsley."

A whimper left me at the familiar voice.

"Pet." Lips pressed against the spot by my ear. "Fuck, baby. Open those beautiful eyes for me."

I did as I was told, Cyrus's handsome face coming into my line of sight.

"That's my girl." He wrapped his arm around my shoulders, pushing his face into the crook of my neck. "I thought I'd lost you," he murmured, his voice cracking.

"Take me home," I told him, needing out of here. I felt exposed. I didn't handle change well. The last time I was at a hospital, they ran test after test. I felt like a damn lab rat. "Please, Cyrus, take me home."

"I can't, baby." He cupped my cheek. "Not yet."

"I can't be here." I realized then that we weren't alone when I saw movement out of the corner of my eye, but I couldn't take my gaze off of Cyrus. My love. The only person who had ever been patient with me. Who took his time to be my friend first and lover second.

"You just came out of surgery, pet," he said gently. "But I promise, as soon as the doctor says it's okay, I'm taking you home and putting you in my bed." He didn't mean it to sound sexual, but it still sent a shiver down my spine.

"What happened?" I asked as Sammy came toward the bed, I was lying in.

Cyrus pulled up a chair, keeping my hand in his and kissing my knuckles. "What do you remember?"

"I remember leaving my apartment. We were walking to your SUV and then that guy shoved into me." I tried thinking back to him and what he looked like, but came up short.

"I called Rowan and he was able to hack into the security footage even though he was complaining the whole time how it needed to be updated. Apparently, even though it's top of the line, it could still be better. His words." Sammy scowled. "He didn't see much but is still looking and will call back once he finds something."

I looked between the brothers. "I knew the guy."

"You did?" Cyrus asked. "His face was covered."

"I know." I shook my head. "It doesn't make sense but it's a feeling. He was the guy who followed me to the deli that day. He's probably the same person who knocked on my door just to scare the shit out of me too. I don't know how I know but my gut is telling me it's the same person."

"Did you ever see his face?" Sammy asked, sitting on the other side of me.

"No." I sighed. "I know it sounds crazy but there was something familiar about the guy tonight. I can't explain it."

"I'm going to call Rowan again," Sammy muttered.

"You save his number in your phone?" Cyrus asked him.

"Yes, he's going to love the fuck out of that." He chuckled but the humor was never there. He went up to the door turning back to us. "Listen, I'm sorry for how I treated you," he told me. "I'm an asshole but you didn't deserve that shit. So, I apologize for it." Instead of waiting for me to respond, Sammy left the room, leaving me alone with Cyrus.

"I wasn't expecting that," I said, more to myself.

"Same." Cyrus's mouth brushed over my knuckles.

I turned my head toward him, giving him a small smile. "Thank you for saving me."

"No." He stood, giving me a soft peck on my forehead. "You saved me, pet. More than I even knew was possible."

"You saved my life." I cupped his face, running my fingers through the dark scruff on his strong jaw. "Even before tonight, you saved me."

A shuddered breath left him. "I thought I'd lost you," he told me for the second time. His mouth found mine, the fear of what happened tonight, sliding between us.

"I'm fine," I whispered against his lips.

"Are you? You were fucking stabbed, baby." He blew out a slow breath and pulled away from me. He ran a hand through his dark hair, dropping it at his side. "Sorry."

"Don't be." I shifted over, patting the empty space beside me. "Sit. Please."

Cyrus sat, grabbing my hand and holding it tight in his.

"The last time I was in a hospital, I was alone. The staff was nothing but nice to me, but it wasn't the same. I also..." I swallowed hard. "I haven't been completely honest with you."

His dark eyes locked with mine, staring into a part of me that had only ever belonged to him.

"Last time, they told me that I can't have kids. I'm sorry for not telling you in the beginning but I didn't want to lose you. I know I should have told you when we first started dating but I was scared. I didn't want this to end. I liked you then and I love you now. I can't...I didn't want to lose you," I repeated, my voice cracking. "I'm sorry."

Cyrus wrapped his arms around me, holding me tight against him. "I love you, Ainsley. We don't need to have kids to be together. We can look into adopting eventually, if that's what you want to do but we don't even have to do that. We can travel. I can get you a cat."

"Two cats, so they're not alone."

He chuckled, kissing my cheek. "Two cats. I'll get you fifty of them if that's what you want."

I laughed, wiping the tears from my cheeks that had unexpectedly fallen. "God, I love you."

"Are you sure you're okay?" he asked, leaning his forehead against mine.

I blew out a slow breath. "I need to go home. I need to be with you." I looked up at him then. "I'm scared this will happen again and they won't stop until..."

Cyrus's jaw clenched. "Don't think about that."

"How can you expect me not to? I was able to get out of that hell and the people who escaped are probably working their way through everyone who's still alive."

"I'm going to make a call." Cyrus pulled his phone from his jacket, pressed a button on the screen and held the cell up to his ear before I could argue with him. "I need you and Locke to come to the hospital. Third floor. Room 308B." His eyes locked with mine. "I'll explain when you get here." He disconnected the call and stood. "I'll have Cheesy and Locke standing outside your door. Even if I'm here, they'll be there as well."

"Is Locke a prospect too?" I asked, still not used to the biker lingo but I appreciated the extra protection.

Cyrus gave me a small smile, but it never reached his eyes. "Yeah, pet. He is. His name is Jamie. He's a good kid. Just like Cheesy. Even though I'm still not a fan of the fact that he knew you before I did."

I snorted, rolling my eyes. "Trust me, baby, he doesn't do it for me."

"Oh?" Cyrus sat back on the edge of the bed, leaning his hand on the other side of me, caging me in. "And what exactly does it for you?"

My stomach tumbled at the sudden flirting between us. I appreciated the distraction, still unsure as to what the hell was going on but thankful for the gesture just the same.

I like my men big, I signed.

Cyrus grinned, opening his mouth to respond when much to my surprise, Jaron came into the room followed by Sammy.

Cyrus's head whipped around. "What are you doing here?"

"I'm your president," Jaron answered like it was the most obvious answer. "You should have called me."

"Piper is due anytime," Cyrus explained, rising from the bed. "I called Cheesy and Locke." He nodded toward Sammy. "And Sam of course."

Jaron stabbed a finger against Cyrus's chest. "You should have called me too."

"I'm sorry." Cyrus looked down at me. "I just thought..."

"I get it." Jaron nodded toward me. "How are you feeling?"

"Better," I whispered. I was sore but the meds were doing wonders for the pain.

Cyrus stared at me, a smile finally reaching his eyes.

You gave me a voice again, I signed quickly for him.

His jaw clenched, something flashing in his eyes. I didn't know what it was, but I had a feeling that I would eventually find out and that I wouldn't like it.

TWENTY-FOUR

CYRUS

I DIDN'T LIKE SEEING Ainsley in bed like that. She was small to begin with but now she just looked almost frail, and she was anything but. She was the strongest woman I ever knew. After what she had already survived, I was worried that this would set her back, or worse, but there was now a hardness to her gaze that made me realize something. These fuckers would never get to her again. They may have had her body, but her mind was hers and hers alone.

"I love you, Cyrus," she whispered, her eyes fluttering closed.

I was lying on my side in the bed with her. We didn't care that there technically wasn't enough room. We needed to be close to each other. We needed to reassure each other that we weren't going anywhere. Which was true. The only place she was going after leaving the hospital, was to my bed at the clubhouse.

"I love you too, pet," I finally said, kissing her cheek.

"Cyrus?"

I lifted my head, finding Jaron and Sammy standing at the foot of the bed. I never even heard them come in.

"How's she doing?" Sammy asked, the anger he once felt for what I had with Ainsley, no longer there.

"Sore, I imagine, but I think the pain meds are helping," I said, my voice low, careful not to wake her.

"We have some news," Jaron said, passing a glance at Sammy.

I pulled my arm out from under Ainsley's head. "I'll be back, baby," I whispered, kissing her cheek.

"Okay." She sighed, her eyes remaining closed.

I followed Jaron and Sammy out of the room, thankful when I saw Cheesy and Locke standing on either side of the doorway.

"What's going on?" I asked, not liking the fact that Ainsley was now alone in the room without me.

"Rowan did some digging," Jaron said when we were out of earshot from anyone who could possibly listen in on our conversation.

"And?" My heart jumped, not liking the fact that Jaron was stalling and didn't come out with the information like he usually did.

"The brothel Ainsley was saved from, was torn down and rebuilt as a hair salon, but it's still just a front for what they really do. Rowan got in contact with some people he's worked with before and found out that this salon is actually owned by..." Jaron hesitated. "Price."

My eyes widened. "Price Davies?" The old mayor of this town who almost destroyed Jaron and Piper's lives. "The fuck?"

"Since he's not mayor anymore, I guess he's really making his rounds through the shady shit he's been known for," Sammy added. "But we still can't prove anything. That guy though, the one who stabbed your girl, he was caught lurking around the apartment complex for the last month. I saw the footage, Cyrus. Whenever Ainsley left the building, he was there. When you dropped her off, picked her up, left in the damn morning, he was there. But we couldn't get a clear shot of what he looked like. All we know is that he's a man, maybe six feet or a little taller and my size. And we know he's Caucasian. That's it."

"Fuck me." I ran a hand through my hair. "That doesn't help. At all. What about Price? Any word on him? Has anyone seen him at this salon? We need to end him."

"Trust me. You know how much I want my hands around that fucker's throat," Jaron bit out.

"Then why haven't we picked him up yet?" I demanded, not liking this sense of urgency rushing through me.

"The guys are on it," Sammy added. "We'll get him and bring him to justice over the shit he pulled with Jaron, Piper, and Brynlee. And we'll get the bastard who's stalking your girl. We'll end them both."

"When Price is caught, I want to be there," I told them, leaving no room for argument. "I don't give a shit how long it takes. I need to watch him die."

Both Jaron and Sammy looked at each other before glancing back at me.

"We wouldn't want it any other way." Jaron paused. "I just hope it's after Piper has the baby. I can't leave her right now."

"Oh don't worry." Sammy clapped his shoulder. "If we pick him up before then, I'll just torture him a bit until you can join."

Before my brother could go on even more about how much Price deserved to be buried, I thought back to what Ainsley had told me about her abduction. "Ainsley said after the raid, there were some survivors like her, some of the captors escaped, and some were thrown in jail. I don't know how many people worked at this damn place, but someone must know something."

"I'll see what I can find out, but I don't know if that's possible, Cyrus," Jaron said gently. "The most we can do, is bring Price in. And that may be all we can ever do."

"Why hasn't he been found already?" I grumbled, wishing like hell that things would move faster than they were.

"Because he paid people off to keep quiet. It's his MO. You know that. He's a fucking pussy and can't take care of shit on his own." Jaron crossed his arms under his chest. "So he hires people to do his dirty work for him."

My hands clenched into fists at my sides. I was on the verge of snapping.

"Cyrus." Cheesy came toward us. "She's asking for you."

Instead of responding, I shoved past him and went back to the one person who could keep me calm.

When I entered the room, I stopped at the foot of Ainsley's bed.

"What is it?" she asked softly, shifting her weight in the bed.

"I don't know what to do," I confessed, not liking the desperation dripping from my voice. I hated not having control. I hated not knowing how to avenge Ainsley.

"Come here." She held out her arms, waiting.

My feet pulled me forward as though of their own accord and right into Ainsley's open arms.

She wrapped herself around me, her mouth finding the soft spot at my ear. "I love you, Cyrus, but you don't need to go after the person who hurt me. You don't need to go after any of them."

I shook against her, wishing I could agree but didn't say anything because I knew if I did, this would end up in a fight.

"I can't wait for the doctor to say I can go home with you."

I leaned back, fisting her hair and crushing my mouth against hers.

Ainsley latched on to my hoodie, pulling me closer.

A groan fell between us. Unsure as to who made the noise, I broke the kiss and ran my thumb along the length of her jaw. "I don't like that there's nothing I can do. I'm not used to this."

"Sometimes you just have to give in and submit."

I stared at her, knowing she wasn't referring to the fact that I couldn't go after the fucker who stabbed her.

"If you saw any of the people again who had been with you at the brothel and anywhere else you were held captive at, would you recognize them?"

"What are you asking me?" She gently pushed my shoulder when I didn't answer. "Cyrus, tell me."

"If I find anyone, someone, one of those bastards, to try and get them to talk, would you recognize him or her?" There was no point in keeping my plan from her. Even though we had only known each other for a few months, she knew me better than anyone.

"Yes, probably but I don't like where this question is headed."

I pulled away from her and rose from the bed.

"Cyrus, come here."

I turned away from her. "I need to do this. I need to find him."

"No, you don't. Leave it alone. You don't have to play God."

I spun on her. "Yes, I fucking do because he almost took you away from me. I can't lose you. I can't. I already lost my parents. I refuse to lose the first woman I've ever loved. The only woman I plan on spending my life with."

Ainsley's breath caught. "I want that too. I want to be with you. I want to spend my life, with you. So please, come here, Cyrus. Stay with me."

"You know I have to do this."

"But you don't even know where any of them are," she cried, slamming her fist down on the bed beside her.

My body stirred at the emotion coming from her. "I love you."

"And I love you but right now, you're pissing me off," she bit out through clenched teeth.

My dick jumped. "Be pissed at me all you want. You can take it out on me later. But you know I have to do this. I won't be able to fucking sleep or eat until I know for sure that you are safe."

"God." She laughed. She actually fucking laughed. "You know that even if you do find this bastard, there are more of them, right? Even if they have nothing to do with the shit that happened to me, you have no control over what tomorrow brings. Or even an hour from now, Cyrus. You of all people should fucking know that."

"Doesn't matter." I knew I could possibly lose her because of this but I couldn't stop my parents from dying. I was too damn young for that. But I was old enough now and I could at least avenge Ainsley.

263

I knew that I was too stuck in my head for this. I got it. I understood it. But seeing Ainsley lying in that bed, didn't sit well with me. She could have died and there was nothing I could have done.

"Cyrus, please come here," her voice wavered.

I looked away and was met by Sammy staring back at me from the doorway. Something switched between us in that moment. We held a silent conversation between us, and I knew right then, the decision I had to make. We had to bring Price in and find the bastard who tried to kill my girlfriend. Even if it ruined what Ainsley and I had, I had to make sure that this fucker wouldn't come after her again or anyone else for that matter.

TWENTY-FIVE

Ainsley

"CYRUS SAID HE WAS going to get a coffee," Sammy told me, pulling up a chair beside the bed I was currently stuck in.

I only scoffed.

"I like you for him. He's been looking for someone like you." Sammy cleared his throat. "I just want to apologize for how I was in the beginning. It's not enough of course but I *am* sorry."

"Don't be." I shook my head. "I get it. I don't have any siblings but if I did, I would probably worry too that someone could come between us. It wasn't like you knew me or what my intentions were."

"Why are you talking to me?" Sammy ran a hand through his hair. "I mean..."

"I know what you mean and I'm talking to you because you're Cyrus's brother. I respect you." I crossed my arms under my chest, wishing I could go to Cyrus, but I had to stay in this bed for observation.

"I think there's more to it than that, Mouse."

I looked at him then, my heart stuttering at the pet name coming from someone like him. "Why do you call me that?"

He gave me a small smile. "It's better than quiet girl." He stood before I could respond and cupped my shoulder. "Whatever Cyrus does, I will be right there with him. I'll make sure he comes back to you safely."

"He can't go. Neither of you can. If something happens..." My voice cracked. "I can't lose him."

"I know but unfortunately, when it comes to the ones he loves being in danger, he will do anything and everything he can to make sure that they're safe. No matter the cost."

"He can't." I went to pull the IV out of my arm when a hand covered mine. "Please," I whispered, my voice shaking.

"He won't do anything stupid."

My head snapped up. "You don't know that. He said he's never been in love before, so how the hell could you know how he'll be? How he'll react when he finds the guy who stabbed me?" I waited for Sammy to answer but when he didn't and his jaw only ticked, I shoved out of his grip and ripped the IV from my arm. "You can't know, Sammy." I pushed off the bed. "I need to stop him."

"Stop." He came around the bed and caught me as I fell against him. "You're too weak."

"I'm fine." I pushed against him, attempting to take a step forward when my knees gave out from beneath me and I fell to the ground.

"Shit. Ainsley." Sammy wrapped me up in his arms and lifted me back onto the bed. "You need your rest. It won't do either of you any good if you go and get yourself hurt even more."

"Please go get him for me," I pleaded. "I don't like how we left things."

"I will." He helped me under the covers. "I'll get a nurse to put the IV back in for you." He went to the door, looking back at me. "I hope to one day have what you and Cyrus do."

"You will, Sammy." I held the blanket to my arm to stop the bleeding while Sammy went to grab the nurse. But I wished I was home in bed or better yet, in Cyrus's bed with him beside me.

Sammy nodded once and left the room. I could hear his deep voice barking orders at someone.

"No one goes in that room unless it's medical staff, Cyrus, or me. You hear me?"

Muttered responses came.

"Good. It's about time you listen to me," he told whoever he was talking to. "Yeah, that's fine." As soon as those words left Sammy's lips, Cheesy appeared in the doorway.

"Hey." He gave me a small smile. "How are you feeling?"

I huffed, crossing my arms under my chest when a nurse entered the room.

"I heard you accidentally pulled your IV out." She gave me a small smile. "Let me get that sorted for you. One more night and you'll be on your way. As long as there are no setbacks of course."

I was stabbed. The only setback would be how it would impact my mental health. But of course, I never said that.

"There you go." She patted my hand. "All fixed."

I wanted to thank her. I wanted to speak to her. I wanted to speak to everyone and not stop. I wanted Cyrus there, encouraging me to use my voice that he helped me get back after so many years of not talking.

"Thank you," I whispered.

Her smile widened. "Of course." She quickly left the room, leaving me alone with Cheesy who I realized was still standing there staring at me.

"You've never...I've never heard you..." He paused. "Cyrus is good for you."

I shook my head. *No, we're good for each other.*

"You are. Well, I'll leave you alone. I just wanted to see how you're doing."

"Thank you," I murmured softly.

Before I knew what he was doing, Cheesy had me in his arms. "I know I shouldn't be hugging you and that Cyrus will probably kick my ass, but I'm so fucking proud of you."

I hugged him back, now thankful for the touch since it bothered me before and for so long.

"You're damn fucking straight I'm going to kick your ass."

Both of us jumped at the deep voice.

Cheesy squeezed me one last time, not caring in the least that Cyrus was now in the room with us. "He'll kick my ass but you finally hugging me will be worth it."

I laughed, pushing him away gently.

Cyrus went up to him, cupped his nape and spun him around before shoving him forward. "Leave. Now."

"You're so grumpy," I teased.

Cyrus grunted, sitting on the bed beside me and pulling me into his arms. "This is where you belong. In my arms only, pet."

Cheesy gave me a small wave before leaving the room.

I sighed, cupping Cyrus's cheek. "He was just saying that he's glad I'm doing okay."

"What happened here?" he asked, holding up my arm. It had extra bandages on it from where I ripped out the IV.

"Oh. I was going to go after you, so I pulled out my IV," I said, like it was no big deal. Which it wasn't because he would have done the same thing.

"You were going to do what?" he asked, staring down at me like I had two heads.

I rolled my eyes, moving higher up the bed. "I was going to go after you and stop you from doing something stupid, but then Sammy reassured me that he would be there with you and that nothing would happen. But again, you aren't God, and neither is he. So you need to stop this *I am man, I take care of woman,* bullshit."

His eyes moved back and forth over my face. "It's my job to take care of you."

"It's our job to take care of each other but to also realize that we can take care of ourselves too." I grabbed his jacket when he went to pull away. "I need you. I need you here with me. Not out there trying to fight the bad guys. Please, Cyrus. I need you. Here."

"I need to make a call." He kissed my forehead and pulled away from me before I could stop him.

"Cyrus."

He stopped, looking at me over his shoulder.

"I love you," I told him, wishing he would stay with me.

"I love *you*." His eyes darkened. "More than you will ever fucking know."

TWENTY-SIX

Ainsley

IT HAD BEEN A couple of days since I was stabbed, and something was wrong. I hadn't seen Cyrus since a few hours ago. Hell, I hadn't even seen his brother. I called out for Cheesy and whoever else was standing guard at the door, but I was being ignored. The only people I saw were the medical staff. The nurses and doctors had been nothing but nice to me. They made sure I was comfortable, and one of the doctors assured me that I would be leaving soon as I was healing nicely. But I had to take it easy, of course. I didn't want to take it easy. I wanted Cyrus to take me out of here and for us to move on with our lives. I wanted him. Every inch. In every way.

He had been calling me pet since the very beginning and I wanted to know exactly what that term meant to him and just how deep it went. I read and read a lot, not just the classics, so I knew things from books and also from personal experience.

Although, I knew with Cyrus, it would be all consensual and he wouldn't have me doing things I didn't want to do. I wanted to find out if it was him playing or if it was a lifestyle he actually wanted to live.

Wanting to find out where he was and why it had been hours since I'd last seen him, I slowly pushed my way out of bed. I grabbed the IV stand, wheeled it along with me, and very slowly and carefully, made my way to the door when a man dressed in green scrubs came into the room.

"Ah, Ainsley, you shouldn't be out of bed." He rushed to me and gently pushed me back.

I tried pulling out of his grip. I didn't like his hands on me. Add to the fact I had never seen him before, he made me nervous. He wasn't one of the regular staff who came in to check on me.

I couldn't ask him who he was because the words were stuck. It was like they were glued to my tongue.

The guy shoved me back onto the bed, a little too roughly if you asked me.

"Let's get you checked out and sorted." He wore scrubs and looked the part but there was something about him I didn't like. There was also something about him that seemed familiar, but I couldn't figure out what it was.

When his back was turned to me, I looked around me to see if there was anything I could use to defend myself with. The thought came on suddenly, sending a ripple of fear down my spine. I wasn't sure why I felt the need to defend myself but there was this feeling nagging at me, warning me about this man, and it made me uneasy. I had seen him before. I just couldn't remember where.

My eyes landed on a pen. I didn't know if it would actually work but I had to try.

I ripped out the IV and bounded from the bed when I was suddenly grabbed from behind and thrown down on top of it.

"Listen you little bitch," the man seethed, his hot breath fanning over the side of my head. "I lost a lot of money because of you."

My eyes widened.

"You don't remember me, do you?" His mouth brushed the shell of my ear, making my stomach churn.

I tried struggling out of his grip. I tried kicking. I even tried screaming but no sound left me. It was like my voice just...vanished.

"I missed your silence." He chuckled. "You were so easy to break."

I glared up at him. His hair was dark and short, almost black but had a brown tinge in the fluorescent lighting of the room. His eyes were green but held so much damn evil in them, it took everything I was made of not to look away. He was younger. Maybe around Cyrus's age.

"When the brothel was raided, I searched for you. I wanted to take you and keep you for myself." He lowered his mouth down to my ear. "Still don't remember me, Ainsley? That's fine. You will. When my cock rips through every single hole you have to offer me, you'll remember."

He lifted his head, a slight smirk pulling at his lips.

My eyes widened as the memories suddenly started rushing back.

He was the one who originally flirted with me at the café. He had been nothing but nice when one of the other customers had hit on me, but I wanted nothing to do with them. They were partners. One guy being a dick, while the other played nice. He wormed his way into my heart, making me think that he was a good guy, but he was anything but.

He was the one in my nightmares.

He was the one who made me wake up screaming only for Cyrus to come to my rescue and console me back to sleep.

He was the one who forced the words from my tongue and took them for his own. He took my voice.

"You took me," I whispered. "This is all your fault."

My mind had clearly tried protecting me because of my past trauma and made it so I never recognized him. But now that he was here, I couldn't stop the memories from rushing back.

"My fault?" He tilted his head. "Nah, baby girl. You just fit the part. You were what we wanted. The customers loved you. I especially loved our nights alone together."

My stomach twisted as memories I tried forgetting slid into the forefront of my mind.

When he was finally finished breaking my body, he kissed my cheek and left the cold damp room. I made a promise to myself right then and there that no matter how many times he used me, he would never get all of me.

But he did. He took my voice. He took every single part of my being.

"Gotta make this quick, Ainsley. I'm sure your little boyfriend will be back any moment."

"You were in my dreams," I said louder that time. "You were in my nightmares. I lost my voice because of you. You were the one who used me every night in that hell. You held me down while they...while they...cut me. You've been here this whole time, haven't you? It was you who followed me to the deli. It was you who stabbed me."

"I had to make sure it was you. Lost you when you left the hospital. I searched for you for over a year and had almost given up. The security in that center was tight. Imagine my surprise when someone notified me that they thought they had seen you in this shitty little town. Of all places. You gained your weight back and you changed your hair color, but I knew it was you." A dark shadow passed over his face. "I saw the fucker you've been with. You proved what we said was right. You are a little slut. That's why we cut you."

"You're sick in the head. All of you were. None of us deserved that."

"You deserved every single thing we did to you." He looked down the length of my body, pressing his arm against my chest, pinning me down. "Let's see what kind of damage I caused." He slid a hand up my hip, inching it beneath the hospital gown I was wearing until his fingers grazed over the bandage on my side. He tore it from my skin, the slight pain burning through me. "Hmm... maybe I should have shoved the knife in deeper." Before I knew what was happening, he shoved his fingers against me, ripping the stiches open.

The pain, God the pain, it was nothing like I had ever felt before. Agony seared through me as his fingers forced the wound apart. Bile rose to my throat, my vision fading in and out.

"Say my name," he demanded.

"I..." A sob tore through me as the sharp pain burned through every inch of my body.

"Say it," he growled, shoving two fingers into the wound.

He wanted me to call him Master but I wouldn't. He had never earned that title. I didn't call him that then. I wouldn't call him that now.

"Say. It," he demanded, his deep green eyes searing into me.

"You can go to hell," I bit out through clenched teeth.

"What the fuck?"

The new voice in the room forced this sudden strength in me. It called out to the strong woman in me, the one who had been taken when she was twenty and who fought to survive ever since.

Fisting the pen in my hand, I brought my arm forward and slammed it into the bastard's eye.

He shouted, pulling his fingers from my wound.

A scream tore through me as I stabbed him repeatedly. "You should have killed me when you had the chance!"

Blood splattered my hands, dripping to the ground beneath us as I shoved him back and off the bed.

I fisted the pen in both hands, slamming it down hard into the man's eye once again.

"Shit, Ainsley." Heavy arms wrapped around me, pulling me away from him.

A commotion sounded in the room, people milling about, barking orders and demands but all I could do was stare at the unmoving form on the floor.

"Shhh...pet, you're fine." Cyrus held me against him, rocking me back and forth. He continued whispering to me, trying to console me as best he could.

The sobs subsided but the terror, the fear that the man would jump up and try and attack me again, forced bile to my throat.

"What the hell happened in here?"

"Is she okay?"

Voices, so many words, but I didn't know who was saying what. All I could focus on was Cyrus holding me. I focused on him because I didn't know how to do anything else. He was all I needed. I just hoped he could forgive me for what just happened. It was a side of me I never knew was there and this bastard brought it out of me. I had feared all along that they would come back for those of us who had survived and escaped, but a part of me hoped that they had moved on. I had done everything I could to change my look and my life. I even moved across the country but clearly, that never helped.

"I got you, baby," Cyrus muttered, holding me tight against him. "I don't know what happened," he told someone.

"Ainsley." A gentle hand landed on my shoulder, making me jump.

My eyes shot to a woman crouching near us. She gave me a small smile and lifted her hands.

Can I check to make sure that you're okay?

I blew out a slow breath. *He ripped open my stitches.*

The smile fell from her face. *Let's get you taken care of, so you can go home. Okay?*

I nodded.

Cyrus kissed my temple. "I'm here. I'm not going anywhere." He pushed out from beneath me, helping me to my feet.

The woman who I realized must have been a nurse, gently grabbed my hand, holding me steady. "Let's get you cleaned up."

I noticed then that the man was no longer on the floor. I glanced at Cyrus.

"They took him out," he said gently. "The police are here and will want to talk to you. I won't leave you and I'll speak for you if you need."

"She needs to be checked first. The police can wait," the nurse told him. "I'm just going to check your wound."

I helped her lift the gown to my waist.

"We'll get you sorted." She lowered the gown, patted my hand and quickly left the room, only to come back with another nurse. "We'll move you to another room but we need to do an ultrasound to make sure he didn't do any more damage than what he already did earlier. I'm assuming he's the one who stabbed you originally?"

I nodded quickly, my eyes welling.

More staff came into the room with another bed. They helped me onto it but all I wanted was to leave and go home with Cyrus.

"I'll be waiting right here." Cyrus came up to the bed. "Wait." He grabbed hold of the bar, stopping them from taking me out of the room. He leaned down to my ear. "Once they fix you up, I'm taking you out of here and somewhere safer." He kissed my cheek.

I love you.

I love you, pet.

(Cyrus)

"What the hell happened?" Sammy demanded as the nurses and doctors were wheeling Ainsley away.

"I went to call Rowan to see if there was an update and then when I went back into Ainsley's room..." I couldn't get the image out of my head of her stabbing that fucker. To say I was proud of her, was an understatement. "She stabbed him in the eye." I slumped down onto the chair in the waiting room, running my hand over the back of my neck. "I knew she had it in her, but I never thought I'd see it."

"Who was he?" Sammy asked, sitting on the table across from me while Cheesy and Locke moved to the empty chairs on either side of me.

"I don't know. He was dressed in scrubs." I looked between Cheesy and Locke then. "That's why you never stopped him from entering the room."

"Yeah." Cheesy stood and began pacing. "If I would have known. I didn't know." He stopped, staring directly at me. "I'm sorry. I swear I didn't know who he was. He looked legit."

"I agree." Locke huffed. "But good on your girl for stabbing him. He's lucky that's all he got. Fucking fucker. I hope he rots in jail, if he doesn't die before then that is."

"If he doesn't die on the table…" My threat went unsaid. Ainsley started it but I would finish it. For her.

"He's alive."

Our heads turned as a cop came into the room, followed by a woman dressed in a suit.

"It seems we meet again, Cyrus." Officer Jaxon approached us with ease. He nodded to his partner. "This is Detective Baldwin."

"You can call me Jessica," she said gently. "Can you tell us what happened?"

"I don't know exactly," I said looking between them. "I went into the room and my girlfriend was stabbing a man in the eye with a pen." I knew there was no point in lying about it, seeing as the room Ainsley had stayed in, was filled with evidence. "I don't know who he was but what I do know is that he was the one who attacked her."

"How do you know this exactly?" Detective Baldwin asked.

"She told the nurse that he ripped her stitches open. I don't know anything more than that. You'll have to wait until she's back from getting her ultrasound." I hoped she didn't need a second surgery but we would deal with it when the time came.

I stood and shoved past them, needing some air.

"Cyrus." Sammy ran up behind me with Officer Jaxon and Detective Baldwin following behind him.

When Cheesy and Locke joined us in the hall, I went up to Cheesy first. "You care for her."

He swallowed hard but nodded anyway.

"Then I need you to do me a favor." I looked between them all. "All of you."

TWENTY-SEVEN

CYRUS

AINSLEY SHOULD HAVE BEEN on her way to recovery, but that bastard set things back to the point she did end up needing a second surgery. Once I was satisfied that she would be safe when she woke up, I went to pay someone a little visit. Money talked but what really helped me get the information I needed was Cheesy. Little did I know that he was such a ladies' man.

I had asked him what he whispered in the nurse's ear but when her cheeks turned pink, I could only imagine. Looked like the kid and I had more in common than I thought.

When I reached the door to the room that held the man who tried to end my girl's life, I clenched my hands into fists before taking a step forward.

"I wouldn't do that if I were you."

I looked to the right, finding a big fucker, leaning against the wall. He was typing away on his phone, but I could only assume he was talking to me.

Ignoring him anyway, I placed my hand on the doorknob.

"You deaf? Or is it just selective hearing? I'm betting on the latter."

"Listen." I spun on him. "I don't know who you are, but this is none of your business."

"Yeah, see, that's where you're wrong." The stranger shoved his phone into a pocket on the inside of his leather jacket. He turned toward me, giving me his full attention.

I frowned, something about him vaguely familiar. I noticed then how tattoos lined both sides of his thick neck. They ran beneath the collar of his white shirt. He was older, with graying short hair and silver in his beard. Intricate designs even covered the sides of his head where the hair was shaved.

A memory suddenly hit me. It brought me back to when Ainsley ran into that deli looking frantic and terrified. He had been sitting at one of the booths watching her. It dawned on me that this guy was the same man I saw at the library I took Ainsley to on one of our dates.

"I don't have time for this shit," I mumbled, not letting it be known that I recognized him.

"I wouldn't want to have to tell Ainsley that her boyfriend wouldn't listen and went off to find the bastards who tried to end her life."

"One of the fuckers who tried, is in this room," I bit out through clenched teeth. "And how the fuck do you know her name?"

The man chuckled, running two fingers along his mouth. A gold piercing in his lip twinkled in the lighting of the hall.

"Who are you?"

"I'm here to help." He came toward me.

"I've seen you before. You were at the deli and then again at the library. You want something from my girlfriend?" It took everything in me not to punch him out but there was something about him that I didn't like. I couldn't explain it, but he had an air about him that would make even Sammy seem like a kitten.

"I have no idea what you're talking about." The stranger closed the distance between us, glancing at the closed door.

I took a step back as he opened the door and walked into the room. I looked both ways down the hall. When I was satisfied that no one was none the wiser, I followed him into the room and shut the door behind me.

The bastard who had attacked Ainsley, laid in the bed. He had a bandage on his left eye. He was unmoving but alive. The fucker deserved more than what he got.

"I don't like people who hurt animals, children, or anyone for that matter. Not when it's not warranted. But it's never warranted when it comes to animals or children." The man walked up to the head of the bed, staring down at the guy who almost took my first and only love from me.

"I don't get why you would do this shit or why anyone does. It's something I've never been able to wrap my head around," he said to the still form. "You were treated well."

I frowned. "Do you know him?"

"Not really," the stranger answered. "My team and I have been following him for a while. Your girl caused some damage. But it's not enough. He doesn't deserve to live for what he did. None of them do."

"How do you know what he did?" I took a step forward. "How do you even know who my girl is?" I didn't like not having answers. I didn't like this confusion coursing through me over the fact that this man was looking down at the guy like he was reminiscing.

"He grew up in an organized household," he said, like I was supposed to know what that meant. Before I could ask any more questions, the stranger bent over the still form and leaned down to his ear. He muttered words I couldn't hear but could still feel throughout my soul. The guy who I had assumed was sleeping, slowly opened his good eye. It landed on me.

"Fuck you," he muttered.

The stranger chuckled. In a quick move, he covered the guy's mouth and nose with one hand and silenced the beeping machines by pulling the plugs with the other. "You will never hurt a single soul ever again, cousin."

My eyes widened.

The guy struggled in the bed, trying to push the stranger's hand away but it was too late.

I watched him die in front of me. I watched his chest rise and fall, only to not rise again as his final breath left him.

"He should have suffered more but unfortunately; we don't have time." The stranger released his mouth and nose, leaned over and kissed his forehead. "I'll see you in hell." He rose back to his full height and came up to me. "Take a walk with me." He left the room before I could wrap my head around what the hell just happened.

Following him out into the hall, we made it to the other end before nurses started rushing past us.

"You know there are cameras that will have us on tape that we went into that room," I pointed out.

"They're already taken care of," he said, pulling his phone out of his pocket and lifting it to his ear. "It's done," was all he said as he shoved it away. "It seems you and I have a mutual friend."

"Rowan." I wasn't sure how I knew that, but the name just slipped out, so there was no point in correcting myself.

He stopped when we hit the beginning of the hallway that led to where Ainsley stayed.

"Maybe him. Maybe someone else." His words were cryptic. I found that even though I had questions, I didn't know where to begin.

Sammy, Cheesy, and Locke stood by Ainsley's door. They looked my way, probably wondering who I was with.

"He won't hurt anyone again." The man pulled a pack of smokes out of his pocket and placed a cigarette behind his ear.

I met the stranger's dark eyes. "I never asked you to do that, and I also could have taken care of it myself."

"I know." He paused. "I've seen you in action."

I frowned. "I don't know what you mean."

He chuckled. "I've seen you at The Ring besides the other places you mentioned. You're quite the fighter. But that doesn't matter. I've been watching you and Ainsley."

"Who the fuck are you?" I demanded a little too loudly when several staff stopped to glare our way.

"I *was* at the deli when Ainsley came running in. I was at The Ring during all of your fights. I was at the library when you brought her there on your date. I was at the deli again when you brought her there, for strawberry milkshakes and pie. Am I right?"

My stomach clenched. "You stalking me now? Or her?" I took a step toward him. "You after my girl?"

He scoffed. "Trust me, I don't want your girl."

"Then why the hell have you...I'm so fucking confused right now, and I don't like it."

"The less you know, the safer it is for her. The safer it is for all of you." He looked over his shoulder. "But I know you won't let me leave without some answers." He met my gaze. "Someone you know paid for me and my team to look out for you. I was impressed that he actually found us."

I thought back to the conversation I had with Jaron so many weeks ago about how he paid a few guys to watch over us. Never thought I would see one of them in the flesh.

"Jaron wouldn't pay you to look out for his family if it wasn't serious," was all I said because I didn't know what else to say.

"Truth." The guy leaned against the wall, crossing his arms over his thick chest. "I was there during the raid. I helped Ainsley escape. We don't usually save adults but one of the girls was related to someone close to me. Unfortunately, she didn't make it. So we did what we could to save the others. Ainsley wouldn't remember me, which is probably for the best. Her mind needs to do what it can to protect her. But I've kept tabs on her and a few of the other survivors, because I wanted to make sure that they were safe and were able to move on as best they could from that hell." A dark shadow passed over his face. "It doesn't matter. Bottom line is, Ainsley is safe and no one else will come after her."

"How do I know that? She said that several people escaped. She doesn't know how many of those were the victims or their captors."

"That's true." He clapped my shoulder. "I guess you'll just have to trust me on this one."

"How the hell can I do that?" I shoved him off of me. "I don't even know you. You show up here after she gets attacked and I find out that you've been stalking us this whole damn time? It doesn't make sense."

"It doesn't need to make sense. Maybe you should ask Jaron a little more about this…situation."

"You come here acting like I should just bend over and let you do whatever the fuck you want. Well it doesn't work that way with me."

The stranger grinned. "I know some people who would have fun playing with you."

I rolled my eyes, stepping away from him. "Tell me one thing. Was he really your cousin?"

"Not by blood. We spent a few summers together. His family is messed up. My parents took him in after he got involved with the wrong crowd. They tried everything they could to turn him, but it was too late. So they kicked him out." He sighed. "I was the only one who could ever get through to him but when he became involved with these people, I realized that I was too late as well. They run brothels, strip clubs with underage girls working at them, prostitution and human trafficking rings. If sex is involved, they have their hands in all of it."

A thought came to me. "Price Davies."

The stranger laughed. "Yeah, we won't even talk about him. That bastard disappeared and went so deep underground, I'm having a hard time finding him."

I grunted. "You and me both."

"But I have a feeling that he'll slip up and reveal his location eventually. Word has it that he's working with someone. Here." The man pulled out his wallet from his jeans pocket and handed me a card. "If you want validation that what I'm saying is the truth, call Rowan and Jaron." He spun on his heel and began walking away from me.

"Wait. Who are you?"

The man looked at me over his shoulder. "The less you know, the better," was all he said before he continued walking down the hall. When he disappeared around the corner, I finally looked down at the business card in my hand.

Three crowns, in gold embossed print, sat on the front, and a phone number sat on the back. I sighed, still confused as ever but put the card away.

While I walked to where my brother and the prospects stood outside Ainsley's door, I called Rowan.

"Yeah."

"I need some reassurance that I didn't just get fucked up the ass by a stranger."

"On it." I could hear the clicking of keys in the background. "Lay it on me, big guy."

I gave Rowan all of the information the stranger gave me. Even though it wasn't much to go on, the fact that he ended a life who almost took Ainsley from me, said more than words ever could. But a part of me wondered if this guy wouldn't come collecting some form of payment when I least expected it.

(Ainsley)

For the second time in who knew how long, I shifted in the bed I was lying on, slowly opening my eyes. The fluorescent lighting burned as I tried blinking through it.

"There she is."

My vision cleared, only to be met by the darkest eyes I had ever seen. It had felt like just yesterday that I had fallen in love with them.

Cyrus pushed my hair off my forehead. "Hi."

I swallowed hard, cleared my throat, and gave him a small smile. "Hi."

"How are you feeling?" he asked gently.

I quickly did a mental scan of my body. When I didn't feel any pain, I let out a sigh of relief. "Numb."

"They gave you some pain meds to make you comfortable." He pulled the chair up to my bed trying to get closer, but I knew that with a guy like him, even if he was inside me, it wouldn't be close enough.

"What happened?" I asked, running my fingers through his dark beard. It had grown in some and lines sat at the corners of his eyes. He looked like he had aged years in only a matter of days.

"You were brought in for an ultrasound and ended up needing another surgery."

My stomach twisted over what I had done. "How...is he..."

"He's dead, baby."

My eyes widened. "I killed him."

"No." Cyrus kissed my forehead. "Someone else did."

I stared up at him. "You didn't..."

"No, I didn't." He leaned his forehead against mine. "But I wanted to. I met someone who knew him and who also knew you. He's the one who killed him. I was just there, watching it happen."

"I don't understand."

"I confirmed with a friend that the information this guy gave me, was accurate. I trust this friend with my life, so I believe him." Cyrus's jaw clenched as he thought a moment. "The guy who attacked you—"

"He was the one who stabbed me too," I said, not remembering if I had already told Cyrus that or not.

"I know." Cyrus pulled away from me.

"No." I reached for him. "Please, I need you here."

He stood and sat on the edge of the bed.

I shifted my weight over, giving him some room to lay down beside me.

He laid down, curled on his side, and brushed his thumb down the length of my jaw. "The guy I met tonight knew your attacker. He's the one who killed him. He also said that he was there during the raid."

My eyes widened.

"He said that he helped you escape. He's older, heavily tattooed and has some piercings." Cyrus waited. "Do you remember anyone looking like that?"

"I..." I tried wracking my brain for those memories when suddenly, something hit me.

"I'm going to help you," the older man said gently. "I know you don't trust men right now, but I need you to trust me. Can you do that, sweetheart?"

I didn't have much to go on when it came to this stranger, but he couldn't have been worse than who I had dealt with for the past several years.

I only nodded which earned me a small smile.

"Let's get you out of here." The man wrapped his arm around my shoulders and led me to an ambulance.

Once the EMT helped me into the back of the vehicle, the man had disappeared. I wanted to ask who he was or where he went but the words were stuck on my tongue. I could only hope that I would see him again, so I could thank him.

"I feel like my mind was playing tricks on me. I didn't recognize the guy who attacked me either. Not at first. But when he started talking and saying awful things, it was like these memories came flooding back and I couldn't stop them." A shaky breath left me. Even though he was gone, I couldn't control the fear rippling over my skin.

"You don't have to worry about it anymore, pet," Cyrus said gently.

"I remember someone helping me to an ambulance after the raid. I never got a chance to thank him." I sat up higher on the bed. "I wish I could."

"You don't need to thank me, sweetheart."

Cyrus shot up in the bed.

My head snapped to an older man standing at the entrance to the room.

"I can't stay long but I needed to see for myself that you're fine." He came toward us, holding a teddy bear in his hand. "This is for you. I know it's not much but I'm happy to see that you're doing better."

"Thank you," I whispered, taking the teddy bear from him.

"I thought you left," Cyrus said, covering my hand that was resting on the bed between us.

"I was going to, but my wife likes to remind me that it's good for me to see the survivors years later and how they're doing." The stranger nodded once. "Clearly, you're doing well."

I looked at Cyrus. "Because of him."

Cyrus brought my hand up to his mouth, kissing my knuckles.

I smiled, looking back at the stranger. "And because of you. Thank you."

The stranger nodded, backing up. "I have to go. I'm happy that you're doing better. Oh and one more thing…" He slowly grinned. "You never saw me." Before either of us could ask what he meant by that, he left the room.

"Did you ever get his name?" I asked, staring after the mysterious man and holding the teddy bear against my chest.

"No." Cyrus kissed my temple. "But you're safe now, pet."

"I remember the police coming in that night. I think a lot of us were more scared of them than the men who had abused us for years. A lot of us were terrified that we would end up in jail even though we were victims. I woke up in the hospital, but I don't remember much after that. I was told I had been drugged. So maybe that's why I don't remember much of him. I don't know. I'm sorry I can't tell you more or even that man's name. He never gave it to me as far as I know."

"That's okay, pet. I just want you to know that you're safe. It's over."

"Is it though?" I asked gently. "There's more of them out there. Even ones who had nothing to do with the place I was kept at. It's always happening, Cyrus."

"I know and there's no way we can stop it all, but people are trying. That's all anyone can do."

I sighed, laying back down and staring up at the white ceiling. He was right but it didn't mean I liked it.

"This bastard won't hurt you or anyone else ever again. I'll take you to the clubhouse. The security is top notch there." Cyrus cupped my chin, turning my head toward him. "And whenever you're ready, we can find a place of our own. But I'll make sure that the security is the best there too. I'll get you your own security detail if I have to."

A laugh escaped me.

His brows narrowed. "I'm serious."

"I know." And I did know because Cyrus didn't mess around. Not with me. Not with his feelings. Not with his family.

Not with life. When he wanted something, he went for it. Me included.

While Cyrus murmured sweet words, I couldn't help but wonder if he was right and this was actually over. One guy was taken out but there were so many others out there.

"You can't worry about them," Cyrus told me a few hours later.

"You don't know what I'm thinking or what I'm worrying about," I threw back at him.

"Yeah, I do because I know you."

I huffed, pushing away from him. "Help me to the bathroom." I looked back at him over my shoulder. "Please."

He slid off the bed and came around to my side. He kissed the top of my head before reaching for my hands. "I got you, pet."

I knew he did, and I should have been elated that I wouldn't have to worry about that guy coming after me again, but the relief was never there. I wasn't sure what was wrong with me.

After Cyrus helped me to the bathroom, he wouldn't leave and give me any privacy.

"I can do this next part myself," I grumbled.

He chuckled. "I know you can but I'm still not leaving you."

I huffed again, went about my business and was washing my hands when I glanced at Cyrus in the reflection of the mirror.

His jaw was clenched, that familiar tick by his ear, beating in tune with my heart.

"What is it?" I asked, my stomach flipping at the mere intensity rolling off of him.

His eyes snapped to mine. "I wish I would have killed him myself."

"I wish you wouldn't have stopped me and let *me* kill him," I blurted, my eyes widening at my confession.

"Thank you," Cyrus said gently.

"For what?" I dried my hands, unsure as to where this conversation was about to go.

"For not making me feel like a monster."

My heart stuttered at Cyrus's soft words.

I finished drying my hands and went up to him. Wrapping my arms around his middle, I leaned my head against his chest. "Thank you for not making me feel like one too."

"Never." He cupped my nape, kissed the top of my head, and led me out of the bathroom.

As he was helping me back into the bed, a male cop and a woman dressed in a suit, entered the room.

"We're sorry for interrupting," the woman said. "I'm Detective Baldwin and this is Officer Jaxon. We'll make this quick, so you can get your rest."

Cyrus looked down at me. "I can translate."

I took a deep breath, shaking my head. "I'm fine."

He kissed my cheek. "I'm so fucking proud of you."

Little did he know, it was all him. He helped me find this strength to speak again. "Please," I said softly. "Ask whatever it is you need to."

TWENTY-EIGHT

CYRUS

LISTENING TO AINSLEY TELL Officer Jaxon and Detective Baldwin everything that had happened, was surreal. The fact that she was actually speaking and not signing, hit a part of me that had never been reached. I was beyond proud of her and her growth over these past few months. Our relationship came on strong and fast, but I fell in love with her even more in that single moment. As each word left her lips, I wanted to kiss her and swallow each and every syllable, keeping it safe within my clutches.

"Cyrus."

My head snapped up, finding three pairs of eyes staring back at me. "Sorry, what did you say?"

Ainsley only smiled, her cheeks turning a beautiful light shade of pink.

"I had asked if you saw what happened to..." Detective Baldwin looked down at her notepad. "Mr. Smith." She frowned. "Why do I feel like that's a fake name?"

"Because it probably is," Officer Jaxon said, coming up beside her and grabbing the notepad from her hands. "Looks like you've been busy."

"Give that back to me, ass—I mean..." She cleared her throat. "Sorry." She ripped it from his clutches and glared at him.

He chuckled. "It's been a long week." He looked between us two, the humor no longer there. "So, Cyrus. Did you see what happened to him?"

"Nope. I was waiting for Ainsley to come out of her second surgery," I told him, the lie slipping easily off my tongue.

"So if we checked the security footage, we wouldn't see you heading into his room," Detective Baldwin added.

"Like I said, I was waiting for Ainsley," I told her, remembering the stranger telling me about the security footage being taken care of. Looked like Rowan had been busy himself.

"Alright." Detective Baldwin sighed. "Listen, I'm glad you're okay and that you survived that hell and what you went through," she told Ainsley. "I did some digging and found out that most of the people who escaped, were survivors like yourself. Any of them who were the captors or who had a part in taking you all, are either dead or locked up already. I'm sure you already know this as well, but Price Davies had a hand in this. It seems the old mayor of our wonderful town just doesn't care anymore and figures if he can't make his money the legal way, he'll resort to illegal dealings."

I grunted. "Has he ever cared? The bastard has underage girls working at his clubs."

Detective Baldwin stared at me. "How do you know about that?"

Officer Jaxon placed a hand on her shoulder. "He's a biker, Jess. They probably know more things about Price and his whereabouts than we do."

"Is that true?" Detective Baldwin asked me.

"I have no idea what you're talking about." There was no way that I would have this conversation here.

"Alright." She shook her head. "It doesn't matter. We're still searching for Price."

"I don't give a shit about him." I did but they didn't need to know that. "As long as my girl…" I caught Ainsley's gaze then. "As long as you are safe, that's all I care about."

She nodded.

"If you notice anything at all or can think of any more information, please don't hesitate to call either of us," Office Jaxon added.

"Okay, thank you." Ainsley snuggled into my side, a yawn trembling through her.

"We'll let you be." Officer Jaxon looked at me. "Can we talk?"

I nodded, kissing the top of Ainsley's head. "I'll be right back."

"Okay," she whispered.

Pulling out from behind her, I followed both Andy and Jessica out into the hall, making sure to stay close to the entrance of Ainsley's room.

"I need to ask…" Andy paused. "You didn't see anything at all."

"That's not a question," I told him. "But no, I didn't see anything."

"Andy, it's sorted," Detective Baldwin told him. "Ainsley was defending herself."

"I get that, Jess, but this…someone her size stabbing the bastard in the eye wouldn't kill him. Just cause a lot of damage. So something or someone else did." He looked at me then. "That's all I'm saying."

"I guess you'll have to wait for the coroner to give you that information, but I will tell you now that whatever or whomever caused his death, has nothing to do with Ainsley or me." I turned and took a step back into Ainsley's room. "I need to take my girl home after she rests." I looked between both of them. "If there's nothing else."

"No." Detective Baldwin placed a hand on Andy's arm. "Let's go."

He huffed, letting her lead him away and back down the hall from where they had come from. I watched as she looked up at him. He scowled while shaking his head, but wrapped an arm around her shoulders, pulling her into his side. It was like I could actually see the tension leaving her body, knowing exactly how that felt. To have that person who could touch you and make everything awful in your life better. Even if it was just for a moment.

"Cyrus."

My head whipped around, finding Sammy coming toward me.

"How's she doing?" he asked, nodding to the room I was about to enter.

"She's resting but I hope to bring her home soon. Where's Cheesy and Locke?"

"I sent them home." Sammy held up his phone, showing me a picture. "Piper had the baby."

My heart swelled for the love coming from the image of Piper staring down at her newborn.

"It's a boy," Sammy said, pulling the phone back and swiping his thumb across the screen. "His name is Maximus Jaron Mercer but apparently they're calling him JJ for short because he looks like Jaron did as a baby."

"I'm happy for them." If anyone deserved some sort of happiness, it was those two.

"I'm heading up to see them and wanted to check if you wanted to come with but..." Sammy shoved his phone back in his pocket. "I imagine you want to stay here with Mouse."

I nodded. "Yeah, I do. After what happened, I just...I can't leave her again."

"I get it." Sammy came up to me and pulled me into a hug. "I'm happy for you too, brother."

I squeezed him, hugging maybe a little too long. Definitely longer than we had in quite a while. "I love you, Sammy."

"I love you too." He pulled away from me. "I want to go see Mom and Dad."

My eyes widened, my chest tightening. He hadn't wanted to visit their graves in years. "Why now?"

"I don't know. I..." He ran a hand over the back of his neck. "I found a letter from Mom. It was in my sock drawer. I forgot I had it."

Eve gave it to us to read a couple of years ago but neither of us had the courage to do so. "We'll read it together," I told him.

"Go take care of your girl. I'll see you at the clubhouse." He walked past me, gave my shoulder a squeeze, and disappeared down the hall.

Taking a deep breath, I went back into Ainsley's room, needing her in my arms.

Her eyes slowly opened, landing on me as I neared her. I realized then that she was where I belonged. With her at my side. Sometimes at my feet if she allowed it and in my life. Definitely in my life.

"Hey," she whispered as I neared her.

I sat on the edge of the bed and leaned over her, crushing my mouth to hers. The kiss deepened. Although it bordered on inappropriate at best, it still pulled those sexy little sounds from the back of her throat.

I broke the kiss, giving her swollen lips a final peck before leaning back. "Hi."

"What was that for?" she asked, breathless.

"Just my little way of letting you know that I love you, and appreciate you, and am so damn proud of you." My heart thumped harder the wider her smile became.

"I already know all of that."

"Good." I kissed her nose. "Just making sure."

She giggled, her eyes shining. "Take me home. Please, Cyrus. I need your bed."

My body stirred at the mere idea of having her beneath my sheets when no other woman had ever had the pleasure of being there.

"You need your rest," I corrected her.

"Yeah, I do, and I can rest in your bed." She sat up, wincing at the movement, but made no complaints about the pain. "Please." She licked her lips. "Sir."

My dick jumped. "I have a surprise for you," I bit out, my voice rough.

"You do?"

"Yeah." I laid her back. "And when the doctors say you can leave, I'll give it to you then."

Ainsley pouted. "Do I really have to wait that long?"

I chuckled. "Actually, I'll give it to you when you're naked beneath my sheets."

She sighed. "Fine. I guess I can wait." She grabbed my hand, pulling me toward her. "Lay with me?"

"You don't have to ask me twice, pet." And she didn't.

TWENTY-NINE

Ainsley

I WAS FINALLY GOING home. It had been almost two weeks since I was stabbed and then attacked again by the same guy who was now dead. A part of me wondered if I should have felt some sort of remorse but I didn't. Knowing what the guy had done, not only to me but to others as well, I didn't feel sorry for him at all.

While Cyrus helped me gather the few items I had, I was practically vibrating with excitement.

"I can see you bouncing over there, pet," he laughed.

I went up to him and wrapped my arms around him from the side. "I'm exhausted. Sleeping in a hospital is damn near impossible. I need your bed."

Cyrus kissed me hard on the mouth. "Our bed," he said with a growl.

I shivered, pulling away before I got caught climbing him. I had to take it easy, which helped when it came to someone like Cyrus. He was patient. Way more patient than I ever was.

Especially now that he had told me he had a present for me. I tried getting him to tell me what it was, but he insisted on waiting and said it would mean more if he could show me.

"Are you sure it's okay for me to move into your room with you?" I asked Cyrus when we were finally in his SUV. I rolled down the window a couple of inches, breathing in the fresh scent of the mid-afternoon air.

"It is. I already talked to Greyson." Cyrus started up the beast of a vehicle and cupped my inner thigh. "Not many people live there, even though there's enough space. Greyson and Eve live in the back part of the house. Tray and Zillah have their own home but also a room at the clubhouse for whenever they're in the area. Same with Catch and Sara. Sammy and I have part of the basement but finally moved into our own rooms. He had that done up while you were in the hospital."

"I look forward to meeting everyone." And I did. Even though I was nervous about meeting new people, especially with my aversion to talking, but being with Cyrus helped me with that fear. Not completely but it was definitely better than before.

"I know they look forward to meeting you as well, but I need you to get your rest, so you can get stronger."

"Do you think we can stop by my apartment first?"

"Actually." He pulled his phone out of the inside of his leather cut. "Text Cheesy and ask him to grab anything you want. He and Locke are going to rent the apartment. They already talked to the ladies who run the center about it."

"Really? But I thought it was for victims of abuse, human trafficking and things like that, only."

Cyrus glanced my way. "It seems Locke fits the criteria."

"Oh." My stomach fell. "That's sad."

"It is, pet." He squeezed my thigh. "But don't worry about that. I'll get you sorted."

We drove the rest of the way to the clubhouse in a comfortable silence. I still couldn't believe I was moving in with him. I had been excited before but after getting attacked, twice, I thought maybe it wasn't meant to be.

"Ainsley?"

I glanced at Cyrus but not before I saw a large house off in the distance. "Yeah?"

"There's somewhere I want to take you. In time. I know you don't do well in large crowds or I'm assuming you don't anyway. You were fine at the library that I took you to, but I imagine it's because you were in your element. Am I right?"

"You are," I said, wondering what he was getting at and why he wouldn't look at me.

As the large house neared, Cyrus's hand on my thigh tightened. "I..."

"Pull over," I told him.

"What?" He looked at me then.

"Pull over and tell me what it is you want to tell me or ask me. If there's something you need to ask me, do it while it's just the two of us."

Cyrus did as I suggested and pulled the SUV off to the side of the road. He turned on the hazards, put the car into park, and leaned his arm on top of the steering wheel. "I never thought I would fall in love. Ever. Sammy and I joked when we were kids that it would just be us two and we would have sex with random women for the rest of our lives and that was it. It was a shitty thing to think and made us sound like assholes but it's how it was for the longest time." He looked at me then. "Until I met you. But even before I met you, I realized that sex wasn't casual for a lot of women like they made it out to be. Some were clingy and made it hard to end things. I don't have a psycho ex or anyone you have to worry about though." He scrubbed a hand down his face. "I'm rambling."

I grabbed his hand, bringing it up to my mouth. "You're nervous. Don't be. Not with me. Never with me, Cyrus."

"I want you to know that everything we do is consensual. If you don't want to do something, if you don't even want to try it, we won't. If we do something and you're not feeling it, we'll talk about it. If there's something that you absolutely refuse to try, we won't even talk about it and skip right over it." He paused, waiting for me to comment, but when I didn't because I was curious as to where this was going, he inhaled a deep breath. "I love you and I realized it when I thought I'd lost you. I can't live without you."

My eyes widened. "Cyrus."

"I'm not proposing but I am making a promise to you." He reached across the center console and opened the glove compartment in the dashboard. "I was going to wait until I had you in my bed but I'm sure Greyson is going to have questions. He'll want to make sure that you are in fact safe." Cyrus pulled out a black velvet bag and placed it on my lap. "If you don't know what this is, let me know and I'll explain."

I opened the bag, chewing my bottom lip in anticipation. I pulled out a dark purple leather case. Pulling it open, my eyes widened. "Cyrus," I gasped. "It's...I...wow..." The item laying on beige leather, looked to be a necklace but something told me that it wasn't. A fairly thick gold chain sparkled. It had a diamond encrusted heart-shaped pendant with a gold key sitting off to the side in its own case.

"Do you know what it is?"

"I was going to say a necklace, but it looks too short to be one."

"It's a collar. This..." He pinched the heart pendant between his fingers and lifted it. "Is a lock and this key is the only one that can open it."

"It's your key. A key to my heart?" I asked, my voice shaking.

"Yes, pet," he said softly. "I love you and I know you weren't introduced to the BDSM lifestyle the right way, but I live it and I want to have you living it with me."

"I started reading romance books and the BDSM scenes I've read in them are nothing like I experienced, but I trust you." I cupped his face. "You saved me, Cyrus. You saved me from falling completely within myself. You helped me get my voice back."

"No." He covered my hand that was cupping his cheek. "You saved yourself. I was just there cheering you on."

"I love you, Cyrus, and yes, I promise. I promise that you have my heart and I promise that I want to spend my life with you. I can't have kids, but I want to do whatever we can to have a family of our own. Even if it's by adopting animals." I pulled the collar from its clasp and handed it to him. "Will you put it on me?"

"Really? Right now?" he asked, his voice thick.

I reached up and cupped his nape, pulling him down to my mouth. "I want your collar around my throat, Sir."

"Fuck." A shiver trembled through him. "I never thought those words would sound so damn hot."

I laughed, turned around, and moved my hair off the back of my neck. "Please."

His dark eyes met mine, a slow grin spreading on his face. He put the key in the hole at the base of the heart and unlocked it. When he had it around my throat, he kissed the spot behind my ear. "This is my promise to you that I will love and cherish you, protect you and help you whenever you need it. I will stand by when you don't need my help and cheer you on. Your voice is mine, and my voice is yours. I will love you until my last breath and beyond that."

My eyes welled at his sweet words. Words that I never thought I would ever hear from anyone.

Once the heart sat at the base of my throat, I turned around.

Cyrus took the small key and locked it, his eyes snapping to mine once the click sounded around us. "You okay?"

I nodded quickly, wiping the tears from my cheeks.

He put the key in his wallet. When he put it away, I was on him.

(Cyrus)

I wasn't expecting her to jump into my arms. With the surgery, two of them in fact, she was still weak and needed to take it easy, but that fierce little sex kitten in her, ignored it all. Her mouth slammed down hard on mine. Her fingers ran through the back of my hair, deepening the kiss, sucking a groan from somewhere deep within my soul. My dick twitched, lengthening the longer we went without being inside her.

"Pet," I murmured against her lips, running my hands down her back.

She ignored me, slipping her tongue into my mouth.

A growl escaped me but as much as I wanted to continue this, this wouldn't be happening in a car and she needed time to heal.

"Hey." I broke the kiss, fisting her hair and holding her head in place when she tried pushing out of my grip. "Baby, as much as I love having your mouth on mine, you need to take it easy."

"I need you," she whispered, licking her swollen mouth.

"Let me take you home and put you in my bed then." I helped her back onto her seat.

She pouted.

I chuckled, running my thumb along her bottom lip. "I'm happy to see this little kitten again."

Her smile widened. "Me too." She kissed the pad of my thumb. "Take me home, my love."

Every cell in my body tingled at the new term of endearment coming from her. Blowing out a slow breath, I sat back, put the SUV into gear, and drove the final distance to the clubhouse.

"It looks so quiet." Ainsley sat forward. "Do you think anyone is home?"

"There should be people home." I pulled the SUV into the large driveway.

Once I had the vehicle parked and the engine off, I turned to Ainsley.

She was looking out the window at the large house sitting in front of us and rubbing the heart-shaped lock between her fingers.

"Hey." I squeezed her inner thigh. "You good?"

She looked at me then, her eyes welling. "I am. I'm very good."

"Why the tears, pet?"

She laughed, wiping under her eyes. "I never thought I'd find happiness. I never thought I'd find someone like you, Cyrus." She turned her body toward me, giving me her full attention. "You are the most patient man I've ever met. I know you lost your parents at a young age, but they did something right with raising you. And then your other family, they raised you well too."

My tongue became thick at the sudden emotion coursing through me. "I remember when I was a kid how my dad would do whatever he could to make my mom smile. Even when she was pissed at him. They constantly flirted, touched, kissed, and so on. They acted like they were dating even though they had been married for years already at that point." I rubbed my chest, trying to ease away the ache of them no longer being here. "I miss them. More and more every day. And I know my mom would have loved you. She would fawn over you and tell you how beautiful you are. My dad would love you too, but he wasn't a man of many words. Not when it came to anyone else but my mom."

"He was the strong, silent type," Ainsley added. "Like you."

"Yeah." I smiled. "Like me."

A bike took that moment to pull into the driveway. I recognized it instantly as Sammy's beautiful machine.

"Let's go," I told Ainsley. "We can get you settled, and I'll get the guys to go to your apartment later and grab the rest of your things before they move in."

She nodded, opening the passenger door.

I went around to her side of the vehicle and slid my hand down her arm.

She shivered, smiling up at me. There was a hint of something behind her eyes. Something intense. Something that wanted more. I would give it to her. Whatever she wanted. She wouldn't have to worry ever again.

"How are you feeling?" Sammy asked, coming up from behind us.

"Sore but getting there." Ainsley stepped into my side, wrapping her arm around my lower back. "I just want to sleep for days."

Sammy nodded, pulling his smokes from the inside of his leather cut. "I feel that."

Ainsley fingered her collar, a notable shiver trembling through her.

Sammy caught the movement, his eyes flicking back to mine. He raised an eyebrow.

I winked.

He chuckled. "It's about damn time."

I grunted. "Could say the same for you, brother."

He scoffed.

I cupped his nape, pulling him against me. "It'll happen."

"Don't worry about me, Cyrus." He returned the embrace, giving me a quick hug before pulling away. He stuck his smoke between his lips and headed toward the house.

"Greyson will kick your ass if you smoke inside," I reminded him.

"Probably," he yelled back but headed into the house anyway.

"Is everything okay?" Ainsley asked softly, pulling me back to her.

"Yeah, pet." I cupped her face, kissing her hard. "You're safe. You're wearing my collar. You promised to spend the rest of your life with me. And I'm about to put you in my bed. So yeah, things are definitely okay."

"You sure no more shit will be brought to my doorstep?" Greyson was pacing back and forth in the room where most meetings were held. Anything having to do with MC business had been few and far between over the past few weeks while Jaron and Piper were getting ready for their new little one. I could have held the meetings myself, but we all needed a break, so Jaron never instructed me to do so.

"Yes." I kept Ainsley's hand firmly in mine. "That bastard is dead, and the authorities are keeping an eye out on if they hear anything new or are given any additional information."

Greyson grunted. "You know they can't be trusted."

I glanced at Ainsley before looking back at the man who had raised both my brother and I. "Detective Baldwin and Officer Jaxon aren't under Price's thumb." We hadn't heard from the man who had tried to destroy Jaron and Piper's life so many months ago. I wasn't sure if that was for the better or for worse.

"And you know this how?" Greyson asked, stopping in his tracks.

"I just do and if anything happens, I'll take the blame but right now, I just need to get Ainsley settled. She needs her rest." And I needed to make love to her before she vibrated out of her skin.

"Fine." Greyson looked between us both. "Ainsley, you're welcome to stay here for as long as you need but if I know Cyrus, he'll be finding you a house soon enough that you both can move into."

I leaned over and kissed her temple. "He knows me well."

"Thank you," she whispered, her eyes shining.

"Of course. I'll keep the guys in the loop and contact a few people I know. We will find Price again before he tries to destroy any more lives," Greyson said, his voice rough.

Leading Ainsley out of the meeting room, I turned to Greyson. "Thank you," I told him. "I don't say it enough, but I really appreciate everything you've done for me and Sam."

"You don't have to thank me." Greyson cupped my shoulders. "And it wasn't just me. It was Eve. It was Tray and Catch. It was their wives. It was all of us. Eve and I couldn't have any more children after Jaron but having you two in our lives, made up for that additional loss. My wife wanted more kids and was hurting because of it. So I should be thanking *you* for putting a smile on my wife's face again." He pulled me into his arms, holding me a little longer than usual. Greyson wasn't a hugger, so I would savor this moment.

"Thank you," I repeated, returning the hug.

"Go take care of your girl." He released me and made his way to the side of the house he shared with his wife.

"Cyrus." Ainsley's soft voice pulled me right into her arms. "I need you," she whispered into the crook of my neck.

Grabbing her hand, I quickly led her down into the basement. I would show her the house later but right now, I really needed to give her a tour of every inch of my cock.

Once we were in my bedroom that was now hers as well, I kicked the door closed and had her in my arms.

"Make love to me," she whispered, kissing my jaw. She fisted my hoodie, pulling me closer.

"I'm scared I'll hurt you." I cupped her ass, pushing her back until she hit the edge of the bed.

"You won't." She laid on the bed and began stripping. When she was fully naked, my eyes dropped to the bandage at her side. "Please, Cyrus. I need you."

Stripping out of my own clothes, I crawled onto the bed between her legs. "We should go slowly."

"No." She wrapped her hands around me, pumping hard, fast, and pulling me toward the spot I wanted to be forever. "We can go slow later. I just need a release. Please, Sir."

Letting her guide me to her sweet pussy, I slowly lowered into her.

A sigh trembled through us both at feeling that connection once again between us.

Reaching up, I wrapped my hand around her throat, running my thumb along the gold collar. It was the only thing she was wearing while the rest of her was completely bare for me.

"I love you," I grunted, thrusting slow and deep.

"I love you, Cyrus." Her hands trailed down my back, cupping my ass and pulling me forward.

I stopped, staring down at her. "Marry me."

"I'm wearing your collar." A cheeky grin spread on her face. "Do you even have to ask me?"

I tilted my head, raising an eyebrow. "Is that a yes, pet?"

Ainsley tapped her mouth.

Lowering my lips to hers, I breathed her in and swallowed her *yes*.

THIRTY

CYRUS

MY BABY BOYS,

If you're reading this, I'm obviously no longer around. I know it's morbid, but I needed to write this letter just in case. With the line of work your father is in, I knew it could happen.

So first, I just want to say how sorry I am that we left you. I had your dad read this. He thought I was crazy and said that we would always be around forever and ever, but I convinced him to look at it realistically. People die. It happens. I'm just sorry that it happened to us.

I never told anyone about this letter. Just him. But I know that someone will come across this one day and give it to you when you're ready. If you're reading this, clearly, that time is now.

My first regret is not showing you both how much we love you. You were definitely a surprise, but know that your father and I loved you endlessly. Even as boys, you're both strong in your own way.

Sammy, your humor and your smiles are contagious. I joked around with your dad once, saying that you were going to grow up to be a comedian.

J.M. WALKER

He was having none of that. He said that his boys would join Hell's Harlem much like their daddy.

I couldn't agree more but still liked to poke the bear anyway.

Cyrus, you're quiet but you listen. You're also a stubborn little boy. Or man, I guess you would be now. It's so weird, writing this, thinking how both of you are hopefully married at this point. Happy. Fathers. And more. So much more.

I want you to have everything that life has to offer you.

But what I want most of all is for you to be there for each other. You're brothers but you're also best friends. Be that until the very end. Never let a woman come between you. Never let the club come between you.

You are brothers first. Always.

I placed the letter back in the envelope and handed it to Sammy.

A shuddered breath left him. "It feels like just yesterday that we lost them."

"I know." We stood shoulder to shoulder, staring down at our parents' headstone. Two months had passed since Ainsley was stabbed. Sammy never pushed to visit Mom and Dad's graves, but I knew he needed it. So after leaving Ainsley in my bed, I called up my brother and we spent the morning together. We hadn't hung out just the two of us in months, so I knew that we both needed this. Some brother time.

"How's Mouse doing?" Sammy asked, changing the subject because he was feeling uncomfortable. I knew because I felt it too. We didn't like talking about how much it hurt to lose our mom and dad because, well, it fucking hurt. They were taken from us far too soon, but I also knew that we weren't the only ones hurting. Every time the crew who had known our parents, saw us, you could see the pain in their eyes because we both looked like our dad.

"She's doing well but she wouldn't want you worrying about her." It was one of the things I loved about Ainsley. She and Sammy became close quickly. He now referred to her as 'Sis' and I couldn't be happier that they were getting along.

"I know." He pulled the smoke from behind his ear and stuck it between his lips. "Red and I started...well...you know."

I glanced at him. "Good."

He nodded once. "It's very good. Only woman I've ever met who can handle my mood swings."

"Poor thing." I playfully nudged him in the shoulder.

"She likes it and I like when she calls me out on my shit. She's a brat and I love that even more." A hint of amusement flashed in his dark eyes. "Anyway, thank you for this morning. And please thank your girl for me."

"I will."

He nodded again, kissed the tips of his fingers and touched the top of the headstone that had our parents' names on them. "I love you, Mama and Pop. I hope to one day have a love as strong as yours. Maybe it'll be with Red like I'm hoping."

A lump formed in my throat, never hearing my brother talk about love at all. I knew he loved me and our extended family, but he never mentioned love once when it came to the women he was with.

"I'm gonna head out of town for a bit," he said, walking past me.

"Drive safe, brother." I shoved my hands in my pockets, staring down at the headstone. "I miss you. Both of you," I muttered.

A gust of wind suddenly billowed around me, sending up a pile of leaves and flower petals. I didn't overly believe in life after death and was definitely not a religious person, but I did believe in signs. I also believed in fate.

Ainsley thanked me often for saving her, when really, she saved me. No, she *rescued* me.

From myself.

From the pain and constant agony of losing our parents far too soon.

Because of her, my beautiful fiancée and sub, I could take a step forward and finally live a life my parents would be proud of.

EPILOGUE

Ainsley

EYES DOWN.

Palms up.

Breathe.

Don't make eye contact unless I'm told to.

Don't utter a single word unless I'm asked to speak.

Do as you're told unless I was feeling uncomfortable or needed to talk about it.

Breathe.

Don't talk back.

Smile.

"Color, pet?" Cyrus whispered in my ear, his lips brushing back and forth over my earlobe, sending a shiver down my spine.

"Green, Sir," I breathed.

"Good girl, thank you for telling me." He sat back in the armchair, the sound of ice clinking against glass, sending a shiver down my spine.

I was kneeling at Cyrus's feet in the living room of our home. Home. I still couldn't believe that we had bought a house together. After being together for a while, we purchased a home and were getting married in the next couple of months. Wedding plans were coming along nicely but that was only because I had people to help me. I met Cyrus's cousin Bee Horsch. She was married and had a son of her own and I fell in love with him instantly.

Everyone had been kind and I couldn't be more thankful for the life and family Cyrus had given me.

One Friday night, we were watching a movie. I was kneeling on the floor between Cyrus's knees, with my hand under his pant leg and my fingers wrapped around his shin.

"How's the pain?" he asked, pulling me from my thoughts.

"Manageable," I told him honestly. A gold chain was wrapped around my neck with two long strands that fell down my torso. It had clamps attached to it that pinched both of my nipples, along with my clit. It had been custom-made much like the gold collar that was locked around my throat.

Cyrus reached around to the back of my neck, pulling until a sharp gasp left me. The slice of delicious pain erupted through me, sending a wave of heat licking over my skin.

"Better?" he asked, his voice low.

"Yes," I breathed.

"Good." He leaned back once again but kept his hand at my nape. His fingers ran back and forth, reminding me with each and every small movement that this was where I belonged. With him. On the floor. At his feet.

I had learned over time that Cyrus meant what he said when he lived the BDSM lifestyle. He just never enforced it until he met me. We spent each and every day learning things about each other. What we liked and didn't like.

We had gone to a BDSM club a few times over the past several months, but I liked the privacy of our home better.

RESCUE US

"In time, I want to be your Master," Cyrus told me, placing a soft peck on my mouth. "We don't have to live it twenty-four seven, but I do want you to be my slave. Even if it's just for one weekend a month."

I looked up at him then, my heart thumping rapidly. "Yes, I want that too."

We did what he suggested and spent one weekend a month, living the Master and slave dynamic. Cyrus would make every decision for me from Friday evening once I got home from work. As soon as my first sip of coffee touched my lips on Monday morning, things would go back to how they were the rest of the month.

No one knew about the lifestyle we lived, except for Sammy. I had learned by accident that he lived it as well when we had gone to a club and one of the submissives asked about him. I also learned that he wasn't quite as gentle as Cyrus was and had his own set of kinks that I was sure would make some submissive happy one day.

"Eyes on me, pet," Cyrus demanded gently, pulling me from my thoughts.

I met his gaze.

"You good?" he asked, pulling a piece of ice from the glass tumbler in his hand.

I nodded. "Yes, Sir."

"Good." He ran the ice along my bottom lip.

The cold feeling sent a shiver through every inch of me. My knees spread of their own accord, my body swaying toward him.

His lips pulled up into a grin. "So responsive."

"For you, Sir."

"Always for me, pet." He pushed the piece of ice between my lips, lowering his mouth to mine, the ice melting between us.

Later that night, we were lying in bed, playing one of my video games. Even though I hadn't needed to play them in a while, it was nice having this little moment with Cyrus. Especially since it was one of the things that started our relationship back in the beginning.

Cyrus had taken the clamps off of me only to put them back on hours later. He had been gentle in the way he first removed them, kissing and touching me while I breathed through the delicious pain. But now that they were once again pinching parts of my body, I was thankful for the earlier reprieve. The slight burn was distracting me from kicking his ass like I usually did whenever we played one of my racing games.

He placed the controller on the nightstand, pulled me back against him, and wrapped his arms around my middle while I continued playing. When his lips found the side of my neck, my breath caught and my car on the screen, crashed into a wall.

Cyrus chuckled, the sound vibrating against me. "Keep playing, pet." He cupped my inner thighs, pulling my legs over his.

"Sir, I can't play like this." My breathing picked up at feeling his hands on my naked body.

"You can and you're going to." His hands slid up my inner thighs. When his fingers came into contact with the clamp pinching my clit, a spark of pleasure slammed into me.

"Oh...my..."

"I'll remove the clamp soon and then give you a break until the next weekend we do this but first, I want you to embrace the pain," he murmured in my ear. While some of the nerve endings in my clit were damaged, we had found different ways for me to feel pleasure in that part of my body.

I chewed my bottom lip to keep from crying out as Cyrus flicked the clamp lightly. He had been teaching me that pleasure and pain could go hand in hand when it was with the right person.

"Keep playing, pet," he demanded, wrapping his other hand around my throat. With his fingers that were still between my legs, he tugged at the clamp until my hips were writhing back and forth.

A moan escaped me, spots dancing in my vision. The controller fell from my hand, landing on the floor with a thud.

"That's it, baby." He kissed my temple, still pushing and prodding at that clamp.

I gripped the blankets on either side of us and began moving my hips in tune with his fingers.

Just when I thought a release was coming, he pulled the clamp off of my clit. The sudden rush of blood flowing to that spot, forced a scream from my lips. The orgasm was hard, ripping through me like nothing I had ever felt before.

Cyrus rubbed at my clit, massaging the swollen nub.

When my shaking body finally calmed down, I fell back against him.

He grunted his approval, lifting me onto his lap. "I never gave you permission to come, pet."

My eyes snapped open, forgetting about that rule when he shoved his pierced cock into my throbbing body. "I..." I whimpered. "I'm sorry, Sir. I forgot."

"That's fine." He shoved me forward, pushing me face first into the mattress. "I'm just going to have to teach my pet a little lesson," he growled in my ear, fisting my hair. "Ask me what kind of lesson."

"What kind of lesson, Sir?" I repeated, my voice shaking.

I could feel his lips pull into a smile against my temple as he reached between us and brushed his thumb over the tight spot at my rear. My eyes widened at what he was suggesting.

"You never said this was a hard limit, pet," he murmured. "Isn't that right?"

I swallowed hard. "Yes, Sir. That's right." We had played with butt plugs, but not once had he even suggested fucking me there.

Everything was on the table unless I said otherwise. Until then, we played and tried everything, and this was no exception.

"Your nervousness turns me on." He kissed my cheek. "Safeword, pet."

"Cyrus." We had agreed that while we spent that certain weekend each month, living out the Master and slave relationship, I wouldn't use his first name. If I did, everything stopped, and we talked about it.

I brought that word, his name, the name of the man I had fallen in love with so long ago, to the forefront of my mind and kept it safe as a just in case. But I had a feeling that I wouldn't need to use it.

"Good girl." Cyrus ran his hands to my breasts, tugging on the clamps pinching my nipples. "I love you, pet," he said, kissing the spot between my shoulder blades.

"I love you, Sir."

While he took his time with me, I couldn't help but wonder what our future had in store for us but one thing I did know for sure...

We rescued...

...each other.

THE END

The Next Generation Series:

https://www.aboutjmwalker.com/next-generation-series

ACKNOWLEDGEMENTS

Cyrus and Ainsley have set the bar high for future books. Cyrus is a hero I've never written before and Ainsley communicates through ASL, which I've definitely never written before. These two are life and I had so much fun writing their story. The words poured out of me, and it was the easiest thing I have ever written. Thank you to Angie, Jennifer and Christina for always helping me fix my many issues, timeline problems and inconsistencies. I really can't thank you enough.

Thank you to Joanne, my wonderful editor and friend. Thank you for taking the time to fix my constant timeline issues and thank you for being patient and for teaching me. I seriously couldn't do this without you.

Thank you to my Jems: I know this is a big series, but I appreciate you being with me and holding my hand every step of the way.

To the authors, bloggers and readers who shared my cover reveals, release information and more: Thank you for making this book community being the amazing thing it is.

We are now book 7 into The Next Generation Series and are more than halfway done!

Thank you for embracing the ride with me.

JM

ABOUT

J.M. Walker is an Amazon bestselling author who also hit USA Today with Wanted: An Outlaw Anthology. She loves all things books, pigs and lip gloss. She is happily married to the man who inspires all of her Heroes and continues to make her weak in the knees every single day.

"Above all, be the HEROINE of your own life..." ~ Nora Ephron

Find me!

https://linktr.ee/authorjmwalker

www.ingramcontent.com/pod-product-compliance
Lightning Source LLC
Chambersburg PA
CBHW051331020726
47501CB00007B/2017